I0614674

THE CAPITAL OF CALIFORNIA

THE CAPITAL OF CALIFORNIA

Incase They Trip in Heaven My Enemies in Hell

Raymond Buchannon

P.M. DON

Copyright © 2013 P.M. Don
All rights reserved
First Edition

Will Tickets Publishing
Copyright© 2016 P.M. Don
All rights reserved
New Edition

First originally published by Page Publishing ISBN 9780997830507 (pbk)
ISBN 9780997830507 (digital)
ISBN: 0997830506
Library of Congress Control Number: 2016912304
Will-Tickets Publishing Inc., Sacramento, CA

PREFACE

There's a time and a place for everything; sometimes our circumstances would make the decisions for us. When the time comes to stand up, then stand up. For never, and I mean never is it ever, a time to give up. We will push, pull and strive, we can't stop and we won't stop. Who say? We say, and who are we?

Will Tickets Publishing Inc.

IN LOVING MEMORIES

May God forever hold you in our hearts?

PAULINE MOORE
BARBRA THOMAS
HELEN HAWKINS
DIANNE WILLIAMS

MACK H. WILLIAMS SR.
JIMMY C. MCCOY
SAMMY J. DAVIS SR.
VIRGINIA GREENLY

To: Chase Gregory Payton.

Given the opportunity to work on a great story such as this has taught me to know that every day in life is the making of a wonderful story, and may you too discover your very own... story. I have also learned and very much so want you to understand that your ribbon is too...in the "sky" and that the "sky" is indeed...the limit! So, shoot for the moon with a certain confidence that even if you shall miss, you'll still land...amongst the stars, my son.

-Darren Payton.

Any events, person or places of similarities portrayed in this novel is entirely coincidental and was built upon by the Author's imagination.

BOOK ONE

Growing up one would venture through the many curves of life. All of of us would make mistakes… some more than others. The object is to learn from as many mistakes that not only you would make, but also the mistakes that others shall make. No one is perfect but I have confidence that our father is often times forgiving and often times returning. Through all of the hate, deceit and murders, we must always remember that there is a power greater than ourselves and he and only he would be the judge of the one… VICTOR RAYMOND.

January 11, 1970

Chapter 1

FBI Special Agent Barrnette was dispatched the furthest of all his investigative peers. Just so happened to be too far away from the city where he was employed, if one were to ask him. The good city of what they called brotherly love: Philadelphia, Pennsylvania. Not quite sure how this particular city has taken on such a friendly moniker, with all of the disorder and mishaps that go down in such a wretched place. Where at any given year this city could go from "yeah, mon," on some peaceful Rasta let's get high shit to a leading candidate for the highest murder rate of the year award, and crime rates could wind up out there in the outlandish section, hence Barrnette's employment to begin with. It wasn't the fact that this special agent was saddened by the idea of leaving such a frostbitten city, no. What depressed him the most was the fact that he was deployed to California?

"Shit!" He thought of his luck. "California?" He questioned his luck again. "California?"

Still not believing his destination, he thought. 'Not Hawaii, no Honolulu or Wailuku for him uh uh, Special Agent Watts had drawn that, the lucky son of a bitch. No Tallahassee, Miami or Palm Beach for this guy, nope. Those destinations had gone to Richards, Mallets and Foreman, respectfully. You know what this guy gets, this guy gets California. He'd swear that if it rained pussy in a hail storm that he would get hit in the head with dicks and, dicks only. He wasn't even deployed to Los Angeles, not even San Francisco or Oakland uh uh, and shit naw. His ass was assigned to Sacramento. "Where the fuck is that?" He thought.

Save for economics in his seventh period he would've never heard of the place. It was no secret throughout the whole department that this Special Agent was both 'least appreciated' and the 'least adorned.' Mainly because the vast majority of his colleagues were of the Ivy League, silver spoon type of people who had their own circles, but not this guy. This guy hailed from the south side of Chicago and from the projects at that.

Agent Barrnette reflected back to the day that turned his life inside out, one that caught him up in this political whirlwind, and vivid was his memory. The .38 special jumped into his hand, then the bullet left spinning... in slow motion. "Boom" was the muffled sound of the gun crack and in slow motion misty blood spray filled the air where it stood suspended for eternity and in slow motion Deontae, who was then Barrnette's best friend reached for his chest.

Hell, the only thing moving in real speed was Deontae falling to the ground in sheer pain yelling, "What the fuck you do that for, why the fuck you shoot me?"

An accident it may have been but the dark night still filled itself with red and blue emergency lights and the sirens still wailed through his shock-filled existence. Accidentally, as it was, he was still whisked away and placed inside of a holding cell where he was constantly reminded by a jailer who had to have come from Tex-Arkansas somewhere because Agent Barrnette could still hear that deep, deep southern drawl as the jailer said,

"Son, you better hope that boy over there pulls through, we ain't got a word yet but they're saying that it don't look too good so far."

This is where Barrnette remembered praying to every God mentioned in his 17-year-old history that Deontae would pull through. Well, by the following day it was the same jailer who came to him and said,

"Son, I got some good news, and I got some bad news. The good news is that I don't have to book you on this matter because that boy over there fought hard for you. Now for the bad news, I think it's better to say that I'm going to have to take you to the bad news, seeing that I don't think you'd believe me no how if I told you."

It took all of eight minutes for Barrnette to come two more punch lines away from falling over. The interrogating officer saw how he hyperventilated and came really close to swallowing his own tongue. And at the age of 17, the young Barrnette was on the brink of having a nervous breakdown. He sweated profusely and trembled uncontrollably until the rest of his system decided to shut down completely. Once he heard that the gun that he'd accidentally shot Deontae with was also used to murder two off-duty police officers, the young Barrnette couldn't hold such a yoke and decided to vacate his own premises leaving the officers to the chore of locating a medic, and fast.

"Barrnette, hey guy, you all right with this California thingy?" Asked Special Agent Watts snapping Barrnette out of his reverie,

"Yeah, I guess, it's a job right?" Said Barrnette,

"That's right, go on out there and give them hell, show them what the alphabet boys are about, you heard me?" Watts, who just like Barrnette was recruited by the same divisions, for all the same reasons, because of their undercover abilities. Where the Ivy League agents found complications, these two found simplicities, because it was their ability to walk like it and talk like it that easily fit the characteristics, that of a thug.

"Uh uh brotha, fuck California,"

"Yeah, I know, I read the briefs."

"How, wait a minute, how the hell you do that?" Asked Barrnette,

"Shoot, one look at that and I was the first to turn it down. What the hell I want to go to California for? To handle a case that the locals should have been put to rest? Shit naw, not when Hawaii has a whore problem that needs my handling." Watts said, punctuating his statement with a smile.

"Hope you catch the claps or syphilis or something!" Said Barrnette,

"Yeah buddy, me too, and I'm going to try really hard to." Watts retrieved his tote before exiting the locker room leaving Barrnette to the chore of cleaning out his own locker.

"Seems like everyone's been briefed but me," he thought. "This is bullshit!" He snapped out loud. It was two off-duty narcs that helped land Barrnette into the feared Federal Bureau of Investigation. The fact that Deontae pulled through helped out a whole lot because he swore without changing his mind that Barrnette had found the gun, plus the fact that Barrnette didn't fit any of the descriptions given by witnesses on the other side of town gave credibility to the story. Therefore, the courts offered Barrnette a plea bargain: it would either be a lengthy jail or prison sentence or enlist in the United States Marine Corps. Well this is where Barrnette knew that he didn't even have to be remotely smart to know a bargain when he heard one. So on his 18th birthday he was headed to Parris Island, South Carolina. Where he was trained to precision on how to protect this country before being shipped further north to Quantico, Virginia, and to the Bureau. Where his dreams to be a Larry Hoover had somehow been rinsed away and replaced with something closer to Edgar Hoover.

Detective Stallworth arrived in Sacramento from the Orange County Police Department. Where he was by far the only African-American in the homicide division, and with this statistic only two things ever crossed his mind on a regular basis. He knew that if ever he were to get his balance back these two issues would have to be addressed immediately. First, he needed to break away from an old flame that has only gotten well, old. "Sabrina," he thought and if by chance the good Lord decided to smile at him, he would send her one of those high-voltage lightning bolts through her windshield while speeding on the high way home from work and zap her for her life in an eight car pileup. Because he knew that Sabrina only had one true job in life, and this was to make him so miserable that he'd often felt like eating his service revolver. Shit, her insecurities made him sick, her public displays even sicker, her infidelities were the worst, and to think that next year they were supposed to marry. "Hmm, fat chances that'll be," he mumbled, concluding his thoughts. Second, God, if you're listening would you please get me the hell out of Orange County? It took exactly one full year of praying the same prayers, ones of lightning bolts and exoduses before Detective Stallworth received a partial answer to his prayers. He was being shipped to Sacramento. Hmm, maybe he was asking for too much hoping for lightning bolts.

"So, how long has this transfer been pending?" Asked Sabrina as polite as she could,

"A long time, a long, long, long time," was his answer when the moment finally presented itself to discuss their future plans.

"So, when were you going to share all this with me?" Oh, she just had to ask.

"As soon as I had everything packed and ready to go and now that I'm ready to go." He shrugged his shoulders'. She sized up the moment then sprinted out the house and out to the car only to find the truth. She discovered a packed rental to be awfully locked and very much secured in the drive way and she didn't like it one bit. In haste she sprinted back inside. Demanding the keys, she said, "Give me the keys. Jerry, give me the keys right now!" Her voice going up an octave each demand,

"Now to that Sabrina, I'm going to have to say no!"

"You better give me the keys Jerry. You're all packed up and shit, and weren't going to tell me until now and shit."

"Mmm, hmm,"

"You're leaving me Jerry, is that it? You're leaving me?"

"Yesssss,"

"You're leaving me?" Her voice now a dangerous whisper,

"Mmm, hmmm,"

"There's somebody else, isn't it?"

"Not yet, but I got high expectations."

"Oh, is that so?"

"Yes ma'am, mmm, hmm"

"No! You're not going anywhere."

"Not true, but what's true is I'm already gone and I been that way for a while now, I just stopped by to give you this." The same box that once held their promises, their circles of engagements, now provided finalization's and had she been paying attention she would've known that no longer was he wearing his ring.

"Is that it? So you want your ring back?" She asked.

"Nope, you could flush that with the rest of that shit you've been talking about." And with that, Detective Stallworth headed out the door to a torrent of insults and wayward confessions.

"You go on ahead then Jerry soon you're going to come back, right when you start thinking about how good my pussy is. The same pussy that I give to Ralphie, he appreciates me Jerry. He makes me say his name, oh Ralphie, not like you, you green dick son of a bitch. You'll come back, watch you'll see I'm the only one that loves you. Jerry, don't do this to me, you'll come back won't you Jerry?" The sound of the door closing was the only answer that she received and for the last six years Detective Stallworth has been in the employ of the Sacramento Police Department's homicide division. "Thank you God for hearing me, I knew you were listening."

Sgt. Spencer Wildey, the fast track charismatic officer who as a Sacramento native emerged from a very, very long line of law enforcement officers dating back to the early 1900s. As his grandfather's grandfather was a beat officer, and his great uncles were officers. His father and his uncles and older brothers and middle sister, were all officers. So, armed with sixth generation squad car information, Sgt. Spencer Wildey, "Spence" as they called him, became the youngest officer in the history to be held in this esteem by the SPD. He possessed what a lot of other officers failed to obtain and that was an acute attachment to all of his senses. He was able to "know" without "seeing" and he could "feel" without reason. Toss in some other abnormal approaches to the 'cracking' of other cases that were once deemed to be "cold" and join all of this up with his other dare deviled ventures that brought fugitives to justice, and presto. What we'd have here is a gung ho psychic who possesses extreme amounts of police intelligence that are sure to land him one day in the captain's seat before long. If and had he didn't kill his self in the process.

Let's see, oh-kay there was the media who captured "Spence" on the West Sacramento Bridge as a rookie, disrobing enough to be charged with lewd acts in public only to later be hailed as a hero when he dove from the bridge and into the river in a perfect swan's maneuver to successfully save a young teenage suicidal girl from plunging to her death. Not to mention, just six months later when he borrowed a cab from a very unhappy gypsy man while overlooking the fact that he was off-duty at the time, yet he rammed the cab, borrowed or stolen depending on how you looked at it, through the front door of a downtown liquor store yelling "Police!" Halting what would've been otherwise a successful robbery attempt. We won't even talk about the toddler that fell into the den of the gorilla's display at the Sacramento Zoo. Who retrieved the child? "Spence" did he swing down like Tarzan yelling his intention in a battle cry or did wrestle with the ferocious gorillas.... No. He eased into the den, cradled the toddler and eased his ass out of there, handed the child to his mother to a large round of applause and made his exit. Nothing fancy at all, no arm wrestling techniques, no guns going off, not that anybody thought a 9mm. Sig Sauer would've mattered much anyway. Nothing fancy there, just sheer finesse but tell me, do you know anybody that would have done that shit? Not even the child's mother inched to make this attempt and we all know about a mother's love. The youngest Sgt. in the history of the Sacramento's Police Department, and no matter how decorated he was Spence had one flaw, yet a flaw that motivated him severely and made him tick. Because everyone who knew "Spence" knew that he took crime fighting seriously and nobody or under any circumstances, man, woman or child, was allowed to commit any devilments on his watch, and with this philosophy of "every means necessary," do know that not all of the arrests that Spence had made were of the Constitutional varieties. Sometimes the bar got raised just a little bit, and the rules somehow got twisted and bent just a little out of shape. As the rumor had it that no one in the whole precinct had more informants than "Spence," and no one had more connections than Spence at all and he always knew how to do it, when to do it and where to do it because of this. And what went un-noticed or unspoken were the ways that Spence obtained his information: bought and paid for was normally correct. Yet, a lot of times narcotics was the currency, and not every bust was a clean bust but so what he worked the OAK PARK beat – thugs, whores and drug addicts whoopee. As crooked as this may seem and if word ever got out Spence knew that he'd be terminated on the spot. But if asked why he lives such a double life on just one single career he would tell you, "Raymond Buchannon." This name had been printed on his brain all throughout his youth; this name had outlasted his father and older brothers and all of their failed attempts to rid this city of this name. He knew that this name had outlasted anyone who was deemed foes and opponents, and from the intelligence that Spence had gathered throughout his life. He learned that there was also no one, and he meant no one more poisonous than "Raymond Buchannon." It was only a name, one that appeared to be a ghost or a phantom but truly a name belonging to very controlling and alive and a living, breathing person. Nothing in the data base supports any investigation. Yet, speak this name and fear washed over the city, not the fleeting version no, but a real deep, genuine, authentic, hope to die and rather kill myself before I help you kind of fear. Even the prostitutes and drug addicts would refuse narcotic payments and would rather have Spence lock them up for life then to aid in the arrest or any other demise of this "Raymond Buchannon."

Every city has its gangster but not every city has a Raymond Buchannon. Anywhere, just go there. New York, New Jersey, Chicago, Nevada or Ohio I don't care. Hell, go to Pittsburgh, Milwaukee or even Denver. You could go to Mars or you could go to hell and resurrect you a gangster and you still wouldn't get a Raymond Buchannon. Who is this gentleman? Hell if I know in fact that's what we are all trying to figure out. O'rieley once made the mistake of calling him a figment of our own troubled imagination and advised the city not to panic, and to allow law enforcement to bring order back to the city of Sacramento. Saying this wasn't the mistake; saying this at a press conference though was colossal, huge. The attempt to wash this fine outstanding gentleman ashore by calling him out only proved to be a fiasco that should never be repeated. Friday, April the 12th. If my memory serves me right, somewhere around noon the department held a press conference. I was then an up-and-coming detective with a very old gold shield and as I said, we held a press conference to honor our new Captain and to address this "Buchannon" issue. The Captain to be honored was Loren O'rieley, who swore to bring this gentleman down. He had hooked up with this profiler that came down from D.C. to profile Mr. Buchannon. Saying that he wanted to be captured, though it never looked that way to me, said that he flicks his nose at authority in a catch-me-if-you-can sort of gesture. Now this I could believe. Even went as far as calling him a coward, which is also a mistake that I'd never make. Captain O'rieley took to the podium to field questions at a quarter to twelve, April the 12th. By the time the questions were over and the spiel was delivered of Mr. Buchannon's cowardice and other profiled intelligences. I would say that it was three minutes next to one p.m. and this was Friday, April the 12th. By Monday, April the 15th our good Captain O'rieley was once again in the public eye and once again was he surrounded by cameras. Only this time gone was the podium and gone was the microphones, and missing was his rooster's strut of confidence as the public saw this once assertive and overpowering individual reduced to tears and despair as the news broke in repetition: There was a misfortune that fell over the O'rieley family. The worst fear was then confirmed, that the woman, two girls and a junior had a Hummer utility vehicle blown to pieces and scattered over the pavement's at 65th Expressway was identified to be the wife and the offspring of our one and only Captain Loren O'rieley. This was Monday, April 15th at six o'clock p.m. Now on April the 17th, the city not yet finished mourning nor coming to grips with the first tragedy, did the news break once more. This time a more desperate cry for help because the news that broke on this day was to inform the city of the loss of our very own good Captain, Loren O'rieley.

Now guess if you will, who would you think to be our suspect? Who should be brought in for questioning or Lord help us, for arresting? Who do you think our hot lines buzzed so much about? Phony sightings and bogus information, right, it wasn't then nor is it now a secret to whom should be brought to justice. Let's just say that even if our guesses were feeble, what brought strength to every detective, inspector or investigator in all of the nine different precincts were the knowledge and the full understanding that with Captain O'rieley, Mr. Buchannon left his calling card. This was a bullet behind the officers' right earlobe. Now, understand that this method of murder was never released to the public for fear of a copycat killer. So in our mind and in all of our hearts we as officers knew whom to blame and who needed to be held responsible for not only these murders but over a dozen other events. No single bodies, I said events! When this fellow comes down with a sad case of the hiccups, then we'll need to borrow meat wagons from neighboring counties to pick up the pieces. CSI units would be dispatched in droves to find fibers, molecules or anything else that could aid in bringing this man to justice.

So you could go anywhere, Japan or Jupiter looking for gangsters and you would never find a Raymond Buchannon. In fact, I've heard tales that some parents would threaten their kids that if they didn't straighten up that they were gonna call Raymond Buchannon, and the results were a straight "A" student in the making. Hell, I could call my wife and tell her that I've been targeted by Mr. Buchannon as a prank if I so desired, and would guarantee anybody that by the end of my shift. A forty-seven-hundred-square-foot Victorian house would be a hollow shell of what it used to be. Carpets included, would be packed and ready for transport. Though I smile at the thought, what is not funny at all is the stronghold that the city of Sacramento lacks in order to repel one individual, whose name has become synonymous, to the Boogeyman. The inner city calls him "Uncle," but here, at this precinct and the eight other ones in this fine city, we call him "Armed and awfully dangerous," and no less than public enemy number one. So, it is written that it is I, the new captain, Marcel Wynn who've brought some of the finest detectives and the one borrowed Secret Intelligence Agent from the Federal Bureau, serial killers and narcotics division to help bring down what we believe to be a half-of-a-billion-dollar-a-year criminal enterprise. May God be with us because to bring down a man who'd make old Al Capone, Bugsy Siegel and Legs Diamond look like fairy godmothers to us. Believe me!

Juice sat at his father's desk and pretended to be his father, as he always had. He'd press buttons on the phone and pretend that he was the president of the world. Though he could never recall a time when his father pressed these same buttons; still he knew that he would carry himself just like his father. Even though he believed in his heart that his mother was trying awfully hard to dissuade him from what he felt was his true destiny: which was to be just like his father.

So now that he was coming to the adult stages in his life, he found that he was at a crossroad. This time, the fork in the road wasn't asking him to go straight. No. This time the fork demanded a decision. A lot of the chips had already fallen. With his father laid out of commission in the hospital, his uncle awaited him, and his mother, though compassionate as she always had been, gave him every indication that not every decision would she be around for and how now was as good a time as any for him to stand up and be a man about it. She decided to give him all the space that he would need as long as he hurried up about it.

Juice fought hard against the odds. He grew up in a rough neighborhood that always seemed to keep a helicopter in the sky making their loud announcements, something about a suspect being in the area and for everyone to go inside because the dogs were being released. A chaotic place where gun shots and sirens filled the nights, so to be able to make it through such a pitiful environment had if nothing else, equipped him for moments like this. Oh, how he could not escape the bitter memories of winos in the front of the club, hungry and begging for his lunch money and often were the times that Juice sacrificed his lunch and snacks because fast was how he forked over the money to them. Just to be able to contribute to the needs of others, too, spoke volumes towards the person that he'd become. To walk to school with his basketball was his only distraction away from the ills of his life. This also kept him from feeling the disgust for the dope fiends that crawled out of tenement buildings or dilapidated houses where they had slept or a place that they would call home, or just a place to fix. Lord only knew the countless orange tops that came from syringes or the empty Visine bottles that he'd see throughout the course of a single day. Both the syringes and the small bottles being paraphernalia for drug use, predominately cocaine and heroin. To be able to beat these odds against a place that lives and breathes pestilence had prepared him for what his future would hold. He needed to choose this way or that way because to choose neither would only mean that the decision would be made for him, and who the hell knew where that would take him. Depression had set in so deep that the only move left was to go through his father's file cabinets and allow his education, along with his father's teachings to guide him. "Yes, that's what I'll do, I'll let my father guide me," Juice said to his self, and there he emptied every file cabinet of its contents. Every folder, every note and ledger or scrawled message arranged on his father's desk, and there he began to read.

Chapter 2

As far back as he could remember, nothing in life had ever come easy for Victor Raymond. Barely made it at birth, his first seven years was spent in an orphanage residence and by his eighth year on earth he was assessed and accepted by the Hornsby's. By the time he turned ten and a half he was returned to foster care by the Hornsby's, seems that the Hornsby's false started on their vows swapping their "I do" for their "I don't" and had welcomed divorce, "ahh, poor Victor." By twelve he was accepted by the Ketchum's and so uncontrollable was he that even this rowdy family was forced to return Victor back to sender. Two more years of orphanage abuse and poor Victor decided that he would take his chances and bet on his self as a fourteen-year-old runaway. With nothing but the clothes on his back he climbed out of the bathroom window; escaping the horny likes of Brenda the "night lady," who gathered this handle by the way she crept around at night visiting room after room, receiving her jollies. Just barely out of the window and the outstretched grasp of the feared night lady and the last of her echoing words:

"You mother fucker, I knew your little ass was up to something, get back in here!" Nope, he was gone. He landed on the side of the house and over the fence he went heading towards a life unknown. He wandered the streets of Sacramento with no clothes, no food and no shelter. As days passed Victor knew for sure that his childhood, as rotten as it may have been, was gone. And that the time to think like a man was now upon him, whatever the hell that meant. However, he knew that he had three essentials that would need his immediate tending to. First, he needed to quiet his stomach rumblings, and for this he targeted some easy pickings, literally. For Victor knew nearly every fruit tree from OAK PARK to ELDER CREEK. He knew where the apples were, the plums were, the peaches, and could spot grapefruits from a mile away. The orange trees never stood a chance, and it was because of this his survival wasn't as complicated as it could have been. Did he need to sneak the fruit from these trees? Not always, only some of the time because, if the orphanage didn't teach him anything else, it taught him how to ask for what he wanted. In his tailor made, well-mannered approach he would often times be granted permission to the yard. Yet, what the orphanage didn't teach him was that it was hard to pull wool over the experienced eyes of an adult. Often times he'd hear, "Child, who your momma is?" or "Boy, have you had anything else to eat?" And sometimes "Yeah, you go ahead and take all the fruit you need and when you finish you come back a knocking on this door, you hear." Here he would be offered hot meals and ill-fitting clothing and sometimes paper money and loose jingles. The biggest problem on his think-like-a-man list to do was to find shelter. This way he would find warmth and have a place that he could store his accumulated belongings that he gathered from roaming the streets that covered one part of Sacramento to the other.

A lot of times sleeping in a tunnel, well this provided temporary shelter but he knew that he needed a warmer place and better habitat than what he had offered his self. Then the idea hit him: "Why don't you just get you a nice house, buddy?" Which seems to most people like the craziest thing to do for a homeless teen, and impossible for every other fourteen-year-old but not Victor Raymond, who now after months of barely eating, barely sleeping and barely doing anything had a mind as open as Lake Michigan. He formulated him a plan that could help him transfer all of his belongings, which weren't that many ranging from the clothes he stole from clothes lines, his transistor radio that he'd always kept batteries for, and several bags of food that he could eat whenever hunger prevailed. The house that he had in mind was located on the corner of Second Avenue and 37th. The tunnel that he slept in when this idea hit him over the head was located on Sacramento Blvd., right across Fruitridge Road next to the highway, which would be a three-mile trek. But to go to and from more than once could range between three to nine miles if he didn't do it right. Regardless of this he knew that this was something that he would do if this is what had to be done, but he also knew that there was a wiser way. Well, since he was now thinking like a new man and all he knew that he could achieve this task in one trek if he could just cop one of those shopping carts that were always left in various places. Twenty minutes later he was on the hunt, finding his small treasure behind a diner that used to provide him with food each time they'd throw it out at closing time, and less than twenty minutes after that he was loading up, preparing to go to his new house.

Now, the house in question was a two-room shack that was left abandoned for as long as Victor Raymond could remember. The yard unattended to for years, the paint was now peeling away and boarding covered the windows. Too late to turn back and head for the tunnel so the young Victor Raymond found his way inside of the shack, which he could tell that the last people to occupy this place were probably still inside, now skeletons, for the stench that it possessed and for the filth that remained. If the skeletons weren't there, he knew that rodents would be. Preparing his self to abort his mission and search for other abandonment's but somehow knowing that this is when "A man got to do what a man got to do," came in to play, so this home became his reality. Not to mention the location was perfect, undisturbed by the way it looked, a lot of activity was going on in all of its illegal assortments, figuring that sometimes he could turn a dollar here and there. "No," he thought, "a man got to do, really what a man got to do." So, he traveled through the vacant shack making mental notes of what needed to be done, not quite knowing what he would do, if indeed he found the skeletons that he'd swore would be present behind door number two, where the stench was coming from. He pushed the door open to the sound of its squeaky hinges to discover a restroom. "My goodness," he thought; flies covered the toilet and the bath tub. With all the courage that Victor could muster, he stepped into the filthiest place in the world and pulled the chain, which he took to be the lever that he needed, and to his surprise he heard the sound of a flushing toilet. Grateful to find the toilet in working order next test would be to check the tub, and sure enough the water poured from its faucet. Completing the tour of the shack, his mind was made. This is where Victor Raymond would call home for as long as it lasted. With the very little light that remained outside, and the only light available inside shined through the cracks of the windows and the boarded doors. One especially, now that Victor removed the board to gain entry. His next task was to make it to a store before it closed, so armed with a few paper dollars and a few jingles, he found a hardware store because groceries were not on his list. He needed lighting and all the cleaning supplies that he could purchase, and may the Lord forgive him because all that he couldn't buy he knew that he was gonna steal.

Light showed through the cracks of the boards which covered the windows, so more cracks were needed, so a screwdriver was purchased. The tub, the toilet and all the sinks were horrible, so a large bottle of bleach was purchased. Ajax and scrub pads, a brush, gloves and a mask were another purchase. The broom was the most expensive. He knew that he'd reached his limit with his purchases, so the hammer and the two boxes of candles were stolen, along with the wooden matches. The same for the insect sprays and the mouse traps and poisons. Before leaving he made mental notes for the lantern and other items that he was sure to need in the near future. With that, he was off to Second Avenue and 37th. Before he entered the shack, he figured he'd out-wait the only onlooker, which was a young woman who appeared to be in no hurry to go anywhere, leaving a situation to be nothing more than a mental Mexican standoff: him, waiting for her to leave; she, waiting for him to say something. So, as minutes passed which seemed like hours, he decided to speak, saying, "May I help you?"

"Listen to you, sounding all edu-ma-cated and stuff," she retorted, and then said, "What are you doing?"

"What am I doing? Why, who's asking?" Said Victor,

"My name is Marlene. What you doing in there?"

"Why you wanna know?"

"Are you going to live in that filth? What, you don't have a place to go?" His silence was answer enough for her, so she continued.

"Are you hungry?"

"No, not really," answered Victor.

She surveyed his contents, then said, "You're gonna clean that place up, aren't you?"

"Yeah, yeah, I am, why? You're going to report me to the folks or something?"

"Boy, please. You want me to help you?"

"Why you wanna do that? You don't have nowhere to go, are you hungry?"

"No, I don't have a place to go, my man don't want me no more. Figure my momma is the best one for him. I walked by and saw you coming out and waited until you left and went inside. So, I waited to see what you were up to. There are two rooms inside and I promise that I won't bite."

"I don't know. Why don't you find your own place?" Said Victor,

"You just barely beat me to this one. If I had the guts to go inside I would've allowed you in once you said you had nowhere to go, plus I could help out a lot."

"Is that so? And how could you do that?"

"Well, for starters I could feed us."

"I eat."

"Yeah, I saw, plums and grapefruits."

"I've been doing oh-kay."

"But, there's one thing that I could help you with that beats all," she snapped.

"I'm listening."

"Neither you nor I would have to be alone. How old are you? What, ten?"

"I am fourteen," he answered.

"Oh-kay, I'm nineteen, which means if the folks come, then I'm your older sister. See the sense in that?"

"Hmm," nothing else to talk about because she knew she had him at "alone" and had killed him with "older sister" because, in this world, alone he was and a sister he never knew. To prove that she scored big, she took the broom and the bags and headed towards the rear of the house where Victor had removed the board from the door.

"It's dark in there," said Marlene once she opened the door.

"I got a bunch of candles," said Victor,

"Well, you're the man, go and light some." Her smile showed the sarcasm she intended, and to prove that she was right because indeed he was the man, he withdrew a handful of candles, lighting one, then the other from the one that was already lit. Somewhat frightened of the unknown himself shit, maybe a cat would jump out or an oversized rat or something, he thought. "So what, a man gotta do what a man had to do," he reminded himself. So, with confidence he'd gone through the shack, illuminating room after darkened room.

"I'm a take it that you don't intend to sleep here under these conditions," said Marlene now standing behind him referring to the filth she saw.

"Not at all," was his reply.

"This could take all night, look at this stuff. Where do we put all this junk?" She asked.

"I saw a dump not far from here; we could use that push cart to help us," he responded.

"You got soap I hope," she said, going through the bags. Finding the bleach and the Ajax, she headed towards the bathroom, splashing bleach everywhere, then to the kitchen, same thing. Behind her he went spraying insect killer just as wild as she splashed the bleach. He closed the doors behind him to allow the poison to take effect while limiting the bugs' escape. Through the shack they went, pointing and spraying, splashing and dashing, until empty were the bags of its purchases leaving the disinfectants and the poisons to work on the filth and parasites. Satisfied with the way things were taking shape, Victor dug through his properties searching for his transistor radio to bring entertainment to the shack.

"I saw a sheet in the room," said Marlene. Not knowing quite, the plans she had for the sheet because he wasn't sleeping on anything but his coat and he knew it.

"Oh-kay," he said, surrendering to his ignorance.

"I figured that we could load a lot of this junk and tie it in a sheet and carry it to the dumpster," smiling she said. "What did you think we were going to do with it?" Searching the rooms, they found other sheets and a few curtains, which could help them transport the mounds of junk.

"I got a pair of gloves," said Victor.

"I saw them and a mask too. How about you tie the junk up first and set it outside and we'll dump it in the morning, and while I'm doing the kitchen and the sinks, tub and the toilet you could sweep the place up? That way we could finish quicker." She finished by turning up the radio to the classic sound of Ole Lady Day. For Victor, this was a better plan than the one that he had conjured up. The one that he put together had "him" in that bathroom, and "him" in that filthy kitchen, and he could tell that she was trying to spoil him because she didn't even ask for the gloves. She just donned the mask and left with the scrub brush and steel wool scrubbing pads. Song after song, hour after hour, the results were a very empty residence, which smelled strongly of bleach. With the job complete, Marlene stepped into the front room and looked around. Satisfied, she sat down and said, "Now, this is much better."

"It's starting to get cold in here," Victor said.

"Yeah, it must be two or three in the morning."

"You're sleepy?" He asked.

"No, in fact I need to go somewhere, if you can go all over looking for holes that look like mice would come from and stick poison inside and try to get you some sleep. We still got a lot of work to do tomorrow."

"Oh-kay,"

His bewilderment was obvious and needed consolation. With her knowing this, she added, "Don't lock the door; I wouldn't want to disturb you if you're asleep when I come in."

"Oh-kay," still bewildered. What was evading him was the truth, Marlene was troubling him; he feared that she would leave and wouldn't return, leaving him alone in this world again. What was even more troubling was his attachment to a person that he'd only met just hours ago. A person who should be free to come and go as they well pleased. The truth was she was not his sister, not even his friend. She was just another person that life had dealt some shitty cards to.

"Don't worry, if you weren't man enough I'd say lock the door." Again, the smile that said she was teasing. Standing to leave she said, "There are a lot of holes in the kitchen, a lot of them." With that she was gone. Not knowing if he was being a good little chap or if it was his fear of rodents that sent him throughout the shack inch by inch but he sprinkled small amounts of pellets per hole until every hole was covered. This was also the time that the last candle flickered out. Through the rear door he noticed that dawn was soon to break. Thinking, wherever Marlene was that hopefully she was safe. With that he made a pillow out of some pants he brought and a blanket with his coat, and regardless of how cold the shack had gotten, it was no comparison to the tunnel by the highway because there, it was freezing. The shack smelled heavy on the bleach and was clean enough to bring satisfaction and with that, sleep came over him.

Chapter 3

Somehow, in his sleep he must have been dreaming of a fancy restaurant because in his sleep he could smell eggs and pancakes. Somebody was serving bacon and sausage together. Making sure not to wake himself from this perfect dream, he rolled over on the hardwood floor in an effort to find a waiter so he could order whatever the cook was serving up. The scent and its tantalizing fragrances traveled through his mental images reminding him, that he was starving. In his dream his coat took on a large amount of heat, for no longer was he freezing nor uncomfortable. Now the green onions and the strong scent of real butter became the wakeup call bringing him out of a dream and to a better reality because the waiter had made her way to the shack with a quilt and a platter of food.

"You up? I don't know if you ate all of your plums or not but I stopped and picked you up something to eat, and some other necessities that I'm sure we'd need. Here, up and eat. We still gotta haul that stuff from the yard."

"Somehow, I was having a dream that I was at a fancy restaurant, and then you showed up." His smile told her something else.

"Oh, well I could go and retrieve you some fruit if you'd like." Again her teasing smile, which was now starting to get on his nerves.

"Have you eaten?" He asked. "Here, share this with me, it's delicious," he said between bites.

"No. Save me a bit, I need to freshen up first."

"Oh-kay, have you slept any?" He asked, with a concern that was well intended.

"There is absolutely no rest for the weary, try to remember that. So much that needs to be done. Look around, you see what we're missing?"

"Yeah, everything," replied Victor.

"Now, before I go to freshen up, we need to set some ground rules..."

"You don't have to worry about me walking in on you," he interrupted.

"I'm not worried about no shit like that. What I wanted to say before I was rudely interrupted is that you don't have to worry about when I leave, would I come back. For some reason I dig you. You got more fire than I seen in a lot of brothers much, much older than you. But as I say, look around and you would see us so far at the bottom. Need I remind you that this is really no place for anybody to start from? But to be truthful, this is where I'd rather be, at the bottom, because from here there is only one direction for us to go, and sweetie, that's up. So, by saying all of this, I need you to know that time and time again I'm going to introduce you to people and to things but I'm gonna need you to trust me, which is rule number one. Second, being that since we gon' live together, I'm gon' need to be able to trust you. I'm saying with anything and with everything, do you understand?" Froze was the plastic fork that hung in midair so long that the eggs were sure to be cold but for a response to her, he nodded in the affirmative.

"No, I need you to tell me that you understand," she pushed.

"I do, I understand, happy?"

"Yes, now what's your name?"

After a long pause, and finally, between chews he said, "Victor." Her stare told him that she didn't believe him. Seeing this, he said, "So, when are you gonna start trusting me?"

"Victor? As black as you are, you take on a Spanish name? All right, Victor it is then."

"Victor, as in Victory Marlene, which is not Spanish by the way, it means that I made it, I won, and I'm a Champion," he snapped, and then added, "You best go freshen up as you say, because this food is getting cold."

"Oooh, nuh uhh, did you just tell me what to do? Victory or should I say Mr. Champion, oh-kay then daddy, let me go freshen up as you say, before the food get cold. Oh, but you're welcome though, since I knew that you was thinking about thanking me later. I'll go and freshen up now, knowing that it's the thoughts that count." Again with the smile,

"Thank you, I mean it, for everything," Victor said meaningfully.

"I know," Marlene said, temporarily suspended.

"Well, now that I'm up, let me go haul some stuff."

"Wait, I'll help you," she said.

"So, you're gonna freshen up just to go dabble in some filth?" He questioned.

"I guess so, just wait, plus I brought another basket. This way we could finish quicker."

"Food, basket, blankets, what else you up to?"

"I brought the bathroom supplies, some money and some good information."

"Oh-kay, some information, you say?"

"Yeah, the owner of this house has been gone for years and years, so let's take the boards from the windows. Maybe we could do something with the yard, perhaps make a home of this place. Would you like that?"

"I would love that Marlene, how 'bout you?"

"Yeah, I really would. So let me freshen up and I'll help you."

"Naw, I got it. You could use the rest, I'm sure of it."

"You sure," she questioned.

"Yeah, I'm sure. Just leave the door unlocked. This way I won't disturb you if you are asleep when I come in."

"Uh uh, you gonna have to knock, mister. You ain't leaving me alone, by myself, without the doors locked," again, with the smile. With that, Victor left the shack through the rear.

By noon he was finished hauling the junk; by two, the boards were off the windows, by three he was copping curtains and blinds for a nickel each, and to his delight two kerosene lanterns were parked right by the door, where he knew that he would grab them on the way out. By four, the curtains and blinds covered the windows, bringing a homey look to the shack. By five, Victor was in the yard pulling weeds. By six, Marlene was right next to him, trying to finish up before night fell completely. By six thirty, Jesus sent a messenger, one bearing gifts. An older gentleman pulled a wagon over to the two and said, "Figured you guys could use some tools and some help." Either he was a friendly neighbor or he was trouble. Marlene accepted the outstretched hand and shook it saying, "Thank you, and you are?"

"Russell, but everyone around here calls me Russ. I see what you guys are doing to the place. An old friend of mine stayed here. Nobody took an interest in this place like you guys. So, the best that I could do is help out. I got an old mower here that would have it done in no time. The kid could get the rake and we could load this wagon and be done before night fall really sets in." And sure enough they were finished before long, and the three of them marveled at the results of their hard work.

"Is there anything else that I could help you with?" Asked Russ, obviously with a good eye for Marlene but who could blame him, thought Victor. Marlene was pretty tall for a woman, with long shapely legs. She sported a Chocolate complexion with almond-shaped hazel-colored eyes, a nice set that anyone could easily get lost in. Plus, she was built like a quarter horse from the waist down and she walked like she owned a bunch of stuff, very confident. But Victor knew first hand where Russell was getting most of his problems from, which came when Marlene smiled at him: her pearly white even teeth had always packed dynamite for a sex appeal.

"In fact, there is something that you could help us with," she said, then smiled her weapon at him; visible was when ole Russ turned to mush.

"Just ask and just maybe you could receive!" His weakness dripped like venom. Two steps later Marlene had her lips to Russell's ear as if keeping a secret from Victor which was a terrible belief, because something sultry had to have been said, because ole man Russ came very close to keeling over. Sensing this, Marlene decided to ease up on him and backed away from Russell, but not before pecking him on his cheek.

"Well, gee whiz. Miss Lady, let ole Russ see what he could do, just give me about an hour before you come a knocking. I'm just two doors down over yonder you can't miss it; there's a trailer in the yard. Don't you worry, I'll leave the light on so you won't kick over some of the junk there you understand?" She nodded her reply, and with that he headed out of the yard and Victor and Marlene headed into the shack.

Once inside, she spoke first "Do you wanna know what that was about?"

Feeling like he already knew, Victor said, "Nah, not at all."

"You sure,"

For an answer he lit a candle and headed to the rest room so he could wash up. When Victor returned, Marlene was gone. Hmmm, that was a quick hour, he thought, turning on the radio to the soulful sounds and the most popular blues which always massaged Victor for his pains. Two oranges later and he was making a pallet from now the quilt and his coat, this way he could lay his weary body down because in this case rest was definitely needed. What seemed like a few minutes had to have been a few hours, because the sky went from twilight to dawning by the time Marlene walked through the door with more covers and more food.

"Sorry champ but I don't recall seeing you eat anything. Maybe you could wolf down some nourishment's while I make it a little more comfortable in here," she said while fluffing up the pillows she brought.

After spreading the blankets and quilts to a more suitable pallet, she said: "Ain't no sense in me using the other room. As cold as it gets in here, we could survive with body heat." And with that, she laid down, giving the sounds of relief.

"Thank you for the food. It was very good. I saved some for tomorrow."

"Good, now come and lie down and get some rest. We got a big day coming."

"A big day you say?"

"Yeah, a really big day,"

"Oh." Obviously confused was Victor, so he voiced his confusion, stating. "Oh-kay, doing what though?"

"Oh, now you wanna know, don't you? I will show you later, now come." She patted the pallet. Not knowing quite sure if he should occupy the pallet with Marlene or not. Save for Brenda "The night lady," who made all of the decisions for him, Victor couldn't place a time when he was this far out there on his own.

"Come, you a man ain't you? Well, you may as well face it. I'm cold, you're cold, I'm tired and you need rest too. Besides, as I say, we got a big day coming." And moments later Victor fell asleep to the soft purr of Marlene's snore.

Chapter 4

Victor awoke to a sun-filled house as Marlene opened curtains and windows together, allowing fresh air to come breezing through.

"Come on Champ, up and at 'em."

"I'm up, I'm up," said Victor, stretching to bring his body to life.

"I got a few bucks; I figure we could stop by the Goodwill and pick out some nice outfits. We need to be presentable at least, from here on out. Not saying that we gotta go all fancy, just presentable, you understand?"

Nodding his affirmation didn't do it with Marlene, so verbally he said, "I got it."

"And the other thing is, Mr. Russell is gonna come down here once we get back and carry us to the school house around that corner. He said that he will sign for you as your guardian. I've heard you talk, so I could tell that you have some sort of schooling, but I must ask that you finish and really go to learn. There is no place on earth for a dumb nigga! Don't worry, I will help you as much as I can, but you will find that there is only so much that I can do. So, before we go, pick from your clothes the most presentable and I will wash them for you. We could toss out the rest, do you understand?"

"I need to go to school?" Victor questioned.

"Yes Sweetie, you do," Marlene replied with conviction.

"Oh-kay, I hear."

"And really go to learn, no jiving around."

"No jiving around," Victor repeated.

"Good, so get ready, the Goodwill opens in a bit."

By nine thirty Victor was dressed, as casual as could be. From their selections was a tweeted sweater, which coordinated perfectly with his slacks, and by the looks of the shoes, you would think Victor to be off to church, way before you would think him off to school. By ten thirty he was registered to the freshman class at American Legion. The castle-looking building on Broadway and Sacramento Boulevard had offered Victor a place for refuge and even to his surprise; he found some things that he'd excel at. Science was his only challenge. Math, English and geographies were a cinch. His study habits were as routine as breathing, which were daily and all day. History was his favorite, and while Victor was practicing to be the Black Mark Twain with Albert Einstein philosophies, Marlene was putting together the shack piece by piece. Until now, their living situation became something closer to a residence than a shabby place for squatters to hide from bad weather. Instead of diners every night, Victor found out the strangest thing: that Marlene really knew how to cook. Within the first few months that Victor knew Marlene, a change had come over him. The people that she brought into his life were nothing less than real-life drill sergeants. These people instructed the rules for engagements on life issues. For two months, every day after studying, he would team up with "Fast Freddy," who barely had patience for anybody. What he needed to show you, you had to learn it now. First, there was dice. Here is where Victor was given two dice and sometimes three, depending on the game that was being taught, and from three o'clock until bedtime, "Fast" would have him tossing the dice.

"This is where you need to develop a rhythm; once you got the rhythm, you ride that rhythm. Listen: right now you're doing good but I'm gonna give you a challenge. Toss the dice and land a point, and that's your point all day. What we wanna do is see how many times you could land that point in a thousand tries. I'll count and you toss. Remember, it's the rhythm." And this carried on for months.

Next on the list was the craziest art in the entire world, the art of shark. In a lot of places they call it different things, like the "Minnesota" or the "Stab." To some, just regular ole pick pocketing. For this he was introduced to "Black." Now, there was no secret to how Black got his name. Everything about him was black. His lips were black; he was the same complexion as his hair, which was very black. His eyes were blood-shot red because he was so black. His fingernails were black and so was his attitude. And just like "Fast," "Black" ain't had a whole lot of patience either but had his own training methods. He'd show you where to stab, and if he felt you stabbing, he'd pop the shit out of you. With the Minnesota, Victor had so many failed attempts that often were the times that he'd gone to school looking like he was living with some awfully abusive parents. Months of this and he was seasoned in two hobbies; like "Black," he became so smooth at the stab that he couldn't wait to reap the benefits. Put on a nice necklace and with one hug Victor would have it in his fist, no one the wiser. From a distance, with eyes like a hawk, Victor would see where you carried your poke and would be tempted to stab at it, but he was smart enough to know that he was still a student.

Next on the list there was Pepe. Whoa, now Pepe knew cards like it was the only thing that God needed him to do. He was so good, that after dealing you a hand and before play, he would be able to tell you in a roundabout way the cards to which you were holding in your hand. So after four consecutive correct guesses Victor began to search the backs for markings, not knowing that he was insulting Pepe. Who figured that he could get Victor's attention better by throwing the whole deck of cards at him, yelling at him saying, "you foolish little punk, never think me the cheater. You think my predictions are so amazing that you need to pull out your peepers and scan the backs for evidence. I'll tell you what, you could bring your deck out here and it'll be the same thing dum-dum, because it ain't the cards I'm reading. It's you that I'm reading. You get a few good cards and you blush like a virgin girl who just heard about sex for the first time. You get some lousy cards and you mope around like the world is coming to an end. Go ahead though, and check 'em all."

He finished by revealing to Victor the deck allowing Victor to scan every last card, and for a reply Victor said, "I didn't mean any harm, Pepe. I should have known better. Tell me how I could get better at hiding what it is that you see." These words were meant to bring soothing to Pepe's obvious anger. So, with a smile, Pepe said, "Don't put no 'con' on me lil nigga, trying to ease me over after insulting me. I ought' a hit you in your throat for wasting my time with this bullshit." Packing up, readying his self to leave.

Victor came to believe that he had just lost a mentor and said, "Thanks for your patience anyways, Pepe," and like a true and grateful student, Victor shook hands and hugged Pepe. Like a son would his father, for he was truly upset for an insult that would halt his education.

"Maybe next time fella you would heed what it is that you're shooting for," Pepe said and turned on his heels to leave.

"Hey, Pepe, I promise if you give me one more chance I would pay more attention," said Victor, and as an afterthought, "plus I will pay you."

"Pay me? Lil nigga, you don't have enough money to pay me..."

"Not money. Pepe, with this," Victor interrupted, holding up Pepe's necklace for Pepe to see. Sending Pepe's hand straight to his chest to find that, yeah, it was true; the great Pepe has just been stabbed, by the "lil nigga."

"Ahh, you motha fucka, give me my necklace"

"Oh-kay, does that mean that I could keep the ring then," and from all of the rings that he wore, the most expensive one that once brought its two karats' shine to his pinky, was now gone.

"Son of a bitch, you dirty motha fucka!"

"Oh, so I'm a lil nigga, a motha fucka and a son of a bitch, and to think that I only insulted you once. Now listening to you, your tic tack toe went three in a row," said Victor.

"Motha fucka!" blurted Pepe, still not believing what just happened.

"How 'bout I give you the necklace and the ring back, and me and you would just take it easy on the insults. But, you gotta bring me up to date with everything. I'm talking 'bout everything, deal?" Victor finished.

"What kind of deal you guys in here making?" Said Marlene as she returned from grocery shopping, setting the bags down, she looked at Pepe.

"Pepe, what's gotten into you?" She asked with concern for her friend because never had she seen him in this condition before.

"This motha.... I mean Victor," he corrected, pointing in Victor's direction.

"Oh, hmm, what did he do, Pepe? Oh, oh, oooh," she concluded after Pepe showed her his bare chest.

"So, what kind of deal was you guys making before I showed up?" She asked with ridicule dripping from her tongue.

"He called me a cheater."

"Aww, Victor." Marlene pinched Victor on the cheek: "You know better."

"So I'm 'bout ready to give up on the boy and leave, come to find out that he has my necklace and my ring," Pepe finished, holding up his left hand to show Marlene his missing pinky ring.

"Whoa! Pepe, are you all right? You look queasy. Here, have a seat, what can I do to help you?" she asked, again with ridicule dripping.

"Well, you noticed that I'm missing some things, don't you?" Pepe snapped.

"I can't tell him to give it back, Pepe. You know the rules, finders' keepers. I know Victor, he's pretty reasonable. Why don't you just ask him for it? I'm sure you don't want it out that you forked over your "poke" to somebody like Victor, now do you?" Again, Marlene with the smile, which at this time delivered the blow of death,

"All I ask for is just one more chance Pepe," said Victor, and with this one more chance Victor became a straight "A" student on how not to wear his thoughts on his sleeve and how to become more difficult to read. Yet, bigger than all of this, Victor learned how to read people like the Great Pepe.

Chapter 5

Next on the list was Nigel. Nigel spoke very little but when he did speak you automatically knew that he meant every motha fuckin' word he said. With him, Victor learned the most serious of lessons, how to divert and how to remain invisible by using the community as a camouflage. Nigel was pretty stable when it came to money but looking at him one would never know it because he never held his ill-gotten earnings up as a banner. In fact, you'd never know that he had any earnings. Riding around with him for months and never had Victor seen Nigel pull over to use a phone, and when asked why, Nigel would say, "Because, the FBI. They would take your calls and doctor them up somehow and ship your ass to Timbuktu forever." When asked the purpose for the binoculars, "Good question. I use these so I could watch who's watching me." When asked, when was the last time that he saw somebody watching him, he'd say, "This morning, this afternoon and right now."

"Right now?" Victor asked, not fully understanding,

"From the time I picked you up there's a red sedan, when we came out of the bait shop, a red sedan, and by the time I drop you off, there would be the same sedan," Nigel said as a matter of fact.

"Oh, well, you got me," said Victor and as an afterthought he added, "Well, if they're always with you, then how do you make money?"

"Now, that right there son, is the puzzle that you have to figure out. I mean I'd love to tell you but that's not you learning, that's me giving, could you dig it?" Not that Victor took to the challenge hard; in fact, it was fairly easy.

"Well, we went to the bait shop but not fishing, we went to the ice cream parlor just to order me a split even after I declined," Victor thought. So one day he relayed this to Nigel and scored a BINGO worth of excitement.

"Son, the only reason that you know that is guess why?"

"Because I've been watching you," said Victor.

"No. Those jerks back there is watching me; you win because you are with me. So, what does that tell you?"

"To be careful of whom I have with me." Victor murmured,

"Right, now with you knowing this, you also need to know that when you use a telephone, guess who you got with you, those guys back there. When you write stuff down and leave it, guess who? Leave your house unattended to then yes, you'll get those guys. Now, do you remember when I said that you could use your community to camouflage? Well, the red sedans and the people that they work for is my community. As long as they are with me, I could knock people off and walk away Scot-free. I mean, look who I got for a witness. You see, they want to know about the money that I'm making, narcotics, prostitution or gambling? No, Victor, I sell fear. Who loves you or who respects you don't mount up to who fears you. Do I worry about shady business deals? No, because at the first sign of deceit or betrayal I bust they head open. Not the second sight of it no, but the first. In this my warning shot is always fatal, still dig it?"

"Hell, yeah,"

"Then, what am I saying entirely?" Nigel asked, putting Victor on the spot.

"That if I camouflage myself right that I could get away with anything, and to scare the shit out of people."

With a smile on his face, Nigel was forced to ask: "And, just how do you go about this thing that you call scaring the shit out of somebody?"

"I haven't the slightest idea", Victor responded, and then, "What's so funny?"

"Nothing's funny, just that every time that I see you, you have this Sunday school thing going on and I try to imagine you this ruthless dude, like the Pope who knocks off Hitler. But never mind the humor; tell me, do you see how you could use that to camouflage your true intents? Be truthful, who would suspect you? But anyways, the answer that you need to be comfortable with is honorable. As long as you're honorable, then the people that you are dealing with, too, must be honorable. If not, tell me, is that not the first sight? A fool would say, 'you know what, if you do that again I'm gonna harm you.' Which means what? You gave somebody action at you twice. No, at first sight you sending a message, a cute little gift-wrapped one called revenge, fresh out of the fridge, nice and cold and that son, is how you scare the shit out of people, by playing for real, amongst those who are playing for funsies. In this I could already say that you got off to a bad start. Don't take this the wrong way, because it's the only reason why I'm taking this time to shape you up to begin with. But there's a nasty rumor going around that says that you got your hands on Pepe for his admired chain and his blue diamond pinky ring. I smiled when I first heard it, then felt like running your ass over once I heard that you gave it back to him. The only thing that I saw was a young blood on the move, only to shoot his self in the foot. Whatever you do, don't do that shit again. Pepe knew better, and now, so do you. It's because of when I drop you off this is going to be our last time getting together, unless of course you climb up the ladder and I see you orbiting higher up. This way, and only this way, would we pour the drinks and raise a toast. Then I would know that you knew how to read the writing on the wall. What I'm a give you is a puzzle and some poke. If you take what you learned from me, it'll help you with the poke. The puzzles however are all you though. Just know that there isn't one set way to be successful. Are you ready? The poke, the strip is full of working girls; the strip is run sloppily with no order to it. The puzzle is how to fix that without jeopardizing your mission. The poke, you live on the corner of a main artery for "HOP," heroin could you dig that. Little brother the spot is known all over town. The puzzle is the same, how do you clean all that up without jeopardizing you, or the mission. Poke, Pepe runs an all-night gambling club that generates a lot of money but guess what? He pays out a lot of money through extortion. The puzzle, how do you knock that off for them and fill that void for yourself, got that? And you got to do all of that without doing what?"

"Jeopardizing me or the mission," said Victor.

"Right, last but not least, Marlene: look out for her with knowledge that I'm a give you. She fucks with you because she wants to not because she has to. But should you trust her a hundred percent? No. Not even fifty. But when you're done with your puzzles you should gather the poke and if it seems like the right thing to do send your designs through her. Now, there's a bag in the glove box. Take it out of there and don't open it until you're in the house. Now, when I pull up, you need to hop out right away and bee line away from the truck before my company hits the corner. Remember, you owe me a drink, but first you need to shoot for the moon with confidence, that even if you miss you'll still land amongst the stars and do yourself a favor and lose the choirboy look. Some nice suits would love you the same. Now here we go, you ready? When I stop, take off you hear, and don't let them pinch you" and Victor didn't. The truck stopped and Victor made the perfect line for a bee; he didn't stop for anyone and fifteen seconds later the red sedan.

"Shit!" So, after one trip around the corner to throw it all off Victor hurriedly cut across the grass and to the front door he went. Yet, before he could twist the knob to enter Marlene hurriedly swung the door open, eyeing Victor with curiosity.

"What was that all about?" She asked.

"What?" He responded

"I saw you get out of the truck and head in the opposite direction, what just happened?" She asked.

"That wasn't about nothing, Marlene."

"Oh, then why do you look like you just got out of a space ship?"

"A long day already, would you do me a favor?" Asked Victor,

"Anything, wait a minute, what is it first," her suspicions were overwhelming her.

"Would you have a drink with me?"

"A drink, where have you been that makes you need a drink? Why you wanna…"

"Is that a yeah or a no?" He interrupted.

"I guess, but you have a lot of explaining to do. What is it that you wanna drink?"

"Anything, I just wanna have a drink with you."

"Ohhh, I mean, you never said anything like this before is why I'm nervous. Victor, is everything all right?"

"Yeah, couldn't be better, which is why I wanna have a drink with you." Saying that, Victor went to his can and retrieved six paper dollars and handed them to Marlene, saying, "We're running out of coals, would you bring some back please?" Marlene took the currency and left the house. After giving her a minute to be long gone, Victor took the bag from his waist to peer inside. From the way it felt in his waist he knew that the hard steely item could possibly be a gun, which was confirmed to be a colt .45 with a lot of loose bullets at the bottom of the bag. The paper that he kept repeatedly touching was an envelope that had nearly five hundred dollars in twenty-dollar notes, and a note that said, "A starter kit, don't keep me waiting drinks on you, remember." Victor, who never saw this kind of money and didn't even know that this kind of money existed, was too overwhelmed with all the information that he obtained over the past years to even be excited with his new wealth. He knew that he needed to hide the "piece" from

Marlene and find a suitable stash spot for the money that he had now and the money that he would obtain for the years to come. You see the poke was always the reason and the puzzles were hardly cryptic. Either he was gonna do it or he wasn't. Peeling away two twenty-dollar notes from his stash he made the decision to finally purchase a bed, which way he and Marlene could now get off the floor. Even though Marlene provided them with couches, carpet, and other furniture that made the shack as homey as could be under the circumstances, leaving Victor to wonder whether Marlene left the bed out on purpose so that she could continue to sleep with him on the floor. "Well, she could sleep with him on a bed now," he said to his self.

Marlene came through the door and headed towards the kitchen, within minutes she found him on the couch. She took the seat next to him, handing him a glass of the strong fiery liquid over ice, and after a couple of sips she said, "So, what are we drinking to?"

For that he reached into his pocket and retrieved the two notes and handed them over to Marlene and said, "How about to the first bed that we'll share together?"

"Oh," she stammered then gulped down her entire drink and headed towards the kitchen for a refill. She was taking too long to return, leaving Victor to say, "Why don't you bring the drink in here?" For this she arrived with the bottle and a bowl of ice. Marlene appeared to be uncomfortable, he asked her to pour him a refill, and sure enough, her hands trembled as she poured. This being the first time that he ever saw this part of her so he asked, "Are you all right?"

"Victor, where did you get this money from?" She panicked.

"Come on now; is that the best that you could come up with on such a short notice?" His smile this time sent the daggers.

"I just wanna know where you could have gotten that money is all."

"I never ask you where you get your money, now do I? Let's be for real right here and tell me, what are you saving me for, some kind of special Christmas or something, perhaps my eighteenth birthday, is that it?" Feeling the effects of the alcohol, he pushed some more.

"Guess what, I was eighteen a long ass time ago. Way before I met you, and after I met you. And from what I hear, two days after I was born I was turning eighteen. So, now you're pampering me as a cross between parents, a sister and then a neighbor to now I'm beginning to get confused by all of this. Sweetheart, you introduced me to a great big ole world with some great big ole people in it. So, you're building me up for whom again? For her is my guess whoever the hell she is?"

"Oh, Victor you're drunk."

"So are you Marlene, but tell me are you gonna go and cop us a bed? You see, I believe it's time for us to get off the floor."

"Anything else you want me to do?" Asked Marlene,

"Yes, there is, Marlene. I want, no, I need you to pledge your loyalty and your undying love for me."

"Oh, Victor I can't do that right now, are you serious?" And for a response she only received from him a stone face because Victor was not drunk, Victor was dead serious, and Marlene could easily be the first person that Victor ever walked away from.

"Oh my God, you are serious." Again the stone face.

"Victor, I don't want to hurt you in any kind of way, you just don't understand." Still the stone face. "Victor, I do love you, only I don't know what to do about it." For this Victor stood and walked to the closet, where Marlene had his clothes neatly arranged and he removed his items in haste before Marlene came to stop him.

"Wait a minute, please, just have a seat and let me explain."

"Explain what, the fact that right now you're a two-bit whore who figures that since her last man ran off that she may as well make her own man, only to discover that she really didn't mean it? Sorry to sound so harsh but I'm only saying what I'm seeing."

"And you're all right with that, Victor, a two-bit whore?"

"Shit no. I was thinking a hundred bits, fuck a short sale. A year ago you asked me to look around here. Now I'm asking you to look around here and tell me: do you see anything missing?"

"Oh my God, Victor, what do you want from me?" Marlene screamed, now trapped.

"I told myself that I was gonna only tell you once and I did; the rest, Sweetheart, is up to you," he said with ice in his voice now.

"Do I love you? Yes, I do, very much, with every bit of my heart. Do I want another? No. I want you Victor, you're right. I made you for me. There's no profit for me if you gave you to her, whoever she may be. Loyalty says I'd rather die with you than to live without you. And, by listening to you right now I don't regret a single minute of it. Just ask me and I'll do it but tell me, Victor, could you offer me the same thing? The same love, the same loyalty, the very same undying kind that I got for you?"

"I knew all of this the very same day I met you Marlene. You need to know that the very young man that you met has changed an awfully whole lot."

"I've been watching, so now what? What do we do now?"

"How 'bout pouring us another drink, this way we could sit and plot a marriage."

"A marriage… A marriage… boy don't play with me like that, Victor please."

"I'm not; now, do like I asked you, Marlene." The truth was, Victor never knew life before Marlene and couldn't imagine life without her. Because, Victor well knew, that it was Marlene who had brought Victor Raymond to life.

Chapter 6

In a two-room shack a promise was made, a quiet engagement that no one heard about but them, Victor and Marlene. No one would care anyways and this they both knew. As far as they were concerned, all they had in this world was each other, but to them even that was enough. Marlene was raised by the streets and was in the streets, she was even of the streets. Still for her even she knew that only certain doors would open up. Conceding that this was "a man's world" after all patients was something that she knew she had to be when she met Victor. Here was a man-child swimming upstream with a spark, not yet a fire, but a spark, a glare that needed nourishment and exposure and being of the streets allowed Marlene to know other hustlers that too, were of the streets. A bond only formed in the streets is called hood love and this is where she ran to in order to help shape Victor. Because of this she was exposed to the best of the best when it came to hustlers, and it was only the best that would do to help groom Victor.

What she didn't know, nor had any way of knowing was that Victor possessed an intelligence quotient that came really close to that of a genius: quote him numbers and it's locked in, quote him lessons of histories and it's like he was there, give him puzzles to figure out, no matter how cryptic, and the pieces would land in order and in the only sequence available. So, to underestimate Victor's dexterities would be fallacious and Marlene had learned this all by herself. So to now be engaged to this man-child, he, who of her own creation, as unorthodox as it may seem had brought her happiness as she slept in the bed that he, Victor had provided for them. So happy that she knew that she was gonna wake up and smother him a steak in her rich gravy and run it over the grits that he liked so much. And she would have too, only when she awoke, Victor wasn't anywhere to be found.

Victor on the other hand slept a grand total of six and a half minutes waiting for the sun to announce its arrival. As far as he was concerned, that was twenty months too long. He spent years and years waiting on this moment to come. To, and from school he saw games that he could play, pokes that he could swindle and people that he could meet that could help him put his pieces together. For weeks he was hidden behind binoculars, watching up and down Second Avenue some of the times, then 37$^{\text{th Street}}$ the other trying with might to heed Nigel's every word. It took weeks for the pattern to show itself. And this only reminded him that nothing ever came easy or overnight, so patience was required. "Bird watching" he called it, and yeah, birds were located on Second Avenue and on 37$^{\text{th Street}}$. As the Police Department traded shifts, so did their methods of surveillance. And the dope spots operated as if no one knew this but Victor. Conceding that it was none of his business to inform any of the dealers or the hustlers that they were under the watchful eyes of the cities finest. His business or not, hell, they were his neighbors, he thought. Basically looking for justifications to intrude on business, not his own. He didn't know for sure whether he should or shouldn't intervene. He relented because the internal argument that boiled within him became unanimous once he directed the binoculars towards the side of the house in question and saw there in the driveway, which was shaded by an overhead tarpaulin, a crap game going on full swing.

"Hell, I best go and warn my neighbors of their unexpected company," Victor thought. After removing the currency notes from the can of ready cash, which was eight dollars in total, and left the shack to encroach upon his drug-dealing neighbors who also doubled as public gamblers. Although everyone in the circle was familiar to Victor because of his "bird watching," no one paid much attention to him as he walked into the driveway, asking if he could play.

"What the hell, my man. Oh naw bra what you selling us we ain't buying, no books, no Bibles, no ...." The insults came from the shooter; he was shaking the dice as he spoke. Logging the insults, Victor pulled out his currency, asking, "Can I play, or is this a private game?" The murmurs took over after seeing the money visible and in plain sight. He was hoping that a gesture like such would grant anyone the invitation a maneuver that Victor was counting on. Then again came the insults as the shooter spoke saying, "Your money is as good as they money. If you're bringing it, then God must have wanted me to have it. I don't care how old you are; it's like taking candy from a baby." The roar of laughter took over the circle.

"Oh, is that right? So what kind of point you got?" Asked Victor,

"Whatever points you want me to have, youngster. How much money you got there?" Asked the shooter,

"I got a few dollars," said Victor.

"What is that, your allowance you came to give me?"

"Yeah, I think so," said Victor, then added, "and seeing that I'm on my way to church, why don't we find a way for me to hurry up and give it to you, or do we need to sit and talk about you having it a little longer before I give it to you." Smiling, Victor looked at the shooter to a round of "oohs" and "whoa" before he continued by surveying his clothing with his hands in an up and down motion, then said, "If I know Bishop like I do, he won't mind me gambling, but he is not gonna take to me being late," this said with a wink to show his humor. Again, the sound effects prevailed, "oohs" and "ahhs" leaving the shooter on the spot.

"Well, hell young one, seeing that you got a few dollars, how 'bout we start you off with a double." For this, two dollars each hit the pavement. The dice stopped on nine, a six and a three and for this the bettors voiced their beliefs. Looking around, Victor saw the dollars exchanging hands in various amounts, singles, doubles, fins and tens. Now, this was a crap game, Victor was thinking. Not bad for his first one, he thought, before a dice that showed a five stopped near his foot and the other one a four stopped by the money, totaling nine. The shooter collected his winnings and said, "Youngster, in this game we don't give the money back. You might wanna quit while you're ahead, go buy some shoes or something." For a response, Victor dropped another double, and the shooter took and shook the dice and again a nine, the same five and a four and again the bettors took flight. To everyone's surprise, Victor was one of them. Here, he let his remaining singles hit the concrete.

"You sure you wanna do that, young man?" Asked the shooter,

"Why not, I mean if I'm gonna get me some shoes, hell, I may as well get me some nice ones." Two rolls later, a five then the four showed itself before finally stopping on a deuce, and the winners gathered their winnings Victor included. Quickly, Victor scooped up the dice and shot them quickly, which was a default because at this time no one covered his fade or his bets.

"Whoa, whoa, whoa fella, maybe you're in too much of a hurry," said another hustler. "I'm sure Bishop would understand if you're just a little late. Somebody gotta cover you in order to shoot." It wasn't that Victor didn't know this, he knew all so well. He also knew that naiveté would bring a lot of attention from the sharks, too. So, in his best primitive impersonation he just said, "Oh," and with this the hook was set and everyone wanted to cover him at the same time. From "bird watching," Victor paid particular attention to this one brother who he came to know as Judah. Judah was always on his hustle, and clearly a hustler that Victor admired. So, when Victor finally got a fade, a cover, and a bet, he shook the dice and tossed them, a three, and then an ace. Countless times Victor copped four for a point, and the much-needed rhythm to revisit this one was no different and deeply rooted. He watched as the bettors fell over each other trying to bet that he'd crap out. So, with ten dollars spread in a circle hitting everyone except Judah, he shook and tossed the same three and the same ace, so he collected his winnings to the sounds of "That was luck" and "You lucky motha fucka" and "See how Jesus works" and a bunch of laughter. It was the eye contact that Victor shared with Judah, hoping that he wasn't as slow as the spend-thrift guys that he accompanied. He found satisfaction when he shook and then tossed a three, and this time a deuce. Again, the bettors left the gates like the Kentucky Derby. Again, Victor spread his bets around, watching and waiting for Judah to place his bets, and two rolls later the circle saw the ace stop first and hoped for a six that never showed, because the dice stopped on the money, showing a four to the sounds of "You believe this shit" and "Ain't that a dirty low down." Victor, in full rhythm now, didn't see any sense in remaining a double ante. So, up went the ante to a fin, which made the bettors a little nervous and began to feel a little bamboozled. Sensing this, Victor made the peter sweeter by saying, "I know what y'all thinking, God on my side and all but what I'm a tell you is gonna crack y'all up, funny as hell I tell you. See, first I threw a four, then I threw a five." Smiling, Victor said, "Now who wanna guess what my next point gon' be?"

"It ain't gone be a six, if that's what you want us to believe." This coming from the man who started with the insults and right away Victor knew that there was nothing anybody could do that would make him like this dude.

"All right, ole timer, what kind of jazz you talking? I still got some poke for shoes and a little more than my allowance," Victor antagonized him.

"You call it, two later points and now you a shark. Call it, I cover everything."

"Oh-kay easy money, being that I got the good sense to respect my elders and all, how about I sock it to you for a twenty, or I give it all to you if you cover two to one? Three to one say I do it twice."

"And by twice you mean?"

"Point six and I pass, simple." Meaning that not only would he land the six but he would do again in order to stay rolling.

The money fell, then the ole timer, "You're on, three to one," and with that Victor shook and tossed the dice, yet before the dice stopped the ole timer swooped the dice up and said, "Back here, young man, we play catch what you don't like and I did not like that shit." Passing the dice back to Victor, who shook the dice, and instead of releasing the pair, he released one dice instead of both just to run a check. And, sure enough, the old timer swooped up the dice.

"Gee whiz, cat daddy," said Victor, "something telling me that you ain't gonna like nothing that I throw out there." This is when Victor found out that the old timer's name was Larry, because another hustler said, "Dang. Larry, would you let the boy shoot the damned dice? You see he's running late for choir rehearsal, fuck." On cue, Victor stood and shook the dice and tossed them both. The shot felt good when it left his hand and he saw as the dice tumbled in perfect unison. In his heart, Victor knew that it was a score, and to prove it he was already picking up his partial payment before the dice stopped on a four and then a deuce. The yard filled with excitement and during this excitement Larry took on a look of embarrassment, and listened as Victor said, "You want some of this bread back, saying that I pass on the six?" Pride, being what it is wouldn't let Larry decline. Victor watched as the old timer released his now-dwindled wad, which stopped at sixty bones. Because of this, the bettors once again left the gates, this time in Victor's favor, meaning that no bets were open to Judah. When at first they all opposed Victor's rhythm, now they were in love with his song for real.

"Nah fella, no bet, I don't feel so lucky anymore. How about a twenty spot? I mean I was always taught to never take a man for his last." While saying this, Victor was sending telepathic signals and obvious eye contact to get Judah to cover the many jumping bets. He found satisfaction once he heard Judah say, "Hell, if he doesn't feel lucky anymore, then I got some bets for all you motha fuckas. Ain't nobody ever told me not to take a man for his last. Shit, where I come from they say 'Get it all, nigga, get it all!" And there is where the bettors pounced to their very own dismay, even though it looked good for them at first. For they all watched as Victor rolled a four, a five, then an eight, a nine, a ten and then a seven, all in that order, leaving only Larry to celebrate, yelling.

"Good try, but every road has got to end somewhere!"

"Yeah, you're right about that and I must say that's it's been fun but now let me run off to church before the good Lord tell bishop where I'm at. You guys have a good one." With that, Victor turned to Judah, signaling him to walk with him. Satisfied that Judah picked up on the message, the two made their exit.

"Say man, where did you learn to shoot like that?" Asked Judah,

"I was just lucky is all."

"Nah, you got a stroke. I saw the sequence. Somehow you skipped over that six, like you were trying to croak me on purpose, and to resuscitate me you skipped over the seven too. Shoot, jack I'm sure glad that you kept me in your prayers when you did that because I didn't know what I would do had you tossed that six on an accident. I got that forty that you waved on my account, choir boy," Judah said, reaching for his wad of cash.

"Uh uh, that's all you, cat daddy. I mean, I showed up with eight dollars."

"You know they ain't gonna let you do that again. Besides, I wouldn't bother if I was you anyways. I'd take that show on the road if I was you that shit was like the damn Ringling Brothers. Anyway, you need me for something?" Cut the chase huh, Victor thought.

"Yeah, something really important has showed up that you really need to heed. Also, I got some selfish reasons that I want to propose to you, a business deal really," Victor dove in.

"Well, hell jack, I like the sound of that already, I mean I'm all for the business."

"Yeah, I've noticed that. But what I'm saying ain't about no bullshit business, not even close. If you could look past the young face and the church clothes without thinking like, hey, here's an opportunity for me to hustle a young nigga out his poke then yeah, we would last. I mean other than that we could just go our separate ways right now, and I would still pull your coat to what could bring immediate danger to you."

"Danger," Judah's eyes widened.

"Yeah, pretty soon the man's gonna start pinching people and hauling them off to the pokey." The sound of "pokey" was enough for Judah, who gave Victor the eyes to show that he was skeptical. He sized Victor up, wondering how could he know a thing like that said, "And how do you know all this?"

"How 'bout this: I'll smarten you up and you pull me into this 'Hop' thang that's going on around here." Quickly Judah did a double take, not believing his ears.

"You're trying to peddle some heroin? What is the good Bishop gonna say to that?"

"Who's Bishop? Oh no, that's the way them dudes was looking at me. So, shit, I just ran with it. Come on now, we're wasting time. Do we have a deal or not?"

"Whoa, lil fella, first to dangers,"

"Deal or no deal Judah, last try."

"I mean, what you have in mind, at least allow me that?"

"Ten times what you make right now."

"How do you even know what I'm making right now?"

"I've been watching, and you said so yourself, plus it still wouldn't matter. I still propose the same thing." Victor remembered reading Judah when he schemed past the six to the eight, leaving Judah to finally exhale when he decided it was finally time to crap out, lest Judah went bankrupt.

"Ten times you say? I'm listening," said Judah.

"Me too" said Victor.

"And if I say no?"

"Then I'm gonna recommend that you hustle somewhere else."

"And if I said yes?"

"Then I'm gonna recommend that you hustle everywhere else."

"That was cute."

"Not trying to be. Time's ticking, Judah"

"Ten times better, huh. Are you serious, though?"

"Follow me?" Victor led Judah through his backyard and to his concealed bird watching spot and said, "Wait here, I'll be back." Victor went into the shack and to a worried-looking Marlene to retrieve his binoculars, while assuring her that he would return shortly he made it back to Judah. First, he needed to make sure for his self that the surveillance teams were still present. Locating them, he passed the binoculars to Judah and pointed, saying, "Green sedan, left side. What is that?"

Judah took the glasses and gave a good gander up the street. "Green sedan, you say?"

"Yeah, what is that?"

"I don't know."

"What you think it is?" Said Judah,

"I think it's the man."

"Why you say that?"

"Look on his chest and tell me what that is," said Victor.

Judah, focusing in on the driver's chest said, "Is those some binoculars, and oh, hell no, is that a badge?"

"You tell me, you got the bifocals."

"That is a badge. How long has this been going on that you know of?"

"Two and a half, maybe three weeks, who knows, maybe longer, plus this is just those guys. There's a new set that'll be showing up later on tonight."

"Fuck. I need to go and warn everybody" was Judah's first impulse

"I could see the loyalty in that but I could also see how that could sabotage the plans that I was putting together," said Victor, already regretting hipping Judah.

"How so?"

"They gotta pinch somebody or they're gonna always lurk and may even increase their numbers once they discover that they've been outsmarted."

"So, they're just like ducks?" Said Judah, pointing towards the dealers' locations,

"Judah, dig it man, if you need to hip them, hip them, but that ain't a problem for me. But you should know that the game came to me that a hustler is only as good as his secrets he could keep," Victor finished, locking eyes with Judah.

"And if I said nothing, you got plans to increase us, me and you times ten?"

"From the front, then it graduates," said Victor.

"How you know? Bishop told you that shit?"

"Nope, common sense told me that shit. I watched you, up and down the street you go, dip, dip split, dip, dip split. The dip ain't bad; it's the split I don't see the sense in. Two dips for you, then five other splits. After all, everybody else over there gotta eat too, right?" Victor said pointing towards the dealers' location.

"And the business deal with you is only a split time's one?" Said Judah seeing the logic in the proposition that Victor was proposing to him, and then came the hook.

"Not an even split either, sixty you, forty me." If Judah wasn't won over before, he surely gave in now.

"Oh-kay, I'm in, even though I know there's a catch, right?"

"Yeah, the catch is that this is the only set you win. The other two sets I win, where the break splits at seventy me, thirty you."

"First set first." Judah knew that the term "set" meant hustle.

"We up the quality of the junk you got and relocate taking as many fiends with us as possible." Victor saw too many fiends decline Judah's pitch and concluded the reason being was in quality control.

"That could run a pretty penny," said Judah, then added, "these fiends are trying with all their might to kill themselves; I mean I know just how to do it only I can't seem to break enough luck to score the poison that they want."

"And if you crunch the numbers, you're figuring?" Victor said, leaving Judah to fill in the blanks.

"Well, if we want to flop everybody around like jelly fish, then that could go four hundred a score. If you want the jelly fish to foam out the mouth between flops, that right there buddy could go to six hundred easy," Judah finished, pleased with his delivery and knowledge on such a topic.

"Oh-kayyy, so who's out here foam flopping?" Asked Victor,

"Nobody, I mean, no-bod-dee. If they were, you'd see the man over here and not parked down there." Victor studied Judah.

"Could you handle that, I mean, if we scored the foam flopping fish kind?" Asked Victor,

"I'd swear my only job would be to keep moving around so the pigs don't pinch but if I know fiends like I do, they would find me. Just to tight rope with the reaper, they would find me, no matter where."

"Six hundred is the root. What's the fruit?"

"After the step, I'd say triples the profit each time," Judah responded with certainty.

"The step, what's the step?" Victor asked, needing clarification.

"If you don't step on it at least a little bit, you're sure to croak 'em. Even stepping on it you still run the risk, and why is you looking at me like that?"

"Maybe tight roping with the reaper is what we need to set ablaze quicker," Victor thought loud enough for Judah to hear him.

"It will, but shit, let's just go with the step. It'll still set ablaze anyways. The seed money, did you hear me when I said six hundred smackers?"

"Yeah, don't worry. Just save your money and I'll find the rest."

"Are you jiving me? Lil daddy, because if you are the shit ain't funny, man."

"No jive. I mean, where they do that at?" Victor responded.

"Oh-kay, saying this is all true then, we come to set two, and this is where I get a thirty cut. Doing what?" Judah asked.

"The same as set three: nothing." Hearing this, Judah was sure that his leg was being tugged a little bit. Calmly he handed Victor back his binoculars and prepared to exit the same way from which he came.

"Thirty slash for doing nothing? You need another jack for that." Judah was nobody's fool and he knew it.

"That's what I said, Judah. You do nothing but hang out with me on my night thang, since I'm gonna pull in a pile of money out of my nights, then I may as well split it with somebody why not you?" This wasn't a sale and they both knew it.

"No, for real, what I gotta do? I'm serious," Judah asked.

"Just be honorable is all I ask, nothing after this."

"Hell, when do we start?" Was all he asked,

"Tonight,"

Chapter 7

For more than a month, Victor impressed upon Judah with maneuvers that made feasible amounts of income. And because of that alone, Judah got rid of the idea that Victor's age would hinder their intents or encumbers their motives towards financial enhancements. Yeah, he got rid of this idea all but quick. Not just the fact that Judah, at nineteen, was only a couple of years older than Victor, no! But because Victor showed Judah many traits that anyone should look for in a friend. Any thoughts of suspicion or thoughts of distrust that Judah could have felt for Victor were erased once he'd gotten to know Victor. From paying attention, Judah discovered that Victor always kept his word, and for a young one this was impressive. Even if the answer was "No," there was no changing his mind. The other thing that Judah found to be special was that Victor had a nice follow-through, and because of that Judah didn't bother to ask a lot of questions, and only found their journey to be more spectacular to wait and put the pieces together on his own. During the last three weeks, and every day of those weeks Judah scored for his self a grand or better behind a system brought about by Victor. Traffic was redirected to a location a half a block from the old location, with plans to move another block over in the coming weeks. They concluded that it was harder to hit a moving target than to hit a standstill one. All of this Judah found to his satisfaction. To prove this to be the best strategy, through twin sets of binoculars, Victor and Judah watched in disbelief the tactics used by the SPD during a raid operated on the dealers just a few doors down.

Cops were on foot, they showed up in trucks, and what appeared to be regular ole citizens and pedestrians transformed into Sacramento's finest and got in on the action. Doors were being kicked in by the officers that sounded like bombs were going off. And moments later produced a successful round up of every dealer. Until both, the dealers and their products were now in the custody of the long arms of the law. Mentally, Judah felt the appreciation for Victor deciding to hip him to the fact that a pinch was on the way, but emotionally Judah felt some kind of way as if he should have been one of the unlucky ones that were being detained. Crazy as that sounded, but awfully true. Well, not entirely true, because now that the cops had come and gone, so did the thought of being unlucky. A thought that cured itself the minute he left the pawn shop with a gem of a watch and let's put emphasis on "gem." There was the flawless diamond-encrusted bezel on the watch that matched perfectly with the spark that showed on every hour in pairs. Then, just one week later Judah bought a brand new Buick Electra 225 that doubled as a motel room on any given Friday for him. Even though Victor didn't like it, this boat of a car sure came in handy now that Judah discovered. Victor, who had yet to buy anything with his earnings complained a lot, but fetched a ride every night now that they started to meet up for their late night escapades. Which was a puzzle in itself, and Judah never understood the importance of the two of them needing to always be downtown at the same place and precisely the same time donning binoculars only to watch prostitutes run up and down the street, hopefully not to see them shaking their damn money makers at the potential johns.

Even though Judah had an idea that Victor lived with a prostitute, still, that didn't constitute a reason to make it to 4th and T Street before she did. Because Judah was about his bread and was old enough to know the principles of it all and one of them being that in case Victor at such a young age was moonlighting as an undercover pimp. Then he, as his dear friend was making his first mistake and a big one. Noted should be the reason you see, pimps, they don't go to the "Ho" stroll because tricks do and ho's do. Granted, since Judah knew Victor like he did, he was smart enough to just wait it out. This didn't last much longer because right when the spying and the snooping began to get uncomfortable, the excitement showed.

"You want to stay here until I get back?" Victor asked Judah,

"Why, you got something going on or something?"

"Something, could be nothing though," Victor responded,

"Nah, I'm with you, would be nice to know what's going on though."

"I'm working," was all Victor said before opening the door and trotting across the street and through an alley with Judah in tow. Slowing a bit to let their senses settle, they discovered that right behind a dumpster were the sexy sounds of a couple indulging in intercourse.

"Oh yeah, oh yeah daddy, give me some more of that white dick." What sounded like sex bought and paid for turned awfully violent.

"You whore bitch, take it in your mouth after I take it out of your ass before I cut you again." Now that was pretty expensive Victor thought, before pulling from his pocket the blue steel colt .45 that Judah would of swore that he never in life saw before, and walked to the dumpster.

"You heard me bitch! Don't tell me that you want me to cut you?" Said the trick, and eying the whole situation was Victor and Judah. So wrapped up in his evil, that the trick didn't notice the two and barely heard when Victor said, "Now, ain't this about a bitch; pinky has come all the way down here to rape darky...again." The trick turned on Victor giving a clear view of Marlene, who was caked in blood.

"You young nigger, what is you doing out here this time of night? Ain't your mammy somewhere looking for ya or ain't you got no mammy?" Victor revealed the blue steel, concealing his anger. He pointed the weapon at the pot-bellied, corn-fed john who flushed red all over.

"Baby, no! Look, I'm all right," Marlene said, scrambling to her feet, fixing her clothing and running towards Victor and Judah.

"He's just a John, nothing else. He's not worth it," Marlene pled with Victor.

"Yeah, I didn't mean it. I really apologize. Look, I'll give you all I have, just let me go. I swear to you I would never come around here again, that's my word," said the trick, now shaking uncontrollably with fear.

"Oh, first you got to give us all you got," said Judah, watching while the trick searched himself looking for valuables and coming up with a few singles and a promise to go to the bank to make things right.

"Nah, you see, trick or not, you just done the unforgivable." The first shot went off to an explosion of red mist and bone fragments as the knee of the trick shattered.

"Whoa, shit! Come on Victor, we better get going," said Judah.

"He's right baby, let's go," said Marlene.

"Nah, y'all go ahead. I'll meet y'all at the car." No one moved, only Victor when he moved towards the John, and three shots later had brains and gore splattered over the dumpster. As if nothing ever happened was how the trio walked back to the car. Marlene took to the back seat and Victor and Judah took to their seats respectively where they calmed themselves.

"Should we get out of here, Victor?" Asked Judah,

"No," and for a punctuation mark Victor donned the binoculars and continued to scan up and down the "Ho" stroll. After a long moment of watching, Judah spoke first.

"Fella, I don't know what all we doing here, but it looks as if everyone is leaving, which tells me that the man is coming pretty soon."

"Yeah, I know. That's the same thing I was thinking."

"Oh-kay, so, umm...," Judah, left the opening for Victor to bring a better understanding than the one that he had drawn up on his own.

"We wait, I mean, unless you got other things that you need to do."

"I'm with you and you know this; I'm just looking for the sense in this, is all." As Judah was speaking they saw cop cars come to a stop and from a phone booth a fella in some awfully loud colors for a night time of leisure gone out to meet the cops. His platform shoes gave him away; he was a pimp.

"Now, would you look at this," said Victor as they saw as the cops took directions from the pimp potna which pointed in the direction that Victor and Judah had gone. They watched as the brother sent the coroners and emergency units through the alley. The trio watched as the professionals worked efficiently and hurriedly and then the calm came back to the stroll a few hours later. Seeing this, Victor said, "Hold up, I'll be right back." Victor got out of the car,

"Baby, wait!" Marlene hopped out of the car and ran to catch him.

"Marlene, I need you to wait in the car with Judah; he's a good dude, don't worry."

"Are you gonna hate me Victor?"

"Not at all, just do like I said you hear me." Like she was shot from a rifle was how Marlene was back in the car, and there she watched as Victor crossed the street and walked with his head low and hands in his pockets. Moments later he was next to "pimp potna," who was entertaining women. The pimp reached into his pocket to retrieve a cigarette, then the two loud explosions announced that a gun had been fired, and with a kick that sent the loud suit and the pimp in it reeling over the hood of a nice-looking Bonneville leaving blood on its windshield. Without appearing to be in a hurry to get back to the car, Victor spoke to the women who saw "pimp potna" get blown out of his shoes, like literally because one of his shoes was displayed on the sidewalk for all to see.

Judah and Marlene didn't know whether to wait or go and get Victor, and they rejoiced when they saw Victor reach into his pocket and fork over some ducats before crossing and heading towards the car, which started up and pulled off once Victor was inside.

"Victor, my man, you know, I'm a good dude, and try awfully hard not to question anything that you do, I swear, but what kind of shit was that?" Judah said, barely holding his patience.

"Like I said, I'm working."

Chapter 8

"Working, working," Judah said through excitement "You call this working?"

"Wooo, I'm so pumped up right now, you should have heard that nigga. He was gurgling and shit, like he was trying to snitch one mo' time before he left." Victor's excitement was apparent.

"Oh, this shit funny now, ha, ha, ha. I done pissed my pants over here waiting and you over there with this comedy and shit."

"I'm just saying though, the sounds that nigga was making, woo, I'm so pumped. Look, let's drop Marlene off and let's get to the Game Room." The Game Room was open all night, only Judah never cared for this kind of stake out. In fact, this is when Judah would hop in the back seat and doze off before his shift started but on this night he knew that sleep was never going to come. Nodding his head, he cut the wheel heading towards the house that Victor shared with Marlene and waited in the car as Victor lead Marlene into the house, only to return in a two-piece suit and a pair of patent leather kicks. Victor was looking rather dapper if Judah had to say so himself.

"So how is she?" Judah asked once Victor was inside the car.

"She's lost; don't know if I'm coming back or not." Victor said, shrugging his shoulders,

"That was some crazy shit, you spending time with the ladies after the wham; the pigs probably out looking for you right now have you considered that?"

"That's what we're going to find out now. So, let's get to the Game Room so I could get Pepe to send me to the back before they show."

"Before who show?"

"The ladies," Victor said with a broad smile on his face as he emphasized the word, ladies.

"What the fuck? You, hell nah, you invited them to the Game Room?" Judah asked in disbelief.

"Yeah, to the VIP section, where I'm gonna be waiting for them at to see how they really feel you know. I mean I know how you like sleeping in the car and all but I brought these and I need you to help me out just a little bit," Victor said, handing one of walkie talkies to Judah, then said. "They should show up in a cab. Once it shows up radio me, or they might show up in a cop car. In that case, radio me then get the hell out of here." Maybe it was because Victor was smiling that gave Judah the impression that he just couldn't be serious, only Judah knew that Victor was always smiling and could have sworn that Victor had a smirk on his face when he shot the gentlemen in the alley. Believing that Victor was very serious, no matter the smile or the smirk which taught Judah that his new friend Victor was out for real, and with no turning back.

"So, why would she doubt your coming back or not?" Judah changed the subject, accepting the walkie talkie.

"Well, she got an idea that I was out spying on her and didn't like what I saw for starters." Victor shrugged his shoulders again.

"Oh-kay, now that you brought it up, why was you out spying on her?"

"I wasn't, not at all, believe me. Marlene is a good girl and she do what she do because she do it. Like, do she know about the business that me and you are conducting? No, not at all, and don't hip her if you could help it. I mean why you think I ain't made none of them extravagant purchases that you're out here making? Nice watch by the way, but believe Judah, I wasn't out spying on her. Look, pull up here so that you could get a good look without being seen. Remember, I need you to stay woke lest a surprise slip past you," Victor said, hopping out of the car.

"Don't worry about shit like that," Judah said to the sound of his car door closing. He watched as Victor made his way to the rear door of the storefront club, one that offered after-hour activities, and saw as Victor rapped a few times on the door. He saw as he spoke through a slide, waited a minute, and then he was admitted through the door of the club.

"Oh-kay, let's see what the night got for you my friend: cop or cab," Judah said to his self, getting comfortable, for he knew that the night could be a long one. "Oh oh," Judah said, scratching a long one from his list as a cab pulled up to the rear just moments later. He waited until he could identify the passengers before he sent the signal. Seconds later, he saw four barely dressed women exit the cab and make their way for the door. With that Judah buzzed Victor, who came on right away.

"What you got?" Asked Victor,

"Cab, I got a cab plus four," Judah responded.

"There's gambling and free drinks, dancing and fast women for you if you're interested," came Victor over the radio.

"What kind of question is that?"

"Hold up, cat daddy. You guys can have a seat, drinks on the house as long as you'd like. Cat daddy, you still with me?"

"Yeah, I'm all in. What I gotta do though?" Asked Judah then, "I'm at the door right now,"

"I'm gonna come and get you." Excusing his self from the ladies, Victor went to hip the doorman to Judah, as he'd done for his other visitors. Both Judah and Victor checked their radios in to the doorman. Victor leaned into Judah and told him that for him the drinks were on the house and not to gamble at Pepe's table, lest he felt like donating to charity.

"Hell, well you just fucked over the rest of my night then; I felt like letting off a little steam anyways, in fact I'm feeling kind of lucky."

"Then go ahead but don't say that I didn't warn you." Victor headed to the bartender and pointed out to Judah; this way for Judah a tab would run. Discreetly he slid the bartender a neatly folded Ben Franklin, then Victor headed back to the VIP section where he'd gone immediately into his spiel.

"First of all, I'd like to thank you guys for showing up. I won't keep you long, and all I ask for is just a little cooperation. For starters, there has been a change made to the way we're gonna make money. If any of you have a pimp, now is the time to hit the door." Victor went to the door and swung it open; nobody stood to leave. "Last chance, not that I despise pimps, because I don't. I don't hate the way anyone decide to put bread on the table, but I work for a very powerful man who don't care one way or the other how he sends his messages. Tonight I saw you share company with a snitch, and he got his rewards for that tonight. Is there anyone here who feels as if aiding the man is a good thing? If so, just know that after me, there will be more to come, just like me or even worse. I'm just a messenger and my message is this: thirty percent of all takes, no fakes, no pull backs. And from what I saw, there's a lot of problems with stragglers, which if you ask me is ruining the hustle. I say move them out the way and your pay increases. Instead of paying a pimp every penny, every hundred dollars you pull back seventy. Minus the stragglers, minus the pimps, I could see it working, you get paid, I get paid and we get paid." Victor paused.

"Well, first, who is the man that you work for?" Asked one of the ladies,

"His name is Raymond Buchannon, any more questions?"

"Yeah, what happens on a slow day?" Said another lady,

"There are no slow days. I've been watching, and always will be," said Victor,

"There's a lot of competition on the street honey who's to say?" Said the first lady,

"We're gonna reduce that at least fifty percent. Whoever ain't with us get ran over by us, simple." And after that night, no one doubted a thing that Victor relayed to them.

"Wow," said the lady who sat in the middle, "Reducing the track that much, honey my pussy would never catch a break." This drew laughter from the other women, but not Victor.

"And just how do you plan for all this to be for real," asked the comedian.

"Well, in this I'm gonna need your help. Tomorrow we'll all meet again, right here, and whoever you believe to be friendly bring them with you. Whoever is in the way could be easily identified that way. Remember who ain't with us, then yeah!" For this, Victor received nods of the affirmative.

"Good, tomorrow let's say midnight, right here. So, anybody feel like a party?"

"Yes," came the chorus, and together they all stood.

"What we want to know is how the hell you got in here. This is a club, ain't it?" Again the comedian commented, who was obviously referring to the youth of Victor.

"Pretty soon I'll own the place." And to four different shocked faces, he said, "To prove it, the drinks are on the house, the dance floor is always happening, the gambling tables are wide open, but I don't recommend that."

Chapter 9

Victor left the VIP section and headed towards the club and found Judah sweating bullets at a Black Jack table.

"What's up, Pepe? What you got going on right here, you taking candy from a baby?" Victor asked then took a seat. "Mind if I play a few hands?"

"Not at all," said Pepe, who began to deal the cards. One card down and one card up dealing Victor's first hand, he drew a three down and a face card up. Seeing how Pepe held a four of diamonds up, he placed his bets. Two "C" notes hit the table in front of him, just in time to see Pepe draw a bust. He remained emotionless, winning or losing, he remained emotionless. For Victor knew that to beat Pepe he would need a stone face no matter the occasion. Three hands in the can, leaving Victor twice a winner and once a loser, Victor shifted to an even more focused avenue. Deep in concentration he was, so deep that he barely felt the brush that came across his cheek, a very soft peck planted by Anna who was the comedian out of the four. She whispered in his ear, saying something about them having enough fun for one night and would rather hop on their assignments. In total agreement, Victor dismissed them all while receiving four soft pecks as the ladies filed out of the club.

"Kid, I don't know what it is that you are up to but it sure looks like you are up to it," said Pepe as the club paid the scarcely dressed women their full attention.

"Shit, me either," said Judah, "and I'm with him every day."

"One more to me Pepe, and are you all right Judah?" Victor said this because Judah still hadn't made it back from the aftershock of watching one bombshell after the next exit the club.

"Yeah, I'm cool, how about a drink you on for one?" Judah asked Victor as he stood to go and juice himself.

"No, nothing for me, fella,"

"Sure ain't," interrupted Pepe, "his *ass* ain't even supposed to be in here."

"In that case Judah, make it a double for me."

"Victor!"

"I was only playing, Pepe." Both watched as Judah left ear shot, then Pepe said, "Your boy is down quite a bit."

"How much he owes you Pepe?" Asked Victor,

"More than a triple can he cover it, or do I gotta give him a job?"

"You may need to rough him up a little bit."

"Yeah?"

"No! Man, what the hell wrong with you? You think I'd bring you somebody like that?" Victor said, shaking his head.

"Oh-kay, oh-kay so, the girls?"

"What about them, Pepe?"

"How often can you bring them through here?"

"How about this: I'll answer your question if you answer mine."

"Shoot."

"Why the sunglasses?" Even though Victor knew the answer to this already, he wanted to hear it from Pepe.

"That, my dear friend, is none of your business."

"Oh, well, let me take some guesses: black Cadillac, two brothers are gonna show up, collect from you, if not they gone punch the shit out of you and demand more, am I right or no? Then, guess what, both of them would stop at 'hop' alley on the way out and cop a bag of black and spike right there in the alley until they are both some nodding and drooling fools, and they are doing all of this guess what, with your money." Victor finished with a smile as he offered up his correct summation.

"What the fuck's so funny? You don't know these guys."

"Wrong," Victor interrupted. "I know everything about them except who they work for."

"No one, they work for no one. I did time in the joint with one of them who made it safe for me to be there is all."

"Hmm, and percentages?" Asked Victor,

"Not here, not now."

"Well, I'll be waiting in the VIP section. You're wrong, we do talk about it here and we talk about it now, because unlike them, I do work for somebody who's way more impatient than those guys in the Cadillac would ever be."

"Is that so, and who is it that you work for Victor? Someone worse off than those guys?"

"In the VIP section, Pepe," Victor left, heading through the ropes, moments later joined by Pepe.

"So, who's the guy?"

Victor almost forgot, and said, "What guy, you talking about the guy that I work for?"

"Yeah, that guy. Normally I wouldn't believe it, but I can't recall a time that you lied to me, and the women add credibility, giving you the overnight success look."

"His name is Raymond Buchannon, real heavyweight, sent me as a messenger is all, Pepe. He'll enhance for a small yet stable percentage."

"Oh yeah, and what could he do for me? What could he do for Pepe, huh?"

"Well, for starters he could get rid of the sunglasses for you, bring in more gamblers, turn this place into a real juke joint, Pepe."

"Is that right? And what kind of percentages would he be asking?"

"Pepe, you are my mentor and I hate to see you like this. You've taught me a lot, so I'm gonna ask that you remain being true to me when I ask you to tell me the truth about the percentages that you are already paying out. I'd rather you tell me because my boss man would make these guys spill it out, so I'm a need y'all numbers to match."

"Oh yeah, so he's one of those kind of guys?"

"Numbers, Pepe?"

"Fifty, fifty,"

"No more, Pepe. How about sixty forty your way, plus the enhancements? Revamp the place, more ladies, more gambling, ultimately more business."

"I'll say that I would love to do business with this guy, this Raymond Buchannon."

"Oh-kay, one last thing, I'll need this section at midnight tomorrow night, yeah?"

"Anything for you, Victor," With that, Victor left the VIP section, only to join a desperate-looking Judah.

"Man, these guys are in me for a nickel already," said Judah.

"That's not a problem, is it? I mean, you could always leave your watch and come back to get it?"

"Man, don't play with me like that."

"Then pay them and let's get out of here. I'll go and get the radios, oh-kay?"

"I was thinking we go to the dice table and you could do that thing you be doing with the sequences and all, you know, help me be the winner."

"I bet you don't remember who it was that told you not to go and gamble with them people in the first place, now do you Judah?"

"Shit, man. Can't you swing some kind of discount for a brotha?"

"No, pay them and let's get out of here. You don't know it yet but it's gonna be daybreak. You know what that means don't you?"

"Shit, already." Judah looked at his watch then cursed again, knowing that his shift was gonna start soon. He dug in his pocket and counted out the sum needed to pay Pepe and before heading out, he offered up a very sarcastic "it's been a riot." When they made it back to the car Victor caught Judah before he started up to leave. Victor put his hands out to stop him.

"Wait a minute, just a little while longer."

"Oh-kay let me guess: another one of your surprises?" Judah couldn't believe it and vented his discomforts.

"Yeah, I got to give it to you; you really had me fooled this time. Now here I am thinking that you were spying on the one girl but noooo, you were casing out the whole damn street. I don't know what you told them back there but I didn't get any kisses, none of those come fuck me looks. It seems like I need to knock me some motha fuckas down just to get some respect around here, is that it?"

"So, how many drinks did you have Judah?" Victor asked, seeing the alcohol's effect on Judah.

"About two or dree, that's all, why?"

"Hah, Judah, that's a drunk answer, what the fuck is two or dree, are you sure you got it today?"

"Fool, I was only playing. Those watered-down ass drinks, that nigga need his ass kicked for that." As Judah was talking the black Cadillac arrived and parked outside of the clubs exit.

"Judah look; you ever see them niggas before?" Victor pointed to the car.

"Hell yeah, every day, broke ass niggas always want some credit and shit."

Victor continued: "Oh-kay, give them some credit. Even let them have the alley with no complaints, just keep them happy is all I'm asking, then clear the alley out of possible witnesses and I'll handle it from there."

"I heard the hell out of that: leave it up to you, huh? While I kick back and watch you get all famous and shit with whores galore? I'm your partner, ain't I? Shit, man, why leave it up to you?"

"I was trying to keep you out of trouble is all." Victor reminded Judah as Judah navigated the streets of Oak Park.

"Fuck that! I've been looking for trouble since last week. Lucky for them niggas in the club I ain't have a pistol when they took me for a nickel or I would have echoed off in that motha fucka for stealing my motha fucking money, while giving me some watered down ass alcohol. The only reason why I'm tripping is because I really needed that drink. I mean, just off dude with the funny socks and shit. I would of just boom, boom, boom in that motha fucka. Like nigga I want my money back."

"Well, anyways, pull up over here so you could do your business."

"So?"

"What?"

"Do I need a gun or what?"

"Maybe so, not for them though. This gotta go as quiet as possible but the message must be a powerful one I know that much."

"In the alley though? Where we do our business at and shit?"

"We could always drop them off," said Victor.

"Are you serious?"

"Mmm, hmmm,"

"I don't know where you learn this stuff, but gee whiz."

"I don't know where I get it either Judah, but on with the radio and let's go to our post."

"Listen, you know they got the homeless people that live in the alley. They very seldom do anything but watch shit."

"How you get rid of them is on you."

"Should I just go in stabbing they ass. Maybe I'll get some respect around here that way."

"I mean, if you want to but I was thinking that when them niggas come to score, you just send everybody to the store or to the diner or something. I really don't care let's just hurry the fuck up and open up shop, it's rounding that time." With that Victor hopped out of the car and walked briskly towards the shack, and through the front door he went. He tiptoed through the house until finding Marlene asleep in the bed, which was a good sign. He concluded that she needed all the rest that she could get. He also knew that she needed all the ice that she could get in order to make the swelling to go down. So, with that for knowledge he packed a bunch of ice and headed to the room and placed the ice on to her face bringing her to full attention.

"Victor, you made it, thank you Jesus."

"Yeah, I made it. Look, I need to make you pretty again, so you're gonna have to deal with the ice, oh-kay?"

"Victor, do you hate me right now?"

"No! I love you Marlene. Love don't let you hate, I mean, ain't that what you tell me?"

"Oh, Victor, who are you changing into?"

"A butterfly; no more caterpillars for us."

"So, now what do we do?"

"Well, I got a job for you to do, a square job."

"Victor, I'm a ho, there's no square job for me."

"Marlene, you are a woman, a lady and an ex-ho. Now, the quicker you realize that, the better off we'll both be."

"Victor, you're trying to starve us to death."

"Nuh uhh, as a matter of fact, that's the job: you get to cook all day."

"And who's gonna eat my cooking? It's a wonder that you do."

"You underestimate yourself," Victor said, and then the sound of his radio came to life.

"Victor, why do you need that thing?" Marlene picked up the radio.

"Now you know how I feel about all the questions."

"I only want one answer, just one, Victor, please."

"Oh-kay, just one,"

"No! Two, Victor, please. Last night, did you do that for me? Was that on the count of me?"

"Yeah, and the other question?"

"Would you ever call me anything other than Marlene all the time?"

"Yeah, how about cutie or baby or honey or sugar or sweetie, something like that?"

"Are you kidding around with me?"

"I am, but still do us the favor and ice up and I'll see you when I get back."

"You're leaving again? Hurry back I'm starting to get lonely again."

"I will be back as fast as I can, and then I'll spend time with you, oh-kay?"

"I would love that, and would you have a drink with me?"

"Of course, what's the occasion?"

"The fact that you are all grown up now."

"I heard that. In that case, I'll bring back a big bottle."

"Yeah, that's what I was thinking, a really big bottle."

"Get some rest, Marlene."

Chapter 10

Victor went through the house, changing his clothes. Doubling up even, for he knew a mess was on the way. He chose his weapons carefully, and then left the house to meet up with Judah.

"Shit, took you long enough," Judah complained impatiently.

"What we got?" Asked Victor,

"In the alley, nearly sleep from the junk. I'm so anxious that it's killing me." Judah continued to pace.

"Where is everybody?" Victor noticed the scarcity.

"Told them that I'm expecting a raid and that got them going."

"Well, ain't no sense in keeping them waiting, I mean, since they like sleeping so much." With that Victor followed Judah through the alley and to the Cadillac, where the two dope fiends were enjoying their high with the seats laid back and the windows rolled down. Upon seeing this, Victor gave Judah a blade and a signal for the count of three using his fingers. When no fingers remained, they both attacked with fierceness, Judah through the driver's side and Victor through the passenger's side. Hacking and sticking, poking and ripping away at the flesh of the two fiends. Seconds turned into minutes, and the once Grey, leather interior was now a rusty crimson color, as blood flowed like a river throughout the car. Tired from the attack and messy was the job, just how Victor envisioned it to be. So, through gasps, Victor said, "You got to drive them through the alley." He thought that this would shake Judah up a bit but found that he had another thing coming once Judah pushed over the dead driver and jumped into the driver's seat and started the car. He watched as Victor hopped into the rear before he drove off. In the back, Victor had gone straight to work, where he carved into the dope fiends flesh the name "Raymond Buchannon."

"Come on and hurry up. Let's wipe it down and let's get out of here," said Judah, and they did. Back through the alley they went, disrobing along the way, Judah now to his undershorts, Victor down to the set that he wore underneath.

"Ain't that a bitch? You ain't say shit about bringing a spare wardrobe."

"Shit, it ain't doing no good. Look, blood soaked through. Hold on, wait here and I'll go and get you something." Victor sprinted through the alley and to the house. Slowing as he came to the door, he pushed it open slowly and through the house he went.

"Victor, is that you?" Yelled Marlene from the room,

"Yeah, I forgot something, I'll be right back." With clothes in hand, Victor was back outside in full sprint to Judah. Finding him crouched between bushes, he handed him some clothes and held watch for him while he got dressed. Once dressed, they were safely tucked away at the far end of the alley away from the Cadillac, and away from suspicion.

"Judah, I need you to take me to the store. I 'pose to have been back with a bottle."

"Shit, I'm ready to go get somebody else, ooh my heart racing. I heard that motha fucka gurgle though, shit man, whoa." Judah's excitement bothered Victor for a minute, and then he calmly reminded Judah that he needed a bottle.

"Look, fuck that. You just go home and take care of the girl and I'll bring back a bottle. I'll handle the fiends, but what I want to know is what do we got for tonight?" Yes, Judah's excitement was a problem.

"There's a lot of work for tonight. Hopefully you could score a pistol by then but whatever you do, bring the bottle back quickly, and trust me, you should get some rest." With that, Victor headed through the walkway that led to the house.

When Judah returned with the bottle of Brandy, Victor had gone out to meet him.

"So, how do you feel, right now?" Victor asked Judah right away.

"My adrenaline is sky high, I'm serious," Judah responded with the obvious.

"Which is what I want to talk to you about, listen to me? Judah I learned it all when I was small about how to survive. With me, survival was my only option, nothing else after that. And the one thing that I managed to learn along the way is that you do wrong when you need to, not because you want to. I fear that you have now given blood to a beast, which scares me because I dig you like I do. But I dig me too, and the game came to me that I need to be careful with the company that I keep, which is also my advice to you."

"And you're telling me this because of why again?" Judah shrugged his shoulders.

"Because with me it's to advance up the ladder, and I fear that with you it's to get respect. I mean I've been wrong before and could be wrong again and even now. I just need to know that me and you are on the same page, which is awfully important."

"I could dig it and I could hear that. But correct me if I'm wrong, you say that you are on your way up the ladder and I can't help but to think that you wish for me to run up that fucker with you. Well, aren't you not just thinking for you, but for me too? I mean what if I felt as if this is where I belonged, in Oak Park. By hearing me say this, does this mean that you and I aren't friends anymore?" Victor, after hearing Judah say this, knew that this being the exact moment that marked everyone as the individuals they were. Some like black, some like white, not that Judah was being intractable, no. Judah was being Judah, his own unique and individual self. Victor, who had to concede to this reality, just shook his head in the negative, and said, "Naw, Judah that's not what that means at all, and my apologies, you hear."

"None needed. So I need to rest up for what again?" Again, Judah shrugged his shoulders.

"Tonight we could score big; we need to rid the stroll of stragglers, who are really messing over the flesh trade, you know."

"Oh-kay," Judah wore obvious confusion for an expression.

"Nothing really serious, just a few nicks and cuts, scare the hell out of some folks to open up a lane for some boss shit to ride through."

"Sounds like pimping to me, potna."

"Just earning a keep, move the stragglers, get them out of the way and I can see some good bread in it for us."

"And you're not scared to show your face on the stroll after last night?" This time it was Judah that showed some concern.

"I thought about it, only thing that bothers me is the timing, that's all. We got some right now poke to tend to, not no few days' later action, some right now dough, you hear that. I just as well as go and get down over there then to sit here and let somebody else wet their selves off our designs," Victor rambled off.

"Mmm, I think I know what's going on. Let me ask you: what do the foxes that showed up in the cab got to do with any of this?"

"Everything, in fact tonight it goes down at Pepe's. I told them to invite whoever got they brain thang going on I mean if they want to get work daily without a hitch."

"And you're figuring that moving the stragglers would increase the take by clearing it out over there for them to handle more cases, huh?"

"That's my belief Judah," Victor said, digging Judah's terminology with "cases."

"Well, dig it? How about you get to Pepe's and I'll handle what's going on over there on the stroll?" Judah suggested.

"At first I said that you wouldn't have to do anything for your split; I sort of wanted to stick to that."

"But?"

"You're right, I run a risk, and I got a plot that cause for me to be two places at one time."

"Same thang I'm saying, so you say just a few nicks and some cuts..."

"And they'll need to know that Raymond Buchannon sent you," interrupted Victor.

"I saw you write that up. Is this who we work for?"

"Something like that but you really do need to push that part as an issue, could you handle that?"

"Yeah, nicks, cuts, Raymond Buchannon, I could handle that, cake and ice cream."

"Judah?" Victor said suspiciously.

"I'm telling you man, I could handle it." And in this case "handle it" took on its own definition. By the time Victor made it to Pepe's, the words began to circulate, that Raymond Buchannon had released a psychopathic butcher with serial killer tendencies on the prostitutes, Johns and the pimps alike, who found 4th and T to be two very unlucky streets on this night. And all of this was to Victor's surprise. Had it not been for Pepe's over willingness to satisfy Victor on every turn, Victor would have remained in the dark a while longer, with no understanding to the events at all.

"Oh-kay Pepe, what the hell's going on? Your debt collectors are here or something?" Victor asked.

"No, why are you saying that?" Pepe sent his brows up.

"Well, for starters, I've been here eight minutes, yet have you stopped asking me if I needed anything? Plus, you're fidgety and you're following me, and never have you ever offered me a drink since I've known you, and tonight it happened twice. What the hell is going on?"

"Well, there's a lot of excitement going down in the city tonight. I don't think I got a debt collector coming in tonight, unless of course that's what you're doing here. The VIP section is full of people, wide-eyed and waiting on you, who I really hope that you could calm down and persuade them into enjoying their selves in this fine establishment that I have here, and did I leave out that I don't think I have any debts to pay out tonight, because the funniest thing came over the radio this evening...."

Victor interrupted him by saying, "A lot of excitement, what you mean by that, the pigs or something?"

"No, this boss of yours has released a hell hound downtown. Better than that, would you mind telling me where you getting these fine threads from? I mean, first you looked like 'we shall overcome,' now you appear to have an in-house tailor. Now I know Marlene, she could cook yes, could hustle of course, hardly the clothing designer though. Last but not least, April." Pepe finished as if Victor should have known the rest; instead he drew a blank, then a measly,

"April what?"

"Not what, who, so how 'bout it?"

"Oh-kay, you win, who's April?" Victor's confusion was broad now.

"Well, only the most beautiful, luscious piece of butter pecan that ever stepped foot in this club, and you know how I like cookies." Now this was true: Pepe had a weak spot for cookies, especially the butter pecan ones. So, to compare whoever this April woman was to the rich flavor of the butter pecan package not only piqued Victor's interest, but it also heightened Victor's anticipation at finally being able to meet something so wonderful.

He said, "Yeah, Pepe, I know how you like cookies." Victor spotted the clock, knowing that it wouldn't be quite midnight, figured she could wait with whoever else was in the VIP and decided to push Pepe for more information.

"So, there's a hell hound downtown you say?"

"Mm hmm, those girls ran in here so quick that most of us clocked a genuine world record from the high yellow one and the pearly white one, and to our amazement, was how these records were registered. Because the first two that made in were both wearing high heels." Pepe shook his head, and taking the toothpick from his mouth, and said, "So how 'bout the April lady that I keep asking you about that got you so slow to talk about?"

"Pepe, I ain't got nothing to do with none of that."

"Yes, you do. I know when something's going on, and especially when you're the one who's got it going on. Don't act like I don't," Pepe said, wagging his finger.

"I'ma go as far as saying that you're on your own when it comes to that, Pepe."

Chapter 11

Midnight found Victor heading through the ropes of Pepe's VIP section, and once through the doors the overwhelming scent of perfumes and body sprays, shampoos and conditioners filled the air. This presented a toxic mixture which could turn this place into a real gas chamber, Victor thought before closing the door. As he entered, the chatter came to a halt and all bugged eyes were on him.

"Glad that you guys could make it. As I said before, I won't take up much of your time, which I know to be a precious thing. But, if you are here, then I can't help but to think that you'd agree to the terms that I'll relay to you right now, lest you'd be one of the unlucky ones that are out there probably getting maimed or murdered," Victor said, milking the looks for what they were worth, and right away, from the twenty-two women dressed as if they were for advertisement strategies, and all whom graced the VIP section. Victor found out all but quick who this April woman was. She stood out from everyone: her beauty was undeniable, a swan amongst the rest. Her neck was visible, her thighs as well, revealing caramel at its most creamy. She moved with a grace all her own; she was regal and she knew it, but never would she showcase the conceit that accompanies such a knowledge. She listened attentively and only asked the relevant questions. Victor could understand in full Pepe's nervousness to approach such a person. Only, Victor didn't miss a beat as he rambled off issue after issue, and once he reached his conclusion, it was established: twenty-two women at thirty percent. The club was the drop and the place for them to bring Johns and other appearances. It was an effort to brighten up "this place" as he called it. The drinks would be on the house; only problem with that came from a nasty rumor that went throughout the city that "Pepe's Game Room" was notorious for its watered-down drinks, and for this a mental note was made to change this shortcoming, and for this Victor would send a runner, who was to locate the real bottles and bless his company with a good time. For the understanding was perfect without mention, that tonight, his company would have as a welcome the rest of the night off, and with that Victor was off to find Pepe, which wasn't hard to do, considering that Pepe was waiting for Victor to bring him a verdict on this April woman.

"Uh hmm," Pepe slid next to Victor, nearly frightening him, and said, "Well?"

"We need to go and talk, follow me?" Victor said, ignoring Pepe's inquiries and led Pepe to the bar, where he now accepted the offer of a drink only to find the rumors to be accurate.

"Pepe, we need to do something about these drinks, we got to. This is the only complaint that I get in regards to your fine establishment." For a response, Victor received a stare that carried excessive amounts of ice.

"Pepe, look at me, I'm serious. It'll be hard to entertain company or anyone once they know that they'll be a fool to order drinks that wouldn't be worth the money or the effort." Still the stare, still the ice, so Victor said, "umm, Pepe,"

"You just marched fifty prime ponies past Pepe and you hide me over here to talk about a damn drank. What about April? You ain't said nothing 'bout that, or have that managed to slip your mind?" Pepe found it hard to check his anger.

"It did."

"Oooh, you slithering snake in the..." Victor swatted away Pepe's wagging finger.

"Pepe," Victor snapped, "Listen, you would see a lot of the ponies if, and only if you change the bar. Victor was sure to emphasize "bar."

"Victor, I've tried that before and nearly had to close the place down because of that. They get in here, and once intoxication sets in, then it turns into a bar fight each time."

"Let me handle that. We'll bring real bottles and more security for that purpose alone, and brief the bartenders to know when an individual has reached their limit. We'll line up a cab service for the over-intoxicated, a little more jazz and class, you know, safe for everybody, extras on the first-time visitors. We'll offer up some nice food during the day and discounted drinks through the night. You'll now have a happy hour as well as the after-hours. What do you think so far?"

"Hell, I think you should run your own damn club and run everybody out of business, including me, that's what I think. And you could make these things happen Victor, these things that you speak about?"

"My boss is a big man, he can make anything happen; only thing, and I need to tell you, whatever you do, don't sham on the splits. And, if you feel satisfied, how about throwing me a nice party for my birthday?"

"Every year Victor, I have no problem with that whatsoever, is there anything else?"

"Yes, and this could be a problem because of my age and all."

"What do you mean?" Pepe became skeptical.

"I could get the ladies to come often, only I'll need to be here for that to happen. They'll walk through the door with Johns, they'll walk through the door with money, and they'll walk through the door with business. Above all that though, they'll walk through the door expecting to see me."

"Ohh, so you've turned into a real lady's man, haven't you. Yeah, I could see where that may be a problem, hmmm, but I think I have the perfect idea that could accommodate you and fix our problems. How 'bout you follow me?" And for this Victor was led upstairs to a room directly above the bar, where Pepe opened the door to a large console of television monitors and a very, very sleepy individual who had laid his head on the desk and gone to sleep, next to a large bottle of rum.

"Gee whiz, Pepe; this must be where you keep the good stuff?" Victor said, pointing towards the bottle with heavy sarcasm.

"At first I didn't think so." Then Pepe stepped closer to the sleepy employee and woke him up in just enough time to fire him on the spot, giving him the bottle for payment then said to Victor, "Here you go, Victor. You could occupy this room. The bad news is, you are now the eye in the sky, which is boring enough to make anyone go to sleep, which is not why I fired that jackass by the way; I fired him for stealing my alcohol," Pepe said loud enough for the fired jackass to hear. When Pepe left to escort the now fired employee to the exits Victor took the time to look around and appraise the roomy quarters with disgust. The smell of take-out leftovers was dominant, the mustiness was unbearable and the dust was the worst but the overall character of the building's structure was appreciated though.

"So, how do you like it so far?" Pepe spoke from the door as he re-entered the room.

"Could use a little work, it smells like a zoo in here. I need it to have that VIP look, like the one that you have downstairs," said Victor.

"Oh, well oh-kay, but you are on your own when it comes to that, buddy," said Pepe as he prepared to leave, fearing that Victor would toss the responsibility onto him.

"Hold up, wait a minute, just hold up a minute. This is what I need you to do. I need you to add the same jazz to this room as you've done to the room downstairs, same carpet, same furniture and assortments, you dig what I mean?"

"Uh uh, uh uh, no, hell nah," Pepe said, shaking his head vigorously.

"Why is that a problem, Pepe?" Victor asked.

"You know how much it took to build that thang down there, five grand, five thousand dollars, which is why I call that the VIP section. Could you see the sense in all that?"

"Shit, how long did it take them to put it together?"

"Well, two weeks. I mean piece here and a piece there, jeez, Victor, I said five grand." Pepe hunched his shoulders, then released.

"Yeah, I could dig it but listen, since you gave me this nice job and opportunity, add the fact of us being friends like we are. How about getting those guys to double back on us to bring the same flavor to this unit as they've done down stairs…" Pepe interrupted Victor, getting to the meat of it all.

"And the five grand is coming from where again. I didn't hear you the first time."

"Tell 'em six. I'll toss up another grand for the express effort."

Shaking his head, Pepe revealed his disbelief, and said, "An extra grand, you say?"

"Yeah, and hire somebody to come in here and clean this joint out and put some shine on the oak and offer up a hundred for that and you would have the payments in the morning."

Chapter 12

For Pepe, shocking was the envelope that Victor gave him but impressive for Victor was the efficiency to which Pepe constructed the remodeling that was taking place upstairs, even during work hours. Judah still couldn't believe the things that was going on around him but was glad that he was part of it. Four days and four busy nights later, the outcome was a very polished and well-decorated quarters. Extravagant and luxurious was the only way to explain the sight they were all seeing, which was the perfect place for Victor and Judah to operate from. There were monitors all over the room; there was a cubicle in the far corner that hid a desk, file cabinet, books and other work-related paraphernalia. The carpet was red, the sofa black velour with red piping. Brass coated the oaks, and the mini bar was lacquered to a fine shine.

"Did we just make it to Hollywood?" Asked Judah once he stepped through the door of the newly remodeled office and work station.

"They've done a good job, huh?" Stated Victor,

"How come you don't have them come and do the house like this, Victor? Ain't you about tired of the old things that we got?" Seeing the plush setting sent Marlene straight into her con-artist personality.

"Nah, I'm not tired of what we got. In fact, I love what we got, more than I like this place here." For Victor this was a truth. Everything around the shack had its own value, a very, very sentimental one, and one that Victor had no wishes to change or tamper with.

"Well, how about you live there and I'll live here," Marlene said, flopping onto the soft sofa closest to her, rubbing her hands on the soft fabrics. Marlene adjusted to her new role as lead cook about as good as a piranha takes to the sandy beaches. She looked around the room and found reason to smile at Victor and her other new best friend Judah. One of those short lived smiles, the kind that freezes on a woman's face once another woman enters the room; in this case, it was women. Judah, who knew that Marlene didn't know the full details for her early retirement, was caught in the middle of drinking from his beverage and sent liquids airborne once he saw the train of ladies enter the room. Thelma held the cake; Anna and Charlotte held two bottles of champagne each, singing congratulations in their hot, steamy sultry tones.

"Ooh shit," said Judah, and then the coughing fit; even the eye signals failed to keep Marlene stabled. She watched long enough, one soft peck after the other before finally seeing enough, decided to stand and leave.

"Have a seat, Marlene. Can't you see that here's a moment worthy of a celebration?" Victor said, motioning Marlene to take her seat next to him. She relaxed once Victor said, "Besides, we still have a lot to talk about." Not bothering to lock stares with Marlene, Victor turned away from her and accepted the gifts from the ladies and headed towards the console, which would offer the sky room the option of music or movie, and plugged in the jack to let music fill the room, bringing instant enjoyment from the ladies as bottles took off in heavy rotation. When Victor returned, it was nice to see Marlene with a bottle as well as in conversation with Judy, Judah and Maxine, but Victor knew that this was gonna have to be some "right now" explaining for him to do. This was so, not the case of "I would explain later." So, knowing this, Victor accepted the envelopes that the girls always hid their homage's in and went to the cubicle while hoping like hell that Marlene missed the opportunity to satisfy her curiosities, but knowing that a snowball would have a better chance in hell than the chance that she would pass up on such a moment.

"So, umm, Champion, anytime you're ready. You know that I am all ears."

"How about being all eyes and no attitude," replied Victor.

"Oh, I don't think that the attitude has showed up yet. Is that money?"

"Yes, ma'am, and a lot of it, come, let's go celebrate."

"A lot of it, what you mean by a lot of it? What the hell's going on here?"

"I would love to talk about it later." She nodded her agreement, and together the two joined the celebration, where Victor found Judah at the mini bar playing bartender.

"Hey fella, let me get a gin straight, and keep them coming," Victor said,

"Not at all, I got 'one' for you, and guess what?"

"Nuh uh, not with the way my luck is going. Why don't you just tell me," Victor exhaled, mentally beat.

"I got an expansion idea I need to talk to you about tonight. Not later, but tonight. I mean this is serious." Accepting the single drink and tossing it back in one gulp before releasing the fumes he handed Judah the glass, then said, "One more."

"Funny, but I hear that a lot around here, it's that bad huh?"

"Don't remind me; lest I'm gonna need two more."

"You know what, you are a hard dude to figure out, and because of that I stopped trying. So I'm just gonna voice my shit. You need a drink because you failed to hip Marlene to your night thang. Which means, um, what? Had I known you'd behave this way, I would have told you that they were coming; only I didn't think that they would show so fast, but that's neither here nor there. It's thirty women in here, and granted Marlene is in the top seven, but it's clear to me that you could have every last one of them. But somehow Marlene is different, um and I'm thinking that this is when you tell me how."

"So, you were thinking about expanding."

"Ahh, don't want to talk about it, do you?"

"Not at all!"

"Well, somehow we're going to have to move this party downstairs. I mean, after all, these are business hours." Moments later the room was cleared except for the three: Victor, Marlene and Judah.

"Before we start, you know ain't nobody came through here yet, right." Victor hinted with hand signals around the room, indicating that the room hadn't been swept yet, not fully knowing the extent of Judah's "business talk." Judah caught on right away and motioned for Victor to follow him out of the room and to the stairway, just in time to run into Marlene, which was now becoming frustrating.

"Marlene, are you all right?"

"Yeah, why of course," Only Victor knew better, because the kisses that Victor received from the women as they entered the room were rated PG. But, the kisses that he received from the women as they made their exits had yet to be rated but were somehow flirting really heavy in the X category. Because of that, Marlene sent her visual daggers to Victor, letting him know that she didn't appreciate none of that shit at all.

"Oh-kay, well do us a favor and keep your eyes on the monitors until we get back. We need to step out for a minute." Without waiting for a reply the two headed down the stairs and out of the building.

"Here, let's take a walk," said Judah as he explained the complications that they were having in "Heroin alley" to Victor. One of the problems being that he barely had enough supply anymore, and the connection that he had made a lot of money for was preparing to back away, opting to play behind the scenes and was wondering if Judah would be interested in copping more, and by this the prices would reduce favorably. While Victor was considering the responsibilities, Judah went on to explain to him that the connection also offered up other territories that would soon be vacated, which meant that Judah would now be the new tenant if he was to agree to the terms of upgrading from a quarter pound twice a day to two pounds a day.

Hearing this, Victor knew that he should have pushed the issue on that other drink, regretting that he allowed Judah to talk him out of it he said, "You were right, this is serious."

"And, that's not all of it."

"Shit, I knew you were going to say that. You sure know how to fuck a motha fuckas high off. What else you got?"

"What I'm trying to say, I mean if you let me is that there's going to be some people who don't like that shit and may decide to get in the way, which means that they could and ultimately would frustrate our quotas and give us a real problem, and I know you you're good at fixing dilemmas. So, what you got for this so far?"

"A headache,"

"No, seriously,"

"I am." Victor thought of the situation, really appreciating Judah for asking his opinions. Because Victor knew all so well that over the past months that Judah had accumulated a large enough sum of money to go about this task alone and on his own, said, "First, we'll need to know the people who are not going to like it." Smiling, he added, "Shoot, maybe we could reason with them."

"Hmm, like maybe have a nice sit down and talk is what you're recommending?"

"Exactly, could you arrange that? I mean, that would be nice of you." The smile broadened.

"What the fuck's so funny? You know what happens if I make the deal with this dude and we don't cover?"

Judah's excitement was indicative enough for Victor, who decided to downplay such the obvious expression by saying, "Nah, you left that part out."

"We could lose a lot of money for starters, may be a little dangerous for us, shit, who knows?"

"I believe that if you could get us all together I could see it working, two pounds a day is a lot for a day's work, though. What I need to know is how much room is this guy giving you to move around?"

"All over the city."

"Shit, you serious? Could you handle that Judah?"

"No, and this is why I'm coming to you."

"Oh-kay, so what's the root on this thing?" Meaning: funds needed.

"Get this, nine heavy," meaning thousand, also a major markdown than the scores before, which now gave way to Victor's raw thoughts.

"And the fruit?" Referring to estimated profits,

"Well, we walk in saving four grand, and guess what, the first shipments on consignment, no cash up front." Hearing this, Victor saw the bait and the hook and believed that Judah saw the same thing. Victor understood Judah's dilemma: one, he was running out of supply for the alley and this move could aid in that. Two, this was an opportunity to spread their tentacles over the whole city, which would indeed increase their incomes abundantly.

Victor thought, and then said, "In that case a meeting is in order. Anything else we need to talk about?" Victor asked, now eager to get back.

"Yes, there is."

"Dammit Judah, I'm doing everything I can to grow to be an old man, and you sneaking days right from under me. Let me guess, you done picked up a venereal disease," Victor finished, smiling to show Judah that he was hipped to him moonlighting with the ladies.

"What made you say some shit like that? Naw, I ain't got no fucking disease. It's another money thing I need to talk to you about."

"Oh, you know what? You give me heart burn. I knew it, and what's this 'set' all about?"

"Girl,"

"Girls, what, the ladies?"

"Almost, just in the alley they asked for "girl" to go along with their "boy." They want coke to go along with their hop, calling it a speed ball. You know anything about that?"

"Not at all but I do know that you gotta give the people what they like, I do know that much."

"It's what I was saying, so how 'bout it?"

"Judah, could you handle all of this?"

"Not by myself I can't." This was the messed-up part, because Victor had never seen his self as a drug peddler, not in this life and hopefully not in the next, and in vision of this he just gave Judah a solitary, "Oh..."

"Victor, listen, I'm not asking you to take to the streets, not at all, but there are some concerns that I have."

"I'm listening."

"Well, packaging for starters. I need you to help with that and storage. I need a little help with that, and as we progress, maybe even a little help with the transportation. Not a lot, but a little."

"Mm hmm, and when is all of this supposed to be cranked up?" Asked Victor,

"First thing in the morning, I'm supposed to hook up with the Mexicans with an answer, and I would be expecting the first shipment within a week."

"Oooh shit, yeah, I really see the seriousness now and this girl thing. You got somebody in mind for that?"

"I do, but not for the good numbers that I get for the boy, I see the root just above a nickel for a pound and the quality being knock-dead gorgeous like it is. The fruit could triple each time we restock, you know."

"And what you need from me Judah, I mean to make this thing work?"

"That's all I need, is for you to make this thing work."

"And where are we on the split?"

"Nothing changes unless you change it, but sixty-forty with me holding the bridge seems feasible."

"To me too, then there's the get-together, so umm, when could we get together?"

"Tomorrow night. You got any idea where, though?"

"Yeah, in the alley,"

"Oh, well in that case let me get out of here and let me get started on this thang here. I'll catch you on the late." The two friends embraced and headed off in separate directions, Judah to his car and Victor to the club, where he knew Marlene was ready with curiosity in hand. On the short walk to the club, Victor gave some good thought to the situation that Judah presented to him just moments ago. A whole city shit, talk about a turn of events, but he also knew that the risk would become greater as well. So the saying goes: "any business without risk is none more than an opportunity unworthy of the follow through." And with this as the last thought on the subject, he was admitted into the club. Without disturbance, Victor took to the stairways that led to his work stations, where he had to knock on the door all but loud to get Marlene's attention so he started making notes to get the keys from Pepe before the night was over. The door swung open to a very tipsy Marlene. As Victor stepped past her, his path was blocked by her presence while closing the door behind him. Victor was surprised by the eagerness to which Marlene pursued his kiss. Sure, he had kissed Marlene plenty of times, but never like this. Never this long, never this passionate. Before he could speak, she shushed him by putting her finger to his lips and one to hers, leading him further into the room. Stopping in the center, she unfastened his coat and let it fall to the floor, and then she started on his shirt. She carried on with a smooth unhindered proficiency, until now the shirt was strewn in a heap next to his coat. With her hands on his chest she found his lips, his ear and his neck. Sending rapid fire signals to his mental, giving it warning that it was now under attack by a pleasure-providing demon.

Then the soft nibbles on his ear, then his neck again which brought on small amounts of pain, which only increased the pleasure by tenfold. Caught so much into the ecstasy of it all that Victor never knew that his belt was gone and his pants were unfastened, not until the warm sensation of Marlene's hands gave notice as she rubbed and stroked him until excitement gave way and brought him to a full throbbing erection. Marlene wasn't satisfied enough, worked her way from his lips to his chest, where she nibbled and teased Victor's nipples until he began to vibrate. The sensation was overbearing as her licks and nibbles found their way south, until her nibbles were now on his penis. She took him into her mouth fully, and for her rewards she was given Victor's response: "Oh, shit." With a bulldog's tenacity was how she held him and gave pleasure to him. Afraid that he may become queasy and faint, Victor allowed Marlene to play around just awhile longer before he raised her and began to work on her clothing, until her garments were in a pile on top of his.

All fears erased, his hands found her breast, flicking her nipples until hardened, and then the heat from his mouth found one. Increasing Marlene's desires until now she embraced him around his head, wishing for him not to stop. Her desires redoubled once Victor found to his delight a very, very moistened vagina. Using his fingers and palms until she cried out, "Oh Victor," and then she shook unto convulsions that were wild and barely controllable, a spasm that nearly got Victor choked to death. Escaping Marlene's vice-like grip while increasing the motions to which he worked his fingers, he grabbed Marlene with force. Using a handful of hair to aid him, he looked her in the eyes to achieve the mental communications that told her through brain language that he loved her. In response, and to let him know that she heard him loud and clear she pushed him on to the sofa and straddled him in slow yet powerful gyrations. She rode him, offering her breast to him. The steam was so intense. The moment was so decorative, and the mentalities were so overpowering that the two, Victor and Marlene, knew for sure that there was no other place on earth that the two would rather be. During his excitement, Victor rolled Marlene over to achieve the traditional position; here he performed so unlike a gentleman. The passion too intense, the desires were overboard, so he struck Marlene like a jack hammer, with pounds that echoed through the room.

"Oh my God Victor, Oh my, my God. Victor, what is you doing to me?" For a response she only received heavy breathing as his stokes rose higher and delivered much deeper. Marlene's face contorted, and seconds later her body convulsed again, this time fighting Victor more aggressively, announcing that she was coming. Victor locked her legs to give him an easier match than this championship battle that Marlene was providing him with, and decided to slow his roll, and for this he was rewarded with a bite to his chest that sent a sharp pain shooting through his body. Throwing his excitement through the roof, giving him the sensation of an explosion to come, and so it did. His body jack-knifed in mid-stride, long enough to find relief, and then he resumed the heavy pounding until he was now spent.

"Victor… Victor."

"Yeah,"

"I love you so much."

"I know."

"Do you?"

"Yeah,"

"I mean; do you really love me too?"

"Yeah,"

"Then, you wouldn't lie to me when I need the truth."

"Marlene, I'm still looking for the first lie that I ever told you."

"Silly, but I've been looking for the first time that I could catch you in one."

"What's on your mind though?" Victor said, handing her the clothing that she lost. Pulling on her under garments, she said, "Care for a drink?"

"No, I'm high as hell already. I mean, shit, is it cold in here? I can't stop shivering."

"No, in fact it's hot in here. I'll have one." She walked to the mini bar, sporting Victor's shirt and her bikini brief panties and mixed herself a fruity drink. Then, she headed to the cubical and retrieved, then brought the envelopes that Victor received as a daily gift and handed them to him and sat down next to him and said, "Count it!"

"I never do that, not until the club closes."

"Oh-kay, then give it to me and I'll count it," she said, wiggling her fingers.

"Is that total more important than the questions that you're gonna ask me?" Said Victor, now tugging on his trousers.

"I only got one."

"Hmm, yeah,"

"Yes."

"Which is?"

"How long have this been going on?"

"Nearly a month,"

"Hmm, now I really want to count it."

"Go ahead, count it, I'm really supposed to be watching the monitors." And to his station he went to the sound of envelopes being torn apart. Victor knew that Marlene would have more than one question once she discovered that she would count more than a grand with more to come, but Victor had other concerns. As he looked into the monitors he noticed Pepe in deep conversation with a Caucasian fella that he took to be a trick the other week, but didn't look like a John so much this night.

"Victor, are you kidding me? There's…."

"Marlene, come here, hurry," Victor interrupted her, pointing to the monitor screen, then said, "Look, you know him?"

"Who, Pepe? Oh, the guy he's talking to? Uh, uh, I sure don't, why?"

"You think you could 'stab' him for his poke and bring it back?"

"Why are you interested in him?"

"He switches around a lot, ever since I've been watching him, about a week now."

"Maybe the man, you think?"

"If that's the case, why haven't Pepe shoo flied him?" Marlene was getting dressed in a hurry. After checking her appearances, she took to the stairs and moments later she was visible in the monitors. Victor watched as Pepe began to look uncomfortable, as if whoever this guy was had him in the pinch then saw Pepe nearly keeled over once Marlene came close enough to be intrusive. Pepe relaxed a bit once Marlene gave all of her seductive attributes to the gentleman, who fished good enough to buy her a drink and lead her to the dance floor. Victor watched as he pawed her up and down. Victor watched the lust that filled his eyes. Victor also watched as Marlene stabbed and withdrew successfully, giving him one more paw before she separated from him after giving him a weak promise, then headed for the stairs. Victor, still with his eyes on Pepe, hoping like hell that Pepe wasn't in communications with the man, saw his hopes diminish as the signal was recorded. The gentleman headed for the front door, and Pepe headed for the rear. When Marlene made it back, smiling because she knew that Victor was watching her get palmed to death, and wondered if he was just a teeny bit jealous.

"You got it?" Victor asked, once Marlene made it through the door.

"He had a wallet," she said, then added, "a big one too."

"Oh-kay… Well" Impatience was taking over Victor.

"I left it. That wasn't a good wallet." Victor was lost because never had he ever seen a bad wallet, stared dumbfounded past Marlene then said, "Oh-kay, so you fumbled the shark?" These were bad words for anyone attempting the Minnesota, a fumble is the worst and Victor well knew it.

"Boy please, I searched it then put it back, but I did bring you this." Marlene held up a business card for Victor to see. Smiling, she said, "Ohh is this showing off or what? Socked it to the wallet, felt the shiny piece of a badge, put it back and took a business card like he gave it to me and you talking about a fumble, boy, here." She handed Victor the card, and for an encore she collapsed on the sofa and sat cross legged and scooped up the money that she left sprawled across the sofa, and said, "Now, you were gonna tell me about this cash. I mean, it's over a thousand dollars here."

"Shit, you think that's something? If you stay woke long enough tonight, and you'll see another stack like that." Smiling, he looked Marlene up and down, spun around and stomped his foot and said, "Now is that showing off or what," still not able to get out his mind the printed black ink on the white card that burned like coal in his pocket which told him that Pepe was in real communication with the enemy. "So that's why he needed protection in the big house," Victor thought.

"Yeah, that's showing off all right. First I was impressed, now I'm nervous."

"Don't be. You ain't raised no fool and you know better."

"Oh-kay, so how are you gonna handle that?" Marlene pointed, finding Pepe on the monitor.

"I don't know yet. I got some guesses to what's going on, though."

"Like,"

"Look out there. This place is standing room only, more drinks being served, more door coverage, more cards tumbling. The VIP now offers high stakes gambling, which was doing none of this until I graced this place. What do you think is going on?"

"He's getting greedy; you think?"

"Mmm hmm, do me a favor and carry on like we not hipped to this shit, cook like you've been cooking, come up and keep me company often as you can."

"Oh, you know how much I like that."

"Oh yeah, well how about giving me another one of those kisses that I've just grown to love?"

Chapter 13

It was nearly noon when Victor awoke to the sound of voices; only after focusing in on the hurried tones did he recognize the voices belonging to Judah and Marlene. Believing that he should wait and find out what all the commotion was about, he looked around the room to find his trousers that were laid across the bed post. Locating them and dressing up enough to be presentable for company he headed towards the door until he heard the voices stop and the sound of the back door open and then closing, leaving Victor with the impression that Judah was now gone so he resumed laying down. Moments later Victor decided that the smell of sausage, eggs and toast was too overbearing and if that wasn't enough, the rumblings of his stomach were sure to make the correct decisions for him that would send him to the kitchen and it did. Only to find a scarcely dressed Marlene, who was surprised to see Victor awake so early. Being that noon was early by Victor's standards ever since he dropped out of education to take on new lessons in vocations.

"What are you cooking Marlene that smells so good in here?" Victor said, barely able to hold the anger that he felt. Believing that being jealous was one thing but outright disrespectful a whole other.

He decided that he would curb his anger and accept things for what they looked like.

"What are you doing up so early? Smelled this food, didn't you? I knew that it would wake you."

"How long have you been up?" Victor asked.

"Maybe ten minutes, long enough to start you some breakfast," Marlene lied.

"Is that so? Thank you, I'm starved, you must have read my dreams."

"I know what my man likes," said Marlene, making sure to drip honey extra when she kissed him on the cheek. "Now, sit down and I'll be done in a minute."

"Yeah, you need to hurry up. I'm expecting Judah soon. Has he been through here?"

"Not yet. Here you go, now eat up before you go." Hmm, more lies fazed Victor heavily but nothing was revealed to Marlene that her treachery was now in the open. Victor ate while pondering the correct way to go about the deceit that was dished out to him by his potna and his best friend. It wasn't until later in the evening did Judah resurface with the news that he now had a society of hustlers who came to Oak Park to see how the hustle went down in his neck of the woods. Victor hid his emotions from Judah as well, with the common of most knowledge's that the way he felt now would only make it personal, and business being what business is, should only be business as usual. He decided that it wasn't Judah's fault that he was crooked, even though Victor asked for loyalty. I mean, after all, who could make straight what God himself has made crooked? Nor was it Marlene's fault that she was raised a whore, as Victor well knew. Not only was there a fine and very skinny line between Eve and Jezebel but sometimes we'll often forget who bit that fruit first. Now, don't all through life a serpent enters our life, he was thinking before saying, "How many of them did you bring with you?"

"There's seven; every last one of them do some nice packages, only every last one of them is skeptical to do business with us black folks when they know to find a Mexican and be just as plugged into a connection as we could offer." Judah rambled off, without detecting any negative vibes that Victor held hidden professionally.

"And you got them out in the alley already?"

"Yeah, they're admiring the traffic I'm getting. They love that, but still converting them is another thing entirely. I'm saying this could be a problem."

"All right, I'll meet you in the alley." With that Victor turned on his heels and headed towards the shack leaving Judah with no embrace, as there always was one upon departure. Moments later Victor emerged in the alley as an all-business individual. In twenty-four hours he had become suspicious of his mentor and now business partner, disappointed by his lover and best friend as well as his hustling partner and best friend, and all of this was on his shoulders as he entered the alley.

Judah had his fellowship standing around the alley when Victor approached to a round of introductions, shaking hands as he went around. Finally, after the last sign of welcome, Victor spoke: "Now, I'm not going to keep you long at all. We all got work to do. First, let's understand that there ain't any more Mexicans, they're all gone. The connection is right here with us. Anybody object to what I'm saying so far?"

"Hell, I got a Mexican right now that could come through here right now and run this place out of business, his poke is so good," said a buck-tooth hustler.

"Nah, I doubt it. You see, the dude that I work for, he told me to come here and offer a life line to you guys. Unlike the Mexicans, we got you even when you don't have the dough to cop in case you run bad on your luck. I could even propose a consignment deal with you..."

"You mean work for you niggas?" Again the buck-tooth nigga,

"I mean only what I just said: the prices will go down for you, the more you get the better the numbers." Victor began to get the attention of all the hustlers, all except buck tooth. So, to him he said, "Now tell me, is the Mexicans that you speak of willing to offer that?"

"And some more, I don't need no niggas doing shit for me, trying to get somebody to work for you niggas, ain't that a bitch..."

"Well, in that case." Quickly Victor removed the colt .45 from his waist and pointed it at buck tooth and said, "Well, Raymond Buchannon said whoever refused to cooperate, to just send them home, and something is telling me that you won't cooperate." Then he squeezed the trigger once, and then watched as buck tooth was felled. His actions froze everyone, including Judah; his eyes were wide, and fear washed over Judah and the six remaining hustlers, who nearly lost lunch when Victor stood over buck tooth and fired four more rounds into the convulsing body.

"Say man, we ain't like that. We came to see how we could establish a good line with the brothers. I'll assure you that you don't have to use that thing on us," said the short stubby brotha, who Victor later found out to be a good dude by the name of Felton.

"But I bet that you don't speak for everyone," said Victor,

"No, but I bet that we could all agree. I mean we heard a lot about this dude that you work for, seems like you guys are on the move, so how about us? We like what you are talking about, and we sure don't want to be sent home. You dig what I'm saying?"

"Nah, I don't, but you could tell me more about it tomorrow at Pepe's. You know where that's at? Broadway and Sacramento Blvd. Come through, all of you, ask for Victor. Oh and this guy...." Victor pointed at the bloody figure that lay mangled in the alley, and then said, "Toss this nigga in the dumpster and push that fucker out of here. Remember, tomorrow night, not next week, but tomorrow." And with that, Victor left, headed once more towards the shack and once again without neither embrace nor acknowledgments for Judah.

Marlene was in the yard when Victor walked up. Upon seeing him, relief rushed over her as she came to Victor and said, "What's going on back there?" She pointed towards the alley.

"Somebody ain't getting along with somebody is what it seems like."

"Victor?" Her brows shot up in question.

"What's up?"

"Are you all right?"

"Yeah, oh no, that ain't had nothing to do with me." Victor pecked Marlene on the cheek and went on to the house. Marlene, who followed close enough to be nosy, decided she needed more information.

"Well, is Judah all right? Ain't he always back there?"

"Yeah, he's all right. That's what I needed to know, too. Listen, they love your fried chicken at the club. Why don't you make meals surrounding that and bring it with you when you come in, oh-kay?" Victor said.

"Why, what are you going to do?"

"I got a lot of stuff to do tonight, so I figured that I may as well get started on it all a bit early." With that said, Victor excused himself and headed to the restroom to bathe before he dressed up for tonight's part. A two-piece keen cut white jacket that matched his white slacks. His maroon undershirt, and maroon with gold specked socks coordinated perfectly with his maroon alligator print patent leather kicks and the maroon hanky that he sported in his breast pocket. Appreciating the fact that the mirror had been so kind to him by reflecting a diamond in its most rough, he cleaned up and left the house to a very suspicious looking Marlene.

Victor arrived at Pepe's in enough time to welcome the night as it came in. Noticed by the bartender who complimented Victor on his attire while offering up a drink, and immediately Victor accepted the wine offered before asking the doorman if he had seen Pepe. The doorman pointed to the VIP, which was where Victor found Pepe nursing a shot glass. Seeing Victor brought surprise to his expression.

"This is a surprise. What brings you in this early?" Asked Pepe, checking his watch,

"Slept all day, I was bored to death." Had Pepe known the full contents of Victor's day, Pepe would have looked for telltale signs of nervousness or irregular behaviors in Victor. Not that he would have found any, but still.

"Ohh, well the club is doing a whole lot better thanks to you and your boss."

"That's the way it seems to me, too. Looks like we're earning our cut and not on the take, right Pepe?"

"Yeah, I appreciate that shit too. I mean it, Victor, I really do."

"Don't worry about it but what I was meaning to do was ask you for the keys to the place. I mean I don't see where you wouldn't be able to trust me at especially the key to upstairs, which way I wouldn't have to find you each day I need a day started."

"Really, I was thinking that now that you beautified the place that you would have changed the locks yourself. A security door wouldn't hurt much either."

"Hmm, now that you bring it up, how 'bout I take that in consideration. Anyways, I need to get to work right away; I got some ideas to ponder. Maybe the solitude could help me out on this one."

"That bad, huh?"

"Yeah, but I noticed that you're in an empty VIP room. What's up, what's going on with you?"

"Don't miss a thing, do you?"

"I thought you knew that already."

"So, you don't appear to be dressed for work, what's the occasion?"

"Oh, this means that I'm at play too, trying to see if I could take the club on but don't worry, I promise not to hit your table. Just keep the drinks coming and the cards tumbling for me."

"Then this brings me back to wanting to know the occasion, and what the hell did I do to deserve that?"

"Well, all work and no play ain't good for nobody, the keys, Pepe!" Pepe retrieved the keys to the upstairs unit and said, "I'll make you a copy of the rear door tomorrow."

Chapter 14

Victor high tailed it out of the VIP and up the stairs he went so he could check the trap that he left for Pepe. He discovered that the bait was still intact, but obviously someone had been invading Victor's work station and privacy, which made him a bit uncomfortable. Removing his suit jacket and hanging it on the coat rack, he sat at his desk and sketched up his situations. Personal, financial and mental, and the most threatened was his mental state because personally, who-ever owes anybody anything? Thought Victor, "Just the night before," Victor said to himself as he looked around the very room that he had made love to someone who said that they loved him more than life. Did he believe that? In some strange eccentric way, he did, but he also knew that a lot of people whom were cut from a certain cloth belonged only to that quilt, the ilk of origin. He also knew from looking around, not from experiences, no! Because he was only a first-time buyer in these regards, that birds of a feather, really did, flock together.

However, he also knew that players would "only" love you "only" when they ass was "only" playing. So, he thought. When he met Judah, though it was through binoculars at the time Judah was hustling, which means that Judah was playing. When he met Marlene she was hustling, which must also mean that she was playing. Victor had nothing else for a thought but the fact that Marlene only prepared him not for herself, but for the fact that she knew that she wouldn't always be there and needed to know that Victor could swim before she left, lest he was bound to drown. Thinking back to the words that she told him really didn't help at all but in another off-centered way he wasn't hurt so much. So yes, mentally he was a little knocked around, and personally, who really gave a fuck? But financially, Victor could declare nearly fifty grand that he had hid under the floor board of the old shack. A place that he knew that he needed to do something about before Judah not only won his jar of honey but also his pot of money. Sad yes, but business is business, and in business who could you really trust? With so much on his plate, Victor figured instead of becoming frustrated he'd go and have some fun. Removing the bait that he'd left for Pepe, he grabbed his jacket and headed downstairs, where he immediately sought a table and began betting. Pepe, who saw the real potential of the club going bankrupt in the event that Victor was on his "A" game, decided that he needed to go and have a word with Victor. Four hands in, with Victor the winner of all four, put the "urgency" in "emergency" for Pepe.

"What you doing, buddy?" He asked. "I mean I thought you were only playing around when you said that you wanted to bankrupt us."

"Not at all but before I do it I need you to do me three favors."

"Anything, just ask Victor, you know I would."

"First thing, I know that this is your establishment and all but I need a no trespassing sign for upstairs."

"No problem. You said three?"

"Yeah, Marlene's due to show any minute with the goods for tomorrow. Just cop them off of her and send her home for tonight I don't feel like being bothered with no domestic shit."

"Got you, and three?"

"Keep the drinks running with the tab?"

"Anything for you Victor, you know that." All of this was all right with Pepe; as long as Victor was distracted and tipsy then the club stood a chance.

"Thanks, Pepe."

"No problem." And for two hours the only interruptions were all welcoming for Victor. The message that Marlene wasn't even admitted past the door was all right with Victor. Then there was the cocktail waitress who ran rampant with the Jack Daniels that Victor had more of in his body than he had operating organs. Then there was Anna, Paula and April, who showed up just moments after Marlene had left. Catching April by the wrist, Victor whispered into her ear and saw as she left the club to Pepe's dismay. Then there were the customary pauses as the dealers stacked chips in front of Victor, who was now up over a grand and counting. So yes, this was a night that he could be thankful for. Just when it appeared that Victor had run out of steam he'd catch a breath of fresh air for the next hour or so. Pepe, seeing the recklessness that Victor was displaying in his character, was again by his side.

"Looks like you had enough, buddy."

"Had e-yuff wut? Money, fffffreinds, wut Pepppspe, yuff wut?"

"Yeah, you had enough. Listen to you."

"Don't worry about him sir, I got him," April said, sitting next to Victor, and again this was to Pepe's dismay. Victor was barely focusing on the cards that he was getting, even in a drunken stupor he couldn't lose. Hand after hand, winner, winner, and a winner. The crowd had drawn around to watch Victor attempt to do exactly as he said, which was take down the house. With April as a bodyguard, watching every move that everybody was making had ordered Victor another drink, only this one would be to go. Victor, hearing this, became immediately upset, "Wuta you dooo dat fo' I don't yeee one a-go." For this April whispered into his ear with the message that nearly sobered him up. She stood and gathered Victor's chips and Victor together and led him upstairs, which only meant that fun times for him was officially over.

Victor awoke to a very, very strange environment. There was no sun that shone through the windows. There was no smell of food being cooked and no Marlene, which was the first time in going on three years, but there were people, women sprawled all over the sofa and the floor. Next to Victor was a very, very light sleeper who looked a bit... It was April, and now that his visions had cleared up, he knew exactly where he was and who he was in the company of, he just couldn't remember how he got there. April, who waited all night for Victor to come to stood guard the whole night and was forced to make the girls stay and help. With fears that someone would either hurt Victor or maybe Victor would even hurt Victor, saw as Victor fought his way back to reality.

"You all right, sweetie?" She asked, coming to her feet as if she needed to help him.

"Yeah, what are you guys doing here? What time is it?" Victor struggled to keep the room from swimming and everything that he ate from coming up.

"You don't remember anything, do you?" April stood to retrieve her purse, which contained a straight razor, some cosmetics, and a vast amount of casino chips. It was after she emptied her purse of its contents between her and Victor, who was now trying to straighten out his horribly wrinkled suit from being slept in overnight did she say, "Last night you kept saying that you were going to send the club into foreclosure, and it looks as if you gave it a nice shot. Look at all these chips."

"How did I do; did I bankrupt them?" Victor asked.

"No, no, sorry, nice try, but no cigar."

"So what happened then? I mean, this is a lot of chips. Did I leave any down there?" Victor pointed to the floor then said, "I mean, if so, then we better go and get them. It's only right that I keep my word, you think?"

"Well, all of that could wait, and it's going to have to whether you like it or not because there's nobody down there." April took on the assignment of color coordinating the chips and said, "So about last night, tell me, are you going to be able to rebound from that or do we need to hire you a nanny to keep watch, while I keep this boat afloat."

"Shit, what time is it, while you keep this boat afloat?"

"I don't know, and yeah, look at this, this is a lot of money, and how much are the black and yellow ones?" April said referring to the chips she held.

"Those are fifty-dollar chips, the green and Yellow ones are twenty, the all-white ones are fives, and the Grey and Red ones are ten, the Blue ones are a dollar."

"Well, you got one hundred and six black and yellow ones, seventy yellow and green ones, forty Grey and red ones, sixteen all white ones.... Are you counting or not?"

"Not really but I believe you if that means anything."

"Well, you got a ton of blue ones too; this is a lot of money."

"But still a long, long way from bankrupting the place."

"Well, gosh, you should have seen you. It was incredible, one time you had a queen and a deuce a for sure loser, but you bet five hundred like you knew that you would win, and right when I was getting scared for you, the dealer bust out. Man, was that gutsy. Then there was the time when you drew two nines, easy for you to stay, but no you split and hit them both, drawing a king and an ace, still with the five hundred apiece and this sent the building into an uproar, again a winner. I don't know where you get your luck from but I could use some of it."

"You know; the thoughts I'm having right now is only telling me that life is bittersweet. My day was horrible; my night was spinning; now my morning got some dough in it that only you could explain."

"Not everything because I had to make a lot of runs so I swore Judy to secrecy and a promise that she wouldn't leave you until I was back, or else I was gonna cut her with my straight razor. Judy is the overweight white woman who proved to be light on her feet when it came to running away from danger."

"Is that right?"

"Yes, man, you were amazing. I mean any other night and you would have really brought this place down," said April.

"Any other night, what was wrong with last night?"

"Aww naw, you over did it on the liquids last night. You didn't have too much left but I made sure that the winnings left with us though. Look at all this money, what are you going to do with it?"

"I got some ideas. Listen, I mean right now I really need a true friend, not the kind that I'm used to but better, somebody that not only could I confide in but that I could rely on. Have you ever been somebody like that?"

"Yeah, yeah, I have been somebody like that. Victor, you're scaring me."

"Could you be somebody like that again? Don't get me wrong sweetheart, and don't anger yourself when I tell you that the game came to me that there's nothing in this world that's as cold as a hooker's heart, and I hold that truth to be self-evident. You see sweetie, my momma was a whore and she tossed me in the garbage can to be rid of me because her pimp wasn't tolerating any of it. The only woman that I've ever had any kind of feelings for made love to me in this room, told me that she loved me more than anything, in this room, and now I ask you to put that together with what you told me last night. Could you; is what I ask you, could you be that person again?"

"And I'm a say yeah again, and I'm going to ask you not to anger yourself when I say not to misconstrue the reason why I'm here. Sure, it's true that I work the street, and true is also that I've only had one pimp in all my life and he's due to turn five in March, which is the only reason why I'm here. If your people was shutting down the strip, then tell me how else was I gonna feed him, pay the bills and the cost of living? Unfortunately, I agree with you, there is some cold-blooded stuff that goes down in the streets but tell me how cold blooded is me sitting with you all night, except when I needed to go and check on my son while you were winning and drunk out of your wits? You see, I loaded my purse up with chip after chip after chip, and just off the top of my head I see seven grand here. Tell me that ain't enough for me to move far, far away from here."

"You got a point, but off the top of my head I want to ask you why you didn't?"

"The thought was repelled because of two reasons: unfortunately, that's also enough money to kill for, and tell me who would look after my son if I died or worst him die with me. The other reason is I'm doing pretty good for myself with this system that you built around us, all of us are which is the reason why we aborted the rest of the night to be here. Since you were there when we needed you we figured that we would be there since you appeared to have needed us, and secretly I got a thang for you. I could say for sure that I've never met anyone like you."

"That was three."

"What?"

"You said two reasons but that was three: you would die, I needed you and you got a thang for me that was three." Victor ticked them off with his fingers, then said, "Earlier you asked rather I'm going to be able to rebound from this and I'm a say barely, I mean who wants to be hurt like this." April nodded her understanding before Victor continued with, "My question is still the same: April could you be that person again or have these streets really took you under?"

"I'm gonna always be that person, Victor; I do what I do because I need to, not because I want to. Do you think that you could try to remember that and whatever it is that you need to say, would you please say it because the suspense is killing me?" Victor stared into her eyes for a good spell then said, "Of all of them, who do you trust the most?" Victor pointed to the sleeping beauties, and then said, "I mean really trust."

"That's really hard to say now because last night they've all showed me something that I ain't seen in them before. I mean once they heard that you were out of whack they appeared right away with their razors out, so shit, I don't know now."

"Enough to call them your sisters or your family," Victor added.

"Umm, I think I'm gonna need to hear what you have to say first before I make any recommendations." So Victor told her the play that came to him in his sleep, the answers, the remedies and the solutions that fixes all.

"Whoa, when did you have time to come up with all of that? I mean shit, now I know that I made the right decision to hang on. So when are we getting started on all of this?"

"I mean if my man is making house calls while I'm gone and my girl is the active and willing participant then on the surface, it looks like I'm a loser all across the table. So what would it matter if we start now or next year? This play is designed for the patient. Do you have patience?"

"Yeah, I do. As for the rest, listen to me for the frankness in which I speak: nobody could predict whether or not the mate of their choosing would prove to be an errant spouse or partner; you've just as well rid yourself of calling this fault yours and remain the wholesome through and through type of guy you are and call this loss theirs."

"And I will, yet surely you could understand my indignation's, which I like to take this moment to rinse off right away because today is a real busy one. With me saying that, I need you to do this, April hop on Pepe right away if you could, spare nothing on that, it'll all come back believe it would."

"What you got to do that's so busy?"

"I ain't gone even play games with you, April. Under this tough armor that you keep tapping on my lady believe it or not but there really is a man under all of this, a young one but one. And I've learned this one for myself that alone, and by myself I've been long enough, and truthfully my only fear is being alone. I'm not meant to be alone, so this wayward chick that I chose, she could keep on doing like she was and whatever is in her blood. So, what I'm a do is go home like nothing ever happened, say that I got drunk and couldn't make it in on time, and act like I'm not on to them. Get dressed and get ready to take care of me somebody new, somebody that's gonna always be there, you know, deep inside me, you understand. Somebody who's also through and through, since birds of a feather is what flocks together."

"And you're just willing to bypass me?"

"Why ever would I want to do that? Who did you think I was talking 'bout?"

"I.... shit, you had me going with the 'get dressed going to find me somebody new.' Don't take so long to get to the point the next time but this loses me: why would you put me on Pepe, especially if I'm gonna let my love come down for you?"

"First, are you really for me?"

"To my last breath."

"Would you put your life on that?"

"And that of my son's."

"Then let's have some fun with it, you know the dough."

"Um kay," April was lost.

"The chips that you got, let's go on a shopping spree, let's rent a car."

"I got a car."

"Uh uh, I saw your car."

"What's wrong with my car?"

"One, it won't fit all of us in it; two, that is not how I wanna show up to go shopping; three, I think you should donate that thang to Judy, which way she can stay with the tabs on Marlene while I'm here and cop you another one, a "short" that looks like you belong to somebody. It's Judy you recommend, right?"

"Yes, are you serious?"

"What about you, are you serious?"

"As the air I breathe, I said that already."

"Then yeah, I'm dead serious. Now about tonight, I got company coming through that the girls need to make friends with in order to orchestrate plan B. The girls need to be convincing, don't hip them to why but don't hide the fact that it needs to be done. Do you have everything so far?"

"Yeah, I'm next to Pepe, Judy's next to Marlene. I don't know the company that you have coming though, but I'm sure that we'll work it out when the meeting's over with and then there's my favorite part: to go shopping and cop a car that looks like I belong to somebody, so, did I miss anything?"

"Pretty good, so, rent a limousine to meet us here at three thirty sharp, which would bring us back here by eight thirty. We could hit the mall and a car lot by that time. Pepe would show up at one, he does it every day, which is when I'll trade the chips in exchange for dough and I have to change the locks and add a security door to this room. So you guys need to get up and get out of here right now, and go take care of whatever business at home and make it back in time to get to the mall while it's warming up. I'll clear the day with my boss but tell me, do you got it all so far?"

"Yeah but the only thing is I can't normally get a babysitter until night, this is the only problem that I have."

"That's not a problem, bring him. Pepe's treating, remember?"

"Yeah, I remember," then she drifted off.

"What's going on with you, are you all right?"

"Yeah, I mean, I really don't like bringing my son around men. I don't need anybody coming in and out of his life. I'm just a little scared, that's all."

"Let me ask you: do you see what Marlene is guilty of? Would you ever do that?" She shook her head. "Oh-kay, then tell me, would you ever steal from me?" Again she shook her head. "Well, hell, would you ever turn me in to the people?" This time she said, "Victor, ain't you been paying attention?"

"Yeah, I have, to everything, which is the reason that I don't think you have to fear me, or me coming in and out of your life. If I would have never found this out about Marlene we wouldn't even be having this conversation and you need to believe that." She smiled, then said, "I do, I mean you don't know how long I've been trying to get your attention or the things that I have tried to get you to notice me?"

"No, I really wasn't paying a whole lot of attention but do you got everything checked off? And, just for comfort, try and find a sitter and offer them triple the wages, Pepe's paying remember."

"I got it. I mean, I'll work it out somehow."

"Then let's wake everyone up." Victor went to wake the girls.

"Wait a minute!" April stepped into Victor's arms, and there they kissed until she was quenched.

"Mm, oh-kay, I always wanted to do that. I guess we could wake them up now, no, one more." Then another kiss, "oh-kay, I'm ready," she finished.

"I mean, you sure?" He asked, she nodded, then together they shook everyone awake. Seeing that he now had everyone up and assuring them that he was all right, Victor told them that he was grateful for them, and to prove it they could go to breakfast on him and prepare for a shopping spree, again on him. They would declare this day "all play and no work day," only Victor and April knew better.

"See you guys at three, no later than three thirty." Then they were all gone leaving Victor to contemplate and concentrate on just how exactly, and when exactly would this dynasty that he explained to April become a finished product. Six months, he told himself, and it was settled.

By one o'clock Pepe was unlocking the rear door that Victor had relocked after letting the girls out. Seeing Victor sitting at the bar nursing a glass of water, Pepe came over to him and asked if he was all right.

"Never better," Victor replied, then, "I'm a little hung over I think."

"I would think so, the way that you were getting rid of it last night but I got a marker for you. It stopped around seventy-six ninety, minus the one thirty that you did in cups. So, you'll get seventy-five sixty." Victor handed him the bag of chips and waited for Pepe to unlock his brief case and issue to him his winnings and he did. Shaking his head, he said, "And to think I'm the one who showed you how to beat me like this."

"You could handle it, right?" Victor asked.

"Oh yeah, thankfully you overdid it, because as soon as you left some real red necks came in that work at the capitol and blew a lot on us in exchange for a good time."

"Is that right? I missed some shit like that?" Victor asked excitedly.

"I had to force myself to come in right now I'm telling you. After the girls had you nice and tucked in last night I stopped worrying about you. I wanted to protest that with the way Marlene kept coming back and forth demanding to see you. The high yellow one said that she was gonna cut whoever showed up at the door up there. First, I thought she was playing, and then erased that thought when I tried it; you know, bamming on the door to satisfy Marlene, you know. The good thing is that I halfway believed her when she told me the first time, or I'd be in the hospital right now. That door swung open and that blade flew out'ta there so fast that I fell down the first four stairs before I finally got it right and ran down the rest. I ran straight to Marlene and told her you were busy and would be home shortly, and not to worry, that you were in "gooood" hands," emphatically Pepe said 'good,' then, "I mean it, Victor, that girl is so mean I had to say I was leaving from down here." Victor knew that Pepe was referring to Sonja and he was. Sonja was quiet, she took care of business and she was as mean as they came, and hearing Pepe speak about her like he was only brought confirmation to what Victor already felt through speculations.

"So, the night worked out for you, huh?" Victor asked.

"Yeah, buddy; I had all kinds of fun last night. Watching you was fun for me, even though you kept betting to clean me out, ultimately your actions brought the gambler out of all of us, the club made a good profit. You get to eat; I get to eat, not bad, huh?"

"And guess what else? You are not going to believe this." Victor put excitement in his voice, drawing Pepe's curiosity to the edge, then said "Nahhh."

"Boy, what, what is you saying? Tell me."

"You are not gonna.... Nahhh" again Victor shook his head in disbelief. Pepe's curiosity stole the rest from him, so he grabbed Victor by both sides of his collar and shook him, saying, "Boy, if you don't tell me what the hell, I wanna know."

"I don't know why you'd wanna know; you're not gonna believe it no how. I mean, shit, I barely believe it."

"Victor, just... tell... me." Pepe shook him again.

"Oh-kay, April." Victor left the rest out of it.

"April? Victor, oh my God, oh my God, oh my God, what about her?" Pepe's eyes took to dinner plates in expectations.

"She said she had enough, asked me would I object if she went out with you a couple of times."

"Oh my God, Victor I've been praying... wait a minute... Victor, you wouldn't be trying to see if I'm ticklish when it comes to this shit, are you?"

"Uh uh, I'm dead for real."

"Victor, I'm telling you I'm too old for this shit, it's bad for my heart. I mean, if you're playing around you need to knock it off!"

"Pepe, I don't play around with you. I knew you wouldn't believe it."

"Oh my God, you're serious ain't you boy. We need us a drink, this is a celebration." Victor knew that the last thing he needed was a drink and decided to pass. "Nah, Pepe, I had enough dizzy for a month, but there's something that I need to tell you. This way you could have one up on her. This way you could decide rather or not you want to pursue her or not."

"Oh-kay, oh-kay, I'm listening!" Said Pepe, now over excited.

"Just twenty minutes before you came in she sat right here and cried to me, saying that the streets ain't for her, that she needed to be a woman of respect. I mean, if I'm gonna marry anybody it's gonna be Marlene and I told her that. She says she wasn't shopping for me, that she had a thang for you. If she would have said anybody else, I would have croaked her on the spot but I know how you is for her. What I'm saying is that she do got a thang for you, only she ain't budging on the one-night man no more. You're gonna have to go about it like a gentleman, you know."

"What! Are you serious, boy! I'm a gentleman extraordinaire. You talk like she wants a diamond or something."

"She do, it don't even got to be a diamond. I believe that she would go for a regular ole gold band. It's the title she wants, and I could tell that she's firm on that. She ain't done a John in a week, said her legs ain't gonna open until somebody says "me," you know what I mean"

"Whoa, you think I should do it, boy?"

"If you don't I bet you that she could wrap a line around the corner with guys who would, and that's just before the days over with."

"Boy, this is good news, ain't it?"

"Not for me."

"What are you saying; you should be happy for ole Pepe."

"Yeah, you're right. I'm wrong there, Pepe. Well, since I gave you one up, do me a few favors."

"Anything, you know that boy."

"Oh-kay, call the people and have them come and put a new locking system upstairs, a security gate and all; call the locksmith and have them come and install a safe in the wall, not a really big one, just big enough to hold receipts, notes and little shits that I don't need laying around. The other day Marlene went over a letter that I wrote to somebody else, which had me drinking and overdoing it last night, plus I need all of this done today, and Pepe, I need whoever is going in my office to stay out of my office. Could you manage that?"

"Of course, no problems at all. So, when should I approach Miss Lady?"

"Tonight! We're going to celebrate her retirement this evening. We got a car coming to meet us all here at three thirty and we're going out on the town."

"Well, hell, if that's the case take some change off me and have her get her something nice."

"Yeah, well, I'll let her know that you send your warm wishes."

"Yeah buddy! I'm never gonna ever forget this Victor, I mean it."

"Just never ever cross what we're doing and we'll be fine," Victor said, accepting the money from Pepe, then said, "Let me get out of here Pepe, it seems like I have a lot of explaining to do. You know I'm gonna tell her that you gave me too much to drink, right?"

Chapter 15

Victor made it home just after two p.m., knowing one thing for sure: that he no longer trusted anything that Marlene had to say. So, when she said, "Victor, I've been up all night worried about you, are you all right?" He let that go through his head without stopping but figured he'd go along with it. He pecked her on her cheek and said, "I know, I miss you so much," and hugged her tightly and even then could he smell the expensive cologne that Judah liked to wear. Pecking her again on the cheek and concealing his contempt, he released her and looked into her eyes and just like he figured, wasn't nothing there. No regret at all, just the will to circumspect her wayward ways, which was all right with Victor. The only problem that he had was how he was going to keep Marlene from following him around the house, his wheels were spinning at 350 RPM, yet nothing took, then an idea hit him.

"Marlene, listen. I need to be five places at one time, do me a favor and run up the street and cop me a bag of herbs. I got somebody coming in that like that shit. I need you to hurry back while I bathe so I could hurry up and get out of here."

"You got to leave again? What's so important that keeps you in and out, but more out than in?"

"Business, you remember that don't you?"

"Well, all right, you're not going to be gone overnight again, are you?"

"I doubt it, now go and hurry back like I asked you." Marlene took the money and headed up the street. Immediately Victor went to the floorboard and raised it, glad to see the pistol and his treasure was still there. He gathered everything quickly and hid everything in the suit that he would wear out of there after he bathed, which was so fast that by the time Marlene walked through the door with the reefer he was already putting on his sport coat. Strapped with sixty thousand dollars and a hand gun was how he pecked Marlene on the cheek, relieving her of the herbs and skipped out of the house and up the street, heading towards Pepe's.

It was after three the time Victor made it through the door to Pepe's, and all that he heard was banging, electric saws and drills in action. Victor sought Pepe to thank him for his efficiency, and found him behind the bar.

"Pepe, the noise isn't distraction enough for you?"

"Not at three o'clock but nine o'clock, done or not, they getting they ass out of here."

"I could dig it, hopefully they finish though." Victor thought that to be an understatement, now that he was carrying around his life savings and everything else that could send him to clinker forever. Just as the thought crossed his mind, the drills stopped.

"That sounds like they heard me, huh," said Pepe.

"Yeah, it did, let me go and give it a gander." Victor slid off the stool to leave.

"Hey," Pepe called to Victor, catching his attention then tossed him the key and said, "Just like I said, don't lose it now." Remembering, Victor nodded and said, "I won't, thanks," then he headed up the stairs to see the locksmith opening and closing the tunnel-like box to make sure the safe was in working order. Satisfied, he turned to Victor and said, "Two fifty-five."

"And this covers the door and the locks?"

"No, those are the other guys."

"Well, catch the old man downstairs at the bar and tell him to cover it."

"Not at all, he made it plenty of clear that you were going to cover. He said something about you winning all the money last night."

"He told you some shit like that? Tell you what; I'll meet you at the bar." The locksmith handed over a folded piece of paper which had the combination scrawled in tiny numbers and left. The door people got the same message, which is where Victor found them to pay his bills, and then back upstairs he went to unload all of his possessions into the safe. Now that he was free of such the burden of worry, Victor looked around the room for a suitable cover-up for the safe, not quite finding the perfect one he decided on the coat rack. Removing his coat and letting it drape over the rack to disguise the work that had been newly performed. With mild satisfaction he picked up the funds that he made available for the outing then hit the door, and then the stairs where Pepe was waiting for him at the bottom.

"Boy, that car outside full of the world's most beautiful women, trust me on this one. I just came from out there and I'm just now getting a regular pulse."

"Oh yeah, so are you going to be ready for tonight?" Victor asked, reminding him.

"Boy, I'm ready right now but go on and get out of here." And he did. By the time he made it through the door the chauffeur timed him perfect. He swung the door open and said something about Victor being a lucky man, then closed the door before trotting around the car to occupy the driver's seat. Indeed, once Victor looked around the car, did he really and truly feel like a lucky man.

The car stopped downtown first; the doors swung open and the car was empty in three seconds flat. They ran through the stores like breadwinners; every last one of them ran to the roses. Stockings and shoes were flying everywhere. Thirty-Fifth Street was next, no difference there it was the same breadwinners and the same roses. The poor chauffeur almost bent his trunk trying to get all the merchandise to fit inside. By six o'clock Victor began to see the fatigue set in on the girls. He told them to have the driver carry them wherever they would like to go, and that he and April were going to meet some people, and the two aborted after Victor paid the driver.

"So, now that we're stranded, what should we do?" April asked, not getting it yet.

"Well, I saw this place on the way over and figured we could hop a cab and catch it before it closes."

"Good because anymore walking around here and you'd surely have to carry me on your back because my feet are killing me in these heels." While in the car Victor explained the sit-down that he shared with Pepe nearly verbatim, explained her role for tonight and was glad to hear that she was prepared to go. The cab stopped in front of the car lot that was located on Riverside Blvd. not far from Seavey Circle.

"Hold up a minute," he said to the cabby, who parked and was glad to keep the meter running. Twenty minutes later Victor was negotiating the price of a Mercedes Benz 350sl, metal Grey with a black soft top. A deal was made and the keys were handed over to April, who sat numbly through the whole negotiation process, unable to believe any of it, not until Victor said, "You ready?"

"Umm, yeah, yeah," Victor left to go and pay the cab driver and was back in time to hear April start the car. The soft purr told Victor right away that he made a good decision, add the fact that the car complimented April just perfect was a plus.

"Where to?" She said.

"I need to get a few things for the office, some pictures and stuff. We could go anywhere for that but I need you to listen. The ride came under contract: it goes one twenty a month, payable before the fifth of every month. You got that? I tell you this just in case it slips my mind, not to burden you with it entirely." Nodding her understanding, she said, "I know a place, and guess what?"

"What?"

"I got something for you, too." For this she pulled out a diamond-studded watch that was three times better than Judah's. For a reaction, Victor just stared at the watch, not really knowing quite what to say or do.

"Well, say something! Baby, do you like it? No, you don't like it, I could tell."

"Uhh uhh, no, April, let me share something with you, oh-kay. April, in a few months I'm going to have the keys to the whole city, mark my words, and what I need you to know is that I do like the watch and I love the thought but I hate the timing. I want to say thank you but no thank you. In the future, if you wish for me to have a watch or anything, while you're at your selections, please think of items less flashy or inviting, anything under the radar would be perfect. Speaking of gifts, I got something for you too." Victor fetched a box from his pocket and gave it to her and smiled when he told her that it was a gift from Pepe.

"Did Pepe select it for me?" She asked.

"No."

"Good, then I'll wear it."

Chapter 16

Nine o'clock found Victor in his office hanging pictures, making the place livelier than before. He sat in front of the monitors and watched the entire club. So far, the patrons were having a good time, nothing was really going on. The girls sported their new dresses and shoes, impatiently waiting for the events to turn. By ten fifteen Judah made his showing with a group of guys that Victor recognized immediately. He even saw when Marlene made her entry and Victor followed her until she faded from view, which meant that she was now on the staircase and on her way up. Seconds later he heard her tapping on the security gate. "This is going to be a long six months," Victor thought, then unlocked the door to allow her to step past him.

"Ooh, look at you, what you doing? You came to shake your groove thang or what. It looks like party time for you, look at you." Victor said, admiring Marlene's beauty.

"No! I came to see you, seems like business is where I need to go to find pleasure," she replied then said, "So, I see you added some things to the place. Still wish you do home like this."

"Home," Victor had to catch himself and resist the laughter that he felt, and said, "You on that shit again? You already know how I feel about that, Marlene," he finished, returning to the monitors before saying, "You wish for a drink?"

"I think I could handle it." She stepped behind the mini bar and made herself a scotch over rocks, obviously aiming to loosen up a bit. Taking a sip from her drink and setting it down, she came over to Victor and said, "You look like you could use a massage, you look wound up."

"Not so; really I'm waiting on you to tell me what's on your mind."

"Let me guess, you're busy."

"I'm afraid so, but never too much to hear what's on your mind though."

"I just felt like getting out of the house."

"Is that right? What did you do all day?" Victor looked to make sure that the picture covered the wall safe.

"Nothing, but sat at home all day and thought about you, wondering what you were doing all day that you found more important than me. So, what you do all day?"

"I had a car come and pick me up to take me to paint the town, turned down the offer of a diamond watch, went to the car lot and bought a Mercedes, then stopped off to eat. I practically enjoyed the whole day."

"Are you serious?"

"No, I'm just playing with you but anyways let's get out of here. Judah came in right before you and I need to meet him and some fellas. If somehow I get lost in the shuffle, I'll see you when I come in, oh-kay."

"Oh, well, oh-kay." Victor grabbed his coat and led Marlene to the door and followed her down the stairs after locking up.

The club was warming up, the tables were filling up and glasses were heard clanking against each other. In the far corner was Pepe and April; if Victor didn't know any better, he would of swore that April just hit him with a couple of daggers when he sat Marlene down at a card table and gave her a few bucks and some pointers, before easing away to meet up with Judah.

"Judah." The two shook hands, then Victor acknowledged the rest of the group. "Let's go upstairs and see what kind of understanding we could come up with," and they all followed. For two hours they made deals and boosted strategies until everything was written in blood. Releasing the fellas to go and enjoy themselves in the club, Victor sat with Judah to discuss the fine prints.

"So, you got the first shipment already, I reckon?" Victor asked.

"Yes sir, like I said, I'm gonna need a little help from you as I explained to you before."

"Right, with the packaging and the storage, huh?" Victor figured Judah was hinting on this in order for Marlene to help out in that area, so he tossed the bait out there.

"Fella, the only one I could see that could help you is Marlene. I can't see none of the girls leaving what they doing to help you do what you doing, and you already know I'm not gonna do it, so what do you think?"

"Hell, I guess Marlene it is then," Judah replied before standing to leave.

"One more thing," Victor stopped him while watching as the girls made their moves. "Let's fix one of those drinks that you put together with the lemon and that fruity stuff, something else we need to cover."

"Oh," Judah had gotten immediately suspicious.

"Nah, it's a cash thing, like a major cash thing, thousands and thousands and thousands of dollars, you would like it." Now Victor had Judah's attention.

"Is that right? Well, you know how I feel about that, Victor. I'm all for it. What's the set?"

"Trafficking. My man come to me saying that he's the girl connection, talking some shit about kilograms, saying that if I could score ten or better that he'll go eight-five apiece but the investigations that I performed with some other guys tells me that in Detroit it's thirteen a piece, Chicago fourteen a piece, Indiana nineteen a piece, is you following me so far?" Victor saw each price hit Judah in his greedy pig.

"Hell yeah, I hear you. How long have you been thinking like this?" Asked Judah,

"Ever since you told me what girl was I've been investigating, so much that I know how to do the turnovers as fast as a cop and drop, that quick." Victor emphasized by snapping his fingers.

"Is that right?"

"Yes, sir," Victor nodded affirmative.

"What's it gone take for all this fantasy to be something that we could get our hands on?" Asked Judah,

"Now, Judah, that's the tricky part but I found a solution for even that."

"Oh-kay, then tell me about it."

"Well, my man came in here to celebrate. Guess what? He having to go turn himself in to knock down a few weeks but said that he'll be back soon but sorry his bail runs out and he gotta go. But he's sweet on me; say that I got fire and how he could see it burning in my eyes. I told him that whenever he ready to come through and I really believe that he is. So, he gives me a sample of his product, only he calls it blow and I give it to a brotha downstairs who goes in the bathroom and smells some of it. He starts freaking out and comes out with his nose bleeding." All of this is what Victor learned from hearing Pepe tell his stories but so what? Judah had the hook in his mouth.

"Oh-kay, so you figure a deal is on its way and you say you got a solution to all of this you talk about?"

"Yeah, right now we are doing what, two, three grand a day, more now that we are spreading out? I could see those numbers tripling if not quadrupling in two months. I could see us investing a quarter million and doubling our money in two to three days each time."

"Whoa, whoa, whoa, whoa, whoa, whoa, Victor who taught you how to talk like that?" Judah began to take on the queasy look from overintoxication of the greedy.

"So, are you in or not?"

"Is this dude really this heavy?"

"Judah, he wore a necklace that could buy you a fleet of cars, and one ring that could buy your house. I'm sure that he could handle it, my investigations are solid."

"And the solution?" Asked Judah,

"Save the dough you make, take it easy on the spending and we'll go in fifty-fifty."

"That sounds like a plan to me but now let me get out of here. I got some dudes waiting on me downstairs!" They shook hands with no embrace, and one thing for sure and by looking at the monitors, Judah didn't have no dudes waiting for him downstairs; them dudes were gone.

Chapter 17

Two weeks had passed, with Victor playing everything and everybody close to his chest. He and April met in shadows, concealed by the night where they would exhaust their heated passions of lust and vows of love. She would bring him reports of progress and of new events. Pepe she believed to be a paid informer who, too, met in shadows with the pure-bred detective "Loren O'rieley," the same guy who nearly lost his wallet on the dance floor with Marlene. Victor still held his business card in his desk, waiting on the day to present it to Pepe. Over the past two weeks the girls would get pinched on a regular basis, which put a dent in the incoming cash flows, not so much, but Victor knew that the pig was making out all right. No secret to how the girls had been tipped off; still, Victor took it all in like a champ. Two weeks was all it took for Victor to find out that his life was in danger in two ways. O'rieley and his outfit of rogue officers were beating down the doors on the Upper East Side looking for a Mafia figure by the name of Raymond Buchannon. Victor searched his memory once he got the news, and the only one who could have sent the pigs out East was Judah because Victor always told Judah that he had to make it to the East side to meet "his boss," and also the words made it back that Felton, Big Kev, Duke, SP, Grass and P.

Baby were waiting on the go-ahead to rid themselves of Victor, who didn't know it at the time but bought himself some more time with this trafficking business that danced dazzles around Judah's greed, forcing him to halt on the go-ahead. Victor heard these words as if they weren't meant for him. Although April never underestimated Victor, she found reason to be frightened for him and said, "Baby do you think six months is too long to wait? I mean looks like the rush is being forced upon us."

Satisfied that she said "us," Victor sat up in the motel's squeaker, in a room they would rent on the strength that April was being real adamant about guarding her kid against outside influences. Getting out of bed, Victor began to pace, then said, "Yeah, I do, and to think I shot for Judah's greed on an accident. I didn't realize that this would buy me time at that time, but sweetie I need you to know something: as long as I've known myself sweetheart, the rabbit has always been in my hat. I'm going to out think these dudes, watch."

"How does this cramp the plans that we've laid though?"

"Big time, but I could buy just a little more time but I don't see the purchase going past another three weeks." Victor thought about the fake connection with the imaginary necklace and the fallacious ring then said, "Three weeks at the most."

She nodded then said, "So, should I really go through with the plans or should I shy away? I mean, I hate my part, if that's any leverage to the decision."

"Yeah, we came this far, let's just finish."

"And the time that you're buying comes from where?" She asked, very concerned now.

"Detroit, Chicago, and Indiana…"

"Oh, then that fixes everything then. I'm going with you, let me go pack!"

"Noooo, no, no, no, no. I'm not really going to these places. I'm a leak it that I'm going to these places and I'm gonna hide out. This way I could watch the ones that wanna sock it to me."

"You want me to team up with you on this hide out? That'll be fun, wouldn't it?" April stood and walked into Victor's arms; sexy is what she was, no other word described her better.

"Not really, just a whole bunch of sitting around watching for weak spots."

"And who's gonna conduct your business while you're hiding out?" She asked.

"I'm thinking Sonja; I tried her with traps of all kinds and all kinds of enticing reasons to betray me, and I don't have any proof that she did."

"No, you won't find any either, that's a good selection. And you're hiding where?"

"That's what I'm working on right now."

"Use my place; you could help with the babysitting."

"Whoa, are you ready for that, girl?" Victor knew her saying this meant a lot.

"Yeah, you could be both of our daddies." Again, the long French kiss.

"Is that right? So when do I actually get to meet little daddy?"

"Soon as you are ready to start is all right with me, just promise me something." He nodded as she went on. "Just promise not to hurt my baby. He's a good boy and he's innocent. I don't want the decisions that I make to be mistakes that he has to pay for. I'd rather pay for my own mistakes, oh-kay."

"Yeah,"

"No, I want to hear you promise." Victor froze, because the memories of hearing Marlene say those very same words came rushing back.

"Victor, did you hear me?"

"Yeah, just I hate when I hear words like that. I'll make these pretty promises only to see the ugly end of it. Listen, you could trust me like that and with anything, you need to know this."

"Oh-kay, that's enough for right now, but I need you to know that I'm not "them." I'm really here, do you hear that?'

"Yeah, three weeks though. Tell me, could you pull Pepe off fast enough?"

"Victor, I could have pulled Pepe off yesterday and the day before that."

"Well."

"Are you serious? What if he gone want some then what? Victor, that man gives me the creeps."

"This is one time when I gotta tell you that in this case he is a paying customer."

"And you all right with that, Victor?"

"Not at all, jealousy had just come over me, but if you remember right, this whole situation is a life and death one. I die, it doesn't matter no how; I live, then that's what I wanna do baby is live, you know. Just because you're breathing, that shit doesn't mean that you're living."

"And Sonja?"

"She gotta collect from everybody, Pepe and Judah included, but you'll have to wheel it in from her, because to her I'm on a road trip and to everybody else I'm on a road trip, you hear me?"

The first time Victor stepped foot into April's flat was like stepping into a Cracker Jack box. If Victor had any phobias towards being cooped up, then he barely showed any symptoms of it. "Wow," he thought. This is what they call barely doing anything. Marlene put the shack together with twice as much room as April's little living quarters. Did Victor care about that? No. The fact that she lived poor made him feel even that much worse for taking money off of April all this time. Thinking that if a woman had to stoop so far down as trading something that's forever precious as womanhood for money, then the least that she could do is live like it.

"So this is my place. It's not much, but it's what I got, you know. Here, give me your bags. I'll put them up for you." Now worth eighty-two thousand dollars, Victor declined to up the bag to her and looked past her to a handsomely dressed and well-manicured little boy who wasn't bashful at all.

"Oh-kay, then I won't take your bags. Are you all right, Victor?" No, Victor was not all right, Victor never really knew life at that age or had a chance to know the secrets of a child; he fell immediately in love with this one.

"Umm, yeah, yeah, here, take my bags but be careful. So this is the man of the house?" Accepting the bags from Victor, she pecked him on the lips and said, "Yeah, you wanna meet him?"

"Like one hundred years ago."

"Juice, come here baby, I want you to meet your daddy. His name is Victor." The sound of hearing April tell her son something so powerful did the strangest thing to Victor; it made him feel needed, really accepted.

"Hi, Victor, you wanna play cars?"

"Yeah, I wanna play cars, you wanna play horsy?"

"Yayyy!" Victor got down on his knees now straddled by Juice and the two followed April throughout the house. April took Victor on the smallest tour ever recorded, while balancing Juice on his back.

"So, would you like to see my dress?" She asked with absolutely no enthusiasm, and just as flat, Victor said, "No." Knowing that April was supposed to be married to Pepe this coming Sunday left them both blue, but only for a second because they both knew that this marriage was ephemeral.

"Good, because I'm only going to wear it one time, then it's getting burned after that."

"So, the bag that you're holding is what I wanna talk about. At first, I wasn't gonna say anything, but now I wanna know what's going on?"

"Oh!" Unzipping the bag and seeing the stacks of greenbacks almost stole April's breath away. "Victor, this is a lot of money and you're just walking around like this?"

"It's light though," he said, still running Juice around the house.

"What do you mean by that?" She asked incredulously.

"It's not all there; that's what I mean by that."

"Well, you could have fooled me. It looks like it's all there to me."

"But it's not; it's light nearly ten grand." Playtime was over for the kid, who gladly accepted the toy Victor picked up to give him and headed towards the couch.

"What are you thinking, Sonja?"

"No, and yeah,"

"I don't understand no, and yeah?"

"I think she's paying off without telling me, which makes me say yeah, but she's coming back with something so I can see the effort in it all, is why I say no. Somebody is putting some weight on her."

"No, that's not her. Victor, I swear, Sonja wouldn't take on a pimp, this I know….." April was cut off by Victor handing her a card that had the name, rank and company plus the number to be reached and a badge on it.

"Oh, my God, Victor, do you think she's being extorted?" Victor nodded his head in the affirmative.

"I know she is, now that this bag is so light I know that she's being pinched from both directions." The look was obvious that April was lost. She said, "From Pepe too."

"Nope, that's the only bread that shows up one hundred percent."

"Oh-kay, then I really don't know what you're talking about."

"Look, it doesn't matter. How about we find out for sure first, before we go knocking people off behind it?"

Chapter 18

All it took was two weeks for Victor to know the whole play. Judah and Marlene stayed making their rounds all over town, and after splitting Victors percentages Sonja would show up and collect, only to be pulled over later and pinched by the law. Even the girls began to come with shorter traps, and Victor saw all of this through his binoculars; the pay off, the pinch, and the attempt to send him to the cleaners. Victor followed Pepe after work; once to a cafe, once to a Spirit of Seventy-Six gas station but mostly to a bar in Old Sacramento, where he would meet to exchange Intel for currency. So the game went down like this: this fine officer was led to Judah by Pepe, who somehow pinched Judah, so this Detective took money and intelligence off Judah, and then started to pinch Sonja. This way he could buy more music off of Pepe. Since the bag was so short, Victor knew that O'rieley pinched Judah hard, due to the bad information Judah provided about a mafia figure in lower East Sacramento. So instead of Judah forking it over entirely, he delegated the task of paying off to Sonja, who performed perfectly under the condition of a pinch by not surrendering all of the poke, and all of this is what he told the girls at the first meeting they had since he'd been so called "back".

"But they said that they were gonna kill me… they were gonna kill my girl, Victor. I did the best, Victor, I did," Sonja confessed through sobs, she was struggling to keep her emotions in order.

"He knows this, girl. You think he doesn't? If he thought otherwise, do you think he would have called you up to sit with us?" April did everything she could to comfort Sonja, knowing that she, too, needed comforting, because since she's been married to Pepe she's been cranky and just as miserable as an old hag.

"I've done the best. I did, April, I did. I didn't want to say nothing until I saved up enough... until I saved up enough to hide my baby. I won't do it again, I'm so sorry." The tears flowed still.

"Well, that all happened already, nothing you could do to change any of this. But we've been talking and we got a plan to change all of our lives, but there's also a code of silence that comes with all of it. Whoever feels as if this is too much for them should leave now, and no one would fault them for it. I'm sure that we would appreciate the honesty that you have with yourselves." April, who knew the whole play by heart, relayed to the girls the plan to let the hammer drop. With eagerness was how they received this information and from that moment on, the plan went into effect. First on the list was to remove Pepe and relieve him of ownership of "Pepe's Game Room." April had charmed him with enough honey to get a signature out of him, which made her co-owner along with Pepe. A deed to the property, and a license to the business, that she was more than glad to sell to Victor, for one single dollar, just as they agreed.

Victor waited until Friday, after closing time to put a tail on Pepe, who was driving his sporty, midnight blue Jaguar that Victor found hard to stay with the way Judy drove. She was obeying all of the laws while Pepe ran stop signs and red lights. Yet, and still Judy was able to maintain a safe and effective distance, using Pepe's tail lights as a guide. Victor asked Judy to park at the Pancake and Waffle House located on Broadway and 19th street and she did. This gave Victor a better view of both April and Pepe, until a white van pulled alongside

Pepe and waited for Pepe to hop into the van, and then the van drove off. Victor waited. On and off went the lights to the Jaguar, the signal that Victor waited for. Seeing this Victor got out of the car with Judy and walked away, only to retrace his steps, and through the passenger's window Victor leaned in and said to Judy, "I know you're scared but so am I, and I need you right now, do you understand?" Up and down went Judy's head. "We are counting on you to hang tight, get your nerves up and when that car takes off, I need you to follow it and come and get us, do you hear?" Again the head went up and down. "Here, kiss me before I leave to bring me luck." Obediently she leaned across the seat and pecked Victor on the lips. He was looking for a tremble or any indication that should worry him. Instead she said, "Don't worry about me baby, I'll be right there to get you guys. Now go and hurry up."

"All right, if you say so, you're the boss." She smiled, and Victor walked briskly across the street to gain position.

It took another twenty minutes before the white van pulled up to let Pepe out. Victor stood with a spray bottle, a wash cloth and bucket posing as a homeless man willing to work for food. Victor saw as Pepe paused, seeing April now in the driver seat and cranking up the car, then saw Pepe reluctantly go to the passenger side and got into the Jaguar. Victor readied his self at the parking lot's exit looking awfully hungry, and really homeless. He was hiding in a wig and he was determined to bring this fiasco to an end. April put the car into gear and headed towards Victor at the exit in enough time to see an SPD patrol car slowly drive by, which drew a pause in the car's movement from April. The patrol car stopped at the light, which showed red.

"Hey, sweetheart, mind if I do the windows of this fine machine you have here, only to get me something to eat, because I'm so hungry." The light turned green and the patrol car drove off; April dug into her purse to fetch change, ignoring Pepe's pleas to move the car, she let some of the change fall out of her hand purposely.

"Don't worry, mister, I'll get that." She opened the cars door to retrieve the change then the unexpected happened to Pepe as the homeless guy hopped into the rear seat of the car and put a gun to the back of Pepe's head and said, "Pepe, now I know what you're gonna say." Victor took off his wig so Pepe could take a nice look at him, then went on: "You're gonna say Victor, it's not what you're thinking or what it looked like." April drove off slow enough for Judy to bring up the rear. She parked under the underpass of highway 99 and got out of the Jaguar. April took off her ring and gave it back to Pepe. Now with recognition in his eyes, he said. "Is this what it's all about Victor, the club?" April took the keys to relieve Pepe of his briefcase, only to take it back to the car to sit and wait with Judy. "This is what you want, ain't it, the club? Go ahead, I'll give it to you Victor, my gift to you, take it."

"Nah, Pepe, it ain't what this is all about." Removing the card from his pocket, Victor gave it to Pepe, who immediately tried to explain.

"Victor, it's not what you think."

"Told you that you were gonna say that, Pepe but tell the truth: you don't know what I'm thinking, do you?"

"Victor, for Christ sakes, you got the money and the club, what else do you want?" This is when the car that held Judy and April got the chance to see fire leave the gun as Victor pulled the trigger. They even got a chance to see Pepe's brains hit the windshield as Victor put a well-placed shot behind the ear of Pepe that proved to be as effective as "one shot and one kill." Victor went back to the car, which now held two highly impatiently waiting spirits in April and Judy. He went to the driver's side and leaned in.

"Are you guys all right?" He asked the two, one then the other.

"Come on, Victor, let's blow this scene baby, what are you waiting for?"

"Hold up a minute." Victor opened the rear door and reached for the gas can from the floor board and said, "Just a while longer, oh-kay, I'll be right back," and he did return, only because he didn't have a match because he left them in the cup holder. Taking them back with him to the Jaguar and with one strike of the match he sent the sporty ride into flames inside and out. The car that held his mentor and business partner was now crackling into flames as Victor walked back to meet Judy and April. He refused to turn around and look back; instead, he got in the car and together the three drove away.

Chapter 19

Victor was still rumored to be out of state while April held a meeting at the club to arrange the new direction in which the club would go. The first thing she did was close the kitchen down and giving Marlene absolutely no reason or a need to come around the club unless she was drinking, dancing or coming to play cards. As far as employment was concerned, her pots and pans sat in the pantry, awaiting her pick-up. The second thing she did was put a temporary closed sign on Pepe's table. The third was to counterfeit everybody's money for the night, meaning that all drinks were on the house, and this spread through the city like a wild fire. This also meant that she made a killing in door coverage. Although she spent a whole lot of her night deflecting concerns about Pepe's whereabouts, April still managed to keep the club running in its lucrative order, which is what Victor needed to know from the front.

Later on at the flat, April, Juice and Victor held a house full of company, who heard how the previous night had gone. According to the briefcase that April sat down in front of them issuing out chunks of hush money, all the girls knew that their part was soon to arrive in a matter of days. They found work to be secondary to shopping for gifts in order to excite their new boyfriends. From the reports that Victor received, boyfriends that were more than happy to know that they were screwing the boss's girls. Victor smiled at the thought of them plotting on his life while planning to take his honey, his sweet things and leave him empty.

On the third week, Victor made a showing to the shack on Second Avenue and 37th street, to find Marlene in the yard. Seeing him, she ran into his arms, where he caught and swung her around.

"Dang, girl, are you getting heavy or what, what are you eating nowadays?"

"I ain't getting nobody's fat, look at you, I miss you so much. For a while I didn't think you were coming back, you been gone for so long."

"Picture that? This been my house, or have you moved me out?"

"Please, are you hungry? I could fix you something."

"Nah, nah, I'm all right but is Judah in the alley that you know of?"

"I don't know; I haven't seen him in a while."

"Is that right?" Victor said, knowing that Marlene was lying.

"He might be over there; you're going around there? If so, be careful; it's a lot of stuff that's been going down over there, some dead people."

"Is that right?" Victor pecked Marlene on the cheek, then said, "I'll be back in a few," giving her his overnight bag, then turned to walk away.

"Wait a minute, that's not all a girl gets, is it?"

"Feeling kind of mushy is you?" Victor said teasingly.

"I mean, yeah, shoot it's been long enough, don't you think?"

"I guess but now let me run through this alley so I could go and conduct some of that damned business."

"Oh-kay, but remember to be careful."

Victor couldn't help but wonder if Marlene was sending him a double message, and said, "Don't worry, I will."

Victor found Judah sitting on a bucket in the alley, talking to some dusty, ill-dressed people who Victor took to be dope fiend junkies. Victor saw Judah as he passed them an item, then received currency in return. Money looked to come easy in the alley Victor thought, as he waited for the fiends to depart. Once alone, Victor approached Judah, hiding the disgust that he felt for Judah's betrayals, as well as the knowledge that Judah had a hit in the making to rid the hustle of the one and only "Victor Raymond."

"What you got going on right here?" Victor stepped to Judah.

"Ahh, look who made it back, looking like you been on vacation and shit."

"Hardly a vacation; nevertheless, my discoveries were pretty dead on with my investigations, only problem that I'm having is that my bag is sort of light. I'm saying, maybe you could help me out with the understanding when it comes to this?"

"Of course, you see I've been resting too, I mean we got some big plans on the table that we're gonna have to be ready for, I mean we're still on, right?" Judah hit Victor with the bullshit package.

"Which is the other thing that I need to talk to you about."

"Shit, talk, that's what I'm here for."

"My man is in town. I'm invited to go and sit down with him tonight. So, tell me, how do you feel about that?"

"What do you mean 'how I feel about it?'"

"The order that I placed is for twenty-five kilograms, how do you feel about that?"

"I feel like I'm scared to damned death. Tell me, do you like the idea?"

"I do, but know that the score could go down as soon as this weekend. This gives us three days to get the money right, and I take it that you are going to ride out with me."

"Whatever position you need me to play, then that's the way it's going to be."

"And, we're going one twenty-five apiece, right?" Victor asked.

"There's some change left over, you know that, right?"

"I do, only with a move like this I figure we could rent some cars and spend the rest at Pepe's. This move means that we're alive, can't you see that?" Victor said this knowing full well of Judah's intentions, his wish was that Victor dies.

"Well, you do the meeting and don't worry about my half. I got it counted out and tucked away, waiting on the play and the trips."

"I'll get back to you with everything we need to know about it by tomorrow night."

Instead of heading home to the shack, Victor skipped in the direction of the ice cream parlor. With no time to waste Victor took a booth in the far corner and ate very slowly his banana split while he leafed through a sporting goods newspaper that was left on the table prior to his arrival. Two hours had passed, and twice he rejected additional orders. He was readying his self to surrender and on to plan "B" he would go, seeing that he had such limited time. Victor began to feel the pressure "no more time could be wasted," he thought upon leaving. Then his wait brought fruit; satisfaction washed over Victor as the old Ford pickup made its way to a parking stall. Victor smiled as he saw the ageless Nigel climb from the truck, so he re-took his seat at the booth and waited for Nigel to conduct his business, and watched as Nigel entered and gone to the rear. Thirty minutes later, Nigel was shaking hands with the store's owner before making his exit. Victor stood and timed Nigel's steps, then fell in behind him. Nigel, sensing this had not yet recognized Victor, felt a bit uncomfortable.

"Little brother, can I help you? Are you lost or something?"

"Yeah, Nigel I am. I've never been this lost before," Victor said, raising his eyes to meet Nigel's, who read the pains in the young man's eyes. He shook his head and said, "Church boy? Man, you almost made me croak you. Didn't anybody tell you not to be sneaking up on people like that?"

"Yeah, I knew better but like I said, I'm lost."

"Oh, that bad huh?"

"Life or death."

"Ohhh, so, how could I help you?"

"By coming to have a drink with me." Nigel's brows arched in suspicion.

"A drink you say, I mean you owe me a drink, don't you? Is this the drink, you know the one you said that you would get me?"

"It is the very same drink. Listen, tonight at Pepe's I'll be waiting, ever so impatiently."

"I'll be there, don't worry. Rum and coke is my order, if you could line them up for us, huh."

"No doubt, rum and coke will run wild for you, believe me."

Chapter 20

By the time Victor made it to the club, April was playing host to a group of mid-day drinkers who gave April their condolences for Pepe's demise. "Such a tragedy" they all said. Overhearing the conversation, Victor approached the gossipers and took a seat at the bar alongside the patrons and said, "April, what tragedy are these guys talking about?" For an answer the gentlemen farthest from Victor offered Victor the newspaper, tapping his index finger on the story, where Victor read on in silence.

"Wow, now that was violent. Who could hate Pepe this much to do some shit like this?" Said Victor,

"Psst, did you see the part where it said police informant murdered?" The patron closest to Victor whispered to Victor, away from April.

"Yeah, I saw that, this is crazy." Victor took to the stage.

"You know what that means don't you?"

"What, nah, what do this mean?"

"That your guess is as good as anybody's. What we all want to know is what is going to become of this club. That's what we want to hear."

"Well, we'll need another dealer to take over Pepe's table," April chimed in, and then added "sure I lost a husband but if I know Pepe, he would want this club to live forever." Her timing was immaculate.

"We'll drink to that," said the farthest patron, and glasses were raised and refilled. Victor signaled to April that he was heading upstairs, so there he went. A lot of thought was needed, a lot of planning. The very last ingredient necessary to any of Victor's plans was patience, for Victor knew that in this case, patience had been robbed of its virtue. The pressure from the presence of police was on the way, according to the Sacramento newspapers. Victor thought packing up to leave would indeed fix all, but he also knew that running away would never solve anything. What he knew for certain, more than running or staying, was that the right amount of pressure and the people who wouldn't ordinarily roll over would indeed roll over, hence Judah and the same for Pepe. With patience as a distant memory, a thing of the past and a luxury belonging to someone else, Victor thought of his fate more than anything. The tap on the door told Victor that April was on the staircase, so he went to grant her entrance. Quietly she entered and took a seat next to Victor.

"Are you worried at all?" April asked, with obvious concern.

"Yeah, but me worrying about it wouldn't change anything. Like I say, we may as well finish what we started."

"Oh-kay, so the lawyers are due to come and reconstruct the paperwork to legalize everything. Is there anything else that I need to do in this area with the lawyers, accountants or the overall ownerships that we are doing?"

"No, it all sounded perfect when you told me about it. Just make everything go like you said, then I could see everything working out."

"Oh-kay, you look like you got a lot on your plate. Is there anything that I could help you with?"

"No, just have the girls ready for Friday no later, Friday. Arrange transportation to provide pick-up for them in the small hours of the morning, you got that?"

"Yeah, everything's ready. They've been prepared weeks ago, so now is the time, I guess. They would like that. Your patience was killing them, I could tell."

"Well, that is something that I just ran out of, so I need you to listen. I'm expecting someone, so brief the doorman that anyone asking for me, to send him straight up. Get somebody to send up a bottle of rum with a coke chaser. I'm sure there's none over there." Victor pointed towards the mini bar.

"Oh-kay baby, so are we going to have time tonight? You know me; I need to be held by you."

"I was thinking, you know, we make it out of this thing all right, why don't we move into this place? We could build a room in here for Juice. This way we could concentrate on the club and our other investments, what you think about that?"

"I think I want a kiss. I think I'm in love with you, Victor Raymond."

"I know. Thank you, I needed to hear that." They kissed and April headed out of the door and down the stairs, leaving Victor to thank God for making him a happy man.

It was midnight the time Nigel arrived; along with him was his personal tech team, who brought with them portable transmitters to case Victor's workplace, so, around the walls they went. Concentrating mostly on the sofas and bar, satisfied that they were now in a safe and secure dwelling, Nigel sat down and said, "Now you, my friend, have a lot of explaining to do," handing Victor the very same newspaper that Victor had previously read earlier in the day. Victor declined the paper and went to the mini bar and withdrew the bottle of Caribbean imported rum and two cans of Coke.

"Ahh, so what are we drinking to young fella?" Asked Nigel,

"Ahh, tonight we drink to the writing on the wall," Victor replied, remembering vividly the very last message that Nigel relayed to him.

"To the writing on the wall it is then." The two men, one old, one younger, tossed back their drinks in one gulp and took a seat to face each other.

"So, I guess your debt's paid then, is it not?"

"Debts paid, Nigel; I could honestly say that I'm orbiting. I'm gracing the skies, but to me and for me this is not a good thing, for this moment is like no other."

"And, do I need to ask you how so, or are you just going to tell me?" Victor told Nigel of Judah and of Marlene, as well as Pepe, leaving out the sensitive details. Victor told Nigel about the girls and how all of this has brought him to the point of near death. Nigel sat in silence; never interrupting Victor's flow because it appeared to him that this young man was overwhelmed by the hard knocks of life. When Victor finished, Nigel sat in contemplation, then shook his head at the thought, then said, "Now, how did you go through all of this so fast, plus how did you do all of this around this new guy who came to dominate everything?"

"What new guy?" Victor became immediately curious.

"Oh, so there's no new guy, I mean if you say there's no new guy, then there's no new guy. But I keep hearing about a new guy."

"What the hell are you talking about?"

"I'm talking about the new guy, this Raymond motha fucka."

"Oh, Buchannon, nah, he's not a new guy, he's an old guy."

"Boy, don't make me come over there and pop you in your lips for bullshitting me. Now I know that there's a new guy," said Nigel, now agitated.

"All right then, there's a new guy but so what, I mean fuck the new guy. We need to do something about me, you know, this guy, how about that?"

"Victor, from what you are telling me, not only do we need to do something, but we need to do something and fast. If this dude had a good mind to do so, he could rub you off the minute you connect your dough to his, and never mind the score, he'll still win regardless. I mean, unless his patience is asking for the tour that you promised him, which by the way wasn't a bad move, but if I was you I'd watch this dude like a hawk, lest he decide to go on tour by his self. So, be careful through all of this."

"I will, and I got this other idea that I wanted to run by you," said Victor

"Run it by me then." And Victor did just that for the next hour or so, while Nigel poured his own drinks and listened as Victor ran in and out of possibilities, concluding with the possibility of Nigel and Victor becoming business partners.

"And, all of this begins this Friday, you say?" Nigel asked.

"Dark and early in the morning," Victor responded.

"How dark are you figuring?"

"The small hours, why are you asking?" Victor asked from curiosity.

"So, this way I could stay up and listen," Nigel reminded Victor of the police scanner that he held in his hand, one that he carried like a side arm.

"You and these damned gadgets; I need you to hip me to those boxes that your guys came in here with. I'm sure glad that they drew a blank, the way I've been conducting my business up in here, whew."

"You got it; I'll send you one on me." Standing to leave, Nigel reminded Victor by saying, "We'll set the meeting spot to be at the old house by the bakery on 33rd and 6th Avenue, and don't worry I'll stick somebody on you. So leave from the house you share with Marlene, let's say eight a.m. don't be late. I can't wait forever; you hear?" Victor nodded, and then followed Nigel down the stairs and nearly out of the club.

"Nah, nah, this is enough, I got it from here." Shaking hands, Nigel turned to leave, then turned to Victor and said, "I'm so very proud of you. That writing on the wall was such a fine print. In that, young man, you win over my own heart." Victor nodded and allowed the club to swallow him up as Nigel vanished.

Chapter 21

By five o'clock Friday evening the girls checked into their assigned motel rooms located on Stockton Blvd. This street became the prime selection for its varieties when it came to choosing motel and hotel combinations. Just as he was taught, Victor cased every last one of them. The girls, once checked into their rooms, had gone off to meet their new boyfriends to share their fruits with them.

Judah, who had some of the town's best product, saw as his alley gained new clients, as Victor sent fiends to cop some junk for him and in return some junk for them. Some fiends didn't care, others were like, "Hey man, you don't look like you're on the junk to me, man" or "Young man, you don't need this stuff in your life, it'll kill you slow, it'll kill you slow I'll tell ya," sometimes "Are you the 'Man' or something?" However, the case, Victor now had his hands on a few bags of the junk.

Anna was the only one of the girls that would call herself a recovering drug addict, had hipped Victor to the scandalous game of "Hook." Hook was evil, it was dirty, it was heartless with small regards for life, but most of all it was much appreciated by Victor the most. Hook is a dirty move put on by the old school pimps to string their women out on drugs to keep them humping for dope. During a sex session the old pimp would place small pieces of heroin into the rectum of their women, and after enough times the women would become so dope-sick that they would welcome death anytime. Then the pimp or whoever would come around, and presto she feels better; it was like heaven once the fella loaded her up again in a sex session. So, it went, if she was sick without him, but heaven with him then all of this was a no brainier when it came to the decision making concluding that she'll rather stay humping. Because mentally and now physically, she just couldn't live without him.

The game would change once the women smartened up to the game of hook. Because now, the women would then pass this game onto their Johns, who would then find that they couldn't live without the whore who put the hook on them. The brilliance in this was that the pimps would keep the whores humping, and the whores would keep the tricks paying, which then created a successful operation to get the money with the buck stopping at the pimps' pocket. Unless he too was on the junk if that was the case, then Victor could now see Judah making a shit load of money. Groggy, was how Victor listened to all of this, because he was tuned in as if he'd just been nominated to take a rocket ship to the moon without his permission, bug-eyed and non-believing. Well, hell Victor thought, as he passed the bags on to the girls who would then pass it on to P. Baby, SP, Big Kev, Duke, Grass and Felton through intercourse, and make it easier for Victor to come down on them.

Once the casing was complete, Victor decided to take April up on her offer of spending some quality time together, a good time of touching and kissing, licking and nibbling.

When Victor awoke, he found that April was already gone. Believing her to be at the club and that Juice would be at the sitter's, and this leaving him to awake to an empty house. Half past midnight, which was the perfect time to get up and get dressed and mentally prepared for the upcoming events. He would blend in with the night, so in choosing his outfit he wore black slacks, black shirt, black shoes and a black maxi coat to warm him through the morning. Seconds ticked by like weeks and minutes, like months; everything would have to go accordingly and he knew it; the window for error had never been so small, as it was non-existent according to the plans. Judah knew to be ready by seven thirty, bright and early in the morning.

"This is how we'll catch the city, when it opens up and comes to life," Victor had told him.

What Judah didn't know was that this time frame was only a design to keep him in the dark to the calamities that would soon fall upon his new potnas. With the only thing left to do was bring the calamity part, Victor thought. And just as the thought hit him, there was the toot of a horn outside that only told him one thing: that his ride was now waiting. It was Judy, the once fearful but now tried-and-true wheel person, who was under gag orders about any events that would transpire throughout the night. It was a few ticks past two a.m. when Victor got in the car with Judy, grateful that she didn't stand him up. He gave her the rundown to the ways that they would behave themselves, and the expectations of the small hours and how to avoid suspicions as they traveled through the morning from one place to the next. Starting on Stockton Blvd. between Second and Third avenues, Victor had Judy park on Third Avenue and asked her to wait.

"Oh-kay, don't worry, I'll be here." Hearing that, Victor turned to leave.

"No," Judy shouted to him, freezing him.

"What?" Said Victor wondering if the girl developed cold feet all of a sudden.

"Come here and give me a kiss again for luck."

"Ah, yeah," He then trotted off to the motel after delivering such a small peck.

It was pre-arranged that the television would act as the signal: a television on, then it was no good; if it was off, then it was a go-ahead. So, when Victor came to room 34 the television was off, so he knocked softly on the door. No one stirred or came to the door, so the test. Victor turned the knob on the door and it opened, revealing an awfully sleepy and non-functioning Grass. His snores told Victor that no other time was better than the very moment, one that Victor seized with no hesitation. He stepped into the room and lined Grass' head up with the barrel of the Colt, and without second guessing Victor blew Grass' brains the fuck out, and just like a thief in the night, Victor disappeared according to plans. One minute later, and to the sounds of sirens he was back in the car. Victor gave Judy directions on where to go then climbed into the rear seat to lay down, obscured from vision. He relished in the fact that no one would suspect a single white woman at these times of the morning. The next stop was on Stockton Blvd. and Parker. Victor got out of the car and dismissed Judy and ran up the stairs and located room 27. Even there, the television was off.

"Shit, that junk must be powerful," he soliloquized, then went into the room to see SP waiting on his ride to go home, and Victor offered transportation by blowing his brains out in the exact same way as he did to Grass and Pepe. Victor left the room at a full sprint, taking the stairs two and three at a time hoping to beat the nosey occupants to the streets before they made it to their windows. Whether he did or didn't, he was at a dead sprint to Stockton Blvd. and Baker, where he barely made it inside of room 7 before the red and blue lights filled the black sky. Cop cars blew past with their sirens wailing, playing their crescendos, and heading towards Parker, just three blocks away. As close as this motel was to the previous one could prove to be a problem, save for the fact that Judy was parked on Baker next to a fence that Victor could gain access to if, and only if he was to climb out of the bathroom window of the motel. A cinch he thought, and it was. The sound echoed, first "Boom," the blood, the noodle lookalikes and then the he made his exit and there P. Baby laid suspended, no more air, and no more thoughts. Duke was no different; he waited for Victor just right across Fruit Ridge Rd. Duke must have had a lot on his mind, because the entry hole was regular like the others, but the exit hole was a whole different scene altogether; anyone could have easily put their fist through the exit hole. And hollow his head must have been because his squigglies hit the wall farthest from the bed. Big Kev's head wasn't hollow, but the slug did find its way out of there, but barely. Victor made it to Mack Road and to Felton. When Victor arrived at the motel room on Mack Road, the television was on, yet Victor knocked anyways and the door was opened by Felton.

"Come on in, Victor. Listen, you could down me if that's what you gotta do, but before you do, I need you to know that I ain't have shit to do with none of that shit those dudes was plotting against you, and to you I was loyal, to you I sent information after information to tip you to the plots of those dudes. I don't do business with brothers who work with the police and back-stab their potnas. There's not one gun in this room but probably yours, and look, the televisions been on all night waiting for you to show. I saw the whole play. I asked Donna if she could, would she help to spare my life. It would be her that I'd owe forever if you decide in favor of keeping me amongst the living. Although she told me that it was out of her hands, she did hip me to the television. I waited here Victor, right here, because I'm not supposed to run from a friend nor somebody that I admire, nor one that I prayed for, because even from here you could hear the music being played by the police, and that, Victor, is all I have to say." Victor pulled from his pocket the Colt and pointed it at Felton, who was now drenched in sweat. Victor's anger was so pure; his hate was so white that the gun vibrated in his hand. So much, that he used the other hand to aid in steadying his aim. He said, "Felton, I swear to God I will kill you so fast, so, so fast that when God get the news that you made it to heaven, your ghost would be a year old if you ever cross me after I spare you of your life."

"I would never, Victor. Can't you see that? I could have been gone."

"There's a job getting ready to open up in just a few hours; the pay is big time. Come to Pepe's and claim it late tonight." Victor put down the gun and headed out to meet Judy, who didn't appreciate being held up like she was, not knowing what to think, but found pleasure once Victor told her to head towards the freeway because Stockton

Blvd. was blocked the fuck off. It was a quarter to five by the time Judy dropped Victor off in front of Marlene's and drove off.

"Victor, is that you?" Marlene yelled from the room. Who else would it be, Victor thought before he said, "Yeah, it's me Marlene." Victor undressed and redressed into something more casual and sat next to Marlene while he waited for April to blow for him, and she did just before seven a.m.

"Victor, what's going on? Victor, you barely ever have time for me anymore."

"I'll see you when I get back. I'm only going outside to get something." And he did, in fact he returned with a suitcase that now held one hundred and twenty-five thousand dollars in it. Marlene, seeing this, knew that Judah was having money like this, but never saw Victor with money of this sort and always wondered if she should leave Victor to his club and women and team up with Judah, the true hustler. Now she burned in confusion as she saw Victor organizing the stacks in the suitcase and watched as he zipped it closed. Before leaving he pecked Marlene's cheek and said, "You look like you seen a ghost."

"Whose money is that, Victor?" She asked.

"Look, I'll see you when I get back." Victor left the shack behaving in an inconspicuous way so Marlene wouldn't be able see him leave with Judah. By seven thirty Judah showed up. Pulling over to allow Victor to hop in and once Victor was in the car he unzipped the suitcase to show Judah the money, but underneath the suitcase was the Colt trained on Judah, just in case. With a calming innocence, Judah retrieved a briefcase from the rear seat and snapped it open to dump the contents of the briefcase into the suitcase. He added his funds to Victor's with confidence that Victor was ignorant to his surroundings, and said, "There you go, buddy. If you count it fair, then it's all there." Victor zipped the suitcase, purposely allowing it to sit on his lap. On the sly he wiped clean the Colt of all its prints, as thoroughly as possible under the circumstances, plus on the sly Victor played his mirror, looking for the tail sent by Nigel. Spotting it, Victor told Judah to get to 33rd. and

Sixth. Judah put the car into gear and drove off in the direction of 33rd. and Sixth. Moments later, Victor told Judah to pull over next to the old Victorian, and there they sat a moment. Victor saw as a cab pulled up to the driveway and let Nigel out of it then proceeded on its way.

"This looks like the time. Judah, listen, don't panic but I'm gonna leave this pistol with you. If anybody comes out without me, gun them down, you got that?" Victor left the now-clean gun on the seat as he got out of the car and headed for the Victorian, until up the steps he went. Nigel followed Victor's every move. He swung the door open, and up the staircase they both went to reach the window that overlooked $33^{rd\ street}$. Nigel put three goons on the case: Tyree, Moon and Peter Boy. It was Tyree who pulled alongside Judah and said, "My man, how do I get to 4th Ave. from here?" Judah gave him the directions then Tyree said, "Hey ain't your name Judas?"

"Nah, my name Judah why, what's up?"

"I thought it was Judas, it is Judas," then the rear window rolled down far enough for a machine gun to fit and spit fire. Judah may have had a chance because his already suspicious mind made him bring the pistol to the ready, except while he was paying attention to the car and its driver, he wasn't prepared for Peter Boy, who too brought up his automatic weapon, and there from the sidewalk he emptied the whole drum into Judah and his car. From the Victorian, Victor and Nigel watched the barrage of gun claps fill Judah from both sides of his vehicle. The song played for two minutes so that Judah could dance his very last dance before the lights went out. Then came the sound of his horn, which blew continuously non-stop until the ambulance, fire department and SPD showed up to quiet the street once more. They were picking up the pieces as they awaited the coroners to show and carry Judah, aka Judas, off to the morgue.

"Well um, it looks like you could go and live yourself a nice and happy life now, doesn't it. You know my next question though, don't you?"

"Hmmm, uh uh, what is it?"

"What are you gonna do with Marlene? Somehow I had that girl pegged as a champ, turns out that she's a chump."

"Man, don't start me to lying, I really don't know." In truth, Victor had dread in his heart and in his mind, hoping that the subject of Marlene would just go away all on its own.

"Well, if you were thinking about nothing at all then let me point out a couple of issues that you may have to deal with. First, let me just toss right off the top of my mind, April. Now, let's just say that I'm Marlene and I see you hugged up with that pretty woman that you gotten your hands on, "Oh my God!" It pains me to think about it. That girl so fine, but picture this scene." Nigel pointed downstairs at the emergency units then said, "Tie that together with that boy down there waiting to get carried out of here, which tells me that she loses all the way across the board. Now, put that with the information that she may have. No telling what that boy done told her and what would you have?"

"I know, I know this shit Nigel, but dammit, man."

"I know, I know, I know, damned if you do, damned if you don't, but if I was you I'd rather take my chance on damned if I do. Because if you pick damned if you don't she would walk out of here Scot- free. And you my dear friend, will smell something crossed between brown sugar and cinnamon when they strap yo' young ass down in that damned gas chamber. I heard that sometimes that gas be so damn strong that ya' eyeballs pop out. I know you don't want your eyeballs popping out, do you!"

"Hell, Nigel, you had me at cinnamon and brown sugar. Man, I don't know what I'm gonna do, but I know that I'm a do it."

"Nobody said that this shit was gonna be easy. If it was, it'll be standing room only, it's not and you know why? Because everybody knows that this is a dirty game."

Chapter 22

The emergency team took hours to wrap up the incident down on the street of 33rd. before towing the bullet-riddled Buick and leaving themselves. Impressively, the same cab that brought Nigel had showed up just two minutes after the last of the emergency teams were gone.

"Looks like you need a lift, don't you?" Asked Nigel, who wasn't impressed at all.

"And I was just wondering how I was gone get out of here with this here suitcase… speaking of suitcase, what's the tab on this thing here?"

"You said it yourself: me and you would become business partners, and as business partners let's just say that you owe me one." Together the two walked out of the house and into the cab, which would drop Victor off at the club.

April showed at the door to admit Victor. As soon as she laid eyes on him, she ran to him and hugged him tightly then they kissed. She said, "Come, hurry, your favorite movie is on." The movie in question was a broadcast interruption that brought to the city of Sacramento a special bulletin, one that shook up the whole city. The news showed tales of the midnight hours, where five laid dead in their motel rooms, and how it all ended with the discovery of Judah H. Mathews just a while ago, said that "Judah Mathews" had gone on a killing spree before being killed himself just moments ago. The news broadcast began at twelve in the afternoon showing repeats of incidents that took place up and down Stockton Blvd. It was a crime scene not likely for the California's capitol where it was nominated the third best place to raise a family. A statistic that has now taken a major hit, and they all knew it. April huddled around with Victor and decided that she would pour them both a drink. Nearly one o'clock and the news took on a different twist: the cameras took to a different venue just outside of the police station, where the Mayor, who at the time was Bob Reynolds, approached the podium in just enough time to introduce the Chief of police, Andrew Tolliver. It was he who brought the news that the police department was headed in a different direction, in a more modern direction and a direction that could handle the likes of the modern-day criminal. So, the first new change was that he accepted the resignation of Captain Olmstead, and introduced to the city the newly appointed captain, the very special detective of the narcotic/homicide division. A detective with curriculum vitae that travels everywhere from traffic to burglary, even the fraud division, and the city should be proud to accept the new captain of police: Loren O'rieley. The venue clapped and applauded the chief's decision, and the city saw as O'rieley stepped to the podium as the new captain of police proceedings. Once at the podium, silence fell over the area occupied by news cameras and reporters and of concerned citizens who needed a better understanding in regards to the tragedies that took place while the city slept.

"My name is Loren O'rieley. Captain, Loren O'rieley, and I'm here to field your questions and address any concerns that you may have." Right away the reporters rushed the podium with a barrage of questions.

"Captain O'rieley, are you now the new Captain because you solved the biggest case in "this cities'' recent history?" Asked one of the reporters,

"I don't know the full reasons to why I've been selected Captain of the Sacramento Police Force, but I'd like to think that this case aided in this decision, yes," replied O'rieley.

"Captain O'rieley, should we now say that the city has been restored to order with the death of Mr. Mathews?" Asked another reporter, a very attractive blonde,

"I would like to think so, yes." O'rieley made his first mistake as Captain.

"Are you then overlooking the fact that Mr. Mathews had been shot sixty times with fully automatic weapons, forcing him to drown in his own blood?" Asked the same reporter who set him up the first time, O'rieley had always hated blondes, now even more so.

"We are not overlooking the fact that Mr. Mathews died a very, very violent death, no."

"Within one year we reported a burning car which contained a body inside, shot to death executioners' style, no different than that used by the mafia. We covered brutal deaths of bodies that were pulled away from an alley of one of the oldest suburban areas in Sacramento with no clues there either. We've even reported the death of one of our own city councilmen, who was found also in an alley with his pants down as if at one time he was entertaining the likes of a prostitute. Add that there's a rumor floating that all of these homicides were committed by perhaps the same person seeing that the very same kind of gun was responsible for most of these killings. Sir, and just within the last twelve hours we reported the multiple murders who, too, died in the fashion most adorn again by the mafia, and again the same caliber of gun is mentioned. Is it safe to say that our city is not in order and that somehow our problem isn't a random problem, but an organized crime problem? Are you saying to us that it was Mr. Mathews that was responsible for all the chaos that has plagued our city? Sir, has the mafia now come to Sacramento?" This reporter, Victor thought, had been hired for only one reason and that was to piss off the now new Captain of police. Who in return turned a dark crimson color, attempting with all of his might to remain composed. He said as calmly as possible, "No, I do not believe the city to have an organized crime problem nor a mafia one. What we have here was Mr. Mathews will to kill, who've found an effective way to do it, none more, and none less." Captain O'rieley steadied himself, then the reporter again: "And the nearly one hundred times that Mr. Mathews has been shot, was that only another person who too, found an effective way of killing?" Then the crimson color returned, and if Victor and April saw correctly it appeared that Captain O'rieley was gonna snap and choke the shit out of the frail lady that kept questions flowing fluently while never missing a beat. Again, Captain O'rieley composed himself, "We will get to the bottom of the death of Mr. Mathews...." The lady interrupted again, "Sir, who is Raymond Buchannon?" Then O'rieley snapped, and spit flew everywhere.

"Who is Raymond Buchannon? Who is Raymond Buchannon? Nobody, that's who Raymond Buchannon is! Nobody! A little bug and soon I will squash him like a gnat! Who is Raymond Buchannon? He's a myth, nothing to be scared of. He is just a figment of our own imaginations, that's all. Each time we want to scare ourselves we'll invent something to help us and that's all. As far as I could tell, we have a coward in our city that hides like a thief in the night, a sissy boy who isn't man enough to reveal his intent, noooo, he hides and he lays and waits to scare the innocent, just asking to be captured! That's who Raymond Buchannon is: nothing, a nobody." O'rieley finished with a speech that stung everybody, even the Mayor, as well as the Chief of police.

"Whoa, are you angered by this gentleman. Glad to know that you know so much about him. Sir, now could you tell us if Mr. Buchannon is mafia?"

"Nooo, Raymond Buchannon is not mafia!"

"How do you figure to bring Mr. Buchannon to justice, sir?"

"There will be no more questions," the Chief chimed in and gathered all of his colleagues and vacated the premises.

"Wow, now this looks like somebody's going to get it," said the stunned April. Victor, who wasn't in any better of conditions, stared at the television long after it went blank. Barely believing his ears or his eyes, he shook his head and took a sip from his glass.

"Well. Umm, now that your favorite movie is over, what now?" Victor shook his head and headed for the stairs. It was April who needed comforting the most; she couldn't believe that it was over completely and followed Victor up the stairs and into the office. Victor went to his desk where he sat the suitcase on top of it and unzipped it to remove the contents. April looked upon it in disbelief. Victor, who never told her the play in its entirety, just ignored her confusions and went to the safe to open it and began to add the stacks on top of the already growing stacks. A few trips later, with the help of April, he was finished. April, who didn't ask any senseless questions had gone to the mini bar and refilled their glasses and said, "Something about all that news down there that got me excited." Then her shirt was off.

"I thought you would be scared for me." Off went his shirt.

"I used to be." Now her bra disappeared.

"Used to be?" His shoes went flying.

"Not anymore." She came closer to him, palming her breast.

Victor kissed April, and then said, "What do you want from me?"

"To be Mrs. Raymond." Her pants fell and she stepped out of them then said, "What do you want from me, Victor?"

"A woman that is good to me and good for me, not one who just look good, but a woman that is good." Then off went his pants and socks. Clothing was removed, until now the new couple had no choice but to fulfill their intentions. Victor hesitated noting that his memory was dominating the moment. April, knowing the reasons for this had come to Victor and reminded him by saying, "I told you, I am not them." Then she straddled him and stayed there until they both were exhausted. Sleep being what Victor needed and he found it there in April's arms and remained there until the first light of the following morning.

Chapter 23

Marlene made it to the club in search of Victor and was told that Victor wasn't in and hadn't been for a few days, now grew concerned and couldn't help but to wonder if he was dead somewhere, upon hearing the news about Judah. Scared and genuinely worried out of her wits for days until she found satisfaction, when Victor made it through the door…

"Victor!" She ran to him. "Are you all right? I've been watching the news and it was just horrible."

"I know, I know, baby, I'm tired, I need some rest and some Marlene tonight."

"Oh Victor, it's about time. I was beginning to think that it was someone else."

"Why ever would you think something like that?" Again Victor looked into her eyes, and again nothing was there. Maybe, he thought Marlene was a cold-blooded viper. Hated her, no, Victor loved Marlene. He was grateful for the life that she gave him, but did he trust her? Not at all, so as they undressed Victor made sure to palm the junk. They kissed, they fondled and she took him inside of her. Rolling Marlene over, Victor gave it to her doggy style, and occasionally he would insert pieces of junk inside of Marlene, small chunk by small chunk until he was certain that a dangerous amount was now inside. Moments later the drug took on its effects and Marlene began to vomit uncontrollably. Victor just watched. Marlene jerked and foamed from her mouth, and Victor just watched. Marlene toppled over the table, knocking over the contents, and Victor just watched. Victor watched as Marlene fought for her life and watched as she searched for answers from her betrayer. Steady with eyes that never apologized Victor watched until Marlene shook and Marlene died and watched until she laid unresponsive, and then he left. The time he made it back to the club, Felton was waiting for him along with Donna. It was April that put the flames out once Victor saw Donna.

"Baby, maybe I should have told you this before but I'm gonna always stay in a woman's place, and who you conduct your business with is none of my business but I saw the way you looked at the girl and knew that I better tell you that a lot of the plans that we made surrounded the information that she brought back. Baby, this may or may not be the only time that I come between you and your likes and dislikes but I must ask as a favor to me and to yourself to just let them be." Without waiting for a response April went behind the bar and continued to mix drinks for her customers, as if what she said was it final. Yet, she stole glances in Victor's direction before sending Felton over to join Victor, leaving Donna to nurse her drink.

"Man, this is one hell of a night," said Felton. Victor knew that Felton would have a lot of these "hell of a nights," considering that he came ever so close to having one bad night that lasted forever.

"Yeah, I'm hipped. Come on, let's go upstairs."

Victor knew Judah's routes by heart and he explained to Felton as much as he needed to know without going over the sensitivities of the assignment. Victor made sure that Felton had a direct connection, only differences that Victor would strongly advise Felton not to cover the whole city but gather some recruits and let them cover their own sections respectively. He advised him that in this case the more would really be the merrier; he told him that everybody has a boss. Victor works for Raymond Buchannon, Felton works for Victor, and so Felton too, should bring forth his sidekicks. Felton sat in quiet while Victor ran down the way the machine would operate. Only the real niggas Felton should recruit, the brute types for times of war, and the smart types for times of advancements, yet they should all appoint their loyalty to none other than Raymond Buchannon, saying that Jesus would run a close second. And, Felton received all of this as somebody that Victor knew, would rather take orders and not offers, for Felton's loyalty was bought and paid for with a currency worth more than money.

Over the next few weeks Victor learned of new discoveries that would paint any other hustler into a corner. A team of local law enforcements got together to rid the city of Raymond Buchannon. As soon as they found him they were gonna sentence him to the law. Then, what followed would be a few lines of punishments that were far from constitutional. In the newspaper there were stories comparing Raymond Buchannon to Bumpy Johnson. Then other papers contended, saying Bumpy couldn't hold a box of tissues to wipe Raymond Buchannon's ass, saying that Legs Diamond would have died an embryo had Raymond Buchannon shared the same space as Legs' mother! During all of this it was the Sacramento Police Department that took the most heat: they were called wannabe soldiers, they were called incompetent and senseless as investigation after investigation had gone sour or grew cold.

Weeks turned into years, and all they ever got was wars and dead bodies for agendas. Seems that cartel groups poured in from Mexico City to rid "one city" of "one figure" who had grown more and more magnified before their very eyes. Any extraneous figures were often wiped away. Public officials swore by one God or the other that the city could do better without this modern day hoax of a gangster, only to leave office to no avail of capturing Raymond Buchannon. Who was accused of every crime in the book, one that bore a bold letter stamp that read "unsolved" across the files folder? Anything from petty theft to grand larceny, yet every officer knew that they would love to bring him in for jaywalking as well, and every judge knew that once this man entered their court room that jaywalking, if nothing else would be sufficient enough to bring a sentence worth a hundred years to the one they called "Raymond Buchannon." The cops had received many leads on where, on how, on when to capture this fine figure and outstanding gentleman. Even those leads proved to be empty and had netted nothing, zip, zilch, and zero. Month after month drugs came in, guns came in, everything: imported woman, liquor and artillery of every kind. If anyone wanted to go into business for himself, guess who sent a message? If anyone was due to testify on a friend or business partner, guess who sent a message? Breech on any contract, guess who, yes, Raymond Buchannon.

Only one person knew the entire truth, only one person knew the reason and that one person followed story after story, one gossip column after the next, one broadcast after the next one, each promise and every fail. Victor would read, watch and listen to the streets, as well as the professionals, one professional especially, the one and only "Captain O'rieley." Although no direct contact was ever made with this particular professional note that Victor always traded envelopes for Intel with this very professional and even though this Captain would sometimes press to even meet the man that works for the man or even the guy or gal that works for that person. Victor made sure that only the most trustworthy of messengers was sent to deliver and collect.

Ever since Victor led the SPD to the shack, where he'd swore that the way Marlene lay now was indeed the exact same way how he discovered her. Without knowing what to do, he alerted the ambulance to come and save her. When asked, how he knew Marlene, he said that she was his older sister. Seeing absolutely no sense in remaining at the shack, he would call the very first place that he ever had in life that offered anything close in resemblance to a regular way of living, a thing of the past. He decided he'd move into April's offerings while the club was being remodeled to fit the upstairs to accommodate the Raymond's with a genuine living quarter of two bedrooms and one bath, which would suffice for the years to come. So it was there that Victor married April, it was there that Juice grew from a young child to a young man, though the name of the club still bore the name of "Pepe's Game Room." People now called it April's, for Pepe was a ghost that so long a time ago had disappeared from memory. It was also the very same place that Victor leafed through the pages at yet another attempt on his livelihood. A new outfit had come from across the country to investigate the northern California way of doing things, perhaps a possible takeover was in order. Victor read through the whole folder before paging Felton, who by this time had built for himself a conglomerate of factions on the street. Victor was glad for Felton's unyielding loyalty, and because of him Victor was always with an army at his disposal. Felton knew that to call Victor was not only against the rules, but would also went without saying, for he knew that Victor hadn't fielded a phone call since he'd known him, just made his way to the club where Victor hardly ever departed from. The message had come, which informed Felton that his presence was requested immediately, and immediately Felton made his showing. Victor sat at the bar to await Felton; he found satisfaction in the way Mrs. Raymond traveled throughout the club as if she was happy to serve the likes of others. He was even satisfied in what she had done to the place, being that Christmas was just weeks away.

Felton arrived and took a seat next to Victor, who welcomed him with gratitude, like the brother that he never had. The two shared a drink together, and then Victor stood and beckoned for Felton to follow him to the VIP section, where Victor took his meetings, deeming upstairs off limits to everybody except Juice and April. Once in the VIP section, Victor asked Felton to have a seat, then presented Felton with the entire folder of the Zapatta's, who made a living through extortion's, illegal gambling and legal gambling, as well as drugs and prostitution. Felton read in silence the file in its entirety. Victor saw as Felton's eyebrows rose, then came together to form a uni-brow.

"What you think about this?" Victor asked.

"I think we better squash it before it gets any bigger," said Felton. Victor really enjoyed talking to Felton, for he was no nonsense eighty-five percent of the time and a real comedian the rest of the time.

"How do we know that it hasn't gotten any bigger already?" Asked Victor,

"Says right here that these fuckers come all the way from Hartford. Where the fuck is that, in New England some fucking where?"

"Close, I mean it's a New England state but it's in Connecticut some damn where."

"Shit, then let's send them back to Connecticut, tell them thank you but no thank you" so the story went. The Zapatta's, who took a rented mini-mansion outside of the Elk Grove district, who loved to host parties, plenty of drink, plenty of coke and plenty of girls, were fallen upon by a party of thugs who played party crashers. From the five Zapatta brothers who laid hog tied and gagged, each one watching the next get slaughtered before their very eyes. The younger Zapatta got the worst end as Felton took his Louisville slugger to the younger Zapatta until his head held no resistance, every piece of his skull turned to mush. Next in line was the oversized Zapatta brother, who had every bone in his body broken before finally deciding to head towards that bright light that everyone speaks about; they call that "bright light" heaven. Before the night was over, only one of the Zapatta brothers was left alive, yet he'd survive knowing that he'd be restricted to a wheelchair as a message to his compatriots. A letter was written to the entire state of Connecticut which would drift on to Maine, even Jersey, New York and Boston. Although it was none of Victor's intentions to send the message so widespread, yet the message was short but very powerfully stated when it read like this:

"We are mindful that at times you want to escape the hard concrete and frozen temperatures and opt to bring your wayward ways to greener pastures and warmer climates. We understand your intentions fully, though you walked in without knocking, you ate, without first saying your grace, even though it was a very small plate, we still say grace around here, we call it respect. This is just a friendly warning to let you know that your kind isn't welcome here. Now let this warning allow you to know and understand that what you call warm could become mighty, mighty, mighty, mighty hot. This time we'll send your bodies back in boxes; next time, we'll send your bodies back in pieces.

Yours truly,
Raymond Buchannon

And this was the message that the Zapatta elders received for New Year's because their Zapatta offspring were massacred on Christmas.

Chapter 24

Although Victor very seldom left the club, he always remained tuned into the streets, their wants, their needs and their appreciations. Victor would often time sponsor events so that poor people could forget their miseries for just a fleeting moment. Although he wouldn't sponsor these events directly, he still found ways to give back to such a troubled community. Victor would keep a window open after normal business hours. This way, instead of tossing the leftover menu out, he would give it away to the homeless people and to the drug addicts. On the corners now you could find a boxing gym or a very sophisticated equipped library or a community center. This was only to help Victor sleep at night, for he knew that he had taken a whole lot from these very streets that he was now contributing to.

Dealings with Captain Loren O'rieley had its benefits, but it also had its drawbacks, five thousand dollars a month no matter what a folder or not. The deal had gone like this, for intelligence, the envelope would grow another five grand, but any intelligence or a threat that Victor was to find out on his own, then all deals were final due to the breach of the contract. The curve ball showed up shortly after the Zapatta file had been forwarded to Victor through the correct procedures and protocols. The good Captain grew to be impatiently greedy and more pressing to meet the boss. Victor grew very impatient himself and decided to avoid the Captain's request of a pay raise and pay altogether, and for this action of no payment, the reaction was the raids that took place through the morning, noon and at night. The presence of the police was so strong that in three days the county jail had become increasingly overcrowded. Did Captain O'rieley then get his payments? No. Victor was sent message after message, and threat after threat, yet and still no payments. Then one day the messages began to slow to a halt, and the next time Victor heard from O'rieley there was a file, a folder of investigations that made its way to the attention of the Chief of police who notified the FBI to help bring down the one Raymond Buchannon. Did this get him a payment then? No. What O'rieley didn't know was that Mr. Tolliver's ambition to become a political figure was the one weakness that Victor could and would exploit at any given time, and Mr. Tolliver had known this a very long time ago and so it went, the entire field was set. Chief Tolliver, who began to inquire about politics, until Victor piled bodies on his front porch due to the wars that had opened up once Judah toppled over. The Mexicans arrived on boats, in vans, in jeeps and on helicopters, only to leave in a meat wagon. Because of this, Chief Tolliver retracted his statements of going into politics and Victor knew why. If a Chief of police could not under any circumstances bring down a villain as big as Raymond Buchannon as a Police Chief, who's to think that he'd be able to do so as a Mayor. To arrest Mr. Buchannon would be altogether different, because an arrest of that magnitude would shoot him straight to the Senate seat and everybody knew it. Even Victor, who figured that as soon as any additional shakedowns shall come and the wrong people were killed, maimed or even hauled off, then this too would be a war and one for the ages Victor thought, tossing the file into his desk unattended to.

Juice was due to turn sixteen within the next twenty-four hours and the planned surprise party was under wraps and hadn't been leaked to him yet. This was a good thing seeing how so many people were invited to the party. The whole basketball class, from freshman to the senior class was all invited. With Juice's enormous talents, he was only a sophomore who had played on the varsity team ever since he was a freshman. Victor knew that Juice would love to share his birthday with his friends and teammates, so the club would be closed in celebration of the only child Victor had ever raised second to his self. Juice had lived the life of the fortunate, good schools and basketball camps, whatever made him happy made Victor happy. April did a fine job of grooming him to look toward his future and he always had. Ask him at age ten what he saw in the next ten years, and he'd say that he could see him hooping at the legendary UCLA. He always wore the Bruins' sweatshirt and sweatpants, even at practice where he was not yet a Bruin, but a Dragon. Though he was awfully proud to be a Dragon, he just wore the warm-ups in tribute of his eyes that he'd always kept on his prize. Victor used to always remind him that if he was the coach, that Juice would never leave the bench but the real coach said only once, and this settled everything, "Whatever makes this boy a better person was enough for him." Victor was able to understand Juice's coach by the way the crack rock epidemic blew through the city and stole the "parent" out of "parenting", so much that it was a norm to see prostitutes arrive younger and younger. These young girls were forced to hustle in order to feed and clothe their younger siblings. Yes, teachers, coaches and principals had their hands full due to this new epidemic. The hospitals were forced to open up an entire wing dedicated to catering to an overpopulated section of crack babies, who only grew to be gun- toting maniacs with heartless mentalities and devil-may-care personalities. This sad reality was controlled by Victor, and no excuse would be good enough so he never made any, for if not him it would be people like the Mexicans, the Zapatta's, and the CIA, even the locals. The "take" on drug trafficking was too big to be overlooked. Anyways, the party came around and people began to file into the club where Victor saw the place fill to capacity. There were jocks, there were nerds, there were thugs, and then there was this lone Caucasian family, an attractive-looking woman who accompanied her daughter. Curiosity overwhelmed Victor so much that he found Juice through all of the other letter jackets and jerseys and said, "Kid, I got a question for you."

"Dad,"

"Who the hell is that?" Juice followed Victor's stare to the white lady and her daughter, who sought and found April and were engaged in deep, concentrated conversation.

"Hmm, now that I don't know but she looks like the girl who plays on our soccer team. I think that's her, yeah, I'm talking about she plays like a grown man, why you ask?"

"I don't remember inviting them; I aimed strictly at hoop, and what you got around here? Look at her; she don't seem too fazed about being around all of this tough stuff," said Victor, observing.

"And she's not. You know why? Her daddy is the police, the big one. Shoot, he'll be over here so fast. Let somebody snatch that lady purse and run if they want to, they'll run straight to juvenile hall. That girl got into fight in a game once and the police had the whole school surrounded, made me miss the end of fourth and most of fifth period to answer questions that I just couldn't have known the answers to. I used to know her name but you know, I didn't know it was gonna be a party, so I didn't invite her. Shoot, you think mom did?"

"That's the way it looks, don't it? Oh, before I forget." Victor dug into his pocket to extract a set of keys and tossed them to Juice, saying "Happy birthday, kid." Juice caught the keys out of the air, a set that would fit a cherry red with a white soft top 1965 Ford Mustang. The car was a combination of gifts: first, it was to show appreciation for the good grades that he brought home consistently; second, it was the way that he studied over time to pass the driver's test. Last, but not least, for being the best kid in the world to Victor, a kid who just so happened to be celebrating a birthday.

"Dad, you didn't, I know you didn't, I mean you couldn't have." Juice's excitement showed obvious signs of contentment, and he said, "Where is it? I wanna see it right now."

"It's parked out back." Before Victor could ramble off anything further, he saw as Juice took off in a hurry, headed towards the rear door, collecting his friends and teammates in his wake. Wanting to share in Juice's excitement, Victor followed the crowd of teens and young adults to the lot out back in enough time to catch Juice dropping the convertible top only to re-raise it, and then he started the engine. Seconds later, the system that Victor had installed to fit the likes of the younger generation of loud music came alive. The woofers hissed before coming to life in their thundering announcements of deep, heavy bass drums that shook the trunk, sending the teens into hysteria as they began to dance in the lot to the sounds of the popular hip hop tune that came from the "highs" that Victor had running throughout the interior. Everyone cheered Juice on in a sing-along of "Happy birthday." Seeing enough, Victor headed back into the club and to his office to arrange his assignments. Let's see, there was the ledger that needed re-coding. There was the meeting with Nigel, and then there was the property development issue that he needed to go over with his lawyers: the trusted Dixon, Juan and Dixon. Who often found creative ways to keep Victor out of the limelight and away from gossips that could only open up speculations that could indeed lead to bright lights. Although Victor used more than one legal group, Dixon, Juan and Dixon only handled the sensitive issues. Then there was the folder that laid on Victor's desk that needed some attention, if not immediate attention. Victor was in deep thought, so deep that he didn't see as April approached him with company in tow.

"Honey, this is...Victor!" She snapped, bringing him back to the realities of the now.

"Yeah, what's going on? You guys having a good time?" Victor said, mainly to the woman and girl, not knowing how much exactly he had missed of the conversation.

"Yes, we are fine, thank you," said the woman, extending her hand to Victor.

"Sweetie, this is Megan," April said to Victor, a bit suspicious.

"Megan O'rieley and this is my daughter Jennie. We'd love to thank you two for the contributions you're making to this city, as well as to our soccer club. Lord knows that it's been difficult trying to raise money in these times," finished Megan. Victor shook her hand and then nodded to Jennie and said, "We're glad we could help," but in the back of his mind he said, how come you didn't ask your husband for the money, being that he has a good mind to rip people off. April knew that Victor had absolutely no idea to what he was glad that he could help for, smiled as Victor played the perfect host. One of these times she was gonna donate everything they owned just to watch him shake hands and say, "Glad that we could help." Victor followed the lady and her daughter to the exit, watching as they walked out of the club, then turned to April and said, "What's so funny?"

"Baby, I love how you are. You're perfect for me in every regards, come here smookums." April pursed her lips in search of a kiss. Victor knew a rat when he smelled one, dodged April's attempt at a smookums and looked her in her eyes and said, "April, what just happened? I mean I know that you just gave something away, but now I wanna know what?" Victor demanded.

"Well, you know how you always say the more money, the more problems, and that more problems only mean more misery?"

"I said that? When did I say that?" Victor's excitement grew.

"You say that all the time...."

Victor hurriedly interrupted. "Oh- kay, so,"

"What do you mean 'so'? I mean, who needs problems and who wants miseries?"

"April, baby," Victor said, barely controlling himself, "what did you just do?"

"Nothing,"

"Nothing, what made you…? Oh." Victor, realizing what April had said, had caught himself and watched as April clutched her stomach in laughter and said, "It didn't matter what I said, you was gonna lose it, baby don't you trust me by now to make sound decisions?"

"Hell, not when you don't want me to have misery or problems. You know how I like problems, and whatever you do, don't give away all the misery either." It went unsaid; really Victor found that he could trust April with any and everything. It was April who took the girls off the streets and gave them law-abiding employments; they were in clothing stores, beauty salons, massage parlors and flower shops. Save for Judy and Sonja, who absolutely demanded to be part of the street life, and joined Felton and Donna, which proved to be an effective idea, because of this, the contacts between O'rieley and Victor could remain anonymous.

"Baby, they only dropped by to say thank you, that's all."

"Oh, anyways, let me get to work, I got lot of that to do, enough to last me through the week. You got a bunch of overly amped kids on the way in. Do you think that you'd be able to handle them?"

"I sure wish you would have saved that car for last. He may not even care for the gifts I got him," April pouted.

"Of course he would," Victor said with confidence, for he knew that all the kids nowadays cared about were electronics and technologies, and April filled his room up with both and been sneaking to do so ever since the party began. She was making sneak trips to and from while Victor found ways to distract Juice.

"Do you really think that he would?"

"I'm sure of it." Victor turned and headed up the stairs to prepare himself for the lawyers.

Between the news and the newspapers, Victor saw how Loren O'rieley had begun to advance in the favor of the public's eye, raid after raid, even declaring a war on drugs. Victor saw press conferences on the regular, saw even when the FBI announced its involvements in this very war that had now been declared on the drugs, the dealers and the users. During these press releases, did the press allow the Captain leniency for the elusive Mr. Buchannon? Hell to the no. As soon as the public shined O'rieley up like a diamond, a reporter would show us where the flaws were located, and this had always chapped Captain O'rieley's hide. So, in one particular press conference O'rieley informed the public that Washington D.C was sending in one of their top profilers to bring a new form of intelligence to the table in a way that could aid in identifying Mr. Buchannon. What the public didn't know, nor did it have any way of knowing because of the tight lips that the department held for this profiler, was that this profiler had been in Sacramento for years and years, in and out. Victor knew that this speech was only a ploy that would keep the public patient with this particular investigation. Often times Victor would smile at the television, each time the Captain released bum information to the press, speaking of new developments in the investigation, and Victor knew all too well that all he needed to do was send an envelope with the correct amount of funding and the press conferences would all go away. Again, Victor heard how Raymond Buchannon was disrespected with name calling and fake profiling, only this time the day's message came to the public that the only way to rid this city of Raymond Buchannon was to knock down the walls around him, which brought on a concern to Victor, who knew that to resume payments was to show signs of weaknesses, which would make effective the press releases. So Victor stood steadfast to his decisions and would go about his days as an entrepreneur, ending his work week with these high concerns and with the sensible advice from Nigel to pull back and retreat without showing the appearance of retreating. Victor called Felton in to inform him of the drought that was to hit the streets for everyone in close proximity to the operation which would then affect even the petty hustlers. They were leaving small amounts of products on the street while guarding the border lines of the city limits against a possible attempt of a takeover.

Everyone knew the demands and the decisions that trickled down from Victor, who supposedly had gotten the word from Raymond Buchannon. And so it was. For six months the city was forced to fight over small pieces of action as Victor released small amounts in sporadic intervals. The raids began to slow until they ceased altogether, seeing the effectiveness in the strategy that brought calm to the news and the city alike. Victor also saw the benefits through pricing. He saw as the prices skyrocketed during these times to nearly doubling in price. So armed with this intelligence, Victor would send a drought two or three times a year, all the while guarding the city limits from threats and other possibilities, which never showed signs of letting up. The pickings were easy, the control much more firm and steady, for Victor had built a dynasty by playing for real and for keeps in the area of foes who indeed played for funsies. His fist was iron clad; his gifts were gold plated. Because of this balance, Victor found favors from both friend and foe alike. Whether they knew it or not, the favors were plentiful.

Victor watched as Juice headed off to school, now in his junior year at his beloved University of California Los Angeles, where he would start as a prominent point guard, team captain as well as conference assist and steals leader with an average of 11.6 points a game. At any given moment without warning, Juice would have an out-of-body experience and go for a triple double, which was a performance that was ever so exciting to watch. Victor found pride as a father while watching Juice produce humility and humbleness, while thanking God for his family, attributes and teammates during interviews. Yes, Juice was definitely raised the correct way.

Chapter 25

Victor continued to give back to the community. He installed clean and sober units throughout the city. He brought communities together in troubled times, though April called his endeavors hypocritical. Victor knew that it was easy to sleep after serving a few drinks here and there, maybe exchange a few chips often enough would get you to toss and turn some. Make you feel a little guilty for taking money off the foolish bettors who challenge the odds in a desperate search for sums of monies. A dream that only goes from gold dust to glitter, and a spark that at the end of the day never shined for us, just turned us all to condors. Still it was April's words that brought on a sense of hesitation each time Victor chose to give back anything, because in a way during all of this giving, Victor really did feel a bit hypocritical.

April made plans for her and Victor to board United Airlines to San Antonio in order to see the first round of the March Madness tournament, where colleges across the nation were magnified under microscopes. The big league players brought the scouts out competing for the chance to land one of these big names. One that could catapult their mediocre teams into contention, or to bring an addition to an already superior team that wished to stay a dominant entity in pursuit of or remain in the championship brackets. Whatever the case for the scouts, the kids knew that to play hard would attract the attention of a scout. The need to produce in times as clutch as a March Madness tournament was indeed an attribute that of a professional athlete, and all the agents had known this and was sure to relay such a wisdom to the players. This alone would be a dream come true for every kid in uniform; even some of the referees had their eyes set on blowing whistles on such a huge stage that of the NBA. Where bundles upon bundles of dollars were being tossed around like green salads. These were the plans that April made, and she made these plans with impeccable organization but through fate they were only plans made in vain. The news came back that a car bomb ended the life of Sonja Marie Tillman, her daughter Kyrin and her daughter's twin sons. Victor read how Sonja lost her life, the life of her daughter's and the lives of her grandsons all in one attempt, and all in one explosion. Victor watched as April cried for weeks, even after the wakes and after the funerals. Victor spared no expenses; still, he knew that no matter how much money he poured into these events, nothing would heal his wounds nor massage his conscience. The blow was too heavy for anyone to bear even Victor, who sat in his office and drunk himself into oblivion as the tournament played on without his awareness or attention. April tried all she could to shake loose the hold that the incident held on to Victor, but nothing seemed to work, so instead of an indirect approach she figured a more direct approach was in order. Relieving her behind the bar was the new hire Eddie, who was an excellent bartender who came in from Portland, Oregon, had watched as April removed her apron and headed for the stairs. When April finally made it to Victor, first thing she collected was the bottle saying, "Oh-kay, Victor, the pity party is now over, there is a great big cloud of reality heading your way." Victor stared at April, who went on with, "Victor, I think it's time for you to share with your wife what tore you to pieces this way; I know Sonja hit you hard, she was my friend as well…." Victor interrupted April by sliding her stacks of folders; April figured that the answers that she sought had to be in the stack of folders, so she started from the top. Midway through her search she collapsed on the sofa, and tears flowed from her eyes in its monsoon effect. Knowing that April was now out of commission, Victor easily located the bottle and poured himself another drink without being interrupted, for now April knew that you must give drink to a soul, one as wounded as Victor's, in its abundance. Now it was April who needed medical attention, as she nearly came close to a nervous breakdown.

It took Victor more than a month to regroup and to summon for Felton to join him in a meeting with Nigel, in order to equate the deeds brought on to the operation by none other than Captain Loren O'rieley, who had now begun to attacked with a deadly force. Felton met Victor at the club and the two shared in discussion the contents of the day's meeting and the actions that were to be put into motion at the most earliest of convenience. After discussing matters between the two, they headed towards the exits and into the waiting Town Car that would take them to the mall and to the meeting. The driver put the car into gear and headed in the direction of the K Street mall, which had not too long ago been built to bring this rapidly growing city its silver lining. Neither Victor nor Felton thought to check for followers, which they too found out to be a grave mistake, as the Town Car was overtaken by a cargo van that bore what appeared to be mercenary soldiers. The driver was hit first as he tried to elude the van in pursuit at speeds reaching the high fifties through the back streets. Victor and Felton held on as the car swerved and collided into a line of parked cars with a thundering crash. Though the impact was dead on, the two survived unscathed. Victor heard the van's screeching tires drawing near and said, "Quick… out," while reaching over the rear seat to relieve the unresponsive driver of the MP5SD sub machine gun. Taking hold of the pistol grip, he followed Felton, who favored the Walther semi-automatic from the car. They made their exits through the driver's side rear door in time to receive fire in repetition from fully automatic, as well as three-round burst as they took cover behind the Town Car.

"Go, I got you, hurry," said Felton, who opened up as the van door swung open, releasing its passengers, which proved too much for Felton, leaving Victor to watch as he was overtaken by the soldiers. This brought anger to Victor immediately, leaving him no choice but to open fire, knocking down soldiers while receiving gunfire himself to his shoulders, midsection and neck. Still, he kept the MP5 in business, claiming the van for its driver and other occupants before finally collapsing his self to the sound of his favorite song: the sirens that filled the air.

Just blocks away from the club the gunshots were going off and April heard every shot and dreaded every one. She heard the sirens and knew the reason for them. She said, "Oh, Victor." Then she was on the pavement in full sprint. She sought the direction from which she heard the commotions and the shots. She heard screeching tires, and a lot of screaming. She followed these commotions until she found her husband, her lover, and her soul mate barely breathing while blood formed bubbles from his lips.

"Victor, baby, come on now, I need you to hold on. You could do it, baby. Oh God, please don't take him away from me! I beg you, please, I don't… somebody help me, please somebody help me, oh my God Victor...Victor!" More bubbles formed as Victor tried to speak.

"No, no, hush, honey, they're on their way. You could do it, come on, momma got you. God, please don't do this, please don't do this!" The ambulance screeched to a halt, releasing its medical technicians.

"Ma'am, let us take it from here. We got a live one over here," one of the techs yelled over his shoulder while prying away April's grip that she had on Victor.

"Ma'am, you gotta let us help him. We got a live one over here," the tech yelled to his colleagues. Quickly Victor was loaded on to a gurney and whisked away to an open ambulance, which barely collected April before it sped away with its sirens blaring. April watched as the techs revived Victor with oxygen and other needed preparations. Precious minutes passed before the ambulance pulled into the emergency unit of the UC-Davis Medical Center. April could still hear the beeping of the machine, which indicated that her husband was fighting for his life more than an hour later. She was forced to wait in the emergency unit's waiting room, and there is where she paced and prayed and repeated her actions repetitiously.

Chapter 26

Victor was not yet stable, and April couldn't find any doctor, nurse or observer that was willing to comment on Victor's condition, which too drove April nuts. By three o'clock a.m. the news came down that he was still fighting. Though it looked good, he was far from out of the woods. By five o'clock a.m. Juice, Nigel and one of Nigel's' henchmen came into the waiting room. Leaving nothing to chance, Nigel had gone to pick Juice up personally. No one knew why Victor was hit in this fashion, nor from whom at this time, but neither April or Nigel was willing to take any chances with Juice.

"Momma, is he in there?" April nodded as Nigel came to console her. "I wanna see him," said Juice.

"Me too, only he's in one surgery after the next. We need to pray that God decides to keep him is all we can do."

"Still, I wanna see him." Juice headed towards the nurses' station in search of anyone who would admit him entrance for him to see his father while he was still alive. Not even the threats would get the nurses to budge. By eight o'clock in the morning the emergency room was beginning to fill with well-wishers, by nine it was explained to the nursing staff and doctors alike that the ICU room which held Victor was going to be guarded around the clock by licensed, gun-toting security whether the staff liked it or not, believing that if word was to leak that Victor was alive, then everyone feared another attempt would be made on his life. With these arrangements as a comfort to all, April, Juice and Nigel left the hospital and headed for the club where there was a group of people waiting on April to make a showing. There were the Dixon's. There was the police, and then there was Marjorie. Marjorie was the homeless woman who once had it all, until drugs took everything away. Yet Marjorie was also one of Victor's favorite people, so much that he always saved her a plate and always gave her a few bucks, not caring at all what she would do with it. It was there in the club that April found her pacing and hinting that April remained closed mouth to the officers. April, not knowing quite why, but something told her to dismiss the officers and she did, saying that she would contact them once she was able to rest and get her scruples together, and the two officers obliged and left the club. Then, April sought out Marjorie, immediately saying, "Girl, what has gotten into you? What's wrong with you, girl?"

"April, it was the police that shot Victor, girl."

"Marjorie, girl, what are you saying?" April pressed.

"You heard me. Those were police that was after that man, the fat one Victor was with."

"How you know all of this? This isn't funny, girl."

"How do I know, April they killed that man on Fifth and Thirty-eighth, remember."

April thought, then said, "Shit, Marjorie were you there, you were there weren't you?" April, remembering now that the vacant buildings on 35th was the living quarters for Marjorie and other homeless people, was then satisfied with the head nod.

"Oh-kay, I need you to come with me." April led Marjorie into the VIP section and forced Marjorie to go into detail as she saw it, excluding nothing, and Marjorie did. After playing both good cop and bad cop, April had all the information that she needed, for Marjorie swore by her life that after the gentleman had gunned down Felton, they were preparing themselves to depart when Victor gunned them down in the process of getting shot himself. April knew that it was a war going on because it was April who first saw Judy's mangled body after being tied to a vehicle and drug down Martin Luther King Jr. Blvd. for nearly half of a mile and way beyond the point of recognition, save for the tattoo on her ankle. No one, not even her mother, would have recognized her. April walked Marjorie to the door after giving her some bucks to stay away for a while, unless it could become dangerous for her. Seeing now why Victor liked this woman so much, April took a drink upstairs and sat at Victor's desk and said, "Oh-kay, sweetie, let's have a look-see, I'm sure the answers are in here somewhere." April pulled out the stacks of folders and read through each one, pausing then continuing until the last folder was complete. Through all the turmoil April still found reason to smile for her husband, for now she knew all of his secrets. Some of the things she knew and others she only had ideas of, but never many real facts. She knew that her husband had killed before because he had done so right in front of her face, but according to these folders her husband was a bad word...oh yeah he was a motha fucka. Well now she knew every secret those of his youth and that of his present, as well as that of the future as he saw it.

"Mom, what are you smiling for?" April didn't hear as Juice walked in. For a reply, April just pushed a stack of folders towards Juice, daring him to read them, and finally Juice sat down to read from the top, as April contemplated on what to do next. Juice read in silence, while April paced the floor; both appeared to have their wheels spinning, both appeared to be pre-occupied with the exact same issues. April paused to view her son's expressions while he read the material that Victor tried all of his life to shield from him. April knew that it would be futile to keep such information away from her son. As far as she was concerned, Juice had every right to know the truth about the man that he'd come to know as his father as anybody else.

"So, what do you think?" Asked April,

"Shoot, I think Uncle Nigel was right."

"Oh, right about what?" April became instantly serious.

"When he told me that it looks like my hoop career was all but over and done with."

"Oh and when did he tell you all of this?"

"As soon as we all laid eyes on Dad. You ran to dad, Uncle Nigel ran to me."

"Oh yeah, and what else did he say, Juice?" April asked, now feeling a bit violated.

"He said that nobody in this world understood Dad like him because he raised Dad; he said that the only weak spot that Dad ever had was me, is this truth? Because, I believe him, even more so now that I've read for myself. But, Uncle Nigel didn't have to tell me, because deep inside I already knew and so do you." All of this was true; a whole empire was built for Juice. There were recording studios, record stores, Foot Locker retail shoe stores and even the popular Afro-centric stores that opened in the mall, the steak house chain that flew through the Midwest. The movie theaters all over northern California had Victor's prints on them, there were Yogurt shops and ice cream parlors, detail and car washes everywhere laundry mats and dry cleaners in every city in California, stocks as well as bonds in the premium varieties, and all of this was done under April's watchful eyes of ignorance to such dealings. Oh and we are not going to overlook the countless amounts of dollars that Victor brought in from the streets of Sacramento because to do so would not only be missing a very large gap of the green stuff but it'd be silly as hell. Yet, and still, in April's defense, she had always respected Victor's space, and by the looks of things it was a lot of space. She was allowing Victor to be "man" about his wants and his desires, continuously remaining in a woman's place, she would call it. Victor never told her how to run this club, so she wouldn't even attempt to tell him how to run his business, and by the looks of things, even if she tried she hadn't the faintest idea of where to start.

"Mom," Juice said, bringing her back from her quick visit to a time ever so far from their present, and to show that she was in tuned to her son's truths, she allowed the tears to roll down her cheek without wiping them away.

"Mom, I believe this to be a decision that I need to make, and you know that I would never entertain the thoughts without you. Uncle Nigel raised Dad, but you are the only one that I have to guide me. You may think that I'm blind to that or naïve to the sordid things that Dad did to build these folders, but I'm not. I also believe that Dad had his reasons; I weigh the ethical ways and exuberant nature that he extended to everyone, not just you and not just me, but to everybody. I believe that you and not Nigel could tell me how; it was that Dad had his hands in so many things, yet and still never did he once deviate from the true things that hold the most value. Reading this," Juice picked up the folder then let it fall from his hand, "this would tell me that the person that has created these was a bad person. Now, Dad was a bad man, no doubt, but he wasn't a bad person." April just stared at her son, then reached for her chest and took a seat on the sofa.

"Are you all right, momma?"

"Yes, baby, I'm all right, I'm just listening to you and…and I don't know you just scare the hell out of me is all."

"Because I sound like Dad huh." For a reply, April just let her head bob up and down like she just saw the Jesus getting struck by lightning.

"Well, I'm on my way to the hospital, you want a lift?" Juice knew that a lift from him would be the last thing that his mother would want; because to do so would only mean bass drums pounding in her ears long after the ride was over. He was shocked when he heard, "Wait a minute baby, let me get my coat." So stunned was Juice that he figured that she failed to hear him, so he decided to repeat himself.

"Boy, I heard you, what did you think that I would say? No, that I'll catch a ride with your father?" Then the dam broke and her tears flowed generously.

"Momma, I didn't mean anything by that," said Juice.

"I know, baby."

By the time Juice and April made it to the hospital, they found Nigel sitting bedside, his little brother as he liked to call Victor, and it was closing in on midnight.

"Nigel," April said, surprised to find him there, especially in the wee hours.

"Oh my God, April..." Nigel took her in his arms and squeezed. Sensing the worst, April began to cry along with Nigel, then eventually Juice and the security guards, as well as the nurses, once they found out that the person who'd done so much for the city in its most positive ways now laid lifeless in a bed, just inches away from them.

"What is it, Nigel?" April asked.

"The doctors could tell you..."

"No! Nigel, you tell me."

"I mean..."

"Nigel, would you just tell me!"

"He's not going to make it, April." At the sound of this, both Nigel and Juice waited for her to pass out, but were relieved when she said, "Well, did the doctors say how long he has to live, Nigel?"

"Well, they say that he could live forever, which is the other thing that poses a problem." April became immediately confused and didn't appreciate Nigel playing with her emotions like this, and said, "Oh-kay Nigel, you've just confused me, so maybe if you said it slower I could catch on."

"Oh-kay, well, he's brain dead. See that machine that you hear beeping, well that's the only thing that's keeping him alive, and the way that I know you, all of this would be all right with you. I'm sure that you'd visit every day of your life. But, I know him too, and this ain't all right with him. Still, let us note that I have absolutely no say in this, and this decision is strictly up to you two." Nigel watched as April went to Victor and kissed him on top of his forehead, then said, "So, where is the good doctor at now? Has he been in and out all night?"

"Not too long ago left for the night, but vowed to return first thing in the morning. I believe that he'll be expecting to hear something by then from somebody that could make a better decision than I could have."

"Then I guess that I better make myself available then now, shouldn't I?" April's demeanor took on a suspicious appearance, freezing both men, leaving Nigel to whisper, "Yeah, I believe so" in wonderment.

"Well, Nigel, it's no secret to who's responsible for this, and since you know Victor so well, tell me, what would Victor do if this was you?" April's smile was challenging.

"Hmm, he would do it." April nodded her approval, then said,

"Then it's settled, allow my husband the same luxury that my husband would extend to you. Could you afford to pay such a debt, Nigel?"

"Nothing else crosses my mind since the doctor gave me the low-down, April, don't worry about that, and you'd have to trust me. I don't know how yet, but I will think of something."

"I'm sure something this big would take time, perhaps a guess maybe, cause as you say, and I agree, Victor would rather I push the button and give him peace then to remain like this."

"It shouldn't take very long, momma, really it's rather simple." Hearing Juice's comment brought both Nigel and April to full attention. April stared at her son, trying to will him to hush his mouth while grown folks were talking found that her attempts were fruitless, now that she heard Juice say, "I mean, if I had the equipment I could do it myself, seeing that it's so easy." Nigel knew better than to get involved and had looked from Juice to April, then back to Juice, and waited for April to "tea kettle" with a burst and a flurry of blows to the strange kid that used to be her son. He was more than amazed when none of his thoughts materialized. April remained silent, with hopes that Nigel would say something, just stared blankly, then said, "Nigel."

"Uh uh, I am not in it, might be worth a listen, but I'm not in it, and let the record reflect that in this room I'm the only one who said that I'm not in it."

"Well, I guess that this covers you. Oh-kay, well, you two get out of here. I will stay here with my husband. Whatever you pick, don't keep him waiting, Nigel, you hear?"

"Yes, ma'am," and the two made their exits from the hospital with Nigel in the lead, fearful of April, now that he failed to remember the first time that he ever saw her in such an aggressive light before. Found that it was safer out of the way and leaving April to sit alone with her husband then to remain in her presence at a time like this. This way she would talk to him through the night and shop for gifts for him through the day. She surfed through the channels, shopping for the special news broadcast that she always liked so much.

"Ooh, look honey, your favorite movie's on again." This time, April found no pride, no excitement, only hate and resentment. She listened to the news as the anchors brought on the breaking news stories of vigilante justices on the streets of Sacramento, said that ex- and retired officers took to the streets to help combat the drug wars starting in the Oak Park district. "Although unauthorized to do so by the public officials, these retired officers moved forward to claim the life of a known drug dealer identified as Felton A. Stringfellow, only to become casualties themselves when an innocent bystander unconsciously decided to aid the drug dealer by picking up a weapon and fired the fatal shots to the personnel of retired officers. This unidentified man was also wounded and rushed to the hospital by ambulance, where it is questionable to whether he'd survive through the night. We'll take you to the scene, where there's a mob of protesters that are angered by the likes of their community being under siege by these unknown officers who've taken to the streets without orders."

Chapter 27

April saw as the scenes unfolded, the community came together to strike out. She watched as patrol cars were being bombed with bottles and bricks and other household products and anything else that they could get their hands on. April saw even the press release that repeated what she already knew first hand. Then there was the good Captain O'rieley who defended the actions of these unlawful officers. Claimed that any type of justice, whether it be vigilante or traditional, should not only tolerated but appreciated as well, saying that the streets now belongs to the city of Sacramento again freed from the injustices that Mr. Buchannon had inflicted on the city as a whole. Even said that this is a night that the city has struck back as a whole, he reminded the viewers.

April saw as the good Captain bounced expertly around the subject of an innocent bystander being gunned down as a result of this fiasco. Not just no regular innocent bystander either but one who made more contributions to the community than Mother Teresa, Loaves and Fishes and the Salvation Army combined. No, this community wanted answers, and they wanted them now. There was no proof available to this community that stated that Victor had aided a drug dealer, only proof that Victor Raymond had aided a fallen member of their community. They were defending themselves against mask-wearing, gun-toting criminals who'd hopped out of a van to sprinkle people with fully automatic weapons if you were to let Oak Park tell it.

"Well sweetie, seems like this time they've really outdone themselves, it looks like it's cool to hide behind a mask and claim lives. At least you never hid who you were or what you represented and they call you the coward." April smiled, because now she knew the truth and knew that every press release in regards to Raymond Buchannon was indeed aimed at no other than the one "Victor Raymond" her husband.

"Wow, what you think of that, Uncle Nigel?" Juice said pointing to the TV as he sat with Nigel, both watching the very same broadcast.

"Shit, I think the world done lost its motha fuckin' mind that's what I think, and fuck all that shit. Did you see all the fuckin' cops he brought with him this time?" Juice smiled at Nigel's concerns and said,

"So what,"

"What you mean, so what? Junior, in case you already didn't know, that's the fucker with the bull's eye on his back, remember that?"

"I know," Juice said, Nigel was watching as Juice's smile became broader.

"I don't know why you sitting up here like cheesy cat; looks to me like that motha fucka done brought the National Guard with him."

"Perfect," Juice said.

"Oh-kay, maybe now is a good time for you to tell me what I wanna know because this all looks like a dead, dead, dead-ass issue to me."

"No it doesn't, it looks like we got them right where we want them Uncle Nigel, and you know it." Juice's smile never left.

"I'm listening." So Juice explained the whole play as he saw it, starting with the Captain's weak spots, then gone into equipment. Once Juice reached his conclusion Nigel began to pace the floor, readying himself to poke holes in all of Juice's theories. He stopped as if he needed to suggest some things. Nothing came, so he re-started his stroll back and forth. Stopping once more, then shook his head and continued to pace, then finally he said, "Well, I can't see why it wouldn't work. Do tell me what happens if he decides not to come alone, then what?"

"Uncle, tell me that if all of yours was wiped out and I called you with information but too scared to meet you out there, that you wouldn't come here."

"I would but I'll bring somebody with me. You may not see them but just in case I would bring somebody."

"Well, in that case let's fix the "somebody" that you say might be there."

"Exactly, that's me. I will handle that part, I could keep point and send you a signal you know, letting you know that every thing's cool, but now first things first, the equipment that you would need for a job like this. The first on the list is the C4, highly explosive, so please be careful or it's no more you and I need you to trust me on this one. It looks like putty you would have to make the stick then hurry back; we'll use a wireless transmitter to send the 'bang' at the press of a button…" Juice interrupted,

"Then I'm making the call, like frantic and scared out of my wits. 'I know who did this and who's responsible, I saw him here in the club, and they kiss his cheek and his pinky ring' and shit like that!" He finished.

"Right, and don't forget, put weight on 'come alone.' Tell him that you would book, nothing else to talk about. Too scared, so, so, scared. 'Hell no, I'll split,' you have to tell him. I mean it: stress coming alone."

"Then, I'm all lettered jacket, wing tips and slacks, glasses with the tape in the middle."

"That ain't funny, I mean it is, because that's exactly how I met your father, he was dressed like that when I met him."

"Is that right? But anyways I'll wait for the signal, which is what again?"

"You'll know it when you hear it trust me; before we forget, you're gonna do the job from where again?"

"The back seat, I know this much but what if he shows in a coupe?"

"I have never met a police who drove a coupe, and I meet police everywhere. But, if you meet one before I do, then guess what you gotta do? Junior, you are gonna have to pimpro...I mean improvise. Excuse me, one of my bones almost fell out."

"Uncle Nigel, uh uh, don't tell me that you were one of those pimp guys."

"Never,"

"So, you never was one of those pimps, Uncle?"

"I meant that I would never tell you something like that."

"Anyways, shoot, it seems like we're just in time for square one," Juice said looking at his watch.

"Ohhh, nah, nah, nahhh, cat daddy, we don't just go from talking about it to being about it. We have to make some preparations and stuff like that."

"Well."

Well, an hour later, preparations found Juice and Nigel parked in the parking lot of Hiram Johnson High School, watching kids fly up and down a field playing soccer, each one attempting to make a goal.

"So, this bitch is a soccer mom or some shit like that?" Asked Nigel,

"Mm hmm," mumbled Juice, trying to locate Mrs. O'rieley.

"Which one is she?"

"I don't know yet, but I'm sure that she's the oldest one."

"Hell, they all look like the oldest one."

"Let me look." Juice reached for the binoculars and scanned the field and said, "Wait a minute, wait a minute."

"Boy, do you see her yet?"

"Nope, not yet,"

"Then what's all of this wait a minute, wait a minute bullshit?"

"She almost scored on that last one; didn't you see it, Uncle?"

"I can't say that I did, I mean unless she looks old enough to buy liquor, then I could honestly say that I'm not paying attention to her. Besides, this is soccer; it could take two days to score."

"Wait a minute, wait a minute, got it."

"What, somebody scored already?"

"Nah, I got her, look, sun visor, all white, pale legs."

"You just described all twelve of them."

"Well, this one got the whistle; see her pointing and explaining stuff?"

"Oh-kay, oh-kay, yeah, now let's keep our eyes open and follow everything that she do." And they did, all the way until she and three other passengers boarded a canary yellow SUV, then followed her as she drove off heading for home they'd bet.

"So, what are we gonna do, Uncle?"

"Well, it's not sharp to follow her home; my guess is that it'll be out of the city anyways. Plus, if I know your dad, this is something that has to go down out in the open for everybody to see."

"Well, shoot, have you spotted anything that you're sure he'd like?"

"Well, you'll hold the button. Whenever the time is right for you, then that's when you push that motha fucka."

Chapter 28

The right time presented itself just after the weekend. Monday evening came and found Juice and Nigel once again in the High School parking lot, this time with Nigel being the watch-out while Juice operated his putty with intensive care. I mean, these instructions were followed out to the damn letter. Twenty minutes later Juice crawled from under the SUV. After double checking to make sure that the antenna was visible enough to receive signal from the transmitter. Satisfaction brought him back to Nigel, who then led them out of the parking lot and to a waiting cab where today Nigel would be the driver, and there they sat until practice was over. Then practice was over. They sat until the O'rieley's loaded up in the Hummer. Then the Hummer was filled.

"Junior, take it easy on that but remember we get up to one hundred feet, no more."

"I got it."

"I know this is fucked up but this has to be done."

"I said I got it!" Nigel heard the steel in Juice's voice, then said,

"Oh-kay, here we go, no turning back now." They let the SUV pass, and then they were behind it avoiding suspicion, sometimes two or three cars back knowledgeable to where the SUV was headed.

"How you feel, kid?"

"Like blowing up a motha fucka if that'll get you to hush while I concentrate over here, fuck…."

"Oh-kay, just checking, but do you got it though…" Juice's stare cut Nigel off. They were stopped at a red light then Nigel said, "Junior. This, umm, you know is not a good time you know, being this close and all, I mean umm, like not at all."

"I think I could have drawn that up all by myself, but thanks for the reminder though. Listen, 65th is coming up. Go on and get directly behind her, then stop." Juice watched as Nigel maneuvered through the traffic until he came directly behind the Hummer.

"Oh-kay, Uncle, time her until she reaches the intersection." The cab stopped, tires screeched and horns blew, then one gigantic explosion shook the concrete. Pieces of the SUV blew as high as thirty feet. Nigel, forever calm and collected, cut the wheel and drove around the burning remains.

"Whoa, did you see that shit? Man, this shit is crazy! Uncle, let's go and blow up some other shit! I swear to God I won't say nothing to nobody." Nigel almost forgot that he was driving after hearing Juice's excitement, just stared at Juice and shook his head and said, "Nah, we need to get off the street, go and see your dad, then get ready to go bright and early in the morning, you hear, and for your own sake, swear to God that you won't say anything anyways, whether you blow up some other shit or not." Nigel waited until Juice promised, then continued his focus on the road until he was on the freeway.

Juice found his mother sitting next to his father, reading to him as she held his hand. Sensing another presence in the room, April looked up and smiled at her son and continued reading until the chapter was finished.

"Are you hungry?" She asked. Looking at the bland hospital food, Juice declined instantaneously.

"They have a cafeteria downstairs that's pretty good," she reminded him and led the way to the cafeteria.

"In that case I'm famished."

She smiled to him and said, "You look it, which is why I asked. This way you could tell me about your weekend." Juice watched as his mother pressed the button on the elevator.

Remembering his promise, Juice said, "How about we'll just never mind the weekend and just eat and discuss dad."

"Oh!" April's brow rose and then, "Oh-kay, then don't talk about your weekend though you don't have to, you know why?"

"Uh uh, why?" Juice became instantly curious and suspicious.

"Because every time your dad had a big weekend, I'd say tell me about it, then he'd get all evasive and stuff, sort of like you're doing now. So, I would wait until he left or became distracted, then I'd catch what he was so secretive about on our favorite movie, do you know what that is?"

Juice shook his head and she found the clock, which told her that it was nearing the six o'clock news. She pinched him on the cheek and then said, "The evening news, so go eat and come up and we could watch it together." She turned, and then headed back to the room.

By the time Juice joined his mother, she was sitting with her hands on her lap with a sneer on her face. She looked up to him then said, "See, now tell me that I don't know what I'm talking about, this is good." Juice looked up to the TV and saw as the Captain was being consoled by other officers. He saw as the Captain's shoulders raised then fell as he heaved in despair and obvious pain. The reporters delivered the news softly, yet no matter how soft, the words were still impacted by such sorrow.

"I wonder what he's thinking right now."

"Mom, that's mean," Juice said, shaking his head.

"Not even close, so should I record this one or is there another movie coming on later tonight?"

"I don't know." Juice went over to kiss his dad on the forehead.

Before he knew it, his mother confronted him, "Son, I'm only gone say this one time, so hear me good. Never ever become so wrapped up that you begin to lie to me. You hear me, boy? I'm your momma."

"I know that, sweetie." Juice pinched his mother playfully on the cheek and said, "and even my beautiful mother never tells her son everything," he said sidestepping the swat that April stuck out there, then headed towards the elevator.

By nine o'clock the following morning, Juice was being awakened by his mother. He was trying to remember the dream that he was having before the interruption. Juice stared at the ceiling, he was due back on the campus after the funeral, if there was gonna be one which sort of posed a problem. Even though Juice loved playing ball, he loved his mother more. So, he rolled out of bed knowing that he had a big decision to make. Luckily, Arizona blew them out of the tournament or this would have been an even bigger problem. Juice found his mother and Uncle talking over coffee while April prepared breakfast for the two. She slid them plates then left the men to their discussion.

"So?" Nigel asked.

Juice, not getting it said, "So, what?"

"How do you feel a day later?"

"I'm all right," he said then pointed towards the VIP section. "Dad always took his meetings there, so why not?"

"Cool with me. So how'd your mother take it?"

"She's faster than me Nigel, and she's good on defense."

"What you tell her?" Nigel became suspiciously interested.

"I told her that it was all your fault and that you made me do it."

"No, you didn't."

"Yes, I did."

"No, you didn't, you know how I know? Because she would have told me that your lips were loose."

"Ahh, is that right, so she was testing me or something?"

"You must have done all right or I'd be hitting you in the throat with the butt of my piece. Never, I mean never, re-live yesterday as long as you got a tomorrow coming."

Juice nodded then said, "So the phone call is next?"

"No, son, the phone call is now. Establish a line with him, tell whoever answers the phone that you got a tip that you would only leave with the Captain and no, you got to refuse to call back and that you would blow the scene."

"And we'll meet here?"

"First establish a line of communication and get a call back number; even if you decide to call back at midnight, you see what I'm saying?" Juice nodded then went to the phone and for the first time in all his life, Juice called the police. Immediately sweat beads began to show while he was adding cushions to pad his cheeks in order to disguise his voice. Nigel saw as Juice ran in and out of his intent, saw even the change as Juice metamorphosed into the evil cobra once the Captain was on the line, and saw as he played frightened with a performance that possessed genuine contents of a person willing to blow town. Would he rather come down to the precinct which was protected by officers, no sir? Then the magic;

"Sir, I saw this guy pay an officer, so why should I believe I'd be safe. This don't feel safe; I think I better go now!"

"No! No! No! Son, I understand, just hold on a minute, now what could I do to help you?" O'rieley nearly panicked at the thought of losing his only line to whom he believed to be Raymond Buchannon.

"No, I don't feel safe, I'll call you back."

"When, when would you call me back?" The captain was desperate.

"Ahh, I don't know, maybe tomorrow, maybe tonight, I don't know." Juice had him on a hook and he knew it, the only thing to do now was to reel him in. He almost gave himself away by choking back the sounds of laughter that O'rieley took to be sobs from fear.

"Now son, you just hold on a bit. Don't cry. Listen, I love ya, and what you're doing is a brave thing. Get a hold of yourself and call me back like you say." O'rieley left Juice with every number that he could be reached, even the time frames that he could be reached there. Juice heard the desperation in his voice before he replaced the telephone on its cradle, then shook his head, removing the cushion from his mouth, and said, "I never wanna be that desperate. Look, I even got the number to his mother's house."

"Well, do everything you can not to be put in that position then."

"For real,"

Nigel stayed with Juice until the midnight hour, when the play called for Juice to re-establish the connection with Captain O'rieley. Juice performed well, and again with the padding in his cheeks, per Nigel's reminded instruction. The contact was made on the first try by dialing the second number on the list, bypassing the direct line that the Captain provided for his desk at the precinct. Juice settled for the mobile number.

"Hello." Juice's normally high-pitched voice now took on a slight baritone.

"Captain O'rieley here, please tell me that you're the kid from earlier," desperation already noticeable.

"It is me, sir; I don't know what to do. I believe the word's gotten out that I been speaking to the cops. I really don't know what to do."

"Do you wish to come in? I'll put my guys on you. My guys are the best, they will protect you."

"No sir, not your guys. Your guys take money and provide stuff. Look what happened to that lady and her kids. No way, I won't come." Juice knew to remind the Captain of the incident, even knew the relationship to the Captain, and so did the Captain once he heard Juice's spiel, he nearly cracked and fell to pieces but remained as composed as possible and said, "Oh-kay, oh-kay, I could understand that. How about I meet you somewhere? I don't care, anywhere."

"Oh-kay, where?" Juice asked, knowing better to then to provide the meeting spot.

"How about a restaurant, there's food and people and…"

Juice snapped in: "No! No people. Don't you get it? They all wanna get me."

"Oh-kay, oh-kay, oh-kay then no people, kid just calm down, calm down now, everything is oh-kay, just take it easy, now where do you wanna meet?"

"I don't care, just no people. I mean it I'll just go home to Georgia and never mind this town."

"No, no, don't do that, we have a chance here, me and you to bring down a very powerful individual. Do you know how much reward is in it for you?" Captain O'rieley checked on Juice's greed, and was satisfied when he heard,

"No, how much, I don't see any reward posters anywhere."

"Boy, you could get thousands upon thousands of dollars." Juice could hear his smile.

"Oh. And what I gotta do?"

"You'll have to help us arrest him first. Then you'll have to testify to what you saw. Then…."

Juice interrupted quickly, "I'm not standing around for that. I got pictures and nothing else."

"You got pictures?" Captain O'rieley couldn't believe his luck and bit the bait, leaving Nigel to do his happy dance because he knew the trap was set, and everyone knows that if you wanna escape, you must beat the trap before it sets. Avoid it while it's in the making. Who's to say that the one who killed your wife and children wasn't attempting to flush you out as well? Yet pride, once it's been pushed by revenge, seems to never allow man the luxuries of rational ways of thinking. Pride could be foolish, yet the enticements that revenge provides are always overpowering.

"Yes, I got pictures, only on an accident. I'm not gonna stay to testify. I need the money to blow this place."

"Oh-kay, oh-kay, I understand, I do, so how about a nice quiet place to meet? Let's say, hmm, something out of the way of cops and people. How about Jackson Road just east near Kiefer Blvd.? It's always very little traffic, if any, lots of cows and stuff, but no people."

"Oh-kay, oh-kay, I'll come," said Juice.

"Do you know the place just before you reach Sunrise Blvd.? You can't miss it. You'll notice that it'll go from concrete to green hills."

"Oh-kay, oh-kay, I know the place, but the money, how much is in it for me?"

"Boy, I could get you five thousand dollars; you hear that, five thousand dollars." Juice felt insulted and Nigel saw it written all over his face. He nodded ferociously for Juice to accept it and keep going.

"Five grand, you say? Oh-kay, I'll go over right now. You got the money?"

"No, but I could assure you that I would swing by the bank and get it first thing in the morning. Just stay with me and I will make sure you get it."

"No, you're trying to trick me. Money and the pictures meet at the same time. If you need to wait until tomorrow, then that's about how long I got to give you or I'm out of here, so quick."

"Oh-kay, I understand. Let's say ten o'clock a.m. I'll be there with the money, don't worry."

"I'll be there too. Come alone, no cops, the cops are bad. And I'll come alone. I see strange stuff and I'll leave. You don't hear from me anymore, you got that?"

"I understand."

Juice cut connection and removed the padding from his cheeks, with hopes that this time being the last time. He sat next to Nigel then said, "So now that we got the spot, what's next?"

"Hell seems like we'll need some pictures."

"I got some pictures upstairs in my dad's desk, they look old school."

"Oh, who are they pictures of?"

"My mom said they are of the guy that once owned this club."

"Is that right?"

"Did you know him, Uncle?"

"Who, Pepe? Everybody knew old Pepe, even this police. Funny is how you bring it up now; show those pictures and he'll get a kick out of this whole ordeal because even he knows that Pepe is dead. But I would love to see his face once he gives those a gander, though."

"So, should we use them or not?"

"Yeah, get them and let's get out of here."

Juice left the VIP headed for the stairs, only to return with a folder of portraits. Giving them to Nigel, he said, "So, what you think?"

"Man, look at old Pepe. Wow, I haven't seen this face in years."

"So, should I show these or not?"

"Why not, come on, I need to make a few stops along the way."

Sensing that Nigel wanted to head to the meeting spot, Juice decided to remind Nigel that the meeting wasn't until following day yet one thirty in the morning seemed a bit premature he said, "You know the meeting is at ten o'clock, right? You know tomorrow, though."

"Yeah, I know that. Would you just get your nerd suit together and come on?"

Chapter 29

Juice was asleep in the car the time Nigel made his second stop, and was shifting gears the time that Nigel made his third and his fourth stops. So, he never saw the meetings that Nigel conducted or the equipment that he gathered into the trunk of the primer-colored Crown Victoria. But, he was fully awake the time that the sun came shining through the windshield.

"Yeah, sleepy head, I was just going to wake you up. Look, it's almost time to put on your suit and let's get ready," and by ready Nigel handed Juice a loaded .357 Python with instructions on loading and shooting. Only thing about the instructions that Nigel gave, they didn't go with the stories Uncle Felton had told him. Uncle Felton told him that his dad had a sure one-shot method that'll blow a man's brains so far from his head that it'll take days to find them all.

Juice already knew what he was gonna do. "I got it, Uncle Nigel, don't worry. I'll get in, show him the pictures, wait for the signal, and blow his brains out, then what?"

"The ride will show, cook the car, get in the ride, and go back to the hospital."

"Cook the car?"

"Yeah, that's how Pepe died, so let's keep it going. There will be plenty of gasoline to do the job, but you got to hurry, don't move so slow, and remember these two things: leave the gun, but not the gas can. Leave the gun, and that's only after you've wiped it clean, do you got that? Make no mistakes."

"I got it!"

"Good, now get out and wait for him. I found a place where I can take the high end to see everything."

"And my ride?"

"Is waiting for the signal too."

"Which is?"

"You'll hear it. If you don't hear anything then he's alone, though I doubt it but if that's the case you'll send the signal, one minute is all it should take from the time he pulls up to the time he's no more. Got that?" Juice nodded affirmative.

"Good, now get out of here." Nigel drove off, headed towards his post leaving Juice to wait, hid in his purple and white leather jacket that said SHS on the sleeves, the initials of Sacramento High School, with Dragons embroidery across the front. He wore glasses that were preppy, minus the tape in the middle. His pants raised high enough to see his socks and his penny loafers made him look anything but dangerous. In his left hand he held the folder. In his right hand, though hidden in his jacket pocket, he held the pistol that was already set to fire. Juice watched as a few cars came and went, and then finally an unmarked car came and stopped.

"Well, it's a sedan," Juice thought, giving it a few seconds before crossing the street to meet the officer. Stick to the plan, Nigel kept emphasizing and reiterating, and because of that Juice reached the car and opened the rear door, leaving it opened just as instructed.

He said, "You bring the cash?"

"I sure did, son how about closing the door so we could talk."

"No, cash, then the pictures you got that."

"Oh-kay, no problem, this is a good thing that you're doing, you know?"

"Yeah, I know, the cash please." Juice sensed that the Captain was stalling.

"Son, why don't we just.... What in the hell was that?" An explosion of gun claps was heard and Juice took this to be the signal.

"That was the sound of a cheating police, now you said that you would come alone," then froze him with, "uhh un, uh un!" As he pulled out the Python, he said "Raymond Buchannon. Well his real name is Victor M. Raymond! So, now you know. Like you said, at least you won't go to your grave until you've known; well now you know." Then fire flew from the python. Juice saw the flame, then saw the gore and the tissue as it hit the dashboard and windshield, then he was out of the car, and seconds later a white limousine pulled alongside him.

The driver opened the rear door, and to Juice's surprise, his mother handed him a gas can and said; "Now hurry, we haven't got all day, go." And he did, April saw gasoline flying everywhere inside and outside as well as underneath the car.

"Boy, would you hurry up!" She taunted.

"I don't have a light," Juice replied back.

"Neither did your father, just get in."

"Wait a minute." Juice wiped the pistol off and dropped it inside of the cop car and climbed inside of the limo in enough time to see his mother get out of the limousine and ignite the unmarked cop car before she hopped back inside of the limousine.

She said, "My husband said that he'll see you when he gets there." The driver collected his composure then drove away and as planned, they headed to the hospital.

Nigel was inside of Victor's room by the time April and Juice made their showing. He and Juice exchanged welcomes and admiration's alike. April went to her husband's side and whispered into his ear, and the whole room thought that Victor was gonna sit up because they all saw him flinch.

"Mom, what did you tell him?" Juice asked.

"Boy, I can't tell you what I told him."

"Well, hell, tell it to him some more, and if you need us to get out of here, just say the words now." Nigel knew what was going on, and Nigel could understand if Victor wasn't ready to meet his Maker yet, neither would he be if someone as fine as April was whispering seductions in his ear because April was aesthetic.

"Naw, it only works sometimes. Believe me, I tried everything." Juice just shook his head, not believing what he was hearing, and almost bumped into the doctor as he was heading out, just in case his mother decided that X-rated medicine was sure to bring his father back.

"I see that I've caught all of his favorite visitors at once." Everyone quieted as the doctor ran checks on Victor. No one expected any miracles, nor did any arrive.

"So, has anyone made up their minds yet to how we're gonna proceed with Mr. Raymond?" Everyone in the room knew that the question was directed to April and to April only.

"I believe we have, sir," Nigel answered in April's place.

"And, what are we prepared to do?"

"Just do the damn paper work!" Nigel was very agitated not only by the doctor, but by fate also, for he knew that never did he ever think that these kind of cards would turn this way again as long as he lived.

"Well, alrighty then." The happy-go-lucky doctor left the room.

"Oh Nigel." April took a seat as the realization of the moment had become overwhelming to her.

"Look, you go sign the papers and this boy will collect all of the personal belongings that are here," Nigel responded.

"Noooo, I can't do it. Noooo! Nooo! Noooo.... Noooo," April began to fight Nigel, and there he let her vent, understanding her pains, for he too was hurting. Juice came to his mother's' side and said, "Momma, come on, I'll walk with you."

"No! Baby, we can't do it. God, please don't let this happen." Juice hugged his mother and whispered into his mother's ear then presto, April calmed a little. Juice led his mother to the nurses' station, where the doctor awaited them with clipboard in hand. Once there, April reached for the board and scribbled her signature across the sheet of paper, then held her head up and calmly stepped towards the elevator.

Back in the room, Nigel sat on the bed next to Victor with his head in his hands, as tears rolled down his face. He watched as Juice gathered all of his personal belonging and headed towards the door still he sat, and for the first time in many, many years, Nigel knelt down beside Victor's bedside and there he prayed one long lengthy prayer. He prayed for his friend's salvation, he prayed for his friend's forgiveness, he prayed that God would show Victor favor during the hour of judgment, and during Nigel's tear-filled prayers, he asked that the Lord forgive him for his actions, then he stood. He began to press buttons shutting the power off, watching as one machine died after the other, until ultimately he watched as Victor shook and Victor died. And with his head held high, he left the hospital.

April sat in the chair that her husband once sat in and worked at the desk that her husband spent many years formulating their future behind, a future that fate disallowed him to be a part of. She would field over two thousand calls of condolences; she held one of the biggest going home parties the city had ever seen. Still, she couldn't let escape from her memory the words spoken from her son. It was a poem that Victor had written to her the day Sonja and her family was killed.

If I die don't cry at the wake; hold your head straight, for I'll be in a safe place. Forever I found heaven, each time I looked into your eyes. I could see rivers on both sides, so I'm positive... that we will die... just so others could live. I been a king, I made you a queen, therefore your head must remain high, nose to the sky, because a jewel, no matter how dirty, is still a jewel......and you are mine. Dirty diamond or not...you are the best peace that I got.

April couldn't help but regain her strength as the days ticked past. As she made funeral plans her head was held, from the flowers she picked to the caskets that she selected, every chore was all done with purpose, for she knew that she was gonna send her husband home in luxury.

The day of the funeral, Morgan and Jones was afforded standing room only. Mourners showed from up and down the state of California. People showed to pay their respect. The pimps and players called Victor a gentleman of leisure. The thugs and the gangsters just called him Unc, being short for Uncle Victor. Yet everyone that showed up knew one thing for sure, that the FBI was parked right outside of Morgan and Jones checking license plates and snapping portraits. So everything was strategically set to grant safety away from the black coats, from the arrival all the way to the departure of the visitors and mourners. Near the end of the service a carriage pulled by six white horses arrived in time for the pallbearers to place the coffins of Victor and Felton on the racks in the rear of the carriage while limousines by the hundreds, all white from all makes, aligned and followed an all-white Silver Shadow Rolls Royce, which carried Juice, April and Nigel as it followed the carriage at a snail's pace on one last tour through the streets of OAK PARK. People chanted and cheered as the procession went up and down the streets and boulevards. A procession that lasted hours, just one last tour that would stop at a memorial lawn to allow the ground to swallow up a legend, the one and only Victor M. Raymond, and his sidekick and partner in crime, Felton A. Stringfellow. The caskets were lowered and two hundred doves were released in a display that stole the breath away from every mourner, as they witnessed nature, as it joined hands with natural.

Nigel picked Juice up in front of the club to take him to the airport to meet flight 59 out of Sacramento International Airport, heading to Los Angeles. Juice knew that the moment would arrive and dreaded as it had drawn near. He knew that something as inevitable as death was sure to change the course of a dream.

"Uncle Nigel," said Juice, "do we have time to eat something I'm starved?"

"We'll see what kind of time we have after we make a stop up here."

"What kind of stop geez, well, is there fast food or anything like that close by?"

"We'll see." The stop that they made was no surprise to Juice, not at all. Often were times that his coaches would lead them to a cathedral, and Nigel was indeed a coach, only one of another kind. A special kind, yet he knew that even Nigel was prone to worship. Juice found out that worship wasn't what the two had come to do, and was shocked when Nigel gave Juice a letter from his father. Letting him know that if he was reading such a missive, then and only then would the situation be best known as Victor being the late Great Victor Raymond, and because of this Juice would now be the man of the house, and he must fulfill to a satisfactory conclusion the remaining chores, that of the household, and Lord what a great big house it is. When Juice was finished reading the letter, Nigel recited the oath, the very same oath that he recited to Victor,

> *"Never forget the difference between a friend and a brother. A friend is worthy of trust. A brother is worthy of honor. A friend you feed with a spoon. A brother you feed with your soul. A friend is one that you*

live for. A brother is the one that you'll die for. A friend will always lie and break your heart. Yet your brother if he does will be the day that he dies. In life there are sizes that you must forever pay attention to. And there are colors that shall never be ignored and a status that you should always shy away from. For sizes there are big people and there are little people. The big people would always feed from the little people until the little people become more and more oppressed. The colors that should never be ignored aren't black or white, for big people go as far as to oppress their own. The white big people call white little people trailer trash, while black big people call black little people nigger. The colors that would make changes are green, gold, and silver, which you must not only get, but you must divide these colors with the little people. Then there's this status that you must avoid, the status of the rich and the famous. Never do you ever feed into this. The media nor the gossips, for if a group of people knew how to count your monies, then a group of people would know how much they'll need to come and get, and they will come and they will get it until it's all gone, for life is always the build-up, only to be struck down. Do you solemnly swear to uphold this oath until the day that you die, no matter how old or how young this day may be?"

Juice nodded his agreements, though dazed and confused, still he knew that his responsibilities had gone way past calling plays, pushing the pill, boxing out and rebounding. Now his responsibilities could help or harm a whole city. It was now his responsibility to take over where his father had left off. Shoes that only a giant could fill, for Victor Raymond was and forever will be a very big giant to the city of Sacramento, California.

Chapter 30

"Oh-kay, now that we are all reassembled, first off, let me extend our appreciation on behalf of our city to special agent Barrnette. Because Lord knows that I thought it was over with the passing of Mr. Stringfellow, I was certain that we had our guy. So to you, Mr. Barrnette I do apologize for needing you back here. It is my understanding that Flight 29 boarded and left without you. So to you, sir, I am deeply sorry to report that our fugitive is still at large."

"No problem and thank you still for having me back." Agent Barrnette spoke the words as cheerfully as he could muster. Only deep in his heart he wished that the fugitive would hurry up and surrender or croak of old age or anything: a swimming accident, cerebral palsy, shit, an asthma attack would suffice if you asked him. All he knew was that if internal affairs were to come down on this city, it would have a hell of a time sorting this place out; Captains and subordinates on the payola sheets of known drug dealers and mass murderers was unheard of. It was indeed his duty to report this behavior, and he would as soon as he was back in Philly, let somebody else come and catch this ghost he figured. Yet and still Barrnette's thoughts had swayed far enough to not know how much of the meeting he had just blanked out on, just said, "The pleasure is all mine."

"So, we go all the way back to the beginning. Did or did not Mr. Mathews go on a murder spree before he himself was gunned down, or can we agree that it was staged?" Said the newly appointed Captain Marcel Wynn,

"I think it was staged if not to do anything but to throw us off," said Sergeant Wildey.

"Me too," said Detective Stallworth.

"Well, how many proofs do we got to dispute this?" Asked Agent Barrnette, playing devil's advocate,

"Only one set of prints came back, this set belonging to Mr. Mathews."

"Then is it safe to say that whoever staged Mr. Mathew's death had wiped the gun clean then decided to pull an assault rifle and gun down Mr. Mathews?" Asked Barrnette, then added, "I recall seeing witness reports saying that a car pulled up alongside Mr. Mathews and fired on him, also an assailant who left on foot after firing on Mr. Mathews. To me it smells like a revenge killing. Over seventy bullets fired on him sounds awfully and a whole lot like a personal hate for Mr. Mathews to me."

"Oh- kay, well let's take what we know so far, all the way back to the very beginning. Let's see." Captain Wynn shuffled through his folders, then said, "Oh-kay, the first time this particular gun was used, a Colt .45 caliber hand gun was in a double homicide just a few blocks away from the Capitol building. Get this, city councilman Albert Renieke was gunned down in an alley, found with his pants below his knees, no possession, even a possible robbery. Then, moments later, after the dust had cleared, we get another call, same weapon, same area, only this time we have a hood named Benny Franks who peddled the flesh in the area, any idea of a connection between the two?" Asked Captain Wynn,

"Do we have anything on Franks?" Asked Detective Stallworth,

"All we have is two minor felony convictions for possession," replied the Captain.

"I think what Detective Stallworth meant was, do we have him in the files of informants," said Sergeant Wildey.

"I can't see anything of the nature, why?"

"Because the old club owner got it with this same weapon only he was cooked in his car and also wore the brand of our late Captain and many others, a bullet through his brain, but I found a file on the club owner," said Stallworth.

"Oh-kay, so let's just say for argument that Mr. Franks has a file, then what?"

"Sir, I won't begin to lie. I'm just as lost by the whole Mathews thing. At first I say it's him, then we hear the recordings of the late Captain who describes his contact as a kid in his late teens, smooth complexion, and then we hear the gun shots, same stamp as the rest, minus Mr. Franks and Mr. Renieke's, yet a kid could not have been active those many years ago. I'm thinking copycat, someone trying to feed off the media's hype of Mr. Buchannon," said Special Agent Barrnette.

"Oh-kay, let's say that you have something there. Is it safe for us to think that to be true?" Said Captain Wynn and simultaneously, all movements stopped and simultaneously everyone spoke in the negative.

"Well, then, I think we gotta beat the streets until we catch a break somehow."

"Somehow there are not a lot of locked jaws surrounding this whole ordeal. I came to make a few buys, make a few arrests then head back, only I had my cover blown not even two minutes after my arrival. How can we be sure that our methods and our tactics wouldn't be leaked to the streets before we get there?" said the Special Agent.

Captain Wynn knew exactly what Agent Barrnette was hinting at stared past the agent in wonder to how many IA Agents would soon be crawling over the city. He nodded and said, "Captain O'rieley is dead, the mistake that he made must also die with him. We must allow him at least that. As far as anyone else who may have turned then, there is no way for me to hide from them other information, but these tactics are between us, and I would ask that each one of you hold your investigations close to your chest with confidence that I chose you guys thinking integrity first, and Mr. Barrnette, you could rest assured that if I catch one of our good guys fraternizing with the bad guys, I'd give you my word that I'll hang them so high that they'd be able to wear their balls as a necklace, and you could mark my word that I will catch them!"

Barrnette seemingly satisfied, subdued; seeing this, Captain Wynn continued: "We have a lot of work to do. We have to make new approaches, none of this vigilante business. I mean this to my heart." The whole room knew that Captain Wynn spoke directly to Sergeant Wildey, because of the Wildey's that were found unresponsive, sprawled across the streets of OAK PARK, were indeed close relatives of this Sergeant Wildey.

Captain Wynn continued, "There will be no leaks to the press, no press conferences by me or any other officer in this regard. This is a type 'M' classified investigation. Type 'M' means that you'll report directly to me, there is nothing in the middle. Any slack, just refer them to me and I'll handle it from there. Do you gentlemen understand? We are not to confide in anyone, not our wives, our brothers, our sisters, dogs or goldfish, do you copy? Our plates are full enough then to have an officer run errant and kill us off before we get started. We'll all break for one week, my orders. Use this time to relax, play golf or fish. We need to come back with fresh ideas for a new investigation strategy, because Lord knows that the old one stinks to high heavens. Now go on and enjoy your break, because it may be the last one that you'll see in a while."

The room cleared, leaving Captain Wynn to stare at his wall of cold cases, knowing that he may never even thaw them, let alone solve them.

BOOK TWO

December 6, 1989

Team ORBITT, which stood for Operation Raymond Buchannon Information and Tactical Team assembled for what they hoped to be the very, very last time. It's been three and a half years since the death of Felton Stringfellow, a dealer who came on the radar as being the best pick from a very small bunch of high profiled criminals who could have been this gentleman of question. Since his death the streets had gone silent for long spells which lead law enforcements to believe even as much. Then violence would erupt and the presence of the very one, "Raymond Buchannon" could be felt, just like the very beast that they'd all remembered. He was alive, and he was breathing and this they knew. Although attacks were sporadic still they occurred in the same punishing, diabolical and deadly fashion. Visible was the traffic all over the city which told this team that business, was business as usual and by the looks of it drug trafficking was a very booming and lucrative business. It's been three and a half years, almost to the date since the city mourned the death of Captain Loren O'rieley. And Since then this team called meetings in bars, in clubs, at bowling alleys or even pizza joints, basketball games and old dilapidated office buildings for never, no matter what the intelligence may have been would it be discussed in or at the precinct. The fear of a leak was constantly on the minds of every officer, and each member of team ORBITT especially. Yet, on this day every one present, from the Captain on down rummaged through their new fact findings. Through thorough investigations, it has now come to a head that the subject in this matter was believed to be very armed and awfully dangerous. This subject was also believed to be cunning and vicious, and never to be trusted under any circumstance or on any occasion because this subject was believed to be the one "Raymond Buchannon."

More than two million serious crimes are committed every year and every year there is a pissing contest between agencies, each one refusing to cooperate with the other. Information and Intel was always held close to chest. On this day it was so not the case. On this day multi-agencies were required to share data, whatever it took to bring this 'Raymond Buchannon' and his operations to a screeching halt. There awaited representative from each faction, there was the DEA, the ATF, the FBI and now ORBITT. The bosses were easily recognizable because they could be seen impatiently waiting, pacing and chewing Rolaids, anticipating the news of Mr. Buchannon's status. Rather or not he was now in the custody of the Sacramento County Main Jail, that, or the Sacramento County Morgue. Whatever the case may have been what was high on everyone's mind, officer or civilian, rather the officer was a military one and the civilian was a Pastor at 'Ebenezer' Baptist Church. At the tip of everyone's mind they believed as they do the coming of Christ, that Raymond Buchannon, if this was him, would not, under any circumstances be taken alive.

So, the plan, in the building of this raid party it was noted that only the most seasoned officers would be selected, the ones who've been through war before. Needed were the ones who wouldn't be shaken, rattled or even frazzled once the team encountered Mr. Buchannon and the guns began to talk. Just right beneath the fact that Mr. Buchannon would refuse to go alive, was the belief that the chances of any officer leaving the scene unharmed were just as slim as the chances of Mr. Buchannon surrendering with ease. This would not only be a surprise if he did, but a very welcoming prayer answered as every officer prayed before their arrival.

Nigel awoke at four o'clock in the morning as always, a routine that he'd developed over the years. So precise was this routine that it would be a norm for him to wake five minutes before four a.m. but never five minutes after. He'd often say that this routine happened upon him ever since he swallowed a stopwatch as a baby. This day was just a little different, granted, the same four o'clock a.m. yeah but save for that nothing else was regular, even his sleep was disturbed and that never happened. Anyone would think with the life that Nigel led was prime time reason for anyone to lose sleep, but this was not the case for Nigel who hadn't found trouble sleeping in years. Something else was a little off cue, because normally Nigel would head towards the kitchen for coffee. Just not this time, this time he would choose to lay and look towards the ceiling a while, giving him an extra thirty minutes of mental imagery before the coffee. Something was troubling him and he knew it but he just couldn't put his fingers on it. I mean he had some guesses though if that meant anything. His universes weren't lining up, his universes as he called his intuitions, they were out of sync. No melody, no harmony, no peace of mind at all, and because of this he found his morning more depressed than others and this made him sullen and gloomy even. He took his coffee to the kitchen table noticing that he felt weary and unprotected even tired, and this was ridiculous. To consider a person of Nigel's financial status one would think there would be armed guards roaming his property, but it wasn't. In fact, you'd think him to dwell in the luxuries and at least the securities of a gated community but he didn't. Nigel took a nice enough for anyone to capture condominium just outside of the Pocket area, not quite upper class yet just past middle class. To the naked eye one could assume that Nigel barely qualified for any of those classes. His place looked oh-kay, really simple even. Nothing extravagant was parked anywhere, no antique furniture or classy paintings. There was no expensive carpeting or piano, no exotic fish that swam around a spacious fish tank. Uh uh, there was barely a sofa, a love seat, a dining set and the few office supplies sprinkled here and there. It was at the dining table that Nigel took his coffee, allowing the hot liquids to soothe such an exhausted spirit. Yet, over his coffee was how he looked around his place. He looked at pictures and at furniture as if indeed he was looking at them for the last time.

Never was he one to ignore his inner voice so he gone into his office and brought his computer to life. He sipped from his hot liquids while the computer received, then transmitted his every desire before dismantling his hard drive and replacing it with a brand spanking new one. If nothing else, Nigel knew how to pay attention and especially to a tech who explained the new way that folks were getting apprehended and how to prevent such an occurrence. Vivid was his memory when the tech said that the United States Prisons were getting filled to the rim with the way the "letter boys" were behaving with their computer techs. Said that they will get your files and get to cracking old cold cases, and before you know it they done took all the money. "Oh yeah, the United States prison is one thing, but them getting all the money is a whole other motha fucka ain't it man." Nigel recalled hearing the words of his late friend Victor Raymond, and boy he ain't never lied which was why Nigel was tuned in awfully close when the techs explained the prevention part of the whole throw off process. He even found satisfaction due to this education now that all signs seem to read the same thing… run nigga run!

Chapter 31

For Nigel the past three years had gone by in a blur, one difficult situation after the next. It seemed like life would switch gears until reaching warp speeds before giving him a break again. Never one to cower from life's unpredictability's or run away from life's lessons, no. In fact, he would even be the first to tell you that if it was going down then hell, let's get it over with. This was the concept that he had taken all around as a man no matter which one, grown man or business man, this was the same approach. Warp speed or any other speed was indeed a hazard and this he knew; it was an accident waiting to happen. The most seasoned businessmen would always say that when life sped up that this being the most opportune time to slow it all down to rolls of pictures that anyone should be able to understand. For every hustler, every businessman or individual, the same rules applied with the true understanding that this issue, wasn't a gender one, no. Because Nigel knew many of women who too hustled hard so this was never a sexist issue but an intellectual one. Many times had Nigel witnessed the demise of those whose personalities landed in one or the two self-sabotaging categories, those being greed and speed. Greed had a way of making one selfish and inconsiderate even. One could easily become a miser with an appetite that would be ever so hard to quench. In one's greedy condition one could and ultimately would, push some precious and beautiful people away, and this he knew. As far as speed was concerned, well think about it was all Nigel would say. "Speed" he thought, at the end of the day was always crash and burn, and in this Nigel would partake in neither, greed nor the speed.

Nigel dressed while allowing his thoughts to mellow, he was able to realign his universes until it all made sense. He granted his mental and spiritual vibrations permission to tick in harmony, allowed his balance to be re-established. Though his morning started off depressing, he knew better than to remain in such a state. Noting that gloomy and sullen were always things that Nigel had heard from others and each time the feeling has always meant the same thing, that the game was either close or it was now "over." And check mated even the best players, would be.

"Well, if it's going down, let's get it on" Nigel soliloquized then headed out to his truck and drove away from his condominium with the feeling so strong that he would never see the place again.

Nigel stopped by the gun, rod and bait shop first. Arriving there before the store opened, and this gave him plenty of time to complete his duty. The store was owned and operated by a good friend of Nigel's, a fella named Benny. His real name Benson but try calling him that if you'd like but at your own risk. Benny ran this particular shop with his son Darrel, turned it into a family owned and operated business. Nigel being a silent partner had keys to the shop as well as the security codes to the alarming systems which he deactivated the second that he walked through the door. Once inside, Nigel headed straight towards the rear of the shop and immediately to the computer and there he proceeded with his chores, and his only reason for coming. Over an hour later Nigel was finished, locating and then relocating all of his precious items and information. With the store due to open for the public in a few moments Nigel waited at the counter for Benny to make his showing and he did. It was only a matter of time management with Benny. He'd arrive in enough time to boot everything up, then open the doors which was easy as one, two, three, same thing he's been doing for years, over and over.

Seeing Nigel made Benny both happy and miserable. He was always happy because Nigel was like a brother to him and this has always made Benny happy. What made him miserable though was the card that he held in his pocket. One that he knew in his heart he would never use except to give to Nigel the very first moment that he saw him.

"Benny," said Nigel, shaking his head at Nigel Benny said,

"Nice to see you, it's always nice to see you Nigel but if you came to balance the books I must say that right now is not the best time." For the punctuation mark, Benny dug into his pocket and retrieved a business card. One that had words scrawled across the back reminding Benny to call if in case he ever made contact with Nigel. Nigel took the card and flinched at the three letters emblazoned across the front of the card "FBI"

"Oooh," was all that Nigel could say, now with confirmations for his troubled sleep.

"Sounded like a lot of trouble the way they came in and showed their pieces, then looked around as if I got you hidden in a soda can or something and if you wait around long enough you would see them parked across the street over there," Benny pointed to the shaded area across the street then continued, "So, if you need to peep the books I'm going to advise you to peep them to go, you need to trust me on this one."

"I do Benny; truth is I've never stressed you on your books we've been thick as blood brothers but I need you to listen to me as I heed you I need you to heed me. Your desktop in the back is hot and I need you to call a tech the second I leave and have them bring you a new one, and destroy that one with no delay." Satisfied to see that he had Benny's undivided attention, Nigel continued with "So, where's the kid?" Nigel asked looking past Benny.

"He'll show in a while, but now don't worry about the books or the box, I got that."

"My man." The two embraced then Nigel uttered, "It's been nice serving with you brother," with that Nigel headed out to his truck and left. Three hours later the FBI stormed the place.

Next stop for Nigel was the "Steak House" this was on Broadway and 65th. The Steakhouse has always opened at six a.m. every morning. Here, Nigel had another business partner named Julius. Although Nigel had done business with Julius he was not like a brother to Nigel and Nigel had only trusted him just so far. At this stop Nigel only needed a steak, eggs and hash browns and to use his computer for a second, this way he could swipe away any mentioning's of property and monies and to change a few codes. He would locate then relocate and plus confirm his transactions. As for the breakfast platter, well he needed to take that right there, to go. So, Nigel never got the chance to see the FBI storm Ju-Ju's Steak House either.

As Nigel traveled to and from so many thoughts crossed his mind, and all of them surrounded the same idea. Like how it would be some nice shit to go ahead to the airport and you know, sort of make a run for it. Yet pride wouldn't let him budge "Maybe I'm just stubborn like that" again Nigel soliloquized. Although he didn't have the slightest idea why the feds wanted to talk to him or see him about some stuff but he knew for sure that he wasn't gonna be foolish about it, no. He knew that if the FBI was inquiring then whatever the news, it would definitely be some "bad news" because the FBI delivered only one kind of news and it was always bad 'hey you, come with us' and by the time you finished listening the airport idea always came rushing back to memory.

Nigel recalled the first time, which was the last time that he'd been inside of a United States court room, which was a whole lot different than a Superior courtroom by the way, at least in Sacramento. Nigel could remember when he sat in to watch the sentencing of one of his business associates, he figured to give him all the support that he could. Which to him was asking a whole lot because Nigel had a phobia to structures involving the government because if Nigel didn't know any better he would have sworn that the walls had a pulse and that there were eyes hidden everywhere. He shivered at the thought 'ooh that was spooky' because to him the United States court room were like a haunted house if you asked Nigel.

Now that Nigel's fears of loss aversion were becoming more of a reality by the minute and each minute the scene of a courtroom drama with him being the protagonist painted some nice pictures that even a fool would be able to understand. It was clear that Nigel needed to arm himself for a meeting with the very agency who "sought his immediate attention" as it was wrote on the back of the card that Benny gave him.

Being armed, Nigel knew didn't consist of him waving a machine gun at the FBI, no. Being armed was speculating what it could possibly be that they wished to speak about or arrest him for and simply make it difficult for them to prove a case. It was very hard for Nigel to fathom himself defensive against a drug or a weapons case because in those areas he wasn't weak in fact he was strong there. Although tax evasion played high on his list of probabilities which was the reason why he spent all morning moving money and any information tied to money. What he couldn't get out of his mind was how easy it was to complete such a task if and had tax evasion being the prime reason for all the chaos that imbued his mind. A task that made it hard for him to discern anything other than the fact that the feds were probably still building a case against him and haven't yet gone to the grand jury to get an all-out arrest and seize.

This forced Nigel to smile at the thought of a gun battle with the law enforcement, 'Oh the fireworks in that' and oh how the "hood" would remember him forever for pulling a stunt like that.

By the time Nigel made it to Pepe's the day had grown into the evening. He drove around to the back of the club to park his truck. He selected to walk the rest of the Blvd. until he was more than certain that the helicopter which hovered over the neighborhood would fail to see his destination. Even though the eye in the sky could indeed be there for any number of reasons, and with this community being the most poverty stricken, drug infested and bullet riddled habitat ever in all of Sacramento that could easily be imagined, but Nigel could ill afford to think that the "ghetto bird" as they would grow to call the aerial surveillance wasn't in the air in search of him.

Nigel knew to run to April. He felt rushed, but not so much that he'd pass up a good stiff Rum then after that a small chain of Rum with a Coke chaser and for that he was never that much in a rush. April followed Nigel through the club until he stopped at the bar. No reason for her to expect a visit from Nigel, so putting that together with the fact that she was now watching him getting rid of the liquids like he was. April aborted the monitors and gone to join him at the bar.

"Nigel," she asked while looking for tell- tell signs, all of which was to no avail.

"Let me guess, the FBI came through here too?" Confused, April's look of consternation was answer enough, still she shook her head then said,

"No, why would the FBI be coming through here?" For an answer Nigel slid April the card as discreetly as he could. April read the front of the card and then it's back. Now she understood why Nigel took to the 'cups', she said,

"Oh-kay, so how could I help you?"

"Well, they got an ole school ghetto bird in the sky, may be nothing. Maybe my time is running out."

"Oh-kay, take your drinks upstairs and I'll be up after a while.

Chapter 32

Team ORBITT was prepared to strike at eight o'clock a.m. the following morning, satisfied to at least have obtained a warrant. Captain Wynn began to see their hard works take on a better light. Not all the way convinced that their long, hard and drawn out investigations would bear a suitable conclusion but everyone well knew that the city was under an extreme amount of heat to bring this city its long awaited promise of Mr. Buchannon's head on the wall, and nothing else. Captain Wynn held the folder into the interiors lighting as it shone brightly from the headlining of his unmarked patrol car and offered up a silent Hail Mary before leafing through the folder. As for warrants, he now had undeniable permission to search and seize anything remotely similar to evidence from the residence of Mr. Nigel Collinson's, the address on record being located on Pocket Rd. He had a warrant to search and again seize evidence from a gun, rod and bait shop on Fourth Avenue where he was known to frequent. The same went for the steak house on Broadway, where one of the tips of Mr. Collinson's operations first surfaced. The warrants were good; the Hail Mary's leaned more towards the wish for evidence that's become an item that has yet to date, become a luxury that neither officer nor agency could claim the pleasure of relishing in, hence the prayers.

The information provided spoke of large quantities of narcotics hid within the folds of the Cafe as would be the same for the Bait Shop. The captain would whence at the date to which the warrants were effective, permitted for the following day and that was a 'drats' because the whole team was ready with the utmost right-nowness. Yet their Honor felt that if she could sign such a weak warrant, then they should be able to wait another few hours. Before signing on the magistrate in question really didn't see a vast amount of evidence nothing solid at all and she announced all of which before the "Hancock". She didn't see a buy or a sell and though she was hoping for a smoking gun none ever surfaced. In fact, there wasn't evidence to Mr. Collinson's mischief at all, however there was the presence of two informants who've in the past presented A-1, dead on, adequate and accurate information before and was willing to present testimony to Mr. Collinson's depraved avocations, and because of that, yes Judge Walker signed on. Even though her Montblanc gold tipped ink pen slid across the page saying that the agents reported under oath that a crime had been committed in the state of California and in the county of Sacramento, the Captain needed to know that she done so reluctantly.

The Captain was forced as a last resort to reach out to the Honorable Judge Walker because judges Peterson and Thomas didn't want to hear nothing, and didn't want anything to do with any parts of the shit so he was grateful. Especially after the last fiasco, "how dare you come in my office after embarrassing us as a county for the thirty seventh time in a row?" Captain Wynn knew that his hands were tied, even more so now that the "Type III" warrants failed to bear any fruits of any kind. They were pulling money as well as manpower away from a Police funding nearing bankruptcy in a hopeless manner of trying to capture Casper the friendly mother fucking ghost for all Thomas and Peterson was concerned. "Yeah," thought the captain a 'Type III' warrant granting permission to wiretap the phone lines belonging to Nigel Collinson and all of his constituents, was an embarrassment and a method proving none more than an imbroglio and a warrant that he found awfully hard to rebound from.

Judge Walker signed on because two solid witnesses being the going rate and if these witnesses were willing to testify under oath that Nigel Collision is indeed the "Infamous" Raymond Buchannon then she was damned if what she was willing to call 'her city,' didn't reserve the right to know about it. Then there was the other thing that motivated the good judge, in the event that the Captain netted the true gentleman of everyone's expectations then she was sure that after playing host to a case this huge, "a man whose omnipresence alone would retire her with astronomical benefits and she liked benefits. Bright lights clouded her mind's eye and she became anxious because even the thought of his presence in her courtroom was terrifying and she loved the rush. There was the fact that the Captain had also played his hard card and painted her into the same corner that he was now in, by reminding her that as long as Raymond Buchannon was on the streets then any case that they would attempt to put together would only become more frost bitten and more complicated to prove with anymore delay. He said that it would be best to lock away Mr. Collinson and build their case against him then to allow him to continue to get away with murder, especially the murder that of their late Captain, Loren O'rieley.

Grateful because his honor decided to sign on in the order of house, bait Shop, and Cafe effective the first thing...tomorrow morning. A signature that came after swearing to monitor every move, blow by blow. So much that if you blow this you could kiss any future favors good-the-fuck bye, was basically how she really put it.

"But Your Honor, no offense but we need to go now," said the Captain in disbelief.

"Captain Wynn, don't make me get that sheet back and tear it into a million little mite sized pieces. I'm already giving you permission to run around town and scare the b'jesus out of every body and let's not forget that there's two places of business listed on that sheet that for all I know could be steady, stable, Christian establishments and not the fronts for the laundering of illegal gains as you put it. It's because I heard you when you sold me the death of our late Captain O'rieley am I gonna say this, if my memory serves me right and yours as well then you would agree that neither one of us heard anything in your pitch about the mention of off duty and retired officers positioned on a crime scene that was better fitting for a gang war. They were all over Oak Park, remember? Ha, they were even wearing ski mask, by the way is the attire most commonly adorn by the criminals if I needed to help you with that. Wasn't that also to the conviction that, who was that again? A Mr. Stringfellow, mmm, known drug dealer true yet we said that he was this Raymond guy which was as we found out to be, not true. I signed on to give you a chance to do as you say and build your case from the inside out. Because, if in fact you now have the right one then Captain Wynn I can't think of a better judge that's willing to send this man to death row than myself. You are permitted for the first thing in the morning and I highly recommend that you take that sheet of paper and get the hell out of my office for I am a judge found famous for changing her mind." Judge Walker never broke eye contact with the Captain and she watched as he disappeared into nothing down the hallway.

"Well, the first thing in the morning it is then Ms. Lady, the first thing in the morning it is" the Captain spoke softly in reminiscent of their earlier conversation before neatly organizing the folder into the gloves compartment of the car before starting the car to depart.

Seven o'clock a.m. the following morning found team ORBITT staked outside of the condominiums plaza on Pocket Road sadly awaiting the signals to knock and crash the doors belonging to Nigel Collinson. Not necessarily in that order, but definitely on the residence belonging to Nigel Collinson also known as the feared "Raymond Buchannon."

The signal would come from a borrowed United States Postal Service mail delivery truck sported by an undercover Agent posing as the fill-in mail carrier. This carrier was instructed to ring the doorbell and do all that he can to determine whether or not the subject was indeed available to answer to their warrants.

The rest of the team held their post, eagerly covering every exit, deeming escape to be futile. Captain Wynn and Agent Barrnette donned their binoculars; the suspense was killing them together. So, impatiently they waited for the signals which would release them from their anxieties. The two followed the truck and saw as it stopped in front of the residence, then saw as the undercover Agent gone to the door and pressed the button. Though no Agent could testify to being able to hear the doorbell still most would swear that they heard a 'ding dong' coming from somewhere. Agent Barrnette was the first to cave in when he mumbled but loud enough for everyone to hear.

"Come on you mother fucker open up, can't you see that we got a special delivery for you, you son of a bitch."

"You think he's home?" Asked the good Captain, the same one that everyone in the field that day thought should be back at the fort with the rest of the brass. So, to hear him ask questions from the field was just about as mindless as the question he was asking. I mean, how the fuck could they know if the subject was home, they only knew that if he was then that being a prime time to unfasten your damned shoulder holster and stay ready, and to concentrate on nothing else.

"I don't know," said Agent Barrnette "but, I really have a strong desire to go and snoop around a little though."

"I know, me too" replied the Captain which sounded like a horrible idea to everyone listening.

"Uh uh, wait here sir. How about I go and get enough of a look for the both of us," said Barrnette after watching their undercover agent posing as today's mail carrier return to his truck failing to signal any positive discoveries.

"Hey, be careful down there would you," said the Captain now feeling his blood simmer a bit fearing a possible realization that their subject may have gotten the word somehow and made a run for it.

The FBI Special Agent Barrnette drove away in his unmarked car heading towards the plaza while the good Captain followed him with his binoculars. He saw the side arm being removed by the Agent which to the Captain didn't make much sense because if indeed their subject was down there then an Agent without a sidearm or any kind of protection, was an agent about as good as a goner. The Captain nearly swallowed his tongue far enough for the Heimlich maneuver when he saw the "Agent" began to bang on the door and excessively ringing the doorbell at the address of question. Sensing that there was no feedback or disturbances the Captain was able to exhale. The sight of seeing the agent go to the windows for a 'look- see' then again the anxiety rushed over the Captain. "We got a runner" was all he thought.

The Captain and every other officer began to relax and strategize for their next location as well as the possibility of a fugitive. The FBI Agent would refuse to depart fruitless for he knew that when in doubt it was simple, 'go and ask the neighbors' and he did. Satisfied to have received an immediate response there at the neighbor's residence he said,

"Excuse me ma'am, my name is Special Agent Barrnette and I'm with the FBI and I like to ask you a couple of questions, may I?" The elderly woman became instantly defensive fearing the Special Agent, one that knew he would fair way better to relax the lady by saying as fast as he possibly could,

"What would be a good way to tell if 'your neighbor was home' I need to see him?" The startled lady looked past the Agent then shook her head and said,

"Him no home," The agent followed her glances then said,

"And, I need to know how you know this?"

"He's truck, look, you see, no truck"

"Truck" ahh thought the agent.

"Yes, no truck, see, noooooooo, truck."

"Thank you, but could you tell me where he would park his truck if he were home, and what kind of truck?"

"Red truck, wait here I show you," the Asian lady disappeared through the interior of her unit and returned holding a photo, one of a family outdoor cook out. Agent Barrnette located the truck and right away he found the license plate, a bit fuzzy but he was damned if he wasn't going to commit to memory the six characters on the plate of an old Ford F350, the plate read NC0456. Enough for him "thank you Ma'am" he gave her back the photo and disappeared as respectfully as he'd come hence his reasoning for leaving his firearm in the first place, he wanted to showcase peace. He didn't want to spook the people that he needed to run to for help.

Benny watched as the agents combed through his place of business, the few customers that were present was more than happy to leave such a strenuous predicament. The Agents walked through the shop slowly, taking their time at missing nothing. It was certain that this place was being slow combed and with a fine tooth Benny reckoned. The instruments' for poking and probing as well as wall tapping were being used a lot and this allowed them to x-ray the walls on occasions, basically on some new and improved shit.

All of this to Benny, who felt that if the dogs didn't net anything then that should be good enough of a reason to pack this shit up and let's all go home, you know do this shit again tomorrow or something. But this was also how Benny was feeling just two seconds after they stormed the place yelling all kinds of bullshit too. So, forgive him for being just a little bit biased in these regards.

The next hour would be entirely different because everyone was able to calm the fuck down and please knock off the fucking yelling 'my goodness' Benny thought. Now all they had to do was await a tech team to come and make sense of the mumbo jumbo that was going on inside of the stores computing system, which was alright with Benny because when the agents kicked everyone out of the shop except for Benny and his son Darrel they let Wesley the geek walk away king of the mumbo jumbo. So Benny knew that it would be just a matter of time now.

By noon the shop was released to its owners and the Agents left, again fruitless. Fifteen minutes later over a dozen squad cars stormed Ju-Ju's Steak House. Barrnette was no longer as enthused as he once was, started to think that they were barking up the wrong tree. The whole concept of informants coming forward all of a sudden sort of smelled a little like garlic. However, two informants were at least worth a listen but two informants and a warrant though, now that'll up the ante a bit and was always worth the fishing expedition. Although Agent Barrnette couldn't see nor remember a time when this guy Nigel or Raymond who the fuck ever had decided to leave loose strings anywhere, he thought, "why be this sloppy now?" To him this thought didn't jingle any vibrations, but he wasn't going to say all of that in front of company.

"Barrnette" said the good Captain.

"Yeah, what you think, we out of here?"

"Uh uh, Wildey got a hit, say they located the truck."

"Oh-kay" then came the jitters again for the Special Agent.

"How you feel about running the Steak House?" Asked the Captain,

"I think we better find the good stuff pretty soon or this is going to get awfully ugly."

"You could say that again, now that I think about it how about we'll just keep our eyes on Mr. Collinson until we finish tearing up this Cafe, like you say I wanna find something to get this guy" and no one needed a break more than Captain Wynn, desperation was starting to set in.

"Well, good luck to us," said the Agent as meek as he possibly could while still refusing to believe that they would discover anything useful at all.

From the moment they entered the Steak House to serve the warrant to Mr. Julius Ivory every agent wore their excitements on their sleeves. So, once they heard the spiel that Mr. Collinson had come by earlier in the day and yes he appeared to have been shaken a bit by something or the other, and when Mr. Ivory said that Nigel needed to use the computer and how he spoke real high on needing to leave the state for a while did the officers began to get a bit stimulated and decided that they weren't going nowhere. He also told them that occasionally he himself was asked to run errands for Mr. Collinson. Although he wouldn't be able to testify that they were illegal errands, but he knew that he was meeting up with some pretty illegal people, you know those with high profile concerns. The Special Agent also heard when Mr. Ivory mentioned that with Mr. Collinson one could never know who was who or what was what. He said that this guy was 'slick', and all of this Agent Barrnette was sure to agree with because this was exactly how he remembered everything to be, especially the 'slick' part.

"Well sir, we have here a warrant to search every nook and cranny of your place of business." Said the Captain with more pride than the Special Agent failed to feel himself.

"Yes sir, if you're looking for anything like narcotics, I mean if there were any here then know that there isn't any here now. I'm sure that Mr. Collinson took all of his property with him." Well, some of this was the truth, because at first there was some narcotics available but it took the police so long to come and get the shit Julius thought, now all of a sudden they show the fuck up. Just like the police, they'll show up late as usual then become awfully demanding with the damned questions.

"So, you're saying that there may have been narcotics at this establishment, you know this fine place of business?" Asked the Captain who was now cheesing at Mr. Ivory indicating that he was beginning to get excited.

"And I'm saying that I have no way of knowing any of that with certainty, and not until recently would I have even decided to entertain the thought of it. Mr. Collinson has free will to come and go as he shall see fit, just today was different. When he came this time I was a little nervous. Yet when he left I was a bit disappointed you know, me being God fearing and all." Somehow Julius delivered all of this even to his own amazement, with a straight face.

"Oh-kay, then you wouldn't mind if our K-9 unit come and gave this a try then, would you?" Captain Wynn found a strong feeling for this God fearing Cafe owner. Pleased to hear him tell his stories, but what was better was knowing that the K-9 Sheppard's would still be able to trace the scents of narcotics long after they've been relocated or even sold and for "this Captain" that would indeed be what he would love to call "evidence." In his mind he knew that if need be, he was prepared to buzz saw every piece of furniture in this Cafe and haul that shit right on down to the basement, the one at the precinct.

"No, not at all I mean as long as we're with the same understanding that food is prepared here than I have no objections at all."

"Ha, listen to this guy will you, of course we will keep in mind that some of the finest foods that this city has to offer is prepared right here and in this building. But, while they search tell me, were you present when Mr. Collinson packed his belongings." Julius smiled inside for he knew where the Captain was heading with his questioning even though he saw clearly through the fake 'chummy.'

"Yeah I was; his locker is there," Julius nodded into the direction of the oversized gym locker. Now this was true, the locker did belong to Nigel and in it were documents and a change of clothing identifying Nigel to be the owner of the locker. What was important to Captain Wynn though were scents and possible prints and Julius knew that all of which were present both the scent and the prints. However, the cryptic puzzled note book and the currency counter were manufactured right along with the dirty cell phone and all of its incriminating text messages. "Hmm, that's evidence ain't it," thought the Captain.

"So this was 'his' locker you say?" Captain Wynn peered inside to take in the locker before the dogs came for the finals.

When the dog showed up the place became excited with expectations. The officers watched as the K-9 officer walked the Sheppard around the Cafe saving the office and the locker for last, and so far they've found nothing, nothing and nothing. Well, the time came and everyone knew that the moment that everyone had been waiting for was now upon them. The dog ran around the office then became interested in the locker and a second later the Shepherd became really interested in the locker. First the Shepherd lost control and attempted to tip the locker over then upon instructions had become settled and laid next to the locker and began to bark and scratch uncontrollably at the locker.

Seeing and hearing the dog's reactions, Sergeant Wildey and Detective Stallworth began to think the same identical thing at pretty much the same time, 'what if there were drugs, let's say…under the locker maybe.' Even then, did the Sergeant or the Detective fail to feel anything but uneasiness concluding that this was just too damned easy. Luck was one thing but this was a whole another other kind of fortunate, all of these pieces of evidence just- a- lying every which-a-where. No, these two was going to look beyond the surface, uh uh they felt. They excused themselves and the two ran down the Special Agent. It was the Detective who leaned into the Special Agent to ask the question that he was sure that he already knew the answer to, he said.

"So, now that we are all here what do you think?" The Special Agent shook his head and said,

"Which one of you guys feel as if our Captain should be out here with us?" Neither of the two bothered to answer, but they both knew that the FBI Special Agent had Internal Affairs connections up the starfish, and already vowed to send for them like the Calvary if on the account any more suspicious behavior or generic conduct came about by the SPD, and a Captain in the field didn't look right at all. He was willing to disregard rank or position. Even the Sergeant and the Detective had some concerns of their own as well.

"I think I speak for both of us when I say that this doesn't sit right," says Stallworth,

"Yes, he does speak for the both of us and what a fine job he's doing" said Wildey who added. "There's at least thirty officers with us who are so wired up that I would pay to see you try to talk some sense into them, none of this makes any sense to me, but who am I to say. I mean I see something else, maybe a throw off or something. I may be wrong, and I'm sure I've been wrong somewhere before." The FBI Agent had to admire a Sergeant who lost a father and a brother to this investigation. Far from an honorable way to pass still they were family, and fallen officers which to some was all the constitution anyone would ever need to go the fuck nuts. So, to hear him speak so justly spoke volumes of his individual character.

"Oh-kay, I hear you talking I mean; you may as well say the rest." Said Agent Barrnette who found a whole new respect for Sergeant Wildey.

"I just got another hit on the box that the truck came to a stop on MLK Blvd. I'm saying cover for me here while I go and give it a gander." Both Stallworth and Agent Barrnette gave the thought no more than a split second worth of energy before the two shook their heads vigorously in the negative but Barrnette was the vocal one when he uttered.

"Hell no!"

"Let me finish," said Wildey "I know what you guys are thinking, that I'll go there with all guns blazing but that is so not the case. I need this to go as peaceful as possible you know with the bad publicity that my family has endured over the years. What I'm proposing is that I go and give this line a gander. I mean I would remain in constant contact with you two and if it looks like I got him don't worry I won't be foolish about it trust me on this one." Stallworth thought about the wired up atmosphere and relented saying,

"He got something, I mean I'm skeptical, but he got something."

"Skeptical?" Questioned Agent Barrnette

"Yeah, the fucker is barely even thirty and he's already a sergeant don't that tell you anything?"

"Ahh, yeah request denied buddy, uh uh, no sir," after a small round of chuckles Barrnette turned to Wildey to establish eye contact before saying.

"I'll cover for you, but I mean it you best to keep us updated. I mean play by play and if you do move on this guy you make sure that it's the good ole justice way, do you hear me?"

"Aye aye sir," the salute before leaving then Sergeant Wildey weaved through the heavy police traffic and disappeared without further questions.

Sergeant Wildey arrived at the location provided to him by Carla the most seasoned dispatcher alive. The Sergeant smiled at the thought of hearing her say "well before I give you the information you have to promise me right now that you won't do anything stupid."

"Stupid?"

"Yes, like go and get your head blown off, that kind of stupid!"

"Oh yeah, hell yeah I promise you that, believe me?" And this was a promise that Sergeant Wildey would love to keep. So, while he stared now at the very truck he became both leery and anxious. He was an officer of the law, rather he wanted to or not he was gonna have to address this matter. After running the plates and secretly wishing for a miss which was none more than a wish denied for the hit came back quickly. The Sergeant radioed for the bird in the sky to vacate and was granted upon demand, he watched as the helicopter circled and left.

The Sergeant took to the streets on foot patrol and after several wrong guesses the Sergeant concluded that the subject could only be inside of one place, which was a watering hole that took on a very familiar name "Pepe's" where he made it through the entrance with no problems at all, there were no shots fired what-so-ever. He saw as the drinks stayed pouring, and the music kept playing on and on without being cut due to his presence. In fact, there was no fear of the law here at all he noticed. This would not escape the officer's recognition as far as first impressions were concerned. He felt if not peculiarly welcomed, way more than he felt of inconvenience.

The sergeant headed to the bar and took a seat, and there a bartender approached him, instantly displaying hospitality. "How may I help you?" Asked the bartender,

"Well, first I'd like a Johnny Walker solo, then I'd like you to stand by with a Johnny Walker with a lemon over, and next I would like very much to speak with the owner. But, before all of that I'm going to need you to lock the doors, all of them because soon as the first person walks out of here I'm going to have to arrest everybody... owner included." Oh, this got the bartender's attention all but quick and instantly his eyes had gone to the door, satisfied that no one had left yet. He signaled for the bouncer to come, and to the bouncer he explained the situation very quickly. The bouncer who looked as if he had just gotten out of prison and could very well still be on active parole, and had exactly no desire to go back, ran to lock the doors and stood chiefly on guard.

The Johnny Walker's slid down the counter towards the waiting grasp of the officer who for sure couldn't think of a better person who needed the drinks more than him. Sergeant Wildey sipped from his drink while the bartender picked up the telephone and accommodated the officers wish to speak with the owner and moments later he was in the presence of a very classy and attractive woman.

"Officer," Was her soft spoken request.

"Ma'am, well I need you to pardon me but there is someone here in this club that I need to speak with. I also must tell you that in seconds if not now there will be over twenty deputies outside of your place of business and all of them, trust me on this one are "all" equally wired up to kill. You see, we have reason to believe that right now as we speak you are harboring a fugitive and a cop killer and all of that amongst other things. At this point you have done nothing illegal unless you continue to deny me and my request to see him, then, well that'll be something different just thought you should know."

"And, you say that person is here, in this club?" Fuck this woman was beautiful! The cop noted that this lady made him nervous.

"Yes ma'am, his name is Nigel Collinson. Now I would love to order another drink, and to share this drink with Mr. Collinson as a peace offering, and as you could tell I am still officially on duty and not allowed to drink, yet and still I must act as the buffer between peace and hostility."

"Thank you much and I appreciate your methods, but you don't have a warrant, do you?"

"No ma'am, not at the time, but I can easily get one and I will assure you that it'll be here by the time I finish this drink! I mean if that's what I need to do. Now, hearing that ma'am I need to also tell you that I wouldn't be this polite and I wouldn't have so many regards for your establishment if I have to go through all of that. Look ma'am, I am on duty, yet I sat down and ordered drinks like your other customers which Ms. is so against the rules but you know what, I am so scared. I'm scared of the bloodshed; I'm scared that there is a chance that we can even end up killing an innocent man. Still there is an arrest warrant and I must serve it you understand?" Nodding her understanding April sized up the officer concluding that there was a trace of sincerity to the man, she said.

"Wait here and please, have as many drinks as you like." The Sergeant watched as April gone around the bar and picked up the same phone as the bartender, and spoke briefly then replaced it on its base then came to the officer and said,

"I'll assure you that there is no threat what-so-ever so please decline to make any aggressive scenes in my club. Mr. Nigel is coming down accompanied by his attorney. Your arrest warrant is good though, right?" Oh yeah she was born to be 'The Boss' and the Sergeant couldn't think of a woman who revealed all of these qualities upon one impression.

"Yes ma'am, if you don't mind me asking, what is it that Mr. Collinson does here?"

"Same thing everyone else does here officer, they come, they drink and have a good time."

"I have one more important question; did Mr. Collinson possess any luggage when he entered your club?" Here is when the Sergeant got the chance to size up April in return.

"Hold up a second?" April beckoned for the bartender who stood close enough to protect his boss to come and he appeared instantly to receive his orders to bring and boot up the laptop computer to reveal today's events, mainly the entrance and the exits. The bartender obliged, even making the computer accessible to the officer who controlled the machine expertly himself. He'd fast forward then he'd rewind.

"Wait!" Said April "go back a little," the Sergeant pressed the button "there" April pointed towards the screen at a casually dressed individual who didn't seem shaken nor agitated at all in fact, he was aplomb. He walked with a confidence that the Sergeant could only wish for. April saw as the officers' brows rose a bit, obviously the officer had stereotyped Nigel she thought. It seemed like the officer was geared to see someone more menacing. He would press play then rewind only to play again until he braved up the wits to ask.

"Who is this guy I'm looking at though?"

"Now, that right there is me sir," the Sergeant was so caught up in the viewing of Mr. Collinson that he almost forgot the very reason why he had come in the first place. The fact that his head wasn't blown off yet said a lot if you asked him. He turned to greet the gentleman in the flesh and not once did he reach for his weapon. He kept his poise even though inside he felt a very high level of anxiety, still he said.

"Mr. Collinson I have a warrant for your immediate arrest." Sergeant Wildey sized up the elderly man and really didn't know what to make of this encounter. Even though he believed the man to be old enough to be "Raymond Buchannon" but that was it and it was all as far as taking first impressions into consideration.

"So I heard," said Nigel, then "and I hear that some people would like to kill me. I mean, you wanna tell me some more about that?"

"Would you mind if we sit and have a drink?" Then to April the Sergeant said "It would be wise to keep the doors locked" smiling he finished "I mean I don't wanna get caught red handed you know, another Johnny please!" April nodded her understanding, she was happy to see that the officer also came with a sense of humor. Noting that his timing was perfect, thinking maybe if nothing else just to lighten up the situation was enough for her.

"So, you come to arrest me you say?" Uttered Nigel but barely loud enough for the officer to hear him.

"Yes sir." The Sergeant said over the rim of his shot glass.

"I would love to know the reason." April stated,

"Me too," said Nigel "I mean, wow, you're kidding me …right?"

"Not at all, and if that was a wow, wait until I tell you the rest."

"I mean we're all grown up here." Nigel said while bracing himself for any surprise attacks.

"Well, just off the top of my head there's murder and then of course there's murder on a peace officer. Then there's drug trafficking, but that of a sophisticated enterprise though I'm sure that they will call it something else later. I brought the black coats with me and that's the part that they are the most interested in. So, to tell you that there's another hundred or so other major infractions wouldn't be nothing but me bragging and I didn't come here to gloat or ruin anyone's day, you know what I mean?"

"Shoot, you could have fooled me. All of this you say was sitting on the top of your head?" Nigel began to feel a little queasy.

"Yes sir, I'm more than sure that there's a bunch of other stuff that every judge in this fine country would like to see you stand trial for, but so what, you know."

"And the paperwork, how much of this is on the good ole warrant sheet?"

"That's the other thing; you see the paperwork that you wish to see is on the other side of that door. Me, I'm just the bad news evil messenger who believes that everyone is entitled to see why they are being detained. So, if it's that important to you then we could go on and get out of here because behind that door are agents of all walks and the deal here is that I don't walk out of here without you. Do you remember that wired up anxious to kill story that I wanted to tell you about? Well, the truth is that I'm only here to make sure that the killing stops. The black coats they like dope, me I don't give a fuck about that, shit no. But, the killing…sir it's the killing that has to stop." The Sergeant turned to April and said "Ma'am I will allow Mr. Collinson that drink and no more than one more then I'm going to have to arrest him one way or the other. Safe would be to let me radio that I have him in custody and all of this needs to happen in the next minute." Sergeant Wildey laid out all of the cards to Nigel who really didn't need to see the papers all that bad, but he did have some concerns that he had to voice.

"So, with you I live and without you it could be disastrous at the front door then?"

"Drastic calls for drastic measures"

"Tell you what, I'll surrender to you peacefully though it seems as if I have no reason to at all, you say warrant, but we don't see one. You say you are a cop well, that's not actually a good thing around here especially a cop who sports Wildey for a last name. But as I say before, I will surrender to you without resisting or argument as long and only if my attorney accompanies us in the same vehicle to ensure my safety and no other way lest the request for peace would grow smaller and smaller by the second," Nigel finished. The Sergeant didn't know quite when somebody turned the heater on, but he sure knew that it was starting to get a little stuffy inside of club "Pepe's". He even began to feel like the main ingredients to a fucking alligator trap, but there was one thing that he knew without a shadow of a doubt and that was a bargain when he heard one. He said,

"Mr. Collinson sir, if that would help put this day behind us then I am more than happy to tell you that you sir, have a deal. Now that I know that there would be folks who may want to accompany you to the main jail only to ensure your safety and I have no problem with that. What I will have a problem with is after I radio that we are coming out that you decide to walk very slow or interview for what could be a very large crowd of people. Our objective here is to speedily get to the transportation vehicle safely and nothing else matters after that, do you understand"

"Well, with all of this hoo-rah we shouldn't keep them waiting." Nigel stood and there Nigel surrendered to the Sergeant of the Sacramento Police Department to the sounds of the officer reading the ever important Miranda to the very one "Nigel Collinson".

It was orchestrated that the doors would be opened by the club's owner and that it would be the owner and her bartender along with legal aid that would accompany the Agents and their Suspect 'who was in custody and for everyone's sake the Sergeant repeated that the subject was now in custody' awaiting transportation to the county main jail. And this is when Nigel began to think airport all the way. The Doors were opened by April who fought back a wave of nausea once she saw the sea of agents, the news crews and the many spectators.

"Nigel" was all that she could say as the many guns were trained on them. In slow motion April saw as agents materialized from thin air and formed a barricade around Nigel as if protecting Nigel as well as themselves. One of the officers said in a hurried tone,

"Mr. Collinson I'm Special Agent Barrnette, sorry for this display but we need to hurry, both for your safety and mine. I need you to follow me and don't stop, do you understand me?" Nigel nodded his response then the agent led the way moving briskly through the many reporters and officers alike. The flash bulbs assaulted them along with the many questions until they were inside of the transportation van. The spectators watched as the officers came and left with three of the communities most positive of people they would say. Though they didn't know much about anything, still they all possessed the idea that the world had just lost its motha fucking mind.

Julius received the message of Nigel's arrest the very next morning. Even though it didn't go exactly the way they planned it you know, a few glitches here and there the desired effect was still achieved. Which was his thoughts while placing the call to his soon to be connection, his soon to be direct line to the good stuff. Julius heard the phone ring on the other end of the line, and then the husky voice that he became well acquainted with.

"Ha-low," said the voice into the phone.

"Yes, this is Julius"

"Ahh, Joo-nee-ous, you do good job Si?" The huskiness always reminded Joo-nee-ous of a soft spoken prize fighter.

"Si Senorita, good job, Si?" Was Julius's response, mentally he was thinking 'well that all depends on what you were willing to call a good job' his thoughts were sweetly interrupted by the huskiness again.

"Uno- momento," Julius waited until another voice came on the line this time a male's voice, this brought Julius to excitement.

"Amigo," it was Antonio, a voice that Julius had come to recognize over the months.

"Amigo," said Julius declaring his respect for Antonio,

"You do good job, Si?"

"We have small problem"

"Oh, there is problem?"

"Remember we moved the luggage? Well, we still have the luggage"

"Television, TV says yes, no?"

"Si, si, television, si"

"Oh-kay, good, good. You sell restaurant?"

"Soon, pretty soon."

"Good, almost ready for business, no?"

"Anytime you ready amigo."

"Si, si, oh-kay I see you soon amigo." The line went dead leaving Julius to revel in his thoughts of power, which was ultimately everything that Julius had worked so hard to be, and that was powerful.

Chapter 33

For Juice, life has been lived a bit different over the past years, for him it was education all day, every day. There was the immediate transfer from the University of California Los Angeles to the McGeorge School of Law and nobody understood that shit at all. Although he didn't like it still above everything he knew that this was the best decision for him to make. "Where the hell is McGeorge School at?" He asked just to be embarrassed once he found out that not only was the law school in Sacramento, but the fucka was in Oak Park and no more than five or six blocks away from the club where he worked and still took for residence with his mother.

It was there where Juice had been groomed under the watchful and over protective eyes of his mother. A figure that have never, not one time allowed him the luxury of forgetting his focus, nor did she ever stop reminding him of the person that he must grow to be. Sure there were women that came in and out of Juices' life, but if they weren't able to walk through the metal detector or bend it over and spread them, squat and cough a couple of times and test clean then they weren't able to get through the front door. Juice would always marvel at the many attempts put on by the opposite sex, many have tried and many have failed. His mother has seen it all and this he knew. She saw every trick play, rather fake hand off or misconception, and every attempt, every time, was no good. The only thing the world knew was that these two played for real and that romance was only a fantasy for Juice. Considering that the only ones protecting his father's dynasty was his mother. An investment with portfolios by the thousands and business ventures pushing past even that was protected by the stiff and iron clad fist of his mother. So he respected that even more with knowledge that parasites would come to balance the books and jackals join the hyenas all in collective attempts at back strikes and laughter. It was never a secret to either Juice or April that the best way to defend themselves was and would be if Juice became knowledgeable and polished to a fine and shine when it came to the law. Under no circumstances whatsoever would they ever stray away from the ways of her husband and Juices' father. A man that April would say moved through the city invisible and transparent like a ghost, yet more feared than even Leviathan and these two knew first-hand the impact that those actions held over the whole city. No, it was indeed the best decision for Juice to attend the McGeorge School of Law where his new major would be in three corporate law arenas and this was indeed intelligent. By looking at this particular young man one could easily draw the conclusion that Juice was none more than a hoodlum. Hooded sweat shirts and Nike Air Max, bald fades and baggy jeans, Rockport boots and puffed bomber jackets. He was pretty good with a basketball they'd say, and rumors had it they would whisper that his dad died and forced him to be a bartender in order to help his mother keep a club running. Oh- kay, even with the rumors being ever so powerful still there were young women climbing the fences and jumping off the roof for him. There were old retired whores and young ones too, willing to help bring him to prominence for they couldn't stand to see such a catch reduced to a bartender and busboy. April used to hear the many tales, some of the stories she was impressed with, and others not so impressive.

Yes, there were many women out for her son but none ever quite made it past the potential prospect stages, except one lady, Savanna.

Oh my God, Juice used to stay up late and up so early knowing that he was going to see her as soon as he arrived on campus. My goodness, oh how she got on his damned nerves, so much that he could choke the shit out of her on account to how she ran through his mind. The way she walked forced him to fight hypnosis even though her attire was often times sported oversized meaning they were baggy. Her shirts were always big, and her jeans were often baggy, and Juice had always been a sucker for hats and a lot of times she wore ball caps, shit! The part that made him the most nervous were the boots, the Timberland styled boots. This gave her the "Tomboy" impression and the tough chick look but to meet Savanna, one would know straight off the bat that tough was only when she spoke for the rights of others and that was as far as tough had gone with her. Her Tomboy look well; this wasn't all the way a throw off because in her own athletic way she was a Tomboy. She could knock down a fifteen-foot jumper on call, and could quote scores and sports trivia maybe even faster than Stuart Scott (RIP) of that ESPN network. Juice had caught Savanna on a weekend once, Sunday, on her way to praise God like she did every Sunday. What Juice had noticed instantaneously was how Savanna walked in heels just as proudly and confident as she did in boots, and sneakers. Oh but her dress, which wasn't oversized at all though, no! That was fitted snugly over her body. Everything about her was shapely, Juice remembered taking her in from her shoes up, and by the time he reached her breast he nearly hyperventilated. He didn't quite remember when he stopped breathing but he knew that his lungs had desperately needed emergency air intake. He had never ever seen her this close before, and he was bedazzled by this. He didn't even know that her eyes were naturally green, with skin as dark as savannas, this appeared to be an impossible that somehow God has made possible, just because and, just to show off.

"Juice.... Juice" he remembered like two minutes ago her voice screaming its melodies in his direction.

"What!" Juice snapped at her, an almost frightening gesture that he really didn't mean. He just couldn't believe that somebody was awakening him from his best dream ever and Lord only knew that he was a dreamer.

"Well excuse me." She said sounding apologetic.

"No, no, I'm sorry. I really didn't mean it like that, just... just, you know." with all the air sucked out of his head made it hard for him to find the correct words to say.

"Oh-kay, if you say so..."

"No, really I didn't mean to snap at you like that, just I've never saw you like this before and I was trying to put this right now you with this day before yesterday you and I mean, you know what I mean hell."

"Oh-kay, whatever, but my car is sputtering and out of gas please tell me that you have a couple of dollars that I could borrow. I'll promise to pay you back I mean it, I promise." To Juice this was not a bad request because the other thing that Juice learned was that students were often times found broke. It was like some kind of hidden scholastic law that cash and books just won't and don't mix. No matter how hard one tried. If you go hustling the books would suffer, if you go learning then the hustle would suffer and Juice liked to think that the same rules applied to Savannah. Though he knew very little about her and only saw here in passing but he couldn't help to believe that she didn't arrive from "money." I mean he knew that she went to Kennedy High School and a couple of years at Sacramento City which is junior college before heading off to the McGeorge School of Law where she studied Criminal and Civil Law. All of this Juice had for information because it was required that each student introduced themselves as well as their majors in their Corporate law classes and this is how Juiced had known this much about Savannah. This is also the way Savannah found out the same information about Juice except that when Juice had gone to introduce himself the class had chanted his name right along with him "Juice, Juice, Juice" everyone in class knew who he was and were proud to have him because he was a local hero amongst them. Although none of his peers and I mean none, possessed the understanding of just how could a person walk away from a basketball program at the historical and infamous UCLA where the ghost of the wizard of Westwood still runs the floor just to come to such a lowly and mediocre, not so popular nor as prestigious school, that sits right smack dabbed in the middle of Oak Park. They were glad to have him but would love to have stabbed him for being so damned stupid.

So to hear Savannah right now saying his name was no surprise nor was her asking for a loan considering that she was a full time student. Juice knew that in any kind of way that he could help her, he knew that he would. So, he looked past her trying to locate her car, not seeing one he said,

"Oh-kay, so where's your car at?"

"It's on Franklin Blvd." Now this was asking for a bit much thought Juice, but said.

"Do you have a gas can or something, a container to put the gas in?"

"I have one in my car." Concluding that she must have walked quite a way's in her heels now that they were on Alhambra and Broadway at a food and deli, where Juice had fallen in love with the Gatorade collection when he was younger, not that far from Franklin Blvd. but in a set heels this was awfully serious.

"So, your can is in the car, you want to go get it, I could give you a lift I mean my mom told me not to talk to strangers too so I can understand if you would feel like walking back to get it, under the safety clause and all that."

"Uh-uh, under normal condition I would avoid it, talking to strangers you know but these heels killed all of that already. Plus, the time I go and come back again the service would sure to be over so if you're offering then thank you."

"Same thing I was thinking so I'll give you a lift if that's what you need. Or I can take you to your service and handle your car situation while you're in service. I believe you will have to trust me with your keys though. I mean you don't want to keep the good lord waiting." Juice smiled at his own charismatic wit.

"Would you really do that for me, seriously?"

"I mean why not, just give me the keys and the location of the car and I'll have it waiting at the church for you by the time you get out of service, how about that".

"Yeah, and how are you going to do that?"

"Roadside assistants, it's Savanna right?"

"Yeah," she giggled attempting to hide her blush "I'm sorry, my manners have been compromised due only to my situation. I'm so sorry but I am Savanna Clayton and I do not have insurance or roadside anything."

"Ahh, don't worry about that I do. Like I say, up the keys and tell me where. But first let me run in this store, it's warming up out here. I came for a drink, would you care for one perhaps a Gatorade, pop, or water."

"Yes, I do thank you, a Gatorade is perfect"

"What kind?" Juice gave Savanna skeptic looks, a Gatorade for the lady in the dress, pa-lease."

"Watermelon," said Savanna "not the green ones, the cucumber ones are yuk."

"You just like the red ones."

"Yep, fruit punch and watermelon," said Savanna who lead the way through the doors of the store. My goodness this lady was cut like a diamond Juices thought while he surveyed the rest of Savanna. Her long hair and her perfectly toned anatomy had always given Juice fits.

Maybe he should have shared more with her, trusted her a little more and maybe then she would still be there with him, he thought in hindsight. Well as it stood his family needed protection even more so now that his father was deceased and because of this Savanna would be none more than a distant memory and a thing of the past.

So, for him it made perfect sense to enter the draft and off to legal boot camp he had gone. He saw classes five days a week at the

McGeorge School from eight a.m. to three p.m. and six days a week he would attend the law offices of Dixon, Juan and Dixon which was only the most powerfully structured building located in downtown Sacramento. Which is the very same law offices that handled his father's estates and wishes and one of his wishes was for them to embrace his son and to provide for him a mentor-ship program. So there in the folds of such experience Juice would get what most attorneys would call the ring side version. Here he logged a thousand hours in raw footage and a thousand hours in research and a thousand hours watching films of the highest profiled cases to date.

Juice had learned things that weren't taught in class and he had learned things that he knew for sure would change him forever. It was never on his list to be an attorney but again, his family needed protection. Through every experience Juice had ventured through, he'd done so with Savanna on his mind and so much that Juice had known that if anybody were to invade his fortress that it would have been her. She was the one who made him truly happy and a little bit of happy shouldn't hurt anybody, should it.

There was one problem with all of this happy shit, self-gratification wasn't for Juice at the time but hard work and study was though, in fact it was at the top of his priority list. Savannah was the perfect person in the world for Juice true, and they had even gone out a few times, twice to the Bruins games which way Juice could support his old teammates at UCLA and once at the state fair. Savanna saw as Juice took to the mini hoop courts and liked to cleared them out of their prizes by sinking basket after basket after basket. So much that the stands ran out of prizes over three feet tall and so much that Juice began to get hated on by the other participant's, one brotha in particular.

"Hey sport, I see you won all the good prizes," Juice had recognized the fellow immediately. Even though he took on a different appearance than Juice last remembered, the swagger was there, the same wicked grin was present to. Surrounded by a bunch of tyrants wasn't all the way new either because Juice knew that his adversary had always portrayed the tough guy appearance on the court.

"Filbert Gilbert," Juice said in recognition.

"That's what they call me, I mean, now that you got all the pieces, how about a friendly wager, maybe I could win some of your pieces." And as an insult Filbert Gilbert scanned Savannah up and down then continued with,

"And look, some very nice pieces you've got." Juice was never one to back down on the court, in the streets, or in a church or aisle six at Wal-Mart, he was built different from the ones that did shy away from threats of aggression.

"Oh yea, I always win everything, don't you remember, oh you must' have forgotten." Which to the audience didn't mean much, only Filbert Gilbert knew that he had just been royally insulted and so did Juice, who decided to pour the rest of it on him, by saying.

"If you've been standing there long enough to see me empty everything out then you must have been here to see me giving the prizes away to the kids. I mean, I still got a little energy in me, so tell me how many kids you got and I'll go ahead and win them something, I mean since they daddy can't seem to do it." The good thing was that Filbert Gilbert's' entourage had carnival visitors already paying attention to them which forced security to keep a close eye on them as well, and it was security who followed this exchange from the beginning. They didn't quite know what all of this mess was about but whatever was going on with this group was way bigger than everything else at the carnival and deserved some immediate attention. It was a good thing that they were there too because the chances of Juice and maybe even Savannah getting their asses whupped was definitely running in the high nineties.

"Bitch ass nigga." Said Filbert Gilbert attempting to get his hands on Juice, maybe to ring his motha fucking neck. Was seized by a member of his group who saw that security was on the scene and fearful with their firearms close by.

"Yea, yea, yea, yea that's what you said the last time and still you're trying to find out what it is I'm doing. Well let me help you, as a Freshman I was a starter at a power house that took a dip and guess who that was that lead them back to Prominence. Dude they called a match up nightmare for whoever showed up, Louisville, Duke, Syracuse, North Carolina, St. John, Kansas or Ohio State. I was a problem for you too, remember." Now this was the straw that broke the bulls back.

"I swear to God you're a bitch ass nigga," said Filbert Gilbert.

"Well, how I know." Said Juice who added "I'm saying you don't see this lady here holding me back, how is it that you got your lady holding you back. She stopping you from getting your ass whupped is what's really going on and you know better." Which too was the perfect insult considering that it was one of Filberts homeboys holding him back which wasn't a lady at all, but a hoped to die killer named J-Dog who too grew up on the east side of Stockton California, right on Market Street. Juice had no way of knowing any of this nor did he care because they were now on the streets of Sacramento California.

"Oh yea, well I'll tell you what, how about we just go out in the parking lot and find a better way to fix this. I mean I'm sure we could fix this thang here if we just went outside so I could beat the shit out of you." For an answer Juice shook his head and walked away. Now all of this about Juice, Savannah liked, he had rough edges, he had education, he was driven by a strong sense of direction and he was always in a position to help others, her ideal man she thought.

"What the heck was that all about?" Savannah asked barely suppressing the pride that she was feeling.

"It's a long story." Said Juice,

"Well, hmm. I mean I'm not doing anything else." She just needed to know and was awfully firm about it.

"Well, if you must know, the dude with the dreads the one that blew his radiator? They call him Filbert Gilbert because he's from the projects in Stockton called Filbert Arms. I knew him in High School, he went to

Edison High School, I went to Sacramento High School. He pushed the pill for Edison I Pushed the pill for Sac. Every year we took our teams to the Sac/Joaquin regional finals." Juice paused for a moment.

"Well, four years in a row I went home with it. The closest that he came was in our last year. I mean we barely got out of there with that one, fifty-four to fifty-three was the final score," smiling Juice said "Guess who knocked down the last two free throws?"

"Who, you?" Juice nodded his answer and Savannah playfully pushed him and said,

"So why are you smiling so much?"

"Because while I was at the line preparing for my charity shots that's when I became a bunch of bitches. The sad part was that Filbert had one of the fastest first steps that I've ever seen and he was ambidextrous too, left handed and right handed penetration and all that. We all knew that when you went to play Edison that you had to really bring it. I mean really, really bring it, from the first whistle to the last buzzer sounded you had to go full throttle.

"Wow, then why is he so angry?"

"The last time I played against him was in Sacramento at the Arco Arena. Everyone knew that Scouts were present and a lot of them, both locker rooms knew this. Our locker room had a secret though; we knew that if we were going to win we had to freeze Gilbert. Our team was banged up, we suffered injuries all through the year, yet not to be bragging but I knew that the only way that we were gonna meet in the tournaments that I was gonna have to put the team on my back and take us there."

"Oh, so you were smart like that were you, how did you know all of this? I mean that sounds like a big responsibility."

"Yeah, I was smart like that and reliable and responsibility was plenty but you know" Juice shrugged his shoulders.

"So, you were ready for it?"

"I had to be, me I didn't have another option I'm a winner. You see, Gilbert he's surrounded by thugs, it's true that he really does come from the streets. His down fall was that he let his environment become the prevailing factor in his life, which was our secret because we knew… at least I knew that so I used all of this to our advantage."

"And, you were smart like that too?"

"Yeah, yeah I'm telling you I was." Juice said giving Savanna a playful nudge.

"And how did you get all of this smart stuff as a high schooler, huh? Savannahs eyebrows rose to show skepticism."

"Well, I had three coaches all of my life, one in high school, one in college and one all through my life. The one that I had all through life was a serious coach, the kind of coach that'll teach you how to think when you're on the floor. I mean I had one of the best games against Christian Brothers, girl that rim was as wide as the state of Texas. I was on fire; I'm talking about everything that I threw up went in. Thirty-eight points, the perfect reason to celebrate if you ask me. This coach that I'm talking about was furious I mean he was sweating and spitting mad. I had never saw him like that before, I mean it was crazy, it was ridiculous.

"Wow, what kind of coach was that again?"

"Well, it was my dad."

"Your dad was a coach?"

"Not on the floor but in the car he was a coach."

"I don't get it." Juice piqued Savanna's confusion.

"An in the car coach is way more serious than an on the floor coach because an in the car coach could break down your whole game for you on the way home. An on the floor coach would watch a film on it for a week or so, my dad had always told me that if he was the coach that I would be benched often and all the time. See my dad didn't miss a thing, thirty-eight points was cool by me but my dad would point out that I missed my open passes to better quality and higher percentage shots. He would point out that I had also accumulated six turnovers and would remind me that the guy that I was guarding had a good game too." Juice shook his head at the memories.

"Oh-kay, so your dad was like your ego guard?"

"Something like that, he was pushing me to be better is all. Sometimes he would seek weakness in my opponent and once he did he would slide his finger across his throat and I would press the gas considering that I always had gas. You know what my dad would do, right after practice he would take me to the Salvation Army and there I would practice some more, five hundred free throws, up and down the court with stop and pops until I felt like telling my mama on him. I mean it was torture at least four times maybe five times a week"

"Was your dad how you learned the secret of that one guy from Edison?'

"Yes, coming in we saw Gilbert in a circle of a bunch of guys and they were all smoking the good stuff. We figure if this was his habit then he could also have a training problem. The secret was in conditioning, I had no idea of how much he was smoking but it was a gamble that I took. As his opponent I notice that each time we met that he didn't go as hard as he could have on every play. He never brought it all game he would lag a little but they had a strong team to make up for this. Our team was hamstrung and plagued by injuries the whole year like I said. My dad told me that it was up to me to carry my team and to strike first and to strike fast the whole game. So, not only in the finals but every game I entered with a chip on my shoulder. So, at the Arco Arena we made a few changes in our game plan poking at Edison's conditioning. We were going to run Gilbert especially, off one screen after the next and from the very beginning all you could hear was pick, pick, pick. The coach had to use precious timeouts just to save Gilbert. We worked him so hard when he was on defense that he didn't have enough in the tank on offence because if he did we knew that they were gonna kill us."

"But the screens worked?"

"Yeah, he came off one pick late so I hit his ass with one of those ole school pump fakes that sent him airborne, and on his way down I took to the sky and picked up a foul off him"

"Ahh, so, that's why he so angry."

"He still argues that call, guess how much time was left…. two seconds, if I make one and miss one it's a tie."

"But you used to practice so much"

"Right, I felt like I could have knocked them down blindfolded, with no time outs they were forced to go the length of the court, no go, game over. Now, do you remember all the scouts that I told you about, guess what? I interviewed for them on the court in front of everybody, I'm saying if the whistle doesn't blow, maybe it was him doing the interview."

"I doubt it,"

"Why you say that?" Asked Juice wanting to see how she viewed everything that he relayed to her.

"You said it yourself, your team was ham strung yet you put them on your shoulder and took the Sac/Joaquin tournament, that's very seldom done. He had a strong team you had a banged up one simple, David and Goliath"

"Ha, that's what my dad said,"

"That always gets fans, everyone roots for the underdog."

"How you know so much about this?"

"Because I pushed the pill for Kennedy,"

"Ahh, so you're a cougar?"

"Ahh, so you're a dragon?" And this is how Juice fell in love for the first time.

"So do you think it's safe to leave?" Asked Savanna,

"We could have left a long time ago, this is Sacramento." Pointing backwards Juice said "Them dudes are from Stockton."

"What that got to do with anything?"

"Sacramento loves me, my daddy was the ambassador of the place, believe me."

"Oh-kay ambassador," still the two left unscathed what Juice never got the chance to tell her, not that he thought it wise to do so, was the minute that the argument took place calls were mad right away to ensure Juices survival. Oh yea, it was oh so true that Filbert Gilbert was a goon and in his company were other goons, but as Juice said, this was Sacramento and by the time these two, Juice and Savanna would have made it to that cherry red with the white soft top and every piece original on a well maintenance, since his sixteenth birthday classic 1965 Mustang, there would have been enough hitters in the parking lot with enough artillery to reenact desert storm only to make sure that Juice Raymond also known as "You bitch ass nigga" drove away safe and sound. Savannah, it was true, could have been shot, stabbed and beaten to a bloody pulp but that "bitch ass nigga" better never catch the hiccups the wrong way or all hell was definitely going to break loose. Sorry, but no one was obligated to the young woman, the young man was altogether different though. To him killers were bound by blood to make every day that he lived a fully protected one. The main reason being was the Raymond's had never left nothing to chance. April arranged the chaperones and their placements and spoke highly of the wiggle room that Juice would be entitled to cover while keeping his appointments. In doing this meant that money would fly this way and that way to loyal servants in that good old minimum wage bracket, ensuring that the weapons needed were able to enter the Sacramento State Fair. Not just the State Fair, no, this was how Juice got around no matter where he decided go, to school, or to church it was the same thing. Obscured to vision were obligated killers, meticulous and methodical...Killers.

No one could ever testify to seeing Juice surrounded by hoodlums or anybody else because to the naked eye Juice was a loner.... which was also part of the Raymond's defense. It took months for the many antics put on by law enforcements to subside after his father's death so these tactics were indeed necessary. Agents of all sorts and maneuvers of every design came to investigate the death of his father. They needed to know that Victor Raymond was in some kind of way and hopefully in a partnership with Felton Stringfellow at the time of death which would justify everything because at the time of their deaths Felton was indeed, a big time dope peddler.

The city saw the community come together and bury the two together, Victor and Felton. Though, the officials didn't know quite why, but they knew they were under a lot of pressure to figure this out. There were the public announcements which would broadcast on every news channel and newspaper alike. Then there were social medias network, leaked or however. Each platform saying that it took Wells Fargo to call in every staff it had, retired or whoever was available to come in and help bring forth the grand total of donations that were acquired from all across the country. This was a clue that this event was wide spread. Two full days it took, working all day and all night by hand and by machine did these bankers work counting funds donated to the Raymond's. And this whole affair was being dictated by one of Wells Fargo clients who stood by and made crying sure that every red nickel was accounted for in enough time to spend every penny of it, burying her husband.

What the city's officials learned ever so quick was that the deaths of these two has now created a brand new movement, one that sported "fuck the police" for a mantra. The Raymond's knowing all of this stuck to the blueprints of their departed, their "Head of house." Juice, aware at times and unaware at others to the presence of law men had carried on with life in the forms of healing. He figured if they were willing to use their monies and man power to follow him around was entirely up to them, they could follow him wherever. Most of the times it was to school and to the gym and if they ever cared for a drink then he was sure to serve up a mean martini. Drawing a blank on the Raymond's the investigation relented over time. Still the Raymond's carried on similar or the same way, slow and sure and as always, beneath the layers of the city while being observant to the city's borders.

Chapter 34

Once Nigel made it into the folds of the county jail, April had all she could take and whispered to her son that he would have to remain until Nigel was booked into the jail safely. The officers saw as April stood and walked out of the reception room where she was given blow by blow updates of Nigel's whereabouts and wellbeing. The word spread quickly that the woman that was inquiring about their prisoner had a late husband that made headlines all across the nation due to their own fiascoes, and they were all certain that this lady could indeed summons an attorney that would be willing to work for free. One that'll possess a skill set enough to close the place if and have anything was to happen to their prisoner Mr. Nigel Collins. So to both, her and Juice the officers were awfully polite yet they all breathed a sigh of relief to now watch the lady head towards the exits. What April didn't say to Juice was that she needed to get to Nigel's wishes right away and this is where Juice found his mother even though he didn't drag his weary soul in until two o'clock in the a.m.

"Well?" Said April the moment she raised her attention away from her laptop and notes.

"Well, he's booked into the jail no problems at all with that, but the press was out there really big, cameras and bright lights were everywhere. I heard the craziest thing; they somehow all got the fiendish assumption that they have in their confines the one and only Mr. Raymond Buchannon. Could you believe that?"

"Gee, if I got a nickel for every time that I heard that one, them branding and renaming somebody. I bet you Nigel got a good laugh out of that one. I hope he didn't have a gun in his truck because I noticed that they hauled it out of here."

"If he did, then I'm sure that they'll throw that out if they could convict him on any one of the allegations that they were saying over there, did you know that they are playing for all the marbles. I heard the DA is walking in from the gate yelling Capital Punishment."

"Who said this?" April didn't quite know what Capital Punishment consisted of but she was a bit curious to how it all went together with all the marbles.

"I just said that they have a full blown press going on at the jail, midnight and everyone's there, the DA over there, the mayor is there, the governor is there, everybody." Juice finished.

"Hmmmm, look at this" April said as she spun the laptop around so that Juice could read along with her and what they were looking at were financial statements, emails, and rough discoveries between Ju-Ju's Steak house and the Greater Law Firm of Dixon, Juan and Dixon. There they read through Nigel's educated guesses as well as through Nigel's logical approaches. The two read each and every column that supported Nigel's fact findings.

"Wow," Juice said as his mother scrolled down so the two could read more. Twenty minutes later Juice stood and began to pace which scared the mess out of April because lord knew that Victor was not Juices real father but somehow thankfully her son had picked up every single quality that she both loved and admired in her late husband.

"So," April leaned back in her seat then said "I'm curious, do tell me, what you get out of all this?"

"Nothing save for the fact that somebody needed to move Nigel out of the way if not but for a while. Aren't those some old ass business statements though somewhere around the time everybody pulled out of Dixon's?"

"I noticed that too, what else do you see?"

"I mean; I see it I just don't want to say it." Juice uttered.

"There's nobody here but me and you." She responded

"Oh-kay, with Nigel out of the way as far as they believe someone else would then be able to walk in and eat. By the looks of it it's going to be Julius who by the way is a coward and definitely not smart enough to know the responsibilities to that he's asking for. Which then leads me to believe that there is someone else other than the Dixon's, who by the way I don't believe that they would betray daddy's trust living or dead because you see that would just piss me off."

"What if it is the Dixon's?" She cut him off in order to keep him focused.

"Then it's the Dixon's but I repeat, I do not see them behaving in this fashion add the fact that I'm over there a billion hours a week and would be able to easily tell."

"Oh-kay, well what if it's not all the Dixon's and you there a zillion hours a week makes up for a good blind fold to me," April countered.

"Oh-kay, first why are you so convinced that the Dixon's have some involvement, something's telling me that you ain't telling me everything."

"Oh-kay, as far as Nigel's guesses we'll just say that his guesses are just guesses, no reason to head for the hills just yet, oh-kay. Even though you and I could both think of a hundred times when his guesses were direct hits, but never mind that oh-kay. Tell me though, do you find truth in Julius being a client of the Dixon's?"

"I saw that."

"Well, did you see when he became a client?" April asked.

"Uh hun," Juice answered sending his mother to her notes.

"He became a client two months after everyone pulled out of Dixon's. Now tell me, do you remember when your mentorship program started...."

"Nah," Juice begun to put his pieces together.

"Getting a little tingly ain't you? Even still that is no reason to head for the hills either. I mean so what Julius is a client whoopee but did you read the financial statements..."

"Yeah, yeah, yeah, yeah,"

"Then what did you get out of that?" She asked

"Nothing"

"Noting?"

"Uh un, was I supposed to see something?"

"Yeah, Julius' assets, Steak house and his home, if you clear all of his debts and he would stop somewhere over a quarter million dollars did you see that in there?" April pointed towards her computer.

"Yeah, I mean what that's supposed to tell me is what I don't know." Smiling at her son April said as remedial as she could possibly muster.

"Baby, we agreed that Julius was a client of the Dixon's and we could also see that Julius even if he sold everything and cleared his sleight that he may could drum up maybe a half mill, right. Son tell me, are there any clients at Dixon's worth anywhere under a million? Although they would wish you to have two could you think of any?"

"Shit naw!" Juice reflected to the reasons why everyone was pulling out of Dixon's to begin with. The world needed to know, if left up to April anyways, that the death of her husband was also the death of their finances and that she could no longer afford their services living solely off of the proceeds of the club. The charity that the Raymond's was receiving was much appreciated though.

"So what should we do is what we need to figure out and soon, it's Nigel's prediction that the Dixon's would pull out and refuse him representation at his arraignment which is in a few days. Tell me, would you be convinced then if that were to happen?"

"I'm convinced now I just don't want to believe that they would do something like this."

"Well they handled a lot of your father's transactions, as far as they know the streets are wide open remember. Well even if they don't pull out I wouldn't want anyone over there to represent Nigel, and whoever is over there behaving like this I gotta agree isn't strong enough to act alone. So, let's say New York maybe even Florida has come down who knows, but it's definitely somebody which means that war is pretty much inevitable."

"War!" Juice muttered,

"Yeah, maybe, I mean we could always let them have this city. It doesn't really have to be blood we could sale the club and move on." Juice looked to his mother searching for signs of hallucinated illnesses or any other reasons for the blatant blasphemies said,

"So you're saying just pick up and leave, just walk away sort of head for the hills then?"

"I don't know, what do you think?"

"What I think? Mom what I think, I think that if dad wasn't dead then hearing you talk like this would have killed him for sure."

"Oh, is that so," said April smiling at her son then continued with "and why is that?"

"I mean the whole idea of walking away is an attractive thought, I mean we could go on living, mansions come to mind, along with all the other perks that come with money. I love my Mustang; it has more value to me than the Ferrari that I dream about every so often. I said the thoughts are attractive but the reality of it all is that if Dad or Uncle Nigel would have been that selfish, then we would have been gone a long, long time ago. Yet this thing that we do, we haven't done this for 'us' in a long, long time. Sure it's a wicked occupation one that draws only the wicked and this is the true reasons to why we're here to begin with. These people, they will come this I know and they would pillage and loot this place that we've always called home. Then they will leave but not us, we don't pillage, us, we won't leave, us we have a strong desire to put back what we've abstracted. Because to leave would only mean that we allowed outsiders to walk in and treat our home like a public restroom and they will eat, as dad would say, without saying grace first." April looked at her son with pride, her smile was the giveaway, and so Juice continued with.

"You weren't thinking about leaving were you?"

"Not for a second, we here and we ain't going nowhere, but the thought of a mansion was nice, all the hired help, they will cook for us and open the doors and stuff."

"You cook just fine thank you."

"Nice come back, so what is it that you have for tomorrow?" Asked April,

"Well, I'm to the office to see what I could dig up on capital crimes considering that they are asking for the death penalty "remember"

"Well, right now this family needs a gator mouth to represent Nigel, and it just so happen that I know of a new attorney that I believe would be suitable for Nigel."

"Oh, yeah," Juice searched his mental Rolodex and couldn't think of anyone fool enough to represent Nigel.

"Yeah, she's awfully new at it, but I have a plan."

"She's awfully new? Who is it?"

"Later, so?"

"So, what?"

"So, are you?"

"Am I what?"

"Are you, Gator?"

"Sure, so what you want me to do? Go and spring Nigel, go in there and spit the benefits and get him up out of there is that it. Because if so, it's only one small problem with that, I am not an attorney."

"No, but Savanna is though."

"Savanna!" Juice snapped,

"Yeah.... Savanna, you remember her don't you?" Oh did he,

"Oh-kay, so you're gonna put Nigel's life in the hands of Savanna, and this is your plan?" This time Juice smiled because somehow he now had for confirmation that his dear momma has now flown over the cuckoo's nest for sure.

"Well, it's part of it, sounds silly but I don't see how the two of you couldn't pull it off. Both of you guys together has all the motivation in the world if not, then Nigel would surely die. No one would give this case the hundred percent that Nigel needs for this but you two. The girl called today and sounded wired up to go and get them. I figured to bring her in at Nigel's preliminary what you think?"

Chapter 35

Nigel laid on his bunk inside of a single man cell in the Sacramento County Main Jail, hardly able to believe the course of his day. Oh what a day, what a day, what a motha fucking day. Even though Nigel had a way of picking up intuition like an old married woman, but never did he see this kind of circus that was being put on anywhere in his near future. He pictured high speed chases but not this; he even pictured being shot two hundred and fifty times, but not this. There was no part of this day that he could actually believe now that he thought about it. He couldn't believe the handcuffs, the cops, the cameras or the allegations, what a motha fuckin' day.

"The best part of the day" by far was the single cell. First he was booked into the jail, fingerprinted and took some mug shot photos, then he was placed into these extra tiny cages that the Sheriff was constantly calling holding tanks. Here people slept on the floor, even though urine ran rampant through these boxes as if the floor was the new urinal. The dope fiends were plenty and no matter how high or drunk these other cons may have been, this whole ordeal was a very sobering experience and none of them was so disoriented that they could overlook the buzz that traveled throughout the cages. The mere mention of Raymond Buchannon being incarcerated was way more sobering than any of the rough realities that one may face by being locked away. Just to know that such a legend was amongst them was enough to snap anyone out of their drug induced or drunken stupors. Still in all the break came once the Sheriff's Deputy came to the final holding tank that Nigel would see and called for him,

"Nigel Collinson?"

"Right here sir." Nigel responded,

"Grab all of your items, roll them up and put them under your arm and bury your hands in your pants and come out of the tank and put your nose and feet up against the wall over here." Once Nigel was out of the tank the deputy began to call other names and instructed them to do the same thing. It was whispered around the tanks to never ever step outside of a tank without first burying your hands inside of your pants, saying that the deputies were always itching to "fuck somebody up" as they called it. Nigel may have been new to the system but his ears were very seasoned and the one thing that he knew for sure and that was good advice when he heard it. So, he was in compliance all the way up to the eighth floor and to intake where he would wait to be classified, even though it all seemed as if he had been classified already. I mean if being inside of an individual cell wasn't any indication then the fact that everyone else that road the elevator up with him had gone east while he went west sure gave him the impression that he had already been classified. Looking at the circus outside of the County Jail, reporters and camera crews, the citizens of Sacramento and other public officials, oh yeah, he was classified all right. Nigel also could take for an impression that the Lynch Mob was sure to show up and string his ass up guilty or not and to him that was classification like a motha fucka.

It took all of two minutes for Nigel to fall asleep. Once he got past the misfortune of such a day, fatigue had taken over him the rest of the way and he finished the day on fumes of anxiety until that was all spent. As soon as he was beginning to think that this was a bad dream or a foolish nightmare, he was awakened by the sounds of an official coming over a loudspeaker that Nigel had no idea was located anywhere in the room saying something about preparing for chow, Nigel spotted the speaker directly above the entrance of the cell. Seeing that the dawn was about to break, he guessed that for the first time in many years that he had slept past four a.m. Granted that this was also the first time in many years that he fell asleep in a state of depression too. He sourly welcomed the news of it being time for chow and to turn on the lights to receive such a meal.

Not only was Nigel "not" hungry, oh his appetite was destroyed a long, long time ago but Nigel had absolutely no idea of how to turn on his light. Yet, and still a sheriff came to unlock what have become known as his tray slot, which consisted of a hole in the door just wide enough and high enough to slide a tray through. Once the slot became open the upper tier which housed Nigel had come alive with groggy, whispered voices, some said,

"Hey Unc," some said "say O.G" and others saying "Say O.G you got to turn on your light if you want to eat." Nigel was clueless at first to any of these sayings because no one had summoned for him directly at least not until he heard.

"Say O.G in two twenty-one," now he knew what was going on because he knew exactly what cell he was occupying. He decided to roll off of his bunk and come to the hole in the door and be friendly by saying,

"What's up with you guys," the sound of this made the whole pod come to life, upper tier and lower tier, for each and every inmate held for a knowledge that the legendary "Raymond Buchannon's" luck had run out, and that they were all blessed enough to finally meet the man, the legend and now the inmate who have dominated the mean streets of Sacramento for so long. Nigel had become confused to the chatter that was aimed into his direction which was plentiful and simultaneous.

"Well hell, I don't know if I could answer all of those questions at the same time. So how about letting me ask a question," Nigel said.

"You want to know how to turn the light on huh?" Said one of the inmates,

"Yeah, how you know?" Nigel did not have a clue to whom he was speaking to but he sure liked a man that could put pieces together.

"Because, that was the first thing that I asked, at least you were sharp enough to want to know off the bat, I went to sleep for two days in a row with the lights bright. I was thinking that the police had to turn 'em off but check it out, follow your light all the way to the end of it. Do you see a button in the middle of it?"

"No, what button?"

"Then go the other way, closer to the bunk." Nigel done as instructed and was rewarded by the light illuminating the small cell. Filth was located everywhere. Graffiti was scrawled all over the wall, a lot of quotes from the bible in some places then gang related writings in others.

"Shit!" He was heard saying, to a round of laughter.

"It's heck of nasty in there huh?" Said the same inmate who took it upon himself to be the spokesperson for everyone else in the pod.

"Lord!"

"Well, we're gonna take that as a yeah," again laughter erupted.

"O.G you know what we all want to ask you right," this time it was another inmate coming from another direction.

"Little brother I don't have the slightest idea." Said Nigel,

"Well, before you came in they had all the televisions on so we could watch the death of a dynasty, and I'll swear to God you were on every channel."

"Is that right?" Nigel became interested.

"Yeah and there's a nasty rumor going on that says you're the man, I'm talking about the big man."

"Oh! Is that right?" Nigel let a smile crease his lips.

"Yeah, so are you?"

"Cat daddy, I don't know what you're talking about. All I know is that I was abducted by a whole bunch of white people and watched as they built a circus around me. Then I was shoved this way and that way until I ended up in this little box with the tricky lights," the pod erupted into a long series of laughter this time.

"O.G you're crazier than a motha fucka," said the young voice. Nigel watched as the sheriff deputy entered the pod followed by two trustees who pushed carts containing what Nigel suspected to be their "Chow" and dreaded every minute of it.

"Say two twenty-one?" Nigel returned back to the hole.

"Yeah what's up?" He said locating the sound to be someone next door to him.

"You see this cop, he's alright, if you want to clean your cell up he's the one to go through the other ones are ass holes for real," said Nigel's neighbor.

"Is that right?"

"Yeah, and by the sounds of things you may be in there for a mighty long time waiting to clear things up."

"I figured that much, so what do I have to tell him, that I want to clean my cell or something?"

"Yeah, and that you need some supplies to clean up with."

"I don't know about all of that, I mean if you've been watching the television as the young man says over that-a-way then you would know that these dudes think that I done some awfully terrible things you know, to a police Captain... you know what I mean?"

"Yeah, I'm hipped. They also say that you done made a billion dollars in one year."

"Boy, they exaggerate a whole lot."

"Well, I don't think it'll hurt to ask. The only thing that they could ever say is yes or no, I mean I could ask for you and probably get it for you, but how many times are you gonna need me to do that though?"

"I'm knowing, hold up, excuse me officer," Nigel yelled through the slot.

"Who is that?" Screamed the officer,

"I'm in two twenty-one." The officer looked towards Nigel then took to the stairs and to Nigel's surprise the officer was polite in speaking when he said,

"How could I help you Mr. Collinson?"

"Sir, if it's not too much to ask I would like some cleaning supplies, it's horrible in here," again to Nigel's surprise the deputy said,

"What would you like?"

"I would like to do the toilet, the floor, the sink and would love to do these walls. Perhaps disinfectants, comet, well anything would work if it's not too much."

"Ahh nah, no problem, you want all of this in this hour, normally everyone else goes back sleep after chow."

"I don't see me able to sleep no time soon." The officer thought then said,

"I wouldn't reckon so. I'll have one of my workers bring it right on up after chow; I don't reckon that you have much of an appetite either do you?"

"Not at all,"

"Normally only a few people could come in and eat right away but I'm gonna tell you, you have to eat something." The officer was kind, but Nigel became really skeptical upon hearing the officer pursue with his good will.

"Ahh, I know what you're thinking," said the officer then, "To me every one is innocent until the courts prove otherwise and even that has nothing to do with me that's between you and God." Nigel and the deputy locked stares. Nigel was able to read sincerity in the eyes of the deputy; a mutual respect was formed. No more words were needed to be spoken. The deputy took a couple of grievances from another inmate then he headed towards the stairs and to the lower tier to field other grievances from the unit below while the trustees had gone from cell to cell fulfilling their duties of passing out the breakfast trays.

"See, I told you that he was alright," Nigel's neighbor was once again at the slot in time to receive his tray.

"Yes, you sure did, say you want another tray though?" Nigel asked his neighbor.

"I would say yes, but you should listen to the man and try to eat what you can. You would find that the food isn't all that bad here. I mean I've been to some places where it was the worst, besides lunch won't be until later on in the afternoon and even a stress diet would have worn off by then, trust me."

"Hmm, if you say so, but now if you change your mind get at me."

"Yeah, and if you change your mind by not letting this situation get the best of you then sit down and eat and thank God that you still stand a fighting chance, by the way I'm Ali." Nigel's neighbor stuck his hand through the slot to offer Nigel a companion.

After a short spell, Nigel had taken Ali's hand and the two shook. Ali had drawn into his cell and Nigel into his where he had sat and forced himself to eat the cold pancakes and oatmeal. He drank the warm milk while given into Ali's words that carried a lot of weight. So Nigel had vowed over a spoonful of bland oatmeal that he would not under any circumstances let this situation or any other one for that matter ever get the best of him. So, instead of anxiety of the situation he was grateful that coffee had come with his not so tasty meal. Instead of reminding himself that he was in a lot of troubles he would assure himself that the great city of Sacramento has built a circus around him filled with empty hopes of killing him, a case built on supposition and speculations under which or either, provides not the comforts of stability. For he knew that there was a plan in the making and that the only way that this plan would draw a successful conclusion is if the puppeteer in this matter would have the powerful means of political supports as well as inside information.

Yet and still, even with such connections the government would or could in this case, still fall a little short of convicting him unless this game played out in some bizarre twist of fate. Nigel really couldn't see where he would be found guilty of being a person that he knew for sure that he wasn't. Noting that his enemy was clever, artful and imaginative and through this adroit sophistication, and all the buzz created that has only proven to be none more than smoke and mirrors. A direction full of misconception, a direction that at the moment was unseen to the puppets. If one should peer through the smoke they would indeed be revealed the obvious, and Nigel recalled explaining this much to April.

Although his teachings were rushed and accelerated Nigel was dwelling in the comforts of knowing that April was a fast learner and once she said, "she got it" then he never needed to worry anymore after that. He was not gonna pick this troubled moment to carry doubt in the person that he knew for sure that he could trust with his life and all of his properties. So engrossed was Nigel into his thoughts that he barely heard when the trustee said,

"Here goes your supplies, once you're finished eating push the button and they will pop your door so you could get them, once you're finished push your button and set them outside of the door and I will come around and pick them up." Nigel heard everything that the trustee had said but didn't know if he should try a conversation with anyone that worked so close to the police, he nodded his understanding and pressed the button.

It was day break the time Nigel finished cleaning his cell, his finished product was a very clean and sterilized cell. He felt a sense of pride in his work, he was able to sit and allow his thoughts to prevail, which was all one could ask for and right before his thoughts could go anywhere past pressing the button to return his borrowed supplies. The deputy had come over the intercom and said,

"Collinson, get fully dressed and come to control for a social visit."

"Yes sir," Nigel said to the police then he had gone to the door and said, "Ali…" then again "Ali"

"What's up brother?" Ali said.

"They need me to go to control for a visit."

"Oh-kay, then go."

"Where is control at though?"

"Oh, look down there, see where it's a door and an all-white wall, but if you look up top you'll see hella windows, well behind those windows is hella police, and that there fella, is control."

"Thank you, sorry if I woke you."

"Oh, no, no, no, once I get up, I'm up."

"Right on."

"Yeah, have a good visit."

"So, I just push the button right?"

"Yeah, just press the button," and Nigel had done exactly that, only to hear.

"So what's your medical emergency?"

"Ahh, I don't need medical, you told me to come to control and ahh, I got to return these supplies and ahh, how do I do all of this?"

"Listen, don't press my fucking button unless your cellmate is beating your ass or you have a medical emergency." Then the last that Nigel heard was the speaker pop.

"Hmm, I guess I just got hung up on," Nigel soliloquized.

"What you say? Are you disrespecting staff? Keep that shit up and I'll cancel your visit right now." Though Nigel was taken aback, he knew better than to say anything further and concluded that this must have been one of the ass hole cops that was hid behind the windows.

After thirty additional minutes of waiting Nigel climbed the stairs to find a very agitated April sitting on the other side of the window holding a phone in her hand. Nigel took his seat across from her and reached for the receiver that would grant him access to April, the one true friend that Nigel would hold as a life line to the free word. He spoke into the receiver.

"So, how are you?" He smiled.

"I'm oh-kay, although that was the question that I held for you. How are you holding up Nigel?" She asked looking for signs of strength while wondering if his situation has broken him even if just a little bit.

"I'm holding up oh-kay, I got a lot of friends already and I just got up here. They say that I needed to be classified, but I have the feeling that I've already been classified. I'm saying everybody that I caught the elevator with all went right, but I'm the only one that went to the left, if that means anything.

"Sounds like it to me, have you been watching any television?" April asked.

"Not at all, but I heard about it, it was my first time ever on TV, so?"

"So? So what?"

"So, how did I look?"

"You looked over weight."

"Hmm, maybe I'll buff up now that I'm here, you know, maybe work out little bit and get me some muscles or something."

"I think I heard you say that before."

"Is that so?"

"I'm sure of it, last time when your back went out, remember?"

"Oh yeah, I done a few jumping jacks and a couple of those sit ups, and a push up"

"Yeah that was last year some time wasn't it? I don't know the real way to work out, but I think you got to be a little more consistent than that."

"Maybe twice a year or three times you think?"

"Yeah, that's what I'm thinking but I think the laws are three times a week though."

"Oh, speaking of laws, do you know that I just got cussed out by one of these officers just a minute ago. The only reason why I didn't say anything was because he threatened to cancel this visit. You know what bothered me the most, this little fucker was probably no older than twenty-two, twenty- three."

"Well, this is they house Nigel, let them have they house, but what you can't do is get any visits canceled we have a lot of fighting to do and I need your help as much as you need mine you hear, now let's talk business."

"My favorite subject, only I need you to remember …"

"I know" April interjected, Nigel nodded then said,

"So, is there anything new?"

"Yeah, I got some news for you, I don't know yet if it's good news or bad news, but you may as well know today considering that you go to court tomorrow."

"Let me guess, Dixon's has backed out?" April nodded in affirmative not quite knowing how she was gonna put it to him, wasn't nearly as surprised by Nigel's guess work.

"Nah, nah. Mah that's not bad news at all, in fact it's the contrary. That's the best news so far." Nigel knew that April was lost on his meanings by the expressions that she gave of confusion, but he also knew that he wasn't in liberty to discuss any of his assumptions over the phone that the two had to speak through for he knew that everything from now on would be recorded and used against him, he just said.

"Don't worry right now, you'll get it after a while but humor me by telling me how did you find out that they were backing out, I mean how did they break it to you?"

"Called this morning they said to tell you that they send their best wishes and all the luck, but everyone in the firm has their hands tied on this one, a bunch of bad publicity on this one," she shook her head.

"Ooh, so what happened to every member of society having a constitutional right to be represented by counsel and all that shit?"

"Oh, they said that too, don't worry I got you though,"

"The kid right?"

"Yeah, don't worry."

"Ahh, throw him to the wolves huh," Nigel smiled.

"Yeah,"

"Well, you know what they say, the best way to teach 'em how to swim... is to throw 'em in the water and tell him to kick his legs. Survival is always the best motivation in the world."

"That was the other thing that they said."

"What's that?"

"Considering that the district attorney is going for Capital Punishment that Juice would be highly motivated to fight for you is what they said but we already knew that though."

"Capital Punishment, what the hell do that mean?"

"Uh uh, you know what it means... you didn't know that?"

"Know what?"

"That the DA was going for all the marbles?"

"Hell nah, for all the marbles! Shit! All the marbles?"

"Yeah,"

"How you know?"

"That's all the television has to say, you should see 'em they got all of these analyst of this kind of law and of that kind. Speaking about each different scenario to how a trial could play out."

"Is that right?"

"Mm hmm, some say that you should ask for a change of venue, some say the fact that this case has an omnipresence allure to it that it wouldn't matter where the trial was held at. Some say that it'll be hard to establish the likes of a fair trial anywhere, for it would be awfully hard to find anyone anywhere who hasn't heard of this case, nor has formed an opinion this way or that way."

"Whoa! And what do you think?"

"I haven't decided."

"Does the kid know that they are shooting for the needle?"

"Yeah, he was the first one to tell me."

"Did he appear to be nervous?"

"Not even a little bit, he's only playing paralegal on this one, Savanna will take the seat with you at preliminary."

"Oh, is she shaken?"

"Nuh uh"

"And if she appeared to be shaken."

"I would have gone out and hired the best."

"But"

"I believe in them."

"Then so do I, now tell me, how far did you get through your assignments," Nigel chose his words carefully.

"Not that far, I needed to know the mindset of 'the kid' as you call him. I mean tomorrow at one thirty you're in department sixty-three and I'm warning you right now to expect a large turnout, and to ask for an attorney."

"Oh-kay, and thanks for telling me. I'll suck in my stomach this time."

"Good luck with that."

"All right, you have a lot of work to do, trust me you have all the answers, just be yourself all right, and that's enough for me."

"We're gonna make it through, yeah?"

"Yeah, right now we're just the puppets, somebody got the strings." April nodded her understandings as Nigel stood to leave, April watched as the man that she has come to call her brother on every aspect of kinship had walked down the stairs. His head was held high, his posture held confidence for she knew that if Nigel had nothing else, that he still had his pride.

Chapter 36

For a Steak House Ju -Ju's was listed as one of the top, if not the top places to grab a nice juicy T-bone or a New Yorker in all of Sacramento. The environment was that of a happening place to eat because in the afternoons Ju-Ju's held a happy hour where drinks became discounted which meant that the patrons flocked in to enjoy a nice meal and a drink. This was one of the few places where reservation was indeed necessary any time after one o'clock p.m. The Jukebox was an antique, it held a lot of classic hits and a lot of up to date tunes but mostly oldies found its way out of the speakers. Ju-Ju's designs gave one a classy, down home, backwoods type of feel that brought people enjoyment on its own. The wood chips scattered over the floor gave Ju-Ju's its very own personality and one that Savanna had taken a real genuine liking to. Her discounted Sherries were rolling in as she took on the chef's salad while she awaited her sirloin, baked potato and rice pilaf dish that the waiter swore was the best in town. In the event that the waiter was exaggerating a bit the atmosphere made up for any shortcomings that a meal may have. When her meal finally arrived it was hard to tell if the world had a better steak but she knew for sure that Sacramento didn't. What she needed to do was find the owner and thank him personally for such a fine meal. Savanna waved to the waitress and after getting her attention waited until the lady made her way through the heavy traffic before stopping at the table in front of Savanna, and said.

"Are you all done here?"

"Yes ma'am this was indeed one of the better places that I've come to eat. The environment is awesome."

"Well, nice that you like it, how may I help you?"

"Well, first I got a tip for you, and may I ask you to help me reach the owner? You see I come all the way from Modesto California just to see this place, now I need to know who put this place together. Modesto has nothing even close to this." Savanna finished handing the girl a twenty for a tip and also the coverage for the ticket. She had run a nice tab on Sherries and meals considering that she also ordered the Cajun craw-fish basket.

"Well, right now he is entertaining company, sorry."

"Oh, is that so." Savanna looked around as if trying to locate the owner, clueless she said, "Which one is he?"

"He's the handsome brother in the corner over there." The waitress pointed in the direction of the booth seats. This booth took the shape of a horse shoe, were seated right in the middle of such a shape was the brother of question. He sat quietly, surrounded by a group of Mexicans that were in a heated and concentrated conversation, a very animated assembly was taking place there.

"Ooh, you're right, he is handsome."

"Yes, he is, can I interest you with dessert? We have a nice cobbler, world renown."

"Oh, are you sure? I mean I wouldn't want to miss the opportunity of such a treat but I recommend that I get that to go. Because I fear that it'll just go straight to my hips." The two shared a laugh forming a sisterhood.

"That it will do, lord knows I done had my share of it, don't worry about the cost I'll fix you up some on the house."

"Oh, thank you, in that case I really would love some and another Sherry, please."

"Coming right up,"

The waitress weaved her way through the diner until she was in the back and out of sight giving Savanna a chance to retrieve her powerful ten-pixel digital camera and sneak a few shots here and there until she had zoomed in on the conference that was going on at the back table. As a throw off she snapped pictures of the bar then the rest of the diner. Then back to the conference table. Only this time, the owner of the diner was not present in the meeting. This threw Savanna for a loop, for she hadn't the slightest idea of where could the brother had disappeared to, at least not until he showed up at her table.

"Hello," came a masculine voice that frightened Savanna for a moment.

"Oh my God, you scared the mess out of me." Savanna said buying time to get herself together.

"My apologies, is there anything that I could help you with?" Julius remained forever the gentleman though he was curious.

"Well, all of that…" Savanna was interrupted by the waitress.

"Oh, I see that you found him. Here you go, I got one Sherry and a cobbler to go, already bought and already paid for." The waitress showed in time to bail Savanna out.

"Thank you very much, yes I did find ahh, him thank you."

"Julius, my name is Julius and you were looking for me? How may I help you?"

"First I wanted to thank you for providing one of the finer meals and one of the better atmospheres to have such a meal."

"Well, you're welcome; I noticed that you needed pictures."

"Yes, it is my intention to one day be your competition. I wanted to study your setup so I could one up you."

"Hah, so, you like this place is that it?"

"I do"

"And you want to top the way I put this place together you say?" Julius smiled to Savanna, for he loved the young lady for her casual dress and her smile, her eyes were killing him soft noticing that they were pools that anyone could swim in.

"I do," she said smiling along with him giving him her sixty-watt appeal. If he kept talking and giving up more and more she was sure to send him her knock dead gorgeous hundred and fifty-watt charmers.

"There's nothing wrong with competition hell, competition runs the world these days, where do you plan to open up at?"

"Wouldn't you like to know?" Now the ninety watts,

"Ahh, playing it close to chest huh, I could understand that, but tell me, how would you like to run me all the way out of business though?" Savanna looked into Julius's eyes trying her best to read them for clues, decided to play along with him by saying.

"I would love to put you all the way out of business," what Julius didn't know, nor could he had any way of knowing, was that Savanna spoke words which carried a double meaning, and the smile that he liked so much on this young lady had he been paying attention he would of swore that it was the same smile that one could easily find on a Boa Constrictor. The facts were, that he wasn't paying attention to anything but his 'right now's' he had his connections in the rear of the cafe, in front of him was a potential buyer, who by the way had the presence of a runway model and in the event that he played his cards right, which if you let him tell it he's been known to do, then a whole new world would open up to him and he knew it.

"Well putting me out of business isn't that hard to do. You see, I'm selling this place, I'm opting out because I feel that my fate lies elsewhere." He said.

"Oh, is that so. So, you're willing to chicken out and leave the steaks up to me, huh. Whatever happened to a little bit of competition running the world?"

"I still believe in that, and hopefully this will remain a Steak House, perhaps the new owners wouldn't change a thing."

"If I owned it I wouldn't touch or rearrange a thing, it's the best."

"Well, maybe you should be the one to buy this place. You would then have no competition at all, trust me? The cooks are extraordinary; the customers are loyal and always hungry. The location has been selected to perfection, no one could ask for more than that."

"You're serious aren't you?"

"Yes, I'm very serious."

"So, are those guys over there potentials or what?" Savanna nodded towards the impatiently waiting group of Spanish speakers. Julius followed her towards his guest then chuckled and said,

"Not at all, if they were to buy I'm oh so sure that this wouldn't be a Steak House long after."

"When are you planning to go public with the announcements?" Asked Savanna playing her part to the max,

"Pretty soon, pretty soon,"

"Well, I love the place; I would like to know your asking price."

"I'm going three quarters of a million. Which means that I'm parting with all the inventory, the building I own all rights to, the place always turns profit, so."

"Three quarters, huh?"

"For openers, unless I somehow I get an offer for a quick sell then I may consider other bids."

"And you're giving me first dibs is that it?"

"Why not, no one has ever come in here in love with the designs or the structure of this place, always the food and the atmosphere, but as an owner one would only wish to have its patrons take on the whole vision, you know, as you have."

"Oh, well how about giving me your card and perhaps I'll have my people get in touch with your people."

"Right, and we'll do lunch. Hold a minute and I'll return shortly." Savanna watched as Julius gone to the back of the cafe and returned waving a card saying,

"Here you are Ms...."

"Freeman, Tanisha Freeman," Savanna reached to accept the card from Julius then continued with "again thank you for such a lovely evening."

"Oh no, Ms. Freeman the pleasure was all mines." The two shook hands and Savanna watched as Julius returned to his guest. To herself she said 'Chile I wish I could afford this place,' before collecting her possessions and heading out to her rental. She removed her camera from her purse and shuffled through the portraits, erasing the images that held little or no use to her. Completing this task to satisfaction, and preparing herself to leave before she noticed that the party of Spanish speakers were making their exits. "Hmm what is this" Savanna whispered as she saw an SUV pull into the lot. She only gave the driver her attention because everyone else in the lot was offering theirs. She was watching as rounds of handshakes took place. Savanna decided to snap pictures of this exchange as well before starting the car to leave.

Juice had made his way to the Sacramento County Main Jail after leaving the Law Offices of Dixon, Juan and Dixon, a place that boasted an interior library that took years to build. Their books were advanced knowledge and up to date, and their technologies were also top rated. Juice needed a break after pulling hours and hours of research. He couldn't think of another place that he'd rather be than at the jail, so, to the jail he'd gone.

Juice registered to visit Nigel, this way he could see the old man that has become the only living uncle figure in his life. He thought to support him before going into court. Juice saw Nigel climb the stairs towards the visiting room then take his seat and picked up the phone.

"Wow, uncle you look like you've been woke since the last time I saw you. What was that three days ago?"

"Yeah, where the hell you been?"

"I went on a date; if you remember right my personal life sucks."

"Your personal life?" Nigel couldn't believe what he was hearing.

"Heck yeah, I spent the night with Savanna, oh my goodness, I found heaven I tell you it's pure bliss... heaven I say."

"Heaven, huh,"

"Yes."

"Personal life you say?"

"Mm hmm"

"So, let me ask, what have you been doing you know, about ahh, me? I mean if you haven't noticed on your own let me tell you, my personal life is pretty messed up too. I mean I think it sucks. I got problems all over the place."

"Oh yeah, I see that, man I noticed that you have a lot of people out there with red eyes for you, my goodness."

"Yeah,"

"Everybody out there wants blood and they want it right now."

"Shit, your mother said it was gonna be a large turnout."

"Yeah, it was large the first time I came up here to register then it became standing room only, now it's a whole sea of people out there. There's all kinds of agents out there. It looks like they are expecting a jail break or something.'"

"Oh-kay, so what are we doing, what do we got?"

"Uncle Nigel, have you ever been to an arraignment?"

"If I have I don't remember what the hell transpired, but I'm not supposed to you're the lawyer, so you tell me."

"Well, we're gonna walk in there and tell the good people of Sacramento that you're innocent and we're gonna walk out of there." Nigel scanned Juice's face, looking for the punch line then said,

"You're playing right?"

"About the last part, yes."

"We'll, see if we could take it easy on the games. Maybe we could know a strategy here pretty soon."

"We got a strategy," said Juice taking on the necessary seriousness,

"Oh, we do?"

"Yeah, what you think I am? I'm your fucking lawyer, your attorney at law, well sort of you know."

"Ooh, how that makes me happy."

"And it should" Nigel and Juice stared into the eyes of one another. Each one with a large respect for the next, it was Nigel that broke eye contact and said,

"So,"

"So what, you mean the strategy?" Nigel nodded his response and Juice continued "First my strategy was to get on your nerves a bit, maybe distract you from the "right now," being that our right now's, as you say sucks. Nothing happens right now, we'll go in there and let them know that you are gonna need representation, go on record with that, they would like to know how you plead and you'll say not guilty then ask for a bail, but I assure you that they will shoot it down."

"Why is that?"

"No judge anywhere would want to be known for granting a bail in a Capital Case."

"So, they deny bail."

"Right, then we'll push for a speedy trial, we'll come to preliminary to relieve your present public defender and whatever you do don't wave preliminary"

"No?"

"Let's get it all first."

"Oh-kay,"

"Besides, no matter who's over there they are gonna bound you over for trial no matter what happens. I mean if you just wanted to rattle a few cages you could wave your preliminary if you like, not that I think the DA would second that. Now like I say, I was with Savanna all night last night. She's gonna take to the table with you, but for the most part..." Juice shrugged his shoulders as if saying anything after that, foul or whatever, was and would be admissible.

"Do we have an idea of which cages to shake up though?" Asked Nigel after taking in Juices words,

"Yelp," Juice said allowing Nigel to know that everyone was on the same page with their assignments. "Savanna, huh?" Asked Nigel,

"Yeah, I mean all I could do is her errands and research, plus I'll help write her briefs and bring you some visits, but that's as far as it goes for me I'm corporate…. remember?"

"Yeah, and may I wish you all the success in the world starting from this case here, huh kid."

"If you say so,"

"Well, shit what are we waiting for, let's go get 'em," for an answer Juice reached into his coat pocket and retrieved an envelope and fished through the contents, stopping only when Nigel needed to see more of the photos that Juice displayed. It was Nigel's smile that troubled Juice the most.

"What the hell's so funny?" He asked.

"Savanna huh?" Nigel mumbled and Juice nodded, then Nigel said, "Oh, now I remember her, cute little number, is this the same one that had you so open that I had to stop you from you crying that one time? How'd you guy's team up?"

"What… anyways yeah, she's the same one though pretty smart too, if it'll help any."

"So, I got two rookies coming to my aid?"

"Yelp, the damned cape crusaders."

"But these pictures were a good move if I don't say so myself, pretty good," Nigel said.

"Wait until you read her report."

"Where is that… her report?"

"I'll have it for you in time for preliminary."

"Oh-kay, could you send me the photos though?"

"Not at all, sending them is pretty reckless but I'll remind Savanna to give them to you pretty soon. I mean, I don't need them, they make me sick anyways."

"Does your mother know anything about those?"

"Yeah, she knows everything. Right now she's stuck behind her computer getting ready to dispatch while she putting all the pieces together. So, you basically have two rookies and a dictatorship."

"Oh… then in that case we may have a shot then, huh?"

"Mm hmm, but now we'll see you when you come up."

Chapter 37

Juice, April and Savanna sat in the rear row of the courtroom. There they watched the courtroom come to life. There was already a buzz going on, but this new sound was more than recognizable. Police filled the room and sealed off every exit as if they 'were' indeed expecting a jailbreak attempt. The press was then allowed inside to set up their equipment. So there was no secret that the moment that everyone was waiting for has now come. Juice saw as the bailiff pressed the button then saw as Nigel stepped through the door. He heard how the court room came to life then again the bailiff said,

"This is case number 07433774; here in attendance is Nigel Collinson."

"Nigel Collinson is that your true name?" Asked the judge,

"Yes ma'am," said Nigel.

"You are being arraigned today on murder which totals forty-seven counts…. that we know of so far. You are being charged with drug trafficking and running a criminal operation, which both made and laundered money through legal activities. Which means that the RICO act applies to you, for those of you in attendance who does not know what the RICO Act is; I'll explain its definition. "Racketeering Influenced Corrupt Organization," for Mr. Collinson is being believed to have run a very dangerous and seriously lucrative criminal enterprise and for this, Mr. Collinson I must ask you do you have an attorney?"

"No ma'am, can't afford one yet."

"We'll go on record to admit a representative for Mr. Collinson. After hearing these charges Mr. Collinson how do you plea?" Asked the judge,

"Your Honor I am not guilty and at this moment I'd like to go on record to push for the earliest trial date available." The crowds buzz took on a new life. The judge asked for order and it took a while for the audience to comprehend the judge's request.

"Mr. Collinson is you asking that the court grant you a speedy trial?"

"Yes and your honor it is my wish for you to also grant me the rights to wave my preliminary hearing." Oh, at first the audience had a buzz to it but now pandemonium better described the courtroom this time for no one in the whole United States of America had anticipated these maneuvers. Not even the District Attorney, but as Juice said they may as well rattle a few cages so when the judge asked the people rather they object or not Nigel could of swore that he heard the District Attorney say 'shit yeah', but for the benefit of the courtroom the DA regrouped and said,

"Yes, the people object."

"And so do I," said the judge. Well, we will see you guys back here in let's say, a week. We'll go on the calendar at 8:30. That's next Thursday Mr. Collinson, see you then sir."

"Yes, ma'am," was Nigel's last words before heading back through the doors from which he'd come and only then were anyone permitted to leave the courtroom.

Julius sat behind his desk going over and studying professional testimonies, he was sure to soon be in court to testify against his former business partner. With him was Jessica, the true professional snitch who had already testified on many occasions before receiving the benefits of being labeled a confidential informant. Everyone knew that in this case somebody would have to testify before the court but Jessica, now she was different. She knew how to really sink a battle ship and get away with it, she already told them that she would clam up unless she was indeed protected to the highest degree of being protected. So, in this case the District Attorney, the one Mr. Mathew Donaldson would fix for the benefit of the court and the rights of the defendant, equipment that would protect the witnesses first and foremost which would then allow the one Mr. Nigel Collinson the right to face and hear testimony of his accusers.

Now the equipment of question was a forty-six-inch monitor that the courts would view as the confidential informer gave testimony from the judge's chambers by speaking into a microphone while facing a camera. This would give her the reporting live via satellite look, which for her has proven to be awfully effective. Time and time again, had she sunk many people in her career of being a hired gun for the District Attorney office in this fashion. Even though she was never hired by any particular District Attorney, they were always glad to see her coming. With her they were sure a victory and this case was and would be the victory of all victories. None would be a more celebrated victory more than this one and everyone knew it. No case was as significant as this case and this was known from the back alleys of Cancun, Mexico to the front office of the Nation's Capital and all of the in between. Even most of the outskirts were all tuned into case number 07433774, of the Sacramento Superior Court.

So together the two sat in the back office of Julius's Steak House and studied together while they waited for the third member of their plot to ruin Nigel, which was another professional who had traveled to forty-five different countries doing dirty works like this. One could see upon first impression that Roberto was a hard case that once worked as a contractor, a very private one. In some places they called him

'Bodies'. In others they called him 'The Grim Reaper' because he was a freelance contract killer. To his credit he has worked for cartels all over the world, one crime boss after the next or whoever could afford his asking price. Rich husbands would call upon his services and gladly pay his asking price to rid them of the headaches brought on by a divorce or even just to collect on the insurance was enough of a reason to come in contact with Roberto. Then the crazy things began to happen, time passed by and more and more laws had come into play.

The laws became stricter and because of this a lot of crime bosses grew scared, and they grew soft. The codes of silence, has long been compromised and Omerta had grew to be none other than just a fancy little saying that carried absolutely no meaning at all. So, because of this a lot of people struck deals. Bosses struck deals, Capos struck deals, and soldiers struck deals. So the empires grew weaker and weaker by the minutes. There was no room for the freelancers because they had belonged to none of the factions whatsoever, and this allowed them to become the easy targets for the fibbies. These new bosses were sacrificing their contacts in exchange for smaller sentences. Roberto had got the wind of these exchanges and struck a deal to wear a wire and approach these bosses, which he did with a sense of pride, knowing that the courts passed such a law to get the bosses to begin with. They were interested in the big fishes not the ones they employed. The same bosses, the very ones who would pay for his works saw as he struck such a deal to see thirteen murder charges go away in the best way that the courts could afford. Reduce each charge to manslaughter, involuntary manslaughter, and ran each charge concurrently with the next. Roberto "AKA" Bodies and Grim Reaper had discovered another way to kill, by using his testimonies to rid the United States of corruption if you let them tell it. What no one knew was that Roberto still worked in the underworld. He still accepted payments from bosses, who found ways to utilize his new services. It was funky, but it was fair. It was cold, but it was real. It was dangerous, but so what. The bosses were now scary and soft, he had never feared anyone that would rather pay him a quarter of a million dollars to do what they could've easily done themselves, and saved their money.

While Jessica and Julius waited on Roberto, Julius found reason to reflect back to the days before. The young lady sat at her table alone, took her drinks alone, spoke with such a rhythm and what a joyous melody it was. Her eyes were so captivating. Secretly he wished he would have asked for her number, maybe even asked her out. Although, he was up in age Lord knew that a younger woman was all he desired. One that made him happy to be alive each time he saw her face. In his bones he knew that this woman, Tanisha she called herself, was the perfect one for the job of fulfilling his days with gratitude and happiness. The fact that she hadn't contacted him yet didn't play such a major part, for he knew that the purchase of a business took time. He knew also that if and had he did somehow get the chance to hear from her he was gonna approach his lonely situation with a suitable solution and a very beautiful one at that. First, he was gonna give her the opportunity to raise the three quarters because to rid himself of any ties that he had to Sacramento was indeed job one. His new plans were to reach outside in, and not inside out. He knew also that after this game played out that his survival would depend a whole lot on his strategies to hit and run, and not to be driven by his lust or yearn to sex one of the most beautiful women that he's encountered in a long time.

"So," said Jessica interrupting Julius' temporary escape, bringing his mental flight down to a crash landing.

"So?" He asked, confused to what she was talking about.

"Did you hear anything that I was saying?" She asked,

"Not anything before, so."

"Oh-kay, I need a drink, you care for one?" Jessica asked standing to make her way to the bar.

"No, does this mean that you're not going to tell me what it was that you we're talking about?"

"I only asked if you trusted all of this."

"Hmm, I don't know what about you?"

"I never trust all of it, but I don't have to because I'm a little less manual than you are, I'm going to tell my story and they'll sneak me out the back door. My payments are already in the bank not so for you is why I ask."

"Hmm, I've been thinking hard about it. I just can't see why the ceiling would fall now. I mean this late in the game?"

"Oh-kay, so no to the drink then?"

"Wait a minute, you sound skeptical."

"I'm always skeptical which is the reason that I ask for mines up front, also why I'm always so scared to talk in front of courts. So, now they hide me close to the back door so I could make my escape with ease, shoot, tell me that ain't skeptical."

"And you figure that I should be, you know, skeptical?"

"Hell yeah,"

"Maybe I should be then," Julius gave her a smile that would assure a lesser person that he was just fine, but Jessica knew better. This was not her first time being involved in such a scheme to crumble the ones who were in the way of a new take over. Another takeover, this was the main reason such a scheme was being plotted against one of the biggest players that Jessica ever stood to deliver practiced testimony against. A tactic that has always crumbled everyone on her list so far and she didn't see a viable reason why this time would be any different.

"Yeah, I think you should, still all of this is up to you. If you like it then I love it." With that Jessica walked out of the office and headed to the bar to retrieve the drink that she so much desired. In her absence Julius gave her words some genuine thought. He bounced in and out of recollections, trying to locate a reason to withdraw even though he had already committed himself to such a dirty plot. Such a plan that could either get him killed or makes him very, very rich. Which was the only thing that his life consisted of, either he'd have it all or move him out of the way and send him on to the next level, whichever way life had brought it. He thought of the lady who came in just the other day, couldn't quite get her off of his mind as a matter of fact. If she could afford to buy a restaurant, then she must come from money and wouldn't be all the way dependent on him or his dough, like so many other women.

As fate had it, and only if he had really known Savanna, then all of those beautiful thoughts that he held precious and dear to heart would have been sure to get erased, oh yeah, right along with all of his other sweet amiable fantasies of bedding her. He would have kicked out every dream of the two of them together, and in exchange he was sure to seek and find a blunt object that would later be identified as a murder weapon had he really known her. Had he known that just right outside of his precious little establishment was a Pontiac Grand AM pointed in the direction of the Steak House, and have been there ever since he opened the doors that morning. If he would've known that, inside of the vehicle that sat his dream was a file being created to destroy him, oh how he would have killed her. If he had only known that she was snapping picture after picture, each time she saw his face, and of each greeting, each handshake, oh was he sure to find a name that would better fit her. I mean, had he known that in her glove box sat a check for a half a million dollars, money that she was gonna use to purchase his company and for the very same individual that he was attempting to bury. Oh how would he have found a name for her, 'Bitch' comes to mind at the thought of his red hot anger. 'Scoundrel' wouldn't have been far off either and 'whore' was sure to run a close second. Sanguinity or any other one of his lustful visions would have been replaced with umbrage forcing Julius to live the life of a misogynist and nothing else. Savanna snapped pictures of each and every smoke break that Julius had taken with his lady friend, a dame that he spent an ample amount of time with, one who brought curiosity the moment that Savanna saw her.

Savanna picked up the very sinister looking Mexican man and again snapped a round of photos for she had taken a genuine interest in the strange man as well. From earlier rounds of photos, she came to believe that his presence to be one of detriment. Seeing that she had captured enough footage she decided to head to the convenient store that provided her film developing within the hour. Considering that she had nearly two hundred shots, she figured to drop off her memory card and then head to the law offices of Dixon, Juan and Dixon and this is where she would spend most of her evening. When she had become hired by the Raymond's she had no idea to what she would be looking for. All that Juice gave her for intelligence was that his uncle was a very important man. Not necessarily saying how, but she had her theories, her speculations. Thinking back to the day that she met Dominic she had felt a vibration from him, one that spoke street but she had absolutely no idea to what degree. Hearing allegations placed on his uncle spoke volumes, but to hear Juice say,

"There is a frame up being orchestrated and we need to find the director. Mommy in order for you to locate any of this you must first believe that everything which has transpired so far is only a play." He told her. Savanna remembered all of this all so well, and she heard all of this while lying on top of Juice, both of them nude and spent, and both of them vowing to never allow circumstances to separate them again no matter how hard any of them shall work or even study. There's a reason for everything and always will be and their lives were no different, he was her reason and she was his.

Savanna found her parking spot deep in the lot and sat waiting and looking anticipating the activities of Chase the attorney that Juice had identified in one set of pictures that Savanna had produced. He had recognized him immediately and smiled once he put the backgrounds together with the company. "So chase is hanging out in the slums." Meaning with Julius,

"Chase?" Savanna asked "who's Chase" and for a response Juice showed her the picture and tapped on the person for Savanna could get a visual of the attorney of question.

"Who are the other guys, you know any of them?" She asked. She had searched her memory and if it served her correctly she could recall seeing this man Chase stepping down from a truck and become chummy with the rest of the lot. Yeah, she was certain that they were all acquainted.

"Uh uh, I barely know Chase, I mean from what I've learned is that he's moving up the ladder towards being a partner thanks to the elder Dixon."

"Do, you think Nigel might know them?" She asked.

"I don't know, maybe."

"Hmm,"

"What is it Mah, you feel something with all of them."

"Yeah, I do."

"Then do your shit, I'm with you." Pleased to know that Juice held her in such a high esteem, he always knew that Savanna performed with confidence and enthusiasm, and this day was no different. So on this day as in the past week Savanna played both sides, the only connection that made sense so far was that this law firm was in cahoots with that Steak House, which was why she was parked just three rows down from the very same truck that she saw Chase arrive in and depart from the very same place to cop a nice steak. She was beginning to grow bored, stakeouts as she learned could provide a monotonous way to spend a day, but the moment, just right before she was preparing to abort her mission, Savanna picked up a very, very peculiar and important piece to their already bizarre and mysterious puzzle.

"Oh-kay, what do we have here now," Savanna soliloquized, retrieving her high powered Fuji film digital camera and loading up a new memory chip just in time for her to begin snapping portraits of the sinister looking Mexican man who pulled up and placed a call, one that Savanna believed to be inside of the firm. She watched as the fella made his exit from the car and she captured it, she saw as another gentleman made his exit from the firm, and headed in the direction of the gentleman of question. Right off the bat Savannah noticed that it wasn't Chase, the very one that she had expected to see and this new twist needed a few shots so she obliged and snapped an abundance of them. Savanna saw as the Mexican man encountered the elder man. Savanna caught the greetings like a professional photographer. Savannah was capturing poses and expressions gestures and indications, and just to be sure that she had captured everything she snapped a few more. Savanna saw as the Mexican man reached through the window of the car that he arrived in and pulled from its interior a folder, and just because Savanna saw the folder before, she decided to go snapping crazy. She captured the folder and the exchange, she recorded the entire transaction all the way until the Mexican got behind the wheel and drove away.

"Oh-kay, so we're even playing against our own team," she thought then decided that this thing was bigger than Chase, and this thing was bigger than her. She couldn't help but to wonder if it was even bigger than Juice, not that she wasn't confident in his ability but she wasn't fool enough to think otherwise, then a chain being 'only' as strong as its weakest link. And by the looks of it, Savanna could say that they had a chain that was awfully full of weak links. Still she knew that she wasn't gonna be one of them. No! She was gonna be strong, come what may come and this she knew. So armed with new footage she was once again off to the convenient store.

"How may I help you?" Asked the clerk,

"Well, I dropped off an order more than an hour ago and I am always assured to have my order filled within the hour. If those are ready, I would like to pick those up plus I need an emergency order filled from my new chip." Savanna said hurriedly,

"Oh-kay, do you have the receipt for the first order?"

"I do," Savanna handed the slip of paper to the clerk and watched as the clerk left then returned with her order which were in separate envelopes. Pleased again with the work done, she thanked the clerk and handed over another memory chip that she begged to have printed right away.

"Emergency huh?" Asked the clerk,

"Life or death, employed or laid off," Savanna replied.

"Oh shit, well I'm a do you a solid and push this one to the front. You could stay here and I'll have you out of here in no time."

"Thank you very much," Savanna took a seat on one of the cushioned chairs made available for customers and shuffled through her photos. Clear ten pixel prints stared back at her. Both pleased and sickened by her discoveries Savanna sought the reasoning for such a deadly game, she knew that it was a high stakes game being played because Nigel had only to tell Juice but once to get her a check worth a half a million dollars to purchase a business that she was sure to be a primary partner of. Even though Savanna had absolutely no idea that Juice could even raise that kind of money in such a short time let alone at all. Well, she had one pulled over on her when she watched how he placed calls and made wire transfers and within minutes all she needed to do was go to her bank and pick up a check made out to Savanna Clayton, for the purchase of a restaurant.

Still dazed from the thought of having access to such a check, Savanna had picked up another theory. Just maybe Nigel, April and Dominic was their own secret society and one that revolves around a lot of money. Not that Savanna was avaricious at all and far from it, but she wasn't stupid either because anyone that could move a half a million without even entertaining the thought of whether or not Savanna would head for the trains with the check said a whole lot too. What was confusing from the beginning was how, Juice, Nigel or April behaved as if there was a surplus of the green stuff. Superfluity never came to mind when viewing any of them. A lot of times when money comes into a room it'll be easy to spot due to the sycophantic and obsequious people that surrounds them which is often times a dead giveaway. Thinking back, Savanna could never recall any of these indications or tip offs. Oh she saw the lot perform in a generous way, charitable and good will's is what attracted Savanna to them in the first place for she has encountered many successful churlish people.

Thinking about it now, she noticed that she was with this new belief, she began to think that there was more than what met the eye, and by allowing this thought to pass through her mind, she must also entertain the true question that she couldn't help but to think about ever since this circus begun, "Is Nigel really Raymond Buchannon?" Lord knew that Savanna had grown up hearing about this person. She had even met and saw others pretend to be him. How was it that this man had influenced even her uncles and her brother she didn't know? So in her mind she wondered until she was beginning to believe that just maybe Nigel was Raymond Buchannon and just for entertainment purposes if nothing else, just maybe Juice is connected in some kind of way and what if he was thought Savanna. "What would that make me?" Because one thing that she knew for sure, she was never gonna leave him again. He was everything that she wanted and more than what she had prayed for. Oh how she loathed their times away from each other. Now that she was this close what would she do if her man was connected?

"I ain't going anywhere Juice," Savanna said to no one particular and surely not to the clerk who said,

"Excuse me."

"Oh girl, I was only thinking out loud, don't mind me none."

"Oh-kay, if you say so, but did you hear me when I said that your order is up though?"

"Oh, sorry how much do I owe you?"

"That'll be seven dollars," Savanna fished out a twenty and told the young girl to keep the change and with her order in hand she headed out to the car and made her way to Pepe's due to the fact that she had a lot of work to do and she could finish it up at Pepe's where everything she needed would be at her disposal, even a Hennessy straight. April saw Savanna when she walked in but she was already preoccupied but later found Savanna at the bar nursing a Long Island Iced Tea.

"Oh-kay, so what's the occasion?" Asked April pointing to the glass,

"I just figured that I'll take me a drink to unwind before I ask you if it was all right to use your work station."

"Oh-kay, you know how to get there, no problems there, unwind you say?" April became suspicious.

"Yes, crazy day."

"That's how you look too, how crazy?"

"Can I ask you a question without you getting mad at me?" April eyed the girl trying to read the troubles that she may have confronted throughout the day. Just nodded and said,

"Of course you can," but knew that she would probably need a drink as well, and told her to hold on a minute. Savanna watched as April went around the bar and after concocting her drink she came to sit with Savanna and said,

"Oh-kay you were saying."

"Mom, if it's none of my business you could just say that and I'll handle that… the best that I can."

"Girl I have nothing to keep from you you're a good girl and you make my son happy which makes me happy."

"What was it like when you first met Victor?"

"Huh," Savanna saw that April was not ready for this question and she knew when someone was buying time said,

"What I'm asking is how did you gain his trust? How did you convince him that his life was your life come what may?" Savanna had to cut her spiel because immediately April began hitting the liquids. Savanna knew that she struck oil once April signaled the bartender to top her off again.

"Mom?"

"I heard you, hold on a minute, you can't just barge in and rush me like that."

"Huh, oh-kay, whatever you say." Receiving her drink April took a healthy gulp and said,

"Now, what are you trying to figure out?"

"Just only what I said."

"Oh-kay um Victor, um my husband..."

"Hah, yeah him that's who we're talking about, don't worry I'll wait."

"Girl hush, you better be lucky that I like you."

"Then tell me, I mean if it's none of my business then I could live with that, but barely," finished Savanna

"Oh-kay Victor was a whole lot different than my son."

"Somehow I'm starting to find that hard to agree with, from what I heard your husband was a man that was both great and puzzling and since these are the same traits that I see in Dominic, especially the puzzling part. I figured that I'd come to you and get advice from you."

"Shit, you aren't making this easy are you."

"No, the truth as I learned it mom is never always easy. Still it is the truth that I ask of you."

"Oh hell naw, you need to call Dominic."

"Well, believe it or not, but that's answer enough for me." Savanna stood to leave.

"Wait a minute," April shook her head then said, "Not like this. Listen I'll meet you upstairs in a minute we'll need drinks, trust me you are definitely gonna need one, or two or five." Puzzled Savanna said,

"That bad huh?" April departed from Savanna and gone about the task of running her business. April had known that a day like this was to come sooner or later, and she had thanked God that it was a person of Savannas ilk. April didn't see where Savanna needed to walk the streets, but she was also with the knowledge that the girl almost reminded her of herself. Savanna had the same wit, same curiosity, same beauty and the very same determinations. April though, was in absolutely no hurry to go upstairs and pour all, in fact she noticed that while she was moving around the club she was putting censorships on what she would reveal and what was definitely none of Savannas business.

While April was downstairs Savanna was upstairs hard at work. The first thing that she done was placed everything in order. All of her pictures were in order. All of her assumptions she put into chronological order along with her beliefs and after nearly an hour and a half she was wrapping up her synopsis. Finally, April came into the office with a bottle of Martel and two glasses along with a bucket of ice.

"Hold on a minute," Savanna said now picking up the phone and placing the call to a number that she had committed to memory. After a few rings Savanna heard the masculine voice say. "Hello."

"Hello, my name is Tanisha Freeman and I'm calling for Julius." Savanna heard an exhale through the receiver.

"Oh, Ms. Freeman how are you doing?" April watched how Savanna had gone in and out of number games. She was in and out of disputes that she may have had with contracts or any other transactions that held her concerns and she couldn't help but to admire the young lady. "Ooh, do Juice have his hands full" she thought before she poured two shot glasses of fine liquor seeing that Savanna was coming to the end of her business call. Hanging up, savanna picked up her glass and took a sip of the fiery contents and said,

"So tell me just one of your secrets."

"Well, tell me can you keep a secret?" April asked with curiosity.

"Yes, I really can." Replied Savanna,

"Well my dear child, so can I. I have thought about what I can and would tell you, if you put the rest together on your own then that's good for you, but some things you best not know."

"I'm satisfied with that." Was the last thing that Savanna said, and for the next two hours she just sat and listened and sipped from her glass. She sat and marveled at the woman across from her. Barely could believe any of it but knew better than to think April, the one other lady that she has ever called mom would sit and entertain her with lies. Trying, but she couldn't think of the first time that April had misled anyone let alone her. Although, it would have been very easy to do so, for Savanna was not only under the influence of alcohol, but she was also under the influence of love and was indeed trapped in a vulnerable state and needed something to hold on to.

April gave it to her, in the very same way that April had also needed when she was oh so deep inside of Victor, even though it was ever so long ago. Still April knew that the only way to give it, that it had to be in the very same way that one received it, the correct way.

April watched as Savanna took shot after shot while she listened on and couldn't help but to concur with the likes of Savannas actions. She knew from being in the business of alcohol that one always tended to get all that they needed in order to deal with or to cope. So, if it took Savanna to get to the bottom of the bottle then who was April to tell her when she has had enough. There was one thing April had known and that was Savanna wasn't fighting nobody, but herself, the fight between wrong and right. The fight between love and lust and the fight between should she leave or should she stay only created a war. This being the very conflict that accompanies the way one was raised and the things that one has learned and acquired along the way. A conflict which is sired similar from what one may hear and how that fails to coincide with the things that one may see. To receive a revelation that has an impact more than what the mind and the heart has become willing to reject then indeed a war will be declared. Well, this has been the very popular reason for anyone to yell "Bartender" and April well knew. Seeing that Savanna began to sway a bit April led her to the sofa and laid her on it and retrieved a waste basket and placed it near her then said,

"I need you to sleep it off oh-kay and if you need to get rid of some of it, please if you can, get as much of it in this bucket, oh-kay sweetie?" With that said she left to go tend to her business with thoughts of her son having found his mate, his soul mate.

Chapter 38

Savanna awoke to the sounds of Juice tapping away on the keyboard belonging to the desktop. She sat up and let the room settle a bit before saying.

"Baby… Baby," Juice was so engrossed with his works that he had barely heard her, but came to her and said,

"Gosh, are you alright?" Savanna saw his smile and said simply,

"I love you so much."

"Yeah?"

"I really do; babe what time is it?"

"A little after four."

"Wow, I had a long day."

"And a long night from what I hear." Nodding her head Savanna agreed with Juice by saying,

"An awfully long night."

"But you're all right though?"

"Yeah, what are you doing up so late?"

"Well, when I got in I noticed that you had your works scattered all over the desk so I read what you had put together. You did a good job, a lot of stuff we already knew, but the confirmations were what we were waiting for."

"I'm sorry for you."

"Why you say that?"

"Because it must suck when you are playing against your own team."

"Yeah, it would, but I'm not wounded by that trust me, plus, that's not my team."

"Why are they doing this, doesn't make much sense to me, your mom said that this firm handled family business, and that your dad didn't trust many people, but he trusted them."

"And my dad is dead." Juice interrupted.

"I don't understand; they've treated you to everything. An education, anything you needed they provided for you out of respect for your father, even took me in as a favor to mom."

"If you look at it like that then yeah it doesn't make much sense, but you can't just look at the surface. You must look beyond the surface, especially behind it. Listen my dad used to tell me this story right, and I'm gonna share it with you. There's this village right, and in this village was a bunch of warriors, but they worshiped spirits and false Gods, like smoke and rain and shit. This village, believed that God was this great big ole giant, who would come down to collect its homage's for bringing forth rain and fire and for allowing fruits to grow and vegetables and other vegetation's, could you picture that? True they were warriors and some really ferocious dudes I mean their swords were large razors, one swing and heads would roll once they got into their zones you know." Savanna nodded that she was keeping up and Juice continued. "Now there was this other village, they grew in the mountains, not a lot of corn or wheat, a lot of rocks and water and unlike the other village of warriors; this village was a college of intelligent people, people who practiced medicines and other traits for the healing. This village was a group of carpenters and painters; they weren't fighters though. So one day the village of fighters needed to conquer the village of intelligence, so they readied themselves to invade and enslave the village of smart people, but the smart people were prepared, they had been waiting for this moment. Then sure enough the warriors had come in a battle cry, and they were swinging their swords wildly. Then fire erupted in a burning hiss, and the night sky lit up and this huge giant appeared. The warriors who had come to kill, maim and enslave this passive group were turned away and returned to their lower village fruitless and had become slaves themselves, you know why?"

"No I can't say that I do, but that was a good story," Savanna said so Juice finished.

"Because the warriors weren't smart enough to look beyond their beliefs to who God is or even smart enough to look behind the giant because if they were then the warriors would've conquered the passive intelligent people because the warriors would of then saw the mechanics of such a giant, the smoke, and the mirrors." Juice stood and walked to the desk then returned saying,

"With this group," he showed Savanna the pictures of his choosing. "These are the passive intelligent people," Savanna received a picture of Chase and of the elderly man who had come out of the firm to meet the strange roughneck Mexican man. Savanna said, "Oh-kay" so Juice had continued,

"And this is their fire breathing giant," and for this Savanna was given the other pictures of Juices choosing. Savanna saw that these were shots of the woman, the Mexican and Julius, still not getting it completely shook her head and said,

"I still don't get why the betrayal."

"That's because as my mom would say, you are looking at it like a lawyer."

"And in order to get it…"

"You'd have to look at it like a gangster."

"But you said it yourself these are passive intelligent people…"

"Who thinks to get rid of the gangsters that they would control every trade. It's just as it was written you know about how the 'meek' shall inherit the earth." Juice said putting emphasis on meek.

"But why, baby I don't understand why? I mean they already have one of the biggest firms in the world."

"It's the same reason every day Savanna no matter where you go or how you get there you would always be around the same two people and the sooner you'd realize that the better off you would always be." Juice became animated.

"And what two people are those?"

"The ones that could control and curb their greed, and the ones who can't and for that matter don't." Savanna had known Juice for nearly four years granted that they were separated for a year for professional reasons, but never have she ever heard Juice speak like this and couldn't help but wonder how much of his life was he willing to censor due to the way she would feel or fail to understand, she said,

"And how did you put all of this together?"

"Well, you were out of it when I came in so I went through your works and decided to go and visit with Nigel believing that he could shine a brighter light on this situation."

"Which he has?"

"Yes, he identified the giants of this play so to say; you see the Mexican fella is an old time contract killer who my uncle knew from a long time ago. Guy's name is Roberto. He was known as one of the best then he began to roll over on his employers. See the woman there, well that is another story, her name is Jessica. We believe that Juan has located her, maybe offered her some monetary supplements to come and give her testimony and then run like hell, and the old guy that you saw, well that is Juan, a partner at the firm. You know who Julius is; in fact, we believe that he's in the process of accepting your bid, so congratulations on that. Now, for the better understanding as far as those people at Dixon, Juan and Dixon I'll admit that they've taught me a lot. Sure, I have access to their libraries which is top shelf if I don't say so myself, just know that they also give me secretaries and paralegals. Do you know what that is good for?" Juice saw as Savanna shook her head so he continued by finding other pictures of the folders and the files that had made it out of the firm, each brief had been double recorded, one for him and the other for the enemy and he showed them to her.

"So, they'll take your research and give it to the hired witnesses, so that everyone would know how I'm gonna bring it then they'll sash squash me in trial."

"Right, the only problem with that though is we already know that so you're gonna bring it a whole different way, allow them to prepare for this, so we could hit them with that."

"And by 'that' you mean?" Savanna let her question hang out there for a moment. Seeing that she now had her man stuck between a rock and a hard spot said,

"You know, by you not saying anything is answer enough but I need you to know something, the sooner that you realize that I for damn sure got you the better off you'd be." After a short spell, a quiet time elapsed before Juice said,

"Savanna, can I trust you? I mean can I really? Don't get me mixed up here, I'd love for me to be you and you to be me, that deep inside of each other you know. Not that I'm comparing you to other people, but I'm aware of many people sitting in the clink that are right now wishing like hell that they had never shared their darkness's with their mates. The ones, who shared their fruits of life with, had become the final nail in their coffin. I would be broken, nothing would be able collect my shattered pieces once I've saw someone that I loved and someone who loved me get up there on the stand and sink me to the bottom of uselessness."

"And you're scared that this may one day be me?"

"Only you know the answer to that question my dear."

"Oh-kay, if that's the case I'll say this right now. It looks as if our family, now hear the emphasis on "our" is in its most vulnerable state, may be easily conquered. As you say we need to look at the mechanics and do something about these operations lest "our" family baby "our" family is going to lose "our" Uncle Nigel. Now, is you gonna trust me or not?"

"Well, shit! The way you are talking it seems like I better. So listen, Juan the very same partner to the Dixon's, with understanding that the Dixon's are probably in on the scheme or they could be just as unaware too, but Juan comes from Mexico, we know for sure has a background of trafficking all around him. We believe that it is he who sports the desire to invade Sacramento and pillage this place like an old pirate. It is also our understanding that Juan believes by moving Nigel out of the way that a takeover would be simple, for they all feel as if Nigel is the one who hovers over this city."

"But he's not though… is he."

"No, he's not, my mother is, so it's not only Nigel that I'm fighting for, but it's my mother that I'm protecting. So, if I have to lose a little sleep, then so be it." Savanna was shaking her head for she barely believed any of the things that she was hearing, but couldn't explain it to herself any other way said,

"So, you're saying that mom is Raymond Buchannon?"

"What? Where'd you get that from?"

"Well, you said Nigel isn't the one."

"Let's not stray from where we're going," Juice had intelligently evaded Savannas request and attempts to run down the understanding that everyone in North America wanted to have, continued by saying,

"Now you said that I needed to trust you?"

"I did." Savanna reminded him,

"Oh-kay, well a war is on the horizon. Now I could book you a plane ticket to anywhere if you like."

"And what would that do?"

"It'll keep you safe."

"And where would you be?"

"Right here, I'm defending my family remember?"

"Especially mom?"

"Right here, we ain't going nowhere!"

"Then what do I need a plane ticket for ain't you hear anything that I've been saying to you Juice."

"I was just giving you a way out."

"But it's the way in that I'm looking for how about giving me that, could you do that?" Savanna now clearly upset.

"Alright listen?" Juice had gone in and out of scenarios. Things that he expected to happen, things that they couldn't allow to happen and the things that were beyond salvage. The two talked and covered issues ranging from court dates to war strategies. For these two together, now knew the mechanics behind the giant.

Breakfast arrived for them, seeing the two had stayed up most of the morning, April prepared for them a large breakfast before announcing that she had errands to run and Juice already knew that she had. He knew that today she was to meet up with Benny of the Bait Shop who was to have their trusted computer tech come in and begin hacking into the files of Julius. Nigel had planted the seed into Julius' computer the day of his arrest. It was April's attempt to gain as much intelligence as she could by using this process with full knowledge that every little bit would help.

"Well I need to go home and get myself together and then we'll meet back here right?" Said Savanna,

"I'll be here, the way I see it it'll take my mom a few hours at least to do what she needs to do, which could give me a chance to take me one of those power naps."

"I sure hope so sweetie, because you need to stop doing yourself like this." The two kissed and Juice saw Savanna down the stairs and out of the door.

Nigel laid on his bunk wide awake for sleep was hard to find. The realizations that he couldn't do with his life as he pleased had set in and found a home in his mind. He couldn't bathe when he pleased, he couldn't come and go as he wished, though he could eat, being that he had drawn from the commissary a box full of cookies, chips, and candy bars. Really a box full of junk is what he called it every time he removed the lid to rummage through such a box. So, yeah he was able to eat when he felt like it, but what he ate didn't register under his list of wants. On this night his list of comforts wasn't the only thing that weighed heavy on his mind. Just a moment ago Juice had paid him a night visit as Nigel saw that the clock read nine thirty-seven p.m. the time the officer came through the speaker telling him to get fully dressed and come to control for a visit. As Nigel thought back in hindsight, he could honestly say that Juice had brought him a visit that he would never ever forget. Juice has now uncovered a part of Nigel's past that he would have loved to have kept buried. The sensitivities of such a memory were "often" and "always" without overlooking "every time" too much to bear. Vivid was Nigel's memory, the blood, the waste, the torment and on this night all of those reminders had come rushing back to clear and limpid pictures as if these events had transpired just moments ago. Nigel laid with his hands rested under his head. Still in his jailhouse garments, the two-piece orange top and bottom and the orange shoes had completed his gear as a prisoner, and if this wasn't enough, the fact that it was stenciled on each piece of clothing "Sac. Co. Prisoner." On the pants, on the shirts and on the under shirts to now it was even written across his mind, wrote clear as day "Sac. Co. Prisoner."

Though Nigel laid in his confines, his mind had wandered back to a time ever so far away from there, way back to a time when jazz filled the streets. Oh how it poured out of the door ways of the speakeasies that were crammed up and down Stockton Boulevard, as well as Sacramento Boulevard before it was converted over into Martin Luther King Jr. Boulevard. For some people these were the good ole days. There was nothing better in the world than getting spiffy in one of the finest suits that money could buy and get the ole lady and go for a spin. Driving slow, making sure that everybody saw as you passed by doing a cool dime in your fifty-seven Chevrolet. In Nigel's case it was a nineteen fifty Buick, olive green paint and tan interior, chrome every which- a-where and gangster white wall tires. Nigel could still vision this car, one of his better purchases in all of his life. The radio stations had always kept Nigel leaning in this car. Only back then they called cars "a short." Duke Ellington, Chuck Berry and ole Muddy Waters used to provide the soundtracks for his real life motion pictures. One of his real life pictures was a fine chocolate complexion girl who sported a tapered Afro and sometimes pigtails. Oh, she was so pretty. She had a single dimple that was pushed so far into her cheek that it became ever so appealing the older she gotten. She had a small waist and long powerful built legs. This girl used to get the toughest brothers around to eat out of her hand, but not Nigel though. This girl used to turn brothers into "two timing" chumps, but not Nigel though! Oh, when this girl hit the dance floor the fellas gathered around for she was a beautiful sight to see. The way she did the monkey, was shrewd enough to invent the asthma pump, they'll later call it the inhaler. When she did the alligator and the cat she'd always send lesser men to the restroom to regain their composure's. She was a dancing machine and not a whole lot after that. She was beautiful, and her steps were seductive. She used to gyrate and thrust her pelvic on purpose just to give brothers fits, but not Nigel though! Brothers used to offer her money and gifts not even knowing that they were offending her in their desperate cries for romance, but not Nigel though! In fact, Nigel never paid much attention to this chocolate wonder. Donna, he said her name softly while he stared through the concrete walls of a jail cell. Donna the tease and this was the name given to her in secret by these lesser men, Nigel smiled as he reminisced. Because there was one thing that Donna never ever respected in all of her life, and that was a weak minded man and in Nigel this was not what she saw when she viewed him. So when Nigel sent her a full dozen roses and a card saying that she was to split them evenly with her mother, Donna was impressed. When he asked her out to see a picture show, and when she declined he merely said,

"Explain to your mother that I would never do anything to hurt you nor dishonor you for I am a man of honor, and a man of respect," boy did that drive her crazy. So, when he asked her out again only this time with an ultimatum when he simply said,

"Ms. Donna, I'll give you my word as a man, it's true that I fancy such a pretty woman such as yourself, but if you refuse to see a movie, have a dinner and a night of dancing. Then I'll promise not to bother you with this matter again." It wasn't that Donna gave in so easily, but she knew better than to continue to play around with someone who has opened by saying that they'll give you their word as a man. So on this very day Donna Macon, also known as Donna "The Tease" had relented to the wishes of Nigel Collinson. It took nearly three years of going steady before Donna visited a doctor who've confirmed what she already knew and what she already felt, that she was indeed, nine weeks pregnant.

Upon hearing this kind of news any man should have been elated, happy and over excited. For some reason Nigel recalled being scared to death. It was something about being a father that was scary as hell to him. Ms. Mable, Nigel's mother used to remind him often that he got that fear from his daddy. She would tell him that as tough as his father was, soon as Nigel was born she had to threaten to cut him in order to get the man to hold his own son. Wherever Nigel got his fear from it didn't matter, but he knew for sure that it was authentic, a real fear of being a father which was both crazy and too late.

Donna had moved in with Nigel and his mother, for Ms. Mable had told Donna not to worry and that her son would come around and until then she would help out as much as she could, and this had relaxed Donna a lot. So when the time came for everyone to panic, everyone meaning Nigel. The world would welcome a seven pound, six ounces, nineteen and a quarter inch baby boy, who Nigel had simply named, Nigel Junior. Nigel used to laugh at his reactions the moment he realized that Donnas' water bag had burst. He had never stuttered so much in all his life and during this time Nigel used to do muscle work for a fella named Pierre.

Oh my God did Pierre have his act together, he would say. Didn't matter which way he turned, it was some money coming from that direction. If he went to the store, it was some money in there for him, if he had gone to the cleaners, it would be some money in there for him. They would get on a boat, a charter and you better believe it, there was some money for him on that motha fucka.

Pierre was so smart that Nigel had to like being around him and Nigel very seldom tolerated anybody. Pierre was sharp. He was debonair. He was suave. He was one of those high yellow brothers that had migrated to California, from Louisiana. One of those Creoles that took everyone a minute to get used to, but once they got used to him it was too late. If there was one thing that Pierre knew how to do, that was utilize everything and everyone around him. Sisters and the 'light bright's' as was called the Caucasian women. Who would find their ways to one club or the next humping for Pierre and Nigel had no problems whatsoever with collecting the 'snaps' as money was called oh so long ago. No, he had no problems whatsoever. Nigel's finer qualities were that he had a way with people; very few problems ever came his way. For years him and Pierre was making money hand over fist. They were able to provide for their family's food and a better way of living. Nigel had never had a situation that he couldn't deal with as quietly as possible. At least not until Ramon Garcia came into the picture. His top coat and greasy slicked back hair, still played in rotation right in front of Nigel's eye lids, each time he closed his eyes. For years and years, same face, same hair, same coat and the exact same piercing eyes. Ramon Garcia had brought a family to Sacramento and had made a home in the Colonial Heights area. Then set their sights on Oak Park. A family of killers, ferocious, heartless and barbaric, and for Pierre they were too much, not for Nigel though. Nigel was the charismatic and artful one, cunning and devious, but Nigel was also under orders, and Nigel was a soldier to the end. Lying in his jail issue bunk, he could still recall the argument that had changed his life forever.

"Sir, I don't think it would be wise to allow them to settle in on us. Tell me that you do not trust those niggas. Tell me that we haven't bargained with these mother fuckas Pierre." Nigel shouted.

"Nigel, you don't get it because you're young still, soon you would be able to see the uniqueness of our friends and what they could offer us, way bigger fish for us to fry," said Pierre.

"No, I say we go knock on their doors and blow their motha fucking heads off, that's what I say. No offense Pierre, but it seems as if these... these punks are putting some stuff on us, now I say that you should listen to me." Argued Nigel,

"Son, let's just give it a week, let's see if the promises come through, if not then we'll ship them back. Is that alright with you?" Pierre's words were final and to prove it he walked over to his fish tank and began to feed his fish. Not fully knowing that a week had never taken so long to show itself. For the next day would mark the day that Ramon Garcia and his family of killers and his youngest son Roberto, who at the tender age of twelve would on this day learn the skillful art, of killing. Nigel had known the minute that he walked through the door that his mother had been the one to open the door. For there she laid, blood covering her face and breast. She was folded over next to the end table. With his heart caught into his throat, he would scour through the rest of the house until there in the kitchen he saw his brand new wife both shot and butchered in the nude with her arms wrapped around her son as if she was trying to protect him from the horrific experience that had befallen upon the Collinson family. He was cursing his higher power for allowing something like this to take place to the only thing innocent that he had ever known.

Nigel called for an ambulance to arrive at his address but didn't wait for them to arrive. Instead he left the door open so that the emergency units could spot the horrible sight, one that brought tears to the eyes of the young Nigel. There was nothing else that Nigel could do at home so he packed his pistol and his desire to make things even and left.

Nigel made his first stop to Pierre's house, he was always glad to see Nigel oh, but not this time. This time Nigel only needed to ring the doorbell and soon as Pierre opened the door Nigel raised his piece and blew two holes into Pierre. One through his teeth and the other caught him just below the left eye socket. Believing Pierre to be a goner, Nigel turned his Buick towards Colonial Heights, where it took all of two hours to locate Ramon and finish him on his front porch, leaving Nigel to step over the corpse of Ramon Garcia to gain entry into the lovely quarters that Ramon Garcia had built for his family. Nigel saw elderly women and men, it was because he saw them did he decide to shoot them, and kill them. He was taking his time as he'd gone throughout the house until he found some of Ramon's killers, who didn't look much like killers to Nigel. They were hugging each other to avoid being shot while hiding in the closet. Sure, there were kids inside of the house and had Nigel known what he had learned years later then the very one Roberto Garcia would have never resurfaced in a portrait, he would of swam with the fish a long, long, long time ago. Nigel saw the preteen killer lying next to a very scared, but beautiful woman screaming, "Ma ma, ma ma," then the child rambled off a dozen or so words in Spanish. Nigel knew that he needed to leave, but not before dismissing the lady's wish as being well, just a wish. "Mr. please don't harm me or my son" without listening to the woman's plea Nigel walked to her and shot her two times in the chest and once in the face. With one bullet left Nigel pointed at the child to see if he was really such a low life scum and a piece of shit. Seeing that he couldn't pull the trigger Nigel made his exit out of the house through the rear and over the fence he went, making his way to his car.

Although it never seemed as if Nigel would ever forget this occurrence, and just when it was beginning to make its way to the back of his mind again, the kid shows up. Now Nigel knew the whole script. He knew now that his good friend Victor, who he loved like a brother was sold up the river slowly but surely and all the way to his death. Although Nigel had his suspicions after the death of his good friend he never allowed his suspicions to come before professionalism. He never accepted his impulses as being anything more than just an impulse and one that didn't carry much weight until now. Now the truth is what it is, and by the looks of it this truth was still very much alive. This truth is a dark truth, one that is designed to re-live yesterday and destroy in the ways of today. It was a bitch but so is life. This truth was also a beast and Nigel could only hope that Juice has discovered ways to tame such a savage beast. For the monster of yesterday and the beast of today has now made a marriage. Nigel knew that the only true shot that he had was to bank on the kid, who has become more and more of an adult each time that Nigel saw him. In this, Nigel could only smile. 'If his good friend Victor was alive to see this shit' Nigel thought then said.

"You would be proud of him brother, you really would, I know, because I sure am." Nigel had spoken these words in a whisper before he rose up and pushed the button which controlled the lights then rolled over and sought sleep.

Chapter 39

Juice and Savanna hopped on the freeway and headed south. The Mustang cruised in the far right lane with the convertible top let back. Juice had never changed anything on the car since his dad gave it to him for his sixteenth birthday. Same cherry red, same white top, same monster in the trunk and Juice sported the same desire to crank it up each time he hopped on the freeway. Savanna had grown used to this maneuver and never argued it at all but made sure that she brought along an agreeable play list for the two to enjoy. Forty-five minutes later the two was pulling up to Stribley Park on the east side of Stockton, California. Here Juice stared through his window at the many thug wannabes' that loitered around the park. The scent of marijuana filled the air along with the loud chatter that took place from various circles and picnic tables. Not seeing what he had come to see or even who, Juice decided to stroke the streets of Stockton until he became fruitful. While he was attempting to put the car in reverse to back out, Juice heard Savanna say,

"Baby, look," Juice followed Savannas gaze to a group of thugs who were paying a lot of attention to them. Instead of Juice shying away, Juice opened the car door and got out and Savanna done the same.

For whatever reason she felt that if her man was gonna get beat the fuck up then she may as well join him.

"You know why they trippin' on us?" Juice said.

"Uh uh, but it looks bad though," Juice noticed that Savanna spoke through fear so he said,

"Don't worry about it; let's see what they got for us." Juice led the way and Savanna fell in step saying,

"Why are they staring at us like that though?"

"Because I got on this red sweat suit,"

"Oh, they think you are a gang member or something?"

"Yeah, I think so," Juice and Savanna made it to the first group of park goers who immediately circled the two and began to pose a genuine threat leaving Juice to say.

"Listen, I'm not a Damu if that's what you're thinking." Juice held no fear because he knew from strict planning that somewhere there were fully automatic weapons with all of their eyes on him and Savanna, following every transaction that the two would make in order for the two to make it back to Sacramento safely.

"In fact I'm in school studying to be a lawyer, and I've come down here because I need to help this lady who is a lawyer save someone that she believes to be innocent." Juice finished.

"You're that lawyer for that dude on TV huh?"

"Yes, I am and they're killing me over there, were suffering." Savanna uttered playing her part to the hilt.

"Look, I had a dude that used to live around here and it is ever so important that I find him. I was hoping somebody could help me, as I say it is very important." While Juice was talking he noticed that the circle was becoming larger and larger around them, but it was obvious that the threat of violence had vanished.

"Who are you looking for?" Asked a young lady,

"Gilbert, I believe yaw call him Filbert Gilbert," Juice said.

"Filbert, what you want with Filbert?" This time Juice located the voice belonging to a hard core wannabe.

"Well, if you could call him, tell him that Juice is in the park waiting on him. Tell him I said he's a chump and a bitch nigga. Tell him that if he don't come and see about me then I put emphasis on bitch nigga. I'm sure that'll get him up here right away. Though I'm pretty sure that you'd have his attention once you tell him Juice is up here, but so what tell him everything if you like he's a chump anyways."

"What kind of business you got with Filbert?" Asked the same thug,

"Now that play boy I'm gonna have to say is none of your business, but I do have some for you if you could get him on a phone though." The crowd burst out into a round of 'oh shits,' and laughter.

"Oh yeah, what kind of business you got for me?"

"How 'bout you get Gilbert and I'll give you a c-note," said Juice pulling a wad of money from his pocket and peeling off a hundred-dollar bill.

"How bout I just strip you for it all," said the hardcore thug nigga.

"You mean rob me, oh you could have the money, but before you do, you know, decide to rob me, you need to know that I wasn't a lawyer all my life."

"So what you saying Cuzz?" Juice noticed that the thug was pumping himself up and before Juice could respond the youngster that recognized Savanna as being the lawyer for dude on TV walked up to Juice wiggling his fingers and said,

"I'll take the c-note," then turned to the other thug who liked confrontations and told Juice,

"Him, see, he don't like money."

"Yeah, I figured that, so where's Gilbert?"

"First give me the money." All seemed fair enough so Juice handed over the bill and the youngster handed over the phone.

"Hello," Juice said into the phone.

"Oh, so I'm a bitch nigga hun?" Juice recognized the voice immediately as belonging to Gilbert.

"I done said what I said already, but it's the shit that followed that is what I need you to concentrate on the most, I mean if you can."

"Come see about you? Is it something about business?"

"Now I'm saying that I see you when you get here and I'm thinking that you should hurry up I mean, before your folks decide that I'm worth a robbery."

"Who's folks?"

"Your folks."

"Right there, right now?"

"Umm hmm."

"Put him on the phone." Juice tossed the phone to the thug and said,

"That's for you my nigga." After tossing the phone Juice took Savanna to the side and said,

"Now umm, this could get ugly, but don't trip."

"I already figured that much out on my own, look." Savanna nodded in the direction of a large group of brothers walking across the park in a heated pace.

"Now, this is brand new." Juice said more to himself than anyone else. Juice waited until the group had made their way to where he stood and to his surprise one of the members that showed up with Gilbert walked over to the fella who posed the most threat to Juice and slapped the mess out of him and Gilbert stood over the fallen brother and said,

"Don't you ever disrespect my company again; you hear me you bitch made motha fucka." Savanna seeing and hearing this whispered to Juice.

"That's not a bad start."

"No, it ain't." The two watched as Gilbert walked over to them, looked Juice up and down as if Juice had just crawled from under the porch then looked at Savanna as if she had just peed on the carpet. Circling the two and scanning them as he traveled in circles. He stopped in front of Juice and said.

"What your bitch ass doing here?" For an answer Juice walked over to his car and retrieved a brand new leather official size basketball, coming over to Gilbert he said.

"So far it's four to nothing," Gilbert caught the high velocity pass.

"I know this ain't the business that you came way over here for," tossing the ball back to Juice with just as much steam on it.

"Not at all, but I knew that you wouldn't let me leave otherwise. I figured that we'd just get the bullshit out of the way."

"Is that right and what you got on it big shot, ain't shit for free over here?"

"Oh, I brought a pocket full of money."

"My nigga, five hundred a game?" Asked Filbert,

"Game to fifteen?" Asked Juice.

"No, no my nigga this is Stockton, I make the rules. I come to Sacramento, you make the rules."

"Call it how you call it my nigga, but call it." Juice stared down his longtime adversary.

"To eleven by ones, she holds the dough? You know how I like getting mines, all the time from a bitch." The crowd that had surrounded them sensed the tension, the latent hostility burst into a large round of laughter. Savanna insulted by this comment just looked at Filbert Gilbert and said through her smile,

"Oh, well I brought my purse, and I tell you what, get one of your bitches, rather man or woman and I'll play with this guy, but I'll do you one better, and go two to one odds in your favor seeing that if you are already a four-time loser than you must suck."

"Whoa!" Went the crowd, oh, they knew the perfect insult when they heard one and this one definitely qualified.

"Girl, you be nice," said Juice smiling to Savanna. Then he aided her by saying "You know Gilbert is a little sensitive."

"Fuck this bullshit talking, what we doing here talking about it or being about it?"

"Game to eleven you say?" Asked Juice,

"Yeah, and I get two to one odds over there." Gilbert said pointing to Savanna which didn't do nothing, but get Savanna to unzip her jacket and walk onto the court.

"My nigga is she serious?" Asked Gilbert, surprised by Savannas actions.

"Yeah, I believe so," Juice wasn't so sure himself because yet had he ever seen Savanna in this light before, this was all new to him too, which was what he told Gilbert as well.

"Could she cover?" Filbert asked.

"I don't think she would've said anything if she couldn't." Juice knew that money wasn't gonna be the issue, and the least of his worries.

"All right my nigga, I was satisfied with just you, but like I say I love getting my money from a bitch!"

"I hear you, me too I tell you what, you go ahead and pick up your other ho, and since this your house we'll let you guys take out first." Juice called Savanna over and the two walked out of earshot.

"Mah did you smell that?" He asked.

"Yea, I was gonna ask you the same thing."

"This is gonna get real physical you know that right, enemy territory and all."

"I'll be alright."

"You control the ball and let me set you up for shots."

"You're making me nervous."

"Don't be."

"Shit! What are we gonna do sport the party over here fuck you over there." Gilbert said loud enough to get the game going. Juice reached into his pocket once to retract fifteen hundred dollars and to his surprise Savanna was the queen of spot shooting. In the corner all net. At the top of the key was all money too. Juice would penetrate and draw a double team before he'd kick the ball out and Savanna would make them pay. Juice watched as the crowd who from the start was against them began to favor them as Savanna knocked down jumper after jumper after jumper. This crowd also booed and became a rowdy bunch each time Gilbert or his team mate became overly aggressive with Savanna. Once they had to take a break in order for Savanna to stop her nose from bleeding.

"You alright, mah?" Juice asked.

"Yeah, I'm good. You think I'm pissing them off?" She asked with sarcasm dripping from her tone.

"Yeah, but we're up two games."

"I thought four was the lucky number."

"It is, but now if you want to quit we could." Juice assured her,

"Hell nah, is my nose swollen?"

"You look like you've been playing hockey."

"That bad hun?"

"Yeah, don't worry about it though; I'm warmed up now, let's run this nigga off picks until his ass throw up."

"Oh-kay, I'm ready," and true to form Juice took over the game using Savanna to shoot behind and then the magic appeared. Filbert Gilbert walked to the side line and blew it.

"Now ain't this a bitch," said Juice walking over to Gilbert, "Dog, this is embarrassing, what are you going to do about all of this embarrassment, tell me that you ain't over here throwing up son?"

"Fuck you," said Gilbert trying to collect himself.

"I know, I know, fuck me, I'm a bitch nigga, but you got to agree the girl is good, huh?"

"Where'd you get her from, she's killing my nigga off the dribble?"

"I swear to God this is my first time seeing her like this."

"Quit lying nigga."

"Uh uh, I swear to god. Listen to me? How about we put an end to this foolishness once and for all because right now, you know that I know that your tank is empty and playboy you already know, that I'll be too much for you baby. It's costing you a stack every time I yell game point. I mean, I don't know your financial situation, but if you just need to go to the cleaners I have just the shot to take you there."

"Or," Gilbert relented.

"Or you could pay the girl for insulting her in public like that and we could talk about some real paper and not these crumbs that we're trying to kill each other over."

"Is that right?"

"Yeah, I really need you playa, I mean you or somebody that got balls that wouldn't mind a few million before it's all over."

"I'm listening."

"Nah, nah, first pay the girl and get who you trust the most and we'll go have a chat, but understand that she's lawyer first, the lady would do a lot of the talking just take into consideration that she's out of line, all right. Even though she's the one that elected to recruit you in the first place just know that it was me to agree so I'm just as guilty in this. While you guys talk I'll make a run to get us some cold ones, only if you tell me that she'll be safe here."

"On my momma, you ain't gotta worry no shit like that."

"My nigga," Juice signaled to Savanna to come over and watched as Gilbert dug into his pocket and forked over the payment to her for the third time. Savanna being the trooper gave it back to him and said,

"How about you make your next round on me."

"Lady who are you?" Gilbert found a new respect for Savanna. He said, "Sorry about the nose."

"It's a contact sport… right sport?" She reminded him.

"If you say so, but you got some business that we need to talk about?" Gilbert asked,

Savanna looked to Juice for approval. Juice pointed away from earshot then said,

"Look, I'm gonna run to the store, you'll be alright." Savanna looked a bit suspicious, Gilbert picking this up said,

"Lady don't worry, like he said, you'll be all right no matter who come through here. Let me get my man to come and listen on, we could cop a bleacher over there this way whatever you have to say would just be between us, you alright with that?" Savanna nodded and watched as Juice and Gilbert headed towards the parking lot.

Gilbert returned with a fella that Savanna had recognized from the state fair and the three of them walked away from the crowd in effort to find a place that would accommodate Savannas wish to be discreet. Finding it the three sat and immediately Savanna filled them in on as much as she could without compromising the defense that she needed to form for her client. The more that she told Gilbert and his close friend J-Dog as he introduced himself. The more Savanna started to believe that either these two hated fuck shit or deep down Filbert Gilbert really had a respect for her man. Either one was alright with her because she was now in her zone, not quite confirming or denying the many acts of deceit and deviltry, but the innuendo's were present. Savanna walked around the villages of intelligent passive people and the giant for its mechanics, as Juice had explained to her, but never did she explain the necessary actions that needed to transpire or to take place that'll fix all. Indirectly, insinuating as in hypothetically providing intimations and sort of leading a little without directly saying out of her mouth, that the people in the pictures that she painted posed a threat to a very important man and that these people deserved a killing.

Savanna never said with any candor or directness based on the simplest of all facts that Ms. Savanna Clayton was a lawyer and she was in no position to forget that. She felt justified due to the fact that she was also a Civil Attorney and because of that she was out to sue people for their wrongdoings and in this matter she was serving the deadly torts because it was plain to see, that her client didn't want the money. Her client was seeking another kind of justice where the payments were in blood. Irreproachable in her actions, guiltless in her delivery. Savanna covered every man, every unethical action and every reason why their stratagems and collusion's must fail to function. Savanna saw and was content at these two, J-dog from Market Street and Filbert Gilbert from Filbert Arms ability to adjust and readjust only to follow and to draw their own conclusion to what needed to be done. The most important part, she discussed payments. It was her idea to take the check worth a half of a million dollars and transfer that into cash, make the purchase of Ju-Ju's Steak House with cold hard cash and it would be a well-known fact that not only would Julius be in possession of one half a million all cash mind you, but nobody not even Savanna gave a fuck about what happened to Julius after the titles were transferred and he no longer was called the owner of Ju-Ju's Steak House. It was clear that on this day and on those bleachers that if somehow these two, J-Dog from Market Street and Gilbert from Filbert Arms were to get their hands on such a payment then that would only be a bonus and one not part of their agreement, she called this act, "paying yourselves."

Juice saw from a distance as Gilbert stood and began to pace, almost as if he had a very important decision to make, one of those life or death ones. Juice couldn't help but to marvel at the way Savanna was conducting herself. He felt a sense of pride for she stood up when it was time for everyone to stand up. She stared into the eyes of the dragon and she delivered. Pretty yes, she's been blessed with good features and this was true. Now take with you the understanding that life on every turn isn't always la-la land and not every time do good looks and nice features make a person beautiful. What Juice was looking at was Savanna in her most appealing and beautiful self because on this day, she didn't offer what a man shall want, but also what a man has always needed, and that to him was a confidante. Someone that a man could turn to on all walks of life for man knows that this world could be a very wretched place and that a lot of times to get along one must go along. As it is said, when in Rome, behave like the Romans.

By the time the conversation was concluded a deal had been structured and the three, Savanna, Gilbert and J-Dog shook hands and made their way towards Juice who was fielding questions for even the people of Stockton, California wanted to know whether or not Savanna was defending the one and the only "Raymond Buchannon." Yet, even to them Juice had remained firm by allowing them to understand his position as a man and as a friend by telling the good people of Stribley Park the same two words that Juice had told everyone else. "No comment."

The trio made it to Juice; not fully knowing that they had showed up just in time to rescue him for his patience was beginning to wear a little thin.

"So, you back everything that she's talking about?" J-Dog said pointing to Savanna eying Juice for the likes of a hoax.

"Yeah, I do," Juice responded.

"You know she was talking some big time shit don't you," J-Dog needed to lay all the ground rules before they started the game.

"Well, this is a big time game," replied Juice, keeping eye contact with J-Dog.

"We heard some pretty impressive numbers over there my nigga, they were intriguing if I should say so myself." This was the first time Juice had ever heard Gilbert speak in the form of eloquence, and decided that perhaps he was actually paying attention when the teachers were teaching, smiled at the thought then said,

"Well, welcome to the big leagues."

"And you stand by even those numbers; you could substantiate the whole thing?" Again Gilbert communicated with impressiveness.

"I can," said Juice.

"What the hell are you smiling for then?" Said J-Dog who never stopped analyzing Juice for signs of fraudulent testimonies.

"It's my life, I could smile if I want to," Juices' retort brought on an immediate reaction from J-Dog who grew tensed until Gilbert settled him by peeping Juice for what he was saying.

"Nah my nigga, you see he thought that the only words that I knew how to convey where bitch nigga, Cuzz and loc because I never called him anything else, but a bitch nigga. I never had another reason to call him anything else; even then I can't say with any certainty that I possess any credible reason to call him a liar. Although the lady is quoting some astronomical numbers that we can't prove rather she's lying or speaking the truth, but I can't picture this nigga coming all the to Stockton all flamed up, risking getting his head blew the fuck off just to bullshit us with numbers that we can't believe" Gilbert spoke these words more to J-Dog then to Juice and Savanna, but turning to the two he said,

"I'm asking you again, could you substantiate and stand by the things that this woman is telling us?"

"And again I'm gonna say yeah and the understanding that you need to get is the numbers that you calling astronomical and ever so hard to believe, you need to know that there is somebody somewhere giving that away to charity every day and the reason why I'm backing what the lady says is because the lady that's doing the talking is with me, and what she says she means and I could vouch for that too. Hear that and with the same understanding note that the only reason why she's making these propositions is because of two reasons. One being, she's a lawyer first and couldn't or shouldn't be caught knowing or having any knowledge of what went down on those bleachers over there and that this is our way for you to see our sacrifice or I would have given you 'my' word 'myself'. Two, it was her that has done the works thus far and found that it should be 'you' that should be propelled by 'me' into an area that it appears that 'you' are so unsure about. Seeing that it was you that pushed me ever so hard to be the best that I could be I decided to go along with it, you know. Even though you didn't know that, but she did and like I said this is a job for you." Gilbert stared from Savanna to Juice as if reading Juices' eyes, he searched the windows to Juices' deepest secrets. Concluding, he shook his head and said,

"Bitch nigga you're serious ain't you?"

"I would love to dance around with you, but you know some of us have a lot of work to do other than hang out with a bunch of losers." Juice responded.

"Bitch, call me a loser again and watch how I fly your ass around this park like a kite."

"Girls, girls, girls, do we have to behave this way each time we see each other." Savanna interjected then said, "could you guys just be nice for one day or at least until we decide on these matters, please," and for this J-Dog had walked up to Juice and said,

"Dog, I'm just now starting to like you, so I got to ask you to please and I'm saying please don't let this be no fuck shit." Shaking his head J-Dog added "Please bro," with frustration Juice stepped close to J-Dog, close enough to become offensive and said.

"Dig my nigga, I know that you don't know me but you need to know that there's a lot of shit that I could be doing right now then to bullshit you or anybody else for that matter." Juice paused to let his words sink in then went on saying,

"If you could handle the job then I'll see you niggas tonight at Club Pepe's that way you could get the blueprint, if you're worried about the dough then don't, go open up you an account right now if you like, if you favor an account offshore then say that shit so we could hurry up and make the accommodations." Juice retrieved a business card and handed it to Gilbert and said, "I'll know by tonight the kind of nigga you are, now I got twenty cases of beer in the car, help me get them and let's have a drink for old times' sake." Filbert thought for a second then said,

"Twenty cases, that's enough for this whole park."

"Exactly,"

Chapter 40

Nigel was enjoying his hour and a half of free time in the day room of pod two hundred. This time, allows inmates one hour to shower, shave and place phone calls or to walk around if one liked. Some deputies were generous by offering an extra thirty minutes as a token of their appreciation. For a lot of these deputies appreciated the days when they could come to work and have an easy day and leave. Enough of this and the deputies begin to show their appreciations by bending a little, but lord only knew that if the deputies arrived everyday behaving like ass holes then the inmates had a way of stacking paper work for them to complete, file and present to the institutions heads by the day's end and this being overtime without pay. So to alleviate any of the bullshit, some deputies would just give a little and the inmates would often times appreciate this token both mutually and respectfully.

Whether or not it was an hour or an hour and a half worth of a day room or free time whatever one shall call it. For Nigel this was prime time to get his chess game up to par and for this he always hid in the corner away from everyone else, and with him would be his good neighbor Ali. Nigel liked Ali because Ali didn't ask a lot of questions. Even though Nigel knew that his presence brought along with it a curiosity that was enticing as hell. He admired Ali for combating his desires to become intrusive. So with him was how Nigel spent his day room time. Add the fact that Ali had one of the more superior chess games that Nigel had seen in a while and because of this Nigel well knew that he now had himself a partner in misery. He never once admitted that this partnership was built on fairness. Never said that their means were parallel at all, neither did Ali. The rules were unspoken rules that favored Nigel the most. Saying that it was fair that Nigel could ask a zillion questions and that Ali would ask not a one. Nigel was excused under the "first termer" act which made him curious about all things. Ali was a repeat offender, which meant that he had the answers to all things that Nigel would find a curiosity to. Nigel was fair by not asking Ali what he was incarcerated for, which meant that Ali was up one because Ali already knew what Nigel was incarcerated for. Thanks to the six o'clock news, the ten o'clock news, CNN and every west coast newspaper that circulated in California.

"Check," Ali said as he moved his knight into position to threaten Nigel's king.

"Mm hmmm, I knew you was gonna do that, boy ain't somebody tell you, that a dog that chases cars normally don't live that long." Nigel moved out of check and watched as Ali studied the board, weighing out his options while wondering what in the hell could Nigel be up to because as the days ticked by, as the chess matches progressed, Ali had known Nigel to be very tricky and awfully cunning. He looked at the board and said,

"So preliminary is coming up, right?"

"Mmm, hmmm," Nigel responded.

"You know what that's about right?"

"Yeah, the kid told me all about it." Nigel watched as Ali reached for his bishop "mm" Nigel hummed so Ali dismissed the thought and prepared to push his pawn, but froze when Nigel hummed again, "hmmm uh," so Ali dismissed the thought of pushing his pawn. The only other suitable option was to reach for his knight yet, and again Nigel expressed himself by saying.

"Uh uh,"

"Well shit Nigel, if it was you what would you do? How about you play your side then come around here and play this side too. Gee-wiz, I'm talking about you done hummed me out of every move so far."

"I was just paying your ass back for trying to distract me with this court shit."

"Is that right, well this right here my brother is what a lot of us call avocation, a game, but preliminary ahh, that's a whole other ball game, now I know that you don't need me telling you this shit it's probably the only thing that you think about, but I was just seeing if you've been laced to the legalities of the whole process." Ali noticed that Nigel wasn't paying him much attention so he followed Nigel's gaze and found that a new arrival had entered the pod said,

"You know cat from somewhere?"

"Nuh uh,"

"Then why are you looking at him like he owes you some of that damned money then?"

"Nah, I don't know him, but I think that they've just gave me a roommate."

"How you know?"

"He just asked for room twenty-one, that's how I know," oh, hearing this had gotten Ali's full attention, so he said,

"And nobody told you that you were double bunk cleared yet?"

"No, which is the reason that I'm confused right now, nobody said that I was gonna get a roommate."

"A celly," Ali corrected then said "Look, you sure is" Ali watched as the brother took to the stairs and stopped in front of cell twenty-one. He moved closer to Nigel and said,

"Listen to me and hear me for what I say; only two things could have happened, they either cleared you without you knowing it or they put somebody in your cell to pay attention to everything that you're talking about. I'm telling you they do that here, give you somebody that asks a lot of questions to get you to talking. Whatever you do, never get to talking," Ali kept his eyes on the new brotha and saw as the door popped open and him go inside of cell twenty-one, continued by saying,

"Right now he's probably reading shit that you have laying around looking for trouble. Do you have anything up there that's trouble?" Ali asked, seeing the concern now displayed across Nigel's face took that as a yes. So when Nigel stated that he had some pictures up there of people that he used to know, not knowing fully what that meant nor in position to have his friend take unnecessary chances Ali acted on his own. Ali took to the staircase until he stopped in front of cell twenty-one, where he tapped on the door to get the brothers attention then said,

"My brother listen, push this button and when the deputy answers, tell him that you wish for day room, over here brothers have mandatory day room could you dig." The brother responded by pressing the button and Ali watched him all the way until the door popped open allowing the brother to make his exit.

Nigel was happy to see this had made a mental note to rip the pictures into itty bitty teeny weenie pieces the moment that he was alone to do so.

"Man thank you, I owe you one." Nigel said to Ali once he made it back and took a seat.

"Nigel, you're a good dude, but I really need you to listen to me, you don't trust nothing or nobody not even me, though I assure you that I'm not a rat, but I never get into anybody's business to be labeled anything, but brotha. But I need to tell you that now a day's cell mates are showing up in court and they're taking the stand. Now I don't know your full situation plus I don't want to know, but this is what you need to do and hear me for what I say. If you have anything that a District Attorney could incriminate you or misconstrue, like get the wrong idea about up in your cell get rid of it, pronto. If dude get in there and ask you a gazillion questions be friendly, but never and I mean never talk about your case, not that you do anyways just don't get comfortable and this is the play. The first chance you get, look at his wrist band and memorize his ID number then let him do all the talking. His ID number, we could run a make on cat and see who he really is. That's play one. Play two, as soon as we get the right deputy then we're gonna suggest a cell move, if they give you one then it's all on the up and up me and you would cell-up together and if they refuse you and give you the run around. Then we'll go into play three." Ali froze for a moment too long for Nigel, who said,

"Oh-kay, and play three is..." Nigel left the blanks open for Ali to fill in, which he'd done by saying,

"Well, we could dead him or we could beat him within an inch of his life, I mean any one of those would work."

"Gee whiz Ali, all because the 'man' gives us the run around about a cell move?" Asked Nigel,

"Mm hmm, you know why? Because the 'man' don't give us the run around that's why! If you and your celly ain't compatible then they would separate you guys on the spot, this is maximum security!"

"Oh, oh-kay,"

"Now like I say, play it all the way out and get his ID and we'll make some calls. Give him a few days and get a feel for him then we'll attempt the cell move and we would see how it plays out from there, could you dig it?" Nigel knew that it was way too late to be liberal, agreed with Ali then changed the subject.

It took Nigel exactly one week before he knew that he was having District Attorney problems, and that Ali was right on all turns. The DA had sent the new brother to cell with Nigel, a brother by the name of Marion who had a flood gate that stayed open. This brother came equipped with one question after the next, and all in regards to Nigel's case. He knew everything about law and if Nigel ever needed his help that all he would have to do was ask. He told Nigel that he was involved in a shooting only on SacSheriff.com, his arrest sheet read domestic violence and false imprisonment. The truth was that he had a horrible night with the ole lady. Somehow he needed to make it better because he already had one strike so whatever time he was gonna get they was sure to double his time up, and all of this appeared to be something good ole Marion wanted to do without. Nigel, with full knowledge of this maneuver continued to play Marion like a piano. So, when Thursday rolled around Nigel informed the deputy who was known to be a righteous one, that he and his celly wasn't compatible at all. The deputy advised Nigel to attempt to work it out. When Nigel told the deputy that this celly thing is too depressing for him and that he would rather move, the deputy told him that there were no openings. So Nigel told the deputy that this situation could get physical the deputy just told him to stop pressing the button unless it was a medical emergency. Well by dinner time Marion made it to the entrance of the pod before he toppled over with blood pouring from his wounds as three inmates beat him to the pulp that they've promised.

Juice had a drink while he sat at the bar discussing strategies with his mother. One of the things that they needed to do was to get Savanna retained as Nigel's attorney, that and retrieve the folders from the Public Defender's office which was their first and foremost. Savanna sat with them sporting a bluish purple colored snot box and April didn't take too kindly to this and said.

"So, you say all of this happened in a basketball game?"

"Yes ma'am," Savanna answered.

"And what were you doing for all of this to happen?" April asked.

"I was playing basketball." Savanna answered.

"You was playing ball! Oh-kay, well this boy here has been playing ball all his life and I've never saw him look like that."

"That's because he doesn't get grimy like I do, I'm good though. I'll take a rum and coke."

"Hmm, I imagine so, would you like a pain killer with that?" Asked April,

"The rum and coke is the painkiller, thank you."

"If you say so," then to her son she said "boy I ought to take one of these bottles and beat the shit out of you with it. Got this girl coming in here looking like Rocky,"

"We had a tough game." Said Juice,

"You could say that again, who was yaw playing?" Asked his mother

"Felt like we were playing all of Stockton for a minute." Savanna interjected

"So, Stockton has done this to that girl…" April was beginning to ask her son,

"Yes ma'am, which is the only thing that Stockton got away with. You should have saw her, she socked it to Stockton too." Juice and Savanna turned in their seats to see the two people that they've been waiting to see, that were also part of their strategy. They stood to receive them.

"Boy, don't I know you from somewhere," April said looking at Gilbert while searching her memory and doing everything that she could to place him. Not able to find it she gave up leaving Juice to come to her rescue.

"He went to Edison momma," hearing this snapped the pictures back into April's memory all but quick.

"That's right, yeah; I thought I knew you from somewhere. You're the one who gave my boy all of those cheap shots aren't you. Wow, now you cheap shooting the girls too?"

"No ma'am, it's quite the other way around. You see I used to have a pocket full of money. That is until your son and this lady here came all the way to Stockton to hustle me out of it. Now tell me that ain't a cheap shot."

"Oh, is that so? And how did he do that?" April smiled at Gilbert.

"He brought the girl," Gilbert said that as if that should explain everything.

"So, you punched her in the nose?" Asked April,

"Yes ma'am, like I say we was playing for money, and a lot of it. It got physical yeah, but anyways I brought a friend of mine with me.

Mrs. Raymond this is James. James this is Juices' mom," April nodded to James.

"Mrs. Raymond," James reached out his hand to April then said "If it's alright may I have what she is having." J-Dog pointed at Savannas' Drink.

"Well she's having a rum and coke," said April.

"I know, I could smell it, it's the only thing that I've been talking about on the way down here, get me a dranky drank in me and then I'm a let my hair down."

April eyed J-Dog suspiciously considering that J-Dog was bald headed. Just shook her head and came back with a drink and a folder and said,

"Gilbert you take this in the VIP section there's no one in there and boy if you gonna let your hair down I sure hope that's not a bad thing because there is a no fighting policy in this club that is strict."

"He'll be on his best behavior," Gilbert said to April then nodded to J-Dog and followed the rope into the VIP section where he stayed until two o'clock a.m. when the club closed. April sent Gilbert a bottle and a plate of food while keeping an open tab for his friend James who had fallen in love with the dance floor and the disk jockey. Often he was spotted next to the DJ requesting songs that he would like to step to.

"So this is what he called letting his hair down," April thought.

When the club found closing time April wished everyone a safe trip home and to make sure that they came back to visit. She found Juice and Savanna nursing a drink in the far corner with J-Dog so she joined them saying,

"Is anyone hungry?" April heard the chorus and decided that nothing would go to waste on this night. She went to the back to gather what was left and brought it out so the kids could eat. When she returned to the group she saw that Gilbert was in attendance so she'd gone back to the kitchen and found more food so that he could have more to eat.

"Oh-kay, is it safe to talk Mrs. Raymond?" Gilbert said once the plates were pushed away.

"Nuh un, child never is it safe to talk. Remember that." April dug into her pocket and retrieved a key and said, "There's a storage room on Freeport and Florin, take Freeport all the way Florin Rd. Anything that you would need is in that storage. Keep the folder and everything in it, there's a check down the way just hold on and I'll get it." April left and came back with a check and told her son to fill it out. Then to Gilbert and J-Dog she waved them close enough to hear her whisper then said, "These people are crooked, they are really, really crooked. If you do as you say, then the world would be a better place. Never and I mean never tell anyone of this arrangement. Not your mama's or your girlfriends. The smaller the circle the better, now, in the storage is everything that you would need, I've seen to it myself. You don't have to show here because in the storage is another key; you would find it in a pouch under a laptop. Take the laptop and send me an email asking about our VIP section, it's famous. So, if I get this message it'll means that the bloodshed has started. Juice tells me that you may be interested in off shore. I would highly recommend that you deal in safe deposit boxes first. Anyways in the pouch the key would fit a box at our bank, a Sacramento Reserve bank. When I say our bank, I mean our bank as in mines and my sons and some other people that we know. You would find fifty grand in that box. Unless I clear it you wouldn't even have access into the chambers of boxes. So please do right by me and my family and you will see that I'm full of favors. My brother is due in court three days from tomorrow; I would love to send a message before then. Savanna tells me that she's due to transfer her check into cash in the morning and that you may be interested in relieving the old foe of his funds?" April looked to Gilbert because J-Dog seemed to be frozen. April didn't know if it was the Rum, or if it was the assignment.

"Ma'am all of this is a surprise but yeah those were the plans."

"And by surprise you mean?"

"I mean it feels awkward sharing these things."

"With me you mean?"

"Yes, I mean I seen a lot of strange things but this has got to be placed way up there."

"I heard that," said J-Dog shaking his head.

"Well you may as well get used to it. It's either that or you could let me down and disappoint me and if that's what you plan to do then it would be good for me to know ahead of time, you understand?"

"Don't worry about that Mrs. Raymond."

"I won't, so if you need a room there's a nice little motel on Stockton Boulevard. Check into there after you've gone to the storage and after you got your pieces together. Take my son with you, because it is no one outside but good guys and bad guys and he'll help you get to safety. Make sure you're up because it is my understanding that she should be conducting her business somewhere around ten- ten thirty in the morning. Then I believe it to be show time for you."

"No problems there, and it's clear that what we find we keep?"

"Finders keepers, loser's weepers," April assured them.

"The boxes would clear the moment the first half is finished. Gilbert could share the folder with you if he pleases," she turned from J-Dog and said "you would find in the folders our strategy; it's the only option that we have. Knock off the back to weaken the front, that's our strategy."

"Mrs. Raymond I will share this folder with James just so you know, he's more than a brother to me, but you are trusting us a lot don't you think."

"I trust my son's judgment. Sure you will have a half a million head start and if you're satisfied with that then yeah by all means take the money and run, which is a good thing because you would then have more than what you walked in with. I don't really care about that; I mean it ain't my money you stealing. I'm more into loyalty and honor.

"I just wanted to make sure that we understood each other is all, we will prove our worth in the morning this is my word and I speak for the both of us." Gilbert said signaling that he also spoke for J-Dog who was stunned by the echoing words, "a half of a million."

"Well, let's have a drink on tomorrow and you guys drive safe." April retrieved a bottle and a few shot glasses.

Juice had noticed that the whispering was over when he returned from seeing Savanna to her car and said,

"You want me to follow you guys?"

"I believe those are the plans, yeah." Gilbert replied accepting his glass from Mrs. Raymond, he waited for the rest to receive their glasses and the four threw back the final shots of the night. Juice had lead Gilbert and J-Dog to the front door and out to the parking lot, grateful that Savanna had convinced him to reach back for Gilbert though the circumstances weren't the best, but still.

"My nigga, you got a hood momma," said J-Dog.

"For real, my nigga this shit is crazy but this shit goes," said Gilbert.

"I sure hope so." Juice got into his Mustang and Gilbert got into a boxed Chevy with J-Dog and they headed towards Freeport Blvd.

Chapter 41

It had been pre-arranged that Savanna would leave the Sacramento Federal Reserve by nine thirty. She will get into a hired car and the chauffeur would take her to collect Mr. Brenner who was to oversee the signings and the transfers as the hired witness. He who was also an attorney himself has done plenty of work for the Raymond's and could be trusted to carry out the wishes of April and Nigel and the same would be for Savanna. After collecting Mr. Brenner, the chauffeur was instructed to head to Ju-Ju's Steakhouse and there he would await the return of Savanna and Mr. Brenner. No matter how long it shall take he was not to leave without his passengers.

Savanna received the call that Gilbert and J-Dog was already in position by eight o'clock a.m. and she smiled at the fact that all was going as planned for they had wagered everything on Filbert Gilbert and his partner. Seeming to have placed a good bet, Savanna decided to reward them by sending them coded text messages keeping them updated on her movements and whereabouts.

J-Dog was the one who couldn't sleep, not because of nervousness, no. Ever since the three of them made it to the storage room the adrenaline of it all was too much. If nothing else Juice found out that J-dog was a fiend for weapons. Talk about firearms and you got yourself a partner playa, everything about guns he was infatuated with. The bullets drove him crazy. Equipped with a laser beam? Oh my God. A fully automatic? Oooooh. Tell him that it comes with a two hundred round drum and that was sure to pass his ass out. So, no, he didn't stay awake on the count of nerve problems uh-uh, he was anxious if that said anything about his character. All night and that until the morning J-Dog examined, unloaded then reloaded the Heckler and Koch MP5. He now found love at first sight. As soon as the storage doors opened he lost his breath then raced Gilbert to the many weapons that were neatly displayed across the table next to the laptop.

"Dog, you better get some sleep, lest you gonna wanna sleep on the job," said Gilbert.

"I'm cool, don't sweat me," replied J-Dog.

"I'm telling you."

"My nigga," J-Dog stood up in his bed and said "picture me running up on that nigga waving this motha fucka?" J-Dog squatted in a crouching tiger stance and pretended to open fire.

"What the fuck is all of this Rambo impersonation shit you doing, nigga point that motha fucka that way you know that it's a hair trigger on that bitch."

"I'm just saying though, I'm a light that nigga ass up, thank I'm playing."

"Man, what the fuck time is it?"

"I don't know, about six almost."

"You were up all this time?"

"Hell yeah," J-dog collapsed on his bed and said,

"Shit, it's taking too long already." Yes, he was anxious.

"You can't wait huh?"

"Hell nah, I'm thinking that we should get a jump on this shit. It's only down the street, we should watch the whole play, we need to be as prepared as we could, this ain't no drive by shit. Something is telling me that this shit is real, and we need to be for real with it."

"I was thinking the same thing. We need to knock this nigga down, but we can't knock him down in the restaurant which was my idea at first, then I read the folder, so now it doesn't go down there, which means...."

"That we need to find out a soft spot," J-Dog finished for Gilbert, nodding his head Gilbert continued by saying,

"Not just any soft spot either, it has to give us time to get the dough too, don't forget about that?"

"Shit, how can I forget about that, this shit gotta go right my nigga? I done already put a down payment on a house and bought me a Lamborghini."

"Kind of shit is that?"

"What kind of shit is sitting up in this room when the money is gonna be down the street."

"I'm hipped, let's roll up some blunts and get out of here." J-Dog agreed with him because the last time they were on a stake out the two blew the whole mission. While they were paying attention to the chore of splitting the swisher and breaking down the tree and by the time they rolled up and looked up, their target had gotten in his car and drove off. Oh how they never forgave themselves for that one. So, with blunts rolled and one in rotation, the two now sat coincidentally in the same parking lot that Savanna had sat just over a week ago and the two watched without knowing exactly what to watch for.

"Hold up, I'll be right back." Said Gilbert and got out of the car and walked across the street in the direction of the Steak House. Gilbert had time to get a physical visual of the man who would soon put J-Dog in his dream house and Lamborghini.

Gilbert took a stool at the counter and placed his order and twenty minutes later he had the visual and two Styrofoam containers filled with steak, eggs, hash browns and grits and two medium cups of orange juice then headed towards the automobile and to an impatiently waiting J-Dog.

"Now that's what I'm talking about my nigga good looking the fuck out." Gilbert handed J-Dog the bags through the window then walked around the building of another cafe and was gone awhile before he returned.

"What the fuck was all that about?" Asked J-Dog through a fork full of steak and potatoes,

"There's a freeway right behind us."

"What we need a freeway for? My nigga I ain't going nowhere, uh uh, this him Jim until it's over."

"I'm saying, my guess is that this nigga is gonna hop straight on the freeway."

"Mm hmm, and we gonna be right there with his ass too."

"On the freeway dog?" Asked Gilbert, curious to the ways of J-Dogs thinking,

"Filbert if that nigga went into St. Luke's I'm a knock him down in there. If that nigga went into a daycare center guess what, mm hmm, I'm gonna knock him down in that motha fucka too. My nigga this shit goes; the steak goes so damn crazy. Nigga the hash browns tasted like they got some kind of sour cream powder on them, this shit is crazy. No wonder they want to protect that motha fucka, you don't want yours?"

"Hell yeah I want mines, nigga I was starving last night, I'm talking about this some new shit I'm on this morning." The two finished their meals and placed another blunt in rotation to recapture the high that had gone away while they were chewing and jaw wrestling with their T-bones and egg platters.

Juice sat at his desk at Dixon, Juan and Dixon and prepared briefs while asking all kinds of questions to the paralegal, Ms. Hillary. Ms.

Hillary, understand had worked on every floor of the firm. She started off as a clerk rearranging files and loading them in alphabetical order into file cabinets. Then she became a full time secretary for the elder Dixon where she spent more than twenty years shuffling and organizing the schedules that kept one of the biggest law firms afloat. Ms. Hillary was reputed to know even more about law than most of the Supreme Court judges and all of the ones who presided over the Superior Courts of Sacramento County. It was also Ms. Hillary that made sure that all of Juices files were being recovered and made available for Juan, who would then provide such intelligences to his hired help. For the sake of fun Juice had kept Ms. Hillary running here and there for information. He had her making millions and millions of copies of documents that only pertained to the case the firm believed him to present. Figuring that if ole Juan was gonna fork over some files he may as well ship them by the truck loads. Juice had begun to know the law for real, and one of the first things that he had learned was that for every section or penal code that he could use to help Savanna there were twelve other ones that told him that it wasn't cool like that.

With this knowledge in mind he sent Ms. Hillary to and from toting large books. Then when it seemed as if she had enough he sent her another hundred places, and right when it seemed as if it was time to quit, he gave her another fifty assignments. It was no secret that Juice was aiding one of the largest cases in the history of all cases, and with preliminary coming in just a few days; this knowledge forced everyone to work overtime. Ms. Hillary for sure and also the one and only Juan, who represented the powerful law firm of Dixon, Juan and Dixon.

For April her job was no less strenuous, she was running on fumes ever since she met up with Benny from the bait shop, pretty much every day for a week straight now. Just the last five days found them cooped up inside of an old Fiat. If April was cooped up she knew not to complain about it, because Benny stood most of six foot seven was in the passenger side catching all the hell. Even though his seat was pushed all the way to the back he was still uncomfortable, a position that he was gonna have to live with considering that the Fiat sported a lot of fine qualities. For starters they haven't gotten their heads blown off yet, seeing that the old clunker blended in just perfect with the rest of the scenery. Then there was the fact that Benny's computer nerd had installed into his personal car a lot of fine technological equipment giving it Wi-Fi and software, which was perfect for spying and researching, and this was exactly what the two were doing. The warehouses where all of this snooping was going down were scattered all over West Sacramento, and all had freight liners that were unloading crate after crate of merchandise that April was sure would act as tools to take over the streets of Sacramento. From where they sat the view was pristine, the concerns were overbearing.

"What do you think is in the crates sis?" Benny asked dropping his binoculars.

"Everything that you're thinking of is in that truck and the other ones too is my guess."

"Guns and drugs is what I'm thinking."

"That would be my bet too. They know that a war would take place so they have come prepared."

"I got an idea though," said Benny.

"Me too, you first," April showed excitement.

"If we're gonna get down, we need to get down right away, like really soon."

"Yes, and we need to get down on them right here and on this bank."

"I'm sure that they are gonna have this place manned and armed to the teeth."

"Oh-kay."

"I know you, you're up to something," said Benny now suspicious.

"Well, one thing for sure, we know that everything that Nigel has predicted is beginning to take place, and I agree that whatever goes down should go down right here."

"April I never doubted that in Nigel, you know I've known Nigel for a long time. Way back when he used to wear these slacks and the suspenders you know, and for fun I used to bullshit him and right in front of my face he used to pick my bullshit apart until the true answers were all that remained. Predictions, oh he acquired that talent way before he was able to pick apart the bullshit." It was true; Benny had known Nigel for a long time. In fact, it was Benny that put Nigel up and held him while he cried for months over the death of his mother, his wife and his son. Benny never said that he knew how Nigel felt; he couldn't even imagine what it must be like to lose something so precious. So he just let Nigel cry it out, until his friend had become strong enough to accept the things that he couldn't change and in exchange the world has indeed created itself a monster.

"So, we know all there is to know right here, what you got next?" Asked Benny,

"Juice has brought a couple of guys down from Stockton; we could go and check on them." And that was what they did.

The stretched Mercedes pulled into the lot of the steak house just minutes after ten a.m. and Savanna waited for the driver to come around to release his passengers. Mr. Brenner was first to exit the car. It was he who carried the attaché case full of hundred dollar bills totaling five hundred thousand dollars. Savanna followed him through the entrance of Ju-Ju's Steak House where Julius was waiting for them in the office. Across his desk was the necessary documents needed for such a meeting. Making their entrance, Savanna could see that Julius was already beginning to pack his belongings and preparing to make his getaway.

"Julius." Said Savanna reaching out her hand to greet Julius, he was timid so Savanna gave him her one hundred and fifty-watt charmer, for it was plain to see that she gave him fits. This time she put the extras on it, she wore her skirt a few inches shorter than usual. She had to go heavy on the makeup to hide her bruises from the day before, but she was expert at applying such an art. Her heels, screamed sex appeal at the top of their lungs.

"Tanisha," the two shook hands and Julius made mental wishes. Mr. Brenner heard Julius call Savanna "Tanisha" and got a wink from Savanna stuck his paw out to Julius and accepted Savannas introduction. "Julius this is my attorney Mr. Brenner, Bobby…Julius."

"Please to meet you Bobby," said Julius then pointed to the attaché case and said, "is that for me?"

"Well, that all depends, are those the documents that I'm looking for?" Said the lawyer,

"Read for yourself," Julius pushed the folder across the desk into the waiting hands of the high priced fast witted attorney, who read through the folder at the speed of light saying,

"Mm hmmm, mm hmmm," each time that he turned the page then, "this looks like it's all there. So, shall we count the money?"

"Well of course," Julius had prepared for the moment because his money counter was in the drawer, a portable little gadget. Together they participated in the chore of getting to the bottom of the attaché case. After nearly an hour Julius was in possession of a half a million dollars and Savanna was in possession of the cafe. Julius was so busy counting that he never bothered to witness the signing session between Savanna and her lawyer who would act as a viable witness. Before leaving, Savanna was ever so polite by saying, "Thank you sweetie, how about calling me sometime, maybe I could cook something for you." It was because Julius lit up like a Christmas tree did Savanna know that she had left Julius on a good note.

Gilbert and J-Dog sat and watched as the limousine made its departure. What Gilbert noticed was how regal Savanna carried herself. Man did Juice have his thing together. The second thing Gilbert noticed was that Savanna and the white man came out of the cafe minus the briefcase. Oh, the limousine was cute, but not as cute as the girl and the game. J-Dog recognized the same things but not as much as he did the time, noting that it was still early.

"Oh-kay, now that the first part is over," he said then pushed in to activate the car lighter so he could smoke.

"That has to be some kind of life my nigga."

"For real, for real, Filbert but guess what, if we play our cards right I could see us making moves like that."

"By playing our cards right you mean..."

"Let's be for real, we could run up in that fucka right now and get the dough, right now the money is in there for us, but tell me if we go get it is that playing our cards right or wrong?"

"I'm listening."

"I know you is, because you know like I know that the best way to play this game is straight up. It's a world that either you or me has ever seen before so because of that we walk slowly and we pay attention to every detail, and listening to people who sit here every day at least until we have developed our own sense of direction. I saw how you followed the chick from the car, through the door, out the door, in the car and you wonder if she's a weak spot for a nigga that you hated all your young life."

"What is this, some science that you feel that I need," asked Filbert with obvious irritation in his tone. J-Dog just looked to his good friend and said,

"Ain't it though? I mean let's be real now, five hundred dollars a game my nigga? I have never seen you do no shit like that. Served your ass right that he brought "Set Shot Sally" with him don't it. My nigga, in this whole play understand that I walked in with you, and I got you first and foremost, but I need you to have me too. I mean, I don't see you hating this nigga for him as a person, I see you hating this nigga for the breaks that he got in life which is crazy as hell because we all choose our own streets. He chose his and you chose yours. Both of yaw is even on that account but Filbert, out of everybody in the world tell me why did he come all the way to Stockton to get you? Now understand that in that place just right across the street from us right now is a half a million dollars. This nigga didn't come and get you and tell you that there were a couple of birds and a few dollars. My nigga it's a half a ticket in that thang, and why did he do this?"

"You tell me, you're the genius."

"Because he doesn't hate you, because he respects you and probably even wished that you would have taken to the skies with him. I saw you niggas trading baskets and both of y'all had some nice moves but tell me, could you picture you two niggas at UCLA?"

"And you're telling me all of this because of why again?"

"Because I see the way you see the chick and that my nigga is not playing your cards right, that my nigga is playing your cards awfully wrong. Nothing good comes out of that."

"So, we're not going in there to get the dough?"

"No, we're gonna wait."

"And you say that because?"

"Because, that my nigga is the plan. Now tell the truth, did you get that this job was just a little splash, tell me that you got the feeling that Juice momma could have cared less if we did it or not."

"Yeah I got all of that but now to be real with you, I was only pulling your leg, I do see the chick, but not in lust. I see her because I measured Juices' life with her, in compared to my life. The hate that you see my nigga is something that I had to let go of and I had to do that shit for me, it wasn't worth carrying all of that around because hate was only for that of myself, the decisions that I made, you know."

"Exactly, and you came up with all of this, all by yourself?"

"All by myself,"

"My nigga!"

"Tell the truth, she is bad though huh?" Filbert said,

"Mm hum, don't trip, you got yours coming," J-Dog reminded.

"I really believe so, somehow I got that feeling."

"Me too,"

April and Benny switched cars and opted for a roomier vehicle. Benny had a Crown Victoria that was perfect for the occasion. With April as a passenger they drove to Sixty Fifth and Broadway hoping like hell that Juice didn't pick some numb skulls for the job. Benny hearing the gang member's story could only see the foul up now, police everywhere, yellow tape and emergency units in the parking lot and a high speed chase taking place in residential districts.

"Oh-kay, so it's quiet still." Said Benny half surprised by such a discovery. Juice had reported the two to have a primer colored Chevrolet with big wheels on it. So, April searched the area, spotting the car she leaned back in her seat and said,

"Go around the corner and find a place to park, I seen them parked in the lot of the Chinese takeout." Benny drove through the light and made a block that gave them access to view the Chevrolet. Satisfied that the Crown Victoria offered a comfort that the smaller Fiat refused to negotiate, the two sat and watched.

It was six o'clock the time Benny started up the "Crown" after seeing the Chevrolet make its exit out of the parking lot. Benny weaved through the traffic until the Chevrolet was now in view. Benny smiled at the efficiency that the two projected.

"They're heading towards the freeway Benny," April was jittery.

"I know, I am interested too," said Benny.

"Do they know what time it is?"

"And it doesn't seem that they care one way or the other either."

"Oh my God, tell me why am I nervous?"

"I wish I could, but I need to tell you that it's too late to turn back now, we done got to the good part, popcorn anyone?"

"That's not funny Benny." April shook her head as the Chevrolet followed the Chrysler 300 onto the freeway, which was moving at a snail's pace.

Gilbert saw their target exit the cafe and climb into a newer model Chrysler. He saw as smoke left the exhaust pipe and saw as it was placed into gear too, but more than anything Gilbert saw that the brother was in possession of the brief case, which was the exact same one that Savanna carried into the restaurant many hours ago.

"Oh-kay, well there go dude that got our money," said J-Dog.

"Yelp, seem like he got to fork that over huh?"

"Look, it looks like he's going to the freeway like you said."

"I figured that he would, niggas would open up a shop in the ghetto but they will live in the burbs, believe that shit?"

"Well, stay with him, don't lose his ass but don't let him know that we with him." Filbert Gilbert followed just close enough to avoid suspicion, and on to the freeway they went.

"Ain't this a bitch?" Gilbert shouted once he saw the traffic moving so slowly.

"Shit, we waited this long, what's another few minutes."

"Or hours look at this shit." Gilbert continued to complain about the traffic.

"We'll be alright, let me hit something to calm my nerves, ooh you see that shit?" J-Dog had gotten excited.

"Uh uh, what is it?" Gilbert saw J-Dog slip on his latex gloves so he looked around.

"Dig, I'm gonna hop in the back," said J-Dog tightening up his hoody.

"Oh-kay and you want me to do what?"

"Look on the niggas passenger side, you see his windows rolled down right?"

"Mm hmm, oh-kay,"

"Time that nigga with the next exit, soon as you get close I'm gonna hop out on that nigga and hop in the car with him and I need you get off on the next exit. I'm gonna flock that nigga and run off the exit, don't leave without me." So much for needing something for his nerves Gilbert thought.

"My nigga bet, don't keep me waiting and remember the message, do you remember?"

"Yeah, blow his brains out, I got it."

"Oh-kay, oh-kay it's a quarter mile to Twelfth Avenue, so get ready."

"Pull on the side of him," J-Dog laid down and out of sight, but felt the lane switch.

"Dog there ain't no better time than right now, soon as you out I'm gone, like I say don't keep me waiting my nigga." J-Dog stole a peek then he was out of the Chevrolet with the swiftness of a cat. Gilbert never saw when J-Dog got into the car with Julius but Julius sure did.

"What the fuck..." said Julius, frightened to death.

"Nigga shut the fuck up before I shoot you in the face. Nigga stop looking at me, look out the window."

"Oh-kay, oh-kay, I got money in my pocket just take it, my watch anything you want just don't shoot."

"Bitch stop looking at me, look out the window, that's the last time that I'm gonna tell you!"

"Oh-kay, oh-kay" Julius looked out of the window of the driver's side; the rainbow bakery was his last sight before his world had gone black. As for the other motorist, the ones that were unfortunate enough to have heard the thunder and saw the flash as J-Dog sent one round behind the head of Julius and watched as Julius' brains flew out the window and leaving sprinkles over the steering wheel before relieving him of the attaché case and making his exit.

"Oh-kay…Um, yeah," Benny was at a loss for words. They both saw the whole entire operation. They saw as the car continued to roll with its passenger side door swung open until it crashed into the vehicle directly in front of it. They saw as the attaché case was removed and they saw as the unidentified man sprint across the freeway to the sound of cars blowing their horns. Benny drove by the Chrysler then stopped the car and looked into the Chrysler for signs of life, not seeing any so he took the Twelfth Avenue exit as well.

Chapter 42

The time Juice made it in he had just enough energy to remove his shoes and none after that. Exhausted wasn't the word most suitable for his condition, fatigue had sat in hours ago and drained he was just shortly after arriving at the offices earlier in the day. Juice had to work double just to achieve the minimal amount of progress, but even that was progress enough but hiding from the ones that were placed to help you was more frustrating than the entertainment. Still he knew what had to be done even if it took all night and it so happened that on this night, all night was an understatement.

Juice could have counted to twelve in his sleep before he knew that it was time to get back on his grind. Only when he made it to ten his mother was waking him up.

"I'm up, I'm up, I'm up," he said knowing that this new day offered up another one that would be listed in the strenuous section. Juice rolled over, fully dressed because he fell asleep fully clothed and made his way to the tiny kitchen that was fitted for such a small family.

"I take it that it was a trying day yesterday," said April.

"What gave me away?" Juice asked.

"Your clothing, first time in a long time that I woke you regretting that I had to do it, so, hurry and eat up." Juice was pleased that his mother prepared for him such a large breakfast because he was starving.

"So, how was your day?" Juice asked.

"Just like yours, long and stressful."

"Not like mine I hope."

"That bad huh?"

"My feet hurt, my back hurt, my head hurt and I done read so much that I've become cross eyed."

"Sounds like you're aging prematurely." Juice was examined by his mother.

"I guess so, anything new happen?" Asked Juice,

"Wouldn't you like to know, Mr. Man?"

"Without a hitch, or was there some problems?"

"Nothing in the news, nothing in the papers," said April.

"But you're smiling." Juice noticed the cheesiness of his mother's beam and right away knew that she was holding something back.

"Well, no mentions, what do you think that means?"

"Do I need to reach them?" Juice asked from skepticism.

"No, I got the email in fact I'm expecting a fax pretty soon. Something about a folder was in the case." Juice heard this with the same confusion that he started with, said.

"Oh-kay, I'm lost."

"Well, the good thing is that we know for sure, even without the news channels, and hopefully this would help Nigel a little bit." April turned away for just the mention of his name gave her anxiety.

"You know what I like, I like that you are holding his wellbeing in such a high regard. When I go see him he holds your wellbeing just as high and while all of this is going on I am being used as the mule to carry both concerns," Juice said shaking his head.

"Well?"

"Well, what?"

"Well, you knew the job was hard when you took it, but we're both glad that you took it."

"So, he's in preliminary tomorrow and we expect a circus for this. We expect the DA to win as many points as possible. I don't see the DA pulling any stops personally."

"Even more so now that, you know," April left the rest unsaid.

"Oh-kay, and what do we know about the back end?" Juice asked of his mother's discoveries then listened closely as his mother took him in and out of the day that she had shared with Benny. Juice listened to the tales of the warehouses and the soldiers. He heard about the borrowed space mobile of a Fiat that came fully equipped with UFO detections. He even heard about the incident which took place on a California freeway. Juice shook his head at the story then gone into the day he had. One of fake hand offs, flea flickers and naked bootlegs and for this he gave his mother a deep down soulful laugh.

"That's what they get, so for today you got what?" Asked April through hearty laughter,

"Uh uh, today I hang around here to make sure that I'm well rested for tomorrow."

"No, no, no, no, no, sweetie. We have already learned that there is absolutely no rest for the weary."

"Which means that you need me to do what?"

"We need to sit here and think of a way to bring our guys back home." April had developed a kink in her operation that had become complicated and hard to knock off.

"Ahh, sit here you say." Now this impressed Juice a bit.

"Yeah, we have a huge problem; I have no way of contacting anyone. Nigel knew that this would occur once he was hooked and booked, for it was already pre-established that in the event something like this was to transpire, that everyone should hit the hills. But we have to find a way to get them back, because now it's time to hit the mattresses." Upon hearing this Juice set his feet in motion, to and from he paced admitting and dismissing one idea after the other. Then he stopped as an idea struck him, one that proved to be both feasible and productive, he said.

"Don't worry about it, I got it. I could bring them home." Especially if they had to hit the mattresses, and this meant that war was inevitable.

"Oh and how are you going to do all of this?"

"Now wouldn't you like to know my lovely mommy dearest?" Juice teased.

"Yes, I would like to know." April's' concern was obvious.

"Don't worry about it, I got us. So is there anything else on our plate, you may find something once..." April heard the fax machine announce its need for attention.

"Oh-kay, this may be it." She said,

Juice followed his mother as she gone around the desk to receive her messages. "Yeah, this is for you." She retrieved the sheets and gave each one the once over before handing the forms to her son then sat at her desk and sent the message of reception. Pleased at the works of Gilbert and the one she called James, she had even more of an admiration now that they refused to take the money and run. April watched as her son read the contents of the forms knowing that he too would be pleased, saw as her son glowed and said.

"If this ain't coaching a witness than I don't know what is."

"Yeah, but you better not say anything or guess what?"

"They're gonna be on to us, wondering how did I acquire such information." Juice said matter of factually.

"Yes, then we begin to unravel at the ends."

"I'll work on the angles of this information and be ready. If this is how they want to get down, then let's get it on."

"Oooh, I always loved when you talk your mess."

"So, you never told me about the younger Dixon, what's his place in all of this?" Juice had spent many days watching the Jr. Dixon and wasn't able to determine his placement in the scheme that was oh so obviously set around him. Juice couldn't decide the innocents of the younger partner of the firm so he made a mental note to re-visit the idea.

"Well, I've spotted him on a few occasions at the warehouse, I've talked to Benny and he believes that there's a company called Farmex which is a front to allow the safety for all three transportations', delivery and reception. All protected and accepted by this front that Juan has. So, we're not sure of Dixon Sr., but we are most certain that Dixon Jr. and Juan are in cahoots."

"Don't surprise me really," said Juice "He always struck me as one being ever so easy to influence." Juice shook his head at his mother's revelation and instantly decided that Jr. Dixon was just as guilty as the rest.

"Same thing that we believe Benny and I, it looks pretty clear that Juan is the primary, the head honcho so to say."

"So, now we play ball right, now that all of the players are here?" April never said that she was offended by the likes of the newspapers refusing to recognize the loss of a known citizen, a well-known member of the county of Sacramento, but April didn't need the coin, no. She knew that the departments held incidents under wraps for a reason, whatever reason that they may say, but somehow April knew the real reason. The operation was to keep everyone's focus on Nigel and the only way to do any of this was to keep any new events of similarity of old cases, under wraps. Only what society didn't know was that April knew how to get her point across, always has. Her methods were always the same; if you ever want to get someone to listen you must first get their attention. Oh so long ago she was taught by her late husband the fine art of political motivation. That if they didn't hear you the first time then park a bunch of bodies on their front porch the next time, then and only then would their fuzzy memories become clear and effulgent, she said.

"And hopefully we'll have a good game but still I need you to devote most of your attention to getting our guys home them we could talk about playing ball as you say."

"I'm sure to pull it off. Did Savanna call today?" Juice changed the subject.

"Yeah, she told me to let you sleep."

"Speaking of sleep, I'll see you when I see you. Good afternoon, I'll see you tonight," and Juice headed for his room.

"Could you believe this shit my nigga?" J-Dog exclaimed, for he felt royally disrespected. He searched channels for reports; he even searched the radio station for even a mere utterance of his handy work, not a peep. "I know what I'm gonna do. Shit when all else fails," he snapped on the laptop, feeling as if the internet was sure to report the news.

"My nigga what's so important about reading about it or hearing about it, look at this though, this is what's real." Filbert Gilbert snapped open the attaché case and pointed to the currency and said,

"Now this is what the fuck I'm talking about," J-Dog saw the excitement in his friend and couldn't help but to wonder if he would eventually allow money to go to his head. Shook his head and was glad to see that the laptop was ready for action and to prove that he wasn't a deranged lunatic. He decided to check the email first and he did. Pleased that Mrs. Raymond had successfully received the fax he was now looking for the good stuff. J-Dog searched the web news, gossip columns, and Facebook to see if friends were gossiping. Nothing, nothing and nothing, closing the laptop he turned to Filbert Gilbert and said,

"Help me understand how is it that we created a traffic jam from here to Wichita Kansas and ain't nobody saying nothing?"

"That shit again bro, ain't you heard anything that I just said?"

"Yeah, I hear you, but did you hear me when I said that we can't lug that thang around everywhere that we go, have it dawned on you that at any given time we may get pulled over or something like that."

"We can't just leave it here" J-Dog agreed with that shit right away saying,

"Ain't no telling who comes in here when we leave, one of those room cleaning bitches would come in here and find that shit ain't nobody gonna understand English after that."

"Put this bitch in that storage until the game is over, what you think?" Asked Gilbert,

"I fucks with that, more than this anyways."

"Well, we better get on that right now it's almost lunch time," by lunchtime these two knew that downtown Sacramento is where they needed to be. With their Chevrolet now cooked to crisps in an alleyway between Fifth Avenue and Bret Harte Rd. the two loaded up the barely reliable and almost never dependable Ford Aerostar minivan that was purchased from a seller out the newspaper. Filbert Gilbert had tucked his dreads into a long curly wig and sported his bifocals after drawing tattoos of three visible tear drops on his face and gone to make the purchase of the vehicle.

"What the fuck is this?" Said J-Dog in disgust,

"The only scraper I could find. I mean if we're gonna cook the bitch anyways what do it matter."

"So, were off to the storage to load it all into the shed before heading down-town to meet up with the girl, do the wop and…." J-Dog paused to let Gilbert fill in the blanks.

"Hopefully we land safely after that. Cook the boat then send the message and wait to hear about our box. This thang here," Gilbert pointed at the case then said "We go fifty fifty and we'll see what life has to offer us then. This shit crazy huh?"

"Yeah, crazy just don't quite say it all my nigga. It seems to be leaving something out like strange, peculiar, bizarre and unheard of."

Chapter 43

Savanna couldn't think of a time when her feet had throbbed so much. Never did she ever think that her life would take on so many turns either. Just a month ago God and Dominic was the only thing that she had ever known. Then she learned something about her man. Then she learned something about herself that she thought would never ever be possible in this life or her next life. The internal argument that has brought to her attention a side of the tracks that she feared was now her reality. Oh, Savanna was no stranger to the rough-shod way of living she came from the inner-city and even lived in the projects, it was hard to miss any transgressions there. She just never thought that she would be buying a cafe from anyone who she knew would never live to enjoy the money, but she had. Never did she ever think that she would be caught dead in a clown suit, makeup, red hair and baggy clothes, a Ronald McDonald look-a-like to act as the point person but she was. Her red nose and flapper boots were drawing all of the attention to herself that she could gather. While passing out flyers and coupons for potential customers to come and eat at the new Ju-Ju's Steakhouse, all the while paying close attention to the entrance and the exits of the powerfully built building. A building made of glass, brick and prestige that sat right across from where she delivered her campaign, known as Dixon, Juan and Dixon.

From Savannas own investigations and from what April had provided for her she came to the understanding that the one Minor R. Dixon had a costly flaw. With him, human nature repeated itself Monday through Friday at a monotonous regularity. Eight thirty a.m. Minor R. Dixon would make his way through the entrance of the power structure. Twelve o'clock sharp would find him coming through the exit where he would head to Mary's' Bistro, which was coincidentally famous for its Bloody Mary's, oyster dishes and chowders. By one o'clock Mr. Minor Dixon could be seen walking through the entrance of the building and back to work with a scent of liquor on his breath. April reported such a movement. Now Savanna was in position to second these facts. So, when her watch read eleven thirty she allowed her visuals to be more attentive towards both, the exits and to her cell phone. Just in case through all the noise that she was making she somehow missed any calls. Then the call came just two minutes after her last check.

"Where are you?" Asked the voice that she had recognized to belong to J-Dog.

"Eighth and L."

"Any news yet?"

"It's been the same each time," said Savanna.

"We're getting off on J Street."

"Go to seventh and make a right, go to L and make the left. You'll see me." Savanna gave the directions.

"You still getting your clown on though," asked J-Dog smiling at his own humor.

"Yeah and I'm running out of everything, flyers, patience and water and my feet are killing me."

"Oh-kay, I mean we can't keep you waiting, no ma'am not if your feet hurt," J-dog reasoned.

"Thank you, you guys off the freeway yet?"

"Mm hmm, we made the right turn already."

"Oh-kay hurry." Savanna said looking at the time on her phone before disconnecting. Moments later she saw the van driven by Gilbert pull over and park just across the street from her then saw J-Dog exit the van. Accepting a flyer from Savanna he smiled and said.

"You might want to point him out and then get out of here; I got it from here, alright!"

"If you say so," less than ten minutes passed and Savanna was packed up and heading towards her rented cargo van after positively identifying the one Mr. Minor R. Dixon who as usual was making his way to Mary's for a chowder and stiff Bloody Mary, an event that was interrupted by an African American male wearing a hooded sweatshirt, black jeans and boots.

"Excuse me sir," said J-Dog getting the attention of Minor R. Dixon, "I have a message for you."

"A message, oh my God!" The younger Dixon nearly fainted at the sight of the firearm that J-Dog revealed only to him, an action that was concealed to the rest of the world.

"Yeah a message, if you want to live, you would follow me, that's my message."

"And if I refuse," said Minor.

"Then I gun you down right here, and right now."

"Well, I guess you're gonna have to do what you have to do young man."

"Oh-kay," the barrel of the Glock .40 caliber spit its flame and Minor clutched his stomach and fell to the ground surprised by the actions of this encounter. Filbert hearing the shot, never took his eyes away from his partner, started up the van and drove on to the sidewalk to collect his friend, seeing as J-Dog grabbed a hold of their target and put the pistol to the head of the pleading white man and squeezed the trigger receiving the desired effect. While in his zone, in his rhythm, J-Dog emptied the rest of the clip into the attorney.

"Come on nigga," Shouted Gilbert snapping J-Dog back to reality. Happy to have gotten his attention and him now loaded into the vehicle. Gilbert pressed the gas and got them away from a scene of people running and screaming and frightened for their lives.

"What the fuck was that?" Shouted Filbert Gilbert,

"He said that he wasn't coming."

"Is that right, shit, shit, shit?"

"Man, would you calm the fuck down."

"Oh-kay, oh-kay start pouring the shit and hurry, hurry my nigga." The sound of sirens filled the air and the fact that the vehicle would be identified was a known one. J-Dog had gone to the rear and picked up the gas can and ran wild with it until he was pleased with his works.

"Look my nigga; I hear them the next block over. Let's pull up and set the flame and I'll meet you at the storage, and hurry." Gilbert brought the van to a screeching halt and the two made their exits. J-Dog put fire to the van and a loud swooshing sound echoed its announcements that the fire was in full blaze. Then he took off running in the opposite direction. Filbert Gilbert had no idea where he was, but he knew that one car after the next flew by him with their lights flashing and sirens blaring, heading in the direction of the burning van and towards the last place that he had saw J-Dog. Filbert Gilbert had slowed his pace to a casual stroll as if innocence was the makeup of his entire nature. He encountered a lot of panic stricken faces and faces of people that were once walking or running and minding their own business were now running and walking towards the scene of the burning vehicle. Amazed as the for black smoke filled the air.

Each member of Team ORBITT was assembled at a Chipotle Restaurant and each one was wracking their brains trying to figure out their new puzzle.

"So, we have Mr. Collinson in custody," says Special Agent Barrnette.

"Yeah, last I checked he was on maximum security, not a lot of movement going on over there," said Detective Stallworth.

"Uh-uh, ain't no movement over there, especially not this kind of wiggling." Special Agent Barrnette said picking up the folder then dropping it on the table, indicating the contents between the pages of the new folder.

"I have to agree," said Captain Wynn. "How do we explain what the hell is going on then?" The Captain was obviously flustered.

"Oh-kay, has anyone thought copycat yet?" Asked Sergeant Wildey, these being the first words that he has spoken all night. For his fears were greater than anyone's. If Nigel Collinson was not Raymond Buchannon then Raymond Buchannon was still elusive and very much active in his dirty deeds.

"Oh yeah," said The Captain. "This is the scariest of all my scariest thoughts."

"I'll second," said Barrnette.

"I agree," said Stallworth.

"You bunch of pussies," said Sergeant Wildey.

"Oh yeah, tell me, could you picture not one, but two Raymond Buchannon's. I mean give that a good visual and tell me… what you see?" Finished the Captain guiding the young Sergeant through his pictures,

"Oh-kay, I'll agree that's too many," The Sergeant relented.

"Ahh" said the chorus of pussies.

"I mean, fuck me running, but let's not get ahead of ourselves. Let's go with what we do have and build from there." The Special Agent recommended settling everyone down to focus.

"Which is?" Stallworth had never pulled punches before, nor was there any appropriate reason to start now.

"Hell, let's open the folder, the very, very skinny not all the way satisfactory when it comes to evidence folder. The one that could get us all ran out of Sacramento folder. The documents, you know, the kind that..." The Special Agent was interrupted by the Captain who couldn't stand the ideas of having such a short file blurted out.

"Alright already!"

"I'm just saying though, is there anybody else getting ready to meet the press." Said the Agent,

"Fuck, fuck, fuck!" Screamed the Captain,

"Oooh, now that's a lot of fucks Cap. You need to tell us something?" Asked the young Sergeant,

"Speaking of press, preliminary for Mr. Collinson is tomorrow." The Captain left that out there as if that alone would explain everything.

"Yes sir and I bet you that that's in the folder too." Said the special agent,

"Would you kill us already," said the Captain.

"And for preliminary you've been subpoenaed to appear right?" Reminded Stallworth,

"Correct-a-mundo," The Captain shook his head at the debacle that was waiting to happen.

"That lawyer that Mr. Collinson has is a young woman that nobody has ever heard of," said Stallworth.

"Oh-kay, I have a question," said Sergeant Wildey, who never lost his focus.

"Hopefully something that could kick start us," said the Special Agent.

"Oh-kay, the young lawyer, what do we know about her. Could Mr. Collinson send hits through her in the event that there is somehow a copycat?"

"Mmm, it listens, so there's the question. Well what do we know about the bartender?" Asked The Captain,

"Well, we know that he has a mean crossover and a jump shot that I would love to name my kids after, and he has a study habit that gave him a 4.0 GPA. Let's see, he left The Historic College of UCLA where he studied business and majored in the art of Black History, then something happened and no offense to our good Sergeant, but his dad met the other Wildey's, the not so good, trigger happy, blood thirsty all guns blazing, ski mask..."

"Enough, enough, enough Special Agent!" The Captain had to slow Barrnette's roll.

"I was only kidding, but anyways, ain't no sense in us getting sensitive. So he goes to the McGeorge School of Law, just four blocks from where his father met his misfortune and I'm expecting him to graduate with honors there."

"McGeorge School of Law," they all seemed to repeat simultaneously after hearing the narration given by Special Agent Barrnette.

"Yeah, that's in the folder too, didn't yaw see it in there?"

"So, Mr. Collinson has put his life in the hands of a rookie from public school and a bartender?" Asked the Captain,

"Did you hear the part when I said about the study habits though? I mean I'll recommend that we don't underestimate this guy or the lady, remember he was a point guard and they are tricky, tricky, tricky if I was you Captain I wouldn't relax on this girl. Keep your good eye on her at all times." Finished the FBI Special Agent just as he was beginning to believe to think that he was the only one who read the folder at all Detective Stallworth uttered,

"So, we get a public display on the highway with the same number, one pop, and one kill."

"Same style, do we think coincidence?" Asked the young Sergeant,

"At first we could have said so, then we get another job, this time an attorney, overlooking the many jokes of a good attorney being a dead one, but this one seemed to have left a bad taste. This reads nine shots, all into the attorney. One main shot to the same exact place as so many before him though, if that means anything. The other eight shows hate, disgust and a point hammered home." The Captain delivered this analogy shaking his head at the thought.

"Any non-similarities are better, that's what we should look for?" The young Sergeant was tuned into solving the riddle.

"Which would prove copycat, right?" Said Detective Stallworth and the sergeant nodded.

"Well, we can't say that he's never killed in public, because he has. We can't say that he's never wore a disguise because he has. We can't say that he has never knocked down any high ranking or public officials, because he has. So, do we see any dissimilarity so far?" Asked the Captain and in return received a round of negatives. For all heads shook their blanks when mentally seeking traits of a copycat.

"Now, my next question," the Special Agent stated bringing the attention onto him.

"Which is?" Asked The Captain,

"What, if anything do we have on Mr. Collinson?"

"I knew you were gonna say that," said The Captain as he reached for the folder then said,

"Well, we got three witnesses, each telling corroborating stories of Mr. Collinson's devilment's…."

"Two," interrupted the detective "we have two Cap., one checked out of here the other day remember."

"Oh-kay, now two witnesses, one who'll testify the functioning of this criminals' operation that was ran by Mr. Collinson…" Again the captain was interrupted, this time by the FBI Agent.

"Supposedly, I mean so far Captain."

"Oh-kay then we have a hired gunman who was paid to carry out ordered hits for Mr. Collinson." The Captain paused to accept any more interruptions not receiving any he continued.

"It is to my understanding that we have the mistress of Mr. Collinson who's willing to take the stand before me; we have information that tells us that she qualifies as being a reliable source. Then we have an old retired professional hit man who has already paid his debt to society by bringing fifteen years total of in and out time. Has a history of working for and then rolling over on one crime boss after the next one until he has been forgiven by the District Attorney. Maybe he really took contracts for Mr. Collinson I don't know." The Captain finished with a sheepish smile.

"So, you're saying that we don't have shit then, and that all we have are some words? What happened to the promise of us delivering the good stuff, the physical stuff they call evidence?" Asked Agent Barrnette,

"I'm afraid we are gonna have to turn up the heat on the streets. We're gonna have to get what we need on a street level." Said the Captain,

"Oh-kay by me as long as we operate in the ways of the good book, even though right now I'm starting to see the case against Mr. Collinson unraveling at the seams. In fact, I may be the only one to say it even though we all think it, but I don't think we have Mr. Buchannon over there in that jail cell. I mean it may take another body to land in our laps before someone else agrees with me verbally, but I myself don't see this young lawyer orchestrating hits for Mr. Collinson, lest she'll end her career before it even starts. Nor do I see the bartender, I see this young man as coming from a family background as American as apple pie. His mother's an entrepreneur who is deep into charitable events state wide. Father died a people's champ, celebrated and highly praised. I could be wrong, but it doesn't play right to me. It all seems flimsy and in return we may all be caught into the eye of the hurricane." The table grew quiet then the young Sergeant spoke up by saying,

"Oh-kay, so preliminary is tomorrow for someone who may or may not be Mr. Buchannon. Although, he's a high ranking candidate do we A. release him or B. see how far the courts can go while we beat the streets?" After a spell of silence, the group was forced to go with the latter, for it was known that Nigel was just as good in custody until the officers has figured out for sure, then for these fine and upstanding gentlemen to live with themselves believing that they had and then released from custody the one very inimical and dangerous "Raymond Buchannon."

Chapter 44

Juice arose from his anxiousness knowing that today was a very big day. In his sleep he was forming strategies and while he was sleep he was keeping track of times and dates. Now that he awoke he was climbing out of bed knowing that all eyes would be on Savanna. Eyes from all over the country would indeed be glued to the television awaiting the outcomes of each court date. Ears would be glued to the streets for hints and clues to what's really taking place in the California's States Capitol. With this for knowledge Juice decided to dress as dapper as he could, and get an early jump on the day. He knew that Nigel wanted to visit with him, because unlike the highway incident that was being played close to chest it would be awfully complicated to shield the public of such a horrifying incident that has taking place in one of the most populated places that downtown had to offer to its high class blasé patrons, and tourist alike. Because of the stature that the Dixon's possess, it was also hard to ignore that the son of one of the world's most powerful legal minds ever, now lay stiff in the morgue either. So, therefore, every channel that broadcasted the news was now ringing their alarms.

Juice knew that Nigel would have gotten this information because of this, and decided that it was best for everyone involved to avoid a visit with Nigel before court, leaving him to concentrate on the task at hand which was to avoid the press until after court. They all needed to focus on leading questions and ways to set their traps for trial in order to create the snowball effect and not to stimulate Nigel's incarcerated comforts. First things first, to avoid the press Juice's plans were to have Savanna enter the courtroom before everyone and take a seat in the jury section and await the arrival of everyone, client included. Emphasis were placed on proceeding with the steps, note for note until it was time to reschedule the next court date which meant that preliminary would then be in the can.

The scheduled time for preliminary was eight thirty. By eight o'clock the courtroom offered standing room only. The press flocked in like a hive of bees. The buzz from the events of the past weeks was too loud to ignore. Juice knew that Savanna would have hell getting out of the courtroom on this day. The doors opened and Juice was in the aisle heading towards the defense table looking all of business and none for the games, he'd gone to Savanna and leaned into her and said,

"Baby, there ain't no better time than right now to prove to the world that you belong here, you hear me?'

"I do, and guess what?" Savanna eyed Juice then said,

"I'm about to act up in here, look you could have a seat knowing that." Savanna held his eyes, satisfied, Juice turned on his heels and went to take a seat directly behind where Nigel was expected to take his seat at the table with his lawyer. He watched as Savanna opened her briefcase and removed her defense strategies and gave them the once over. The audience grew impatient and over excited. Each member of the court felt Nigel's presence a full minute before he arrived. Once he was inside of the courtroom Savanna was on her feet and headed directly to the deputy who escorted Nigel into the courtroom and said to the deputy in a voice that dripped ice and venom.

"Take those cuffs off of my client right now! And any other time that this man enters a courtroom after you decided to allow the audience and press in before you bring my client. From now on you better make sure that he isn't tied up like a criminal, before you prove him guilty or I'll call a mistrial right away, try me!" Oh, she was spitting mad.

"I'm sorry counselor, but I have my orders." Savannas eyebrows rose a bit at the sound of orders. The District Attorney was present and eying everything ran to the deputy shouting,

"Take the cuffs off of him right now, and who gave you orders to not only bring Mr. Collinson in late, but to allow the press entry way before you bring in Mr. Collinson?"

"Sorry counselors, Mr. Collinson." The deputy removed the cuffs and lead Nigel to his seat then positioned himself behind Nigel, just enough to allow the defendant breathing room and enough space for a view to the defendant by the audience and the press alike. Savanna reached the district attorney and said,

"Next time miss trial. I'll call it right away!" Savanna shouted, and before giving the DA time to respond Savanna walked away knowing that there will be more shenanigans coming from the other side of the courtroom. One that grew quiet and still as the Honorable Judge Walker took her bench, the court heard the Bailiff,

"All rise for the Honorable Judge Walker!" As if everyone was set to pledge allegiance they all stood then the Bailiff reminded everyone why they were all present.

"This is case number 07433774 the State of California versus Nigel Collinson."

"You may be seated," said the Honorable Judge Walker to the packed house of onlookers, supporters and press.

"Mr. Collinson we are here to have a preliminary to see if there is enough evidence to bind you over for trial do you now understand the functioning's of a preliminary hearing?"

"Yes, ma'am," was what his lips said, but in his mind he was saying "you dumb bitch there wasn't enough evidence to have brought me down here to begin with." To the District Attorney Judge Walker looked down her glasses as if the real Mr. Matthew Donaldson had better show up said quietly,

"Are you ready to call your witnesses?"

"Well Judge I would like to go on record as saying that my witness list has been compromised severely…"

"I object your honor." Savanna was on her feet.

"On what grounds counselor?" Asked the judge,

"Unless it is the people's intention to book my client then we need only to hear what's relevant, the people's witness list last I checked your honor is plenty of long enough to proceed with preliminary" and to the DA she said "may we please stop playing for the press."

"So your grounds are relevancy then?" Asked the judge holding Savanna at eye level,

"Yes, it is Your Honor."

"Well, are you prepared to charge Mr. Collinson for anything Mr. Donaldson?" The judge said "anything" knowing that everyone had knowledge of past events.

"No Your Honor."

"Then the objection is sustained, call the witnesses that you do have." Savanna had known that the DA would attempt to play for the cameras was satisfied and took her seat.

"The people would like to call Captain Marcel Wynn." Everyone turned their attention to the rear of the courtroom where there was a sea of law officers now guarding the exit while scanning the audience for potential trouble. The door opened and Captain Wynn made his way to the witness stand and there he stood.

"Mr. Wynn would you raise your right hand," The Captain complied. "Do you swear to tell the whole truth so help you God?"

"I do." Captain Wynn took his seat and the district attorney ran through a line of questioning starting with the years of employment. The fact that the Captain has been employed by the Sacramento Police Department for many years gave the people in the entire courtroom, Juice included, the idea that professional testimony would soon follow. The District Attorney relived the day of arrest and the tactics used to bring in Mr. Collinson. While the DA questioned the Captain Savanna wrote in her folder allowing the line of questioning to commence without objection until it was her turn.

"Counselor do you have any questions for The Captain?" The judge asked her,

"Yes, Your Honor, Mr. Wynn while you were instructed to proceed with caution of Mr. Collinson's arrest did any incident follow upon encounter of my client, any resisting or any squabbling, a gun fight or anything physical sir that we should know about?"

"No."

"Did he run from you?"

"No."

"Sir in my client's possession did you find any firearms or weapons that posed such a threat?"

"No."

"So as far as you're concerned you caught him at an opportune time when resisting proved to be ineffective and futile?"

"I'd like to think so."

"Oh-kay, sir I'm sure that God smiled on us all on that day. May I ask you whether or not you had a warrant to search my client's home?"

"Yes, we did. Everything was done officially, correctly and by the book." The Captain needed the city to know the department's fidelities.

"You've also had a warrant to search the one… Benny's Bait Shop is that correct?"

"Yes, it is correct."

"Did you search the residence of Mr. Collinson?" Savanna repeated.

"Yes, we did."

"With the appropriate permission I assume?" Captain Wynn was wondering if the young attorney was shooting for an illegal search nodded and said,

"Yes, we entered the home of Mr. Collinson with the proper paperwork."

"Oh-kay, so did you remove anything from this residence and if so what were the fruits of your findings?"

"Well, we believe that Mr. Collinson had been tipped off to our investigation giving him time to clean up…"

"So your fruit of findings were shall we say, fruitless?"

"That'll be correct."

"Did you take anything from this residence that would be later introduced as evidence Captain?"

"We removed a computer that appeared to be very cleaned, we believed was used for Mr. Collinson's operation."

"And what gives you this belief sir?"

'Well, the fact that a new hard drive was installed felt suspicious enough for us to remove it from the residence."

"And the Bait Shop, I'll guess that you had the proper credentials to enter and seize there as well?"

"Yes ma'am."

"And could you tell us why you needed a warrant to enter and seize from a business that had absolutely nothing to do with my client. I'll say that you were thorough with your investigations which told you before obtaining such a warrant that my client was not an owner or partner or even an employee. So, why did you need a warrant for a bait shop, Captain?"

"Well as you say our investigations were thorough and it was during our investigations that led to this Bait Shop by Mr. Collinson. We observed many of times Mr. Collinson deliver to this Bait Shop."

"Oh, and by deliver you mean what exactly?" Now this was the reason that everyone had all gathered here today, to hear the answer to that question, even the camera crews who had their eyes through the focuses of their cameras raised up to view the Captain with a naked eye. The audience that followed this line of questioning had somehow all leaned forward in their seats simultaneously in expectation, for this was the question of the decade and one that needed an answer right away. Everyone had come to the same conclusion that if the District Attorney could prove drugs then murder would not be far away. Everyone needed this answer which was at the moment somehow, more important than their next breath, but nobody needed this answer more than Savanna.

"Well, we observed Mr. Collinson carrying boxes as well as duffel bags into this place of business on many occasions." This was true because after Victor died Nigel helped April rearrange Victor's office and rid it of its documents and other sensitive items that would allow April to go on living without the trace of his dear friend's demise.

"Oh-kay," Savanna wore a look of confusion for an expression. Everyone felt as if the Captain had let them down, including Savanna, who said,

"And in the boxes and bags were...?" Savanna broke her question and walked to the defense table and for entertainment purposes only she picked up a folder and winked at Nigel, who was listening more attentively than anyone else though complicated and close to impossible that may have been, but true. He received Savannas wink like everyone else in attendance that caught the sly gesture and in return Savanna had received many smiles for now they all knew that the young attorney was now up to something. Flipping through the pages she turned to the Captain and in her staged irritations she slammed down the folder and said,

"Oh-kay Captain I give up, what was in the boxes and the duffel bags?" Savanna's smile gave way to a round of snickering from the audience. Judge Walker had brought order back to the court and warned Savanna of her theatrics and allowed her to continue.

"Sorry Your Honor," Savanna said then "Captain you were going to tell us what was in the boxes that you observed my client on many occasions deliver to this business of question?"

"We have no idea." The crowd took off again, a crowd that felt clearly let down and disappointed, someone said.

"We came all the way over here for this shit!" There was an "ain't that about a bitch," mumbled somewhere. Judge Walker took to her gavel and began to bang as if she too was being let down. Once order was restored she warned the audience,

"The next time that I need to bring order to this courtroom I will empty this place so fast," she left the rest to the imagination.

"Oh-kay," Savanna said shaking her head as if she too had been cheated and dissatisfied said to the judge.

"I have no more questions." Then walked away from the witness stand and a very ashamed Captain Wynn who sat searching his memory for exactly how did he get himself into this disaster to begin with. Who led him here, then he remembered.

"Counselor," Judge Walker said to the District Attorney. "You have any more questions for our Captain?" Donaldson didn't see where any questions that he would ask would undo any damage already done, just said,

"I have no questions as of now," then took his seat.

Savanna sat next to Nigel and read the notes that Nigel had taken during her performance. She leaned into him and said, "This is only the preliminary, I am only trying to get everything in the police report on record; I don't see us escaping without trial." Although Nigel nodded she knew that Nigel didn't understand all the way that very few people walked away from preliminary with charges dismissed unless the tactics used by the (AOS) arresting officers were so shabby that there was nothing left to do but rid themselves of such integrity issues but never in a murder case or a Capital Case has this been reported in any of the books that she read so far, which were plenty. Savanna made a mental note to give Nigel the education on preliminaries and trials. The preliminary was only a hearing to see if there was enough evidence to bound one over for trial with the true understanding that a police report alone has a lot of the times proven sufficient enough of a reason.

Savanna sat and ruffled through her file, now knowing which witness to prepare for seeing now that the bailiff was wheeling a television into the courtroom and positioning the set to give everyone the opportunity to view the screen. It has already been prearranged that one of the people's witnesses had been listed under protection so therefore she would not be giving her testimony in its traditional fashion, but in this protective one. It is the law that every defendant has the constitutional right to see and hear testimony from their accusers and Nigel would not be prejudiced this way, no. He would see and he will hear testimony from his accuser only it will be live via satellite so to say. For this testimony would come from the judge's chambers.

"What the fuck is this?" Nigel whispered into Savanna.

"This witness, let's see Jessica Malan," smiling Savanna said, "Do you know her?"

"No. What's so funny, girl I'm nervous. I'm scared to drink some water lest they're gonna have me figured out. My hands are trembling, my teeth are chattering and it's cold as hell in here, is you cold too?"

"Get a hold of yourself," said Savanna.

"No, I can't. Who's the Jessica lady?"

"She's gonna come in and say she loved you all of her life and that you always sold drugs as long as she has known you and that you are the most violent person that she has ever met."

"Yeah."

"Mm hmm."

"How you know?" Savanna smiled and said,

"I got my sources."

"Good ones?" Nigel looked hopeful.

"Mm hmm, watch and listen."

"That's what I'm doing and probably the only thing that I'm doing. You know I was thinking you know, about how I should have gone to the airport you know, and skied the fuck up out of here." Said Nigel,

"What, and disappoint all of these good people."

"Blood suckers, all of them. Trust me; everyone in here is hoping that you lose." Nigel reminded.

"Well, shoot, do I get a chance to disappoint some people. I mean you can't be the only asshole in here?"

"That a tiger," Nigel said. This volley of words between client and attorney had given the audience something else to pay attention to while the Bailiff worked on the mechanics and the technical issues.

From a distance it appeared that nothing was going on around them and everyone saw the smiles then the confusions then the barrage as the two switched from using their ears, then their lips, then their ears back to their lips as they whispered into one another than the laughter came from the client when Savanna said,

"Well, here comes the bride." The two smiled as the judge sent the Bailiff and another deputy to get Ms. Malan situated into her chambers where they would remain until her statements were delivered and she was delivered to safety.

"Your Honor I would like to call Jessica Malan to the witness stand," said Mathew Donaldson the District Attorney who knew for sure that the star witness would deliver. The whole courtroom saw as the witness took her seat in front of the camera. The Judge, who was fitted with a microphone also, spoke softly into it as if she was comfortable with the little black stem that sat atop of her bench, she said.

"Ms. Malan would you raise your right hand," the courtroom saw the conservative but very attractive woman stand to take her oath "I do," she said then took to her seat. Savanna sat next to Nigel and stared at the television and the two listened to the District Attorney create a buzz that generated throughout the courtroom.

"Ms. Malan, I could tell that you are accustomed to a certain life, one of glitz and one of glamour." The courtroom saw as Ms. Malan glowed with innocence. Her smile radiated a show of confidence. When she spoke she wasn't nervous in fact she was confident and stable in her delivery.

"Thank you," she said.

"How is it that you could afford such a life style on an income that of a.... tell me again Ms. Malan what is it that you do?" Asked the District Attorney,

"I am a hairstylist."

"You're a hairstylist? Wow, you must cater to the rich and famous," uttered the DA.

"Sometimes."

"But not all of the times?"

"No."

"So how is it that you could afford the diamonds and the pearls so to say, a nice automobile, home, fur coats and all of the expensive getaways?"

"Well, each of those items that you've listed was all received as gifts."

"Oh, so you mean being a hairstylist didn't do any of those things for you?"

"No, no way could it have, I'd have to save for months."

"So, tell us did Mr. Collinson give you any of those things?"

"All of those things I've gotten from him."

"You were asked the moment that we subpoenaed you to give us a list of your possessions to which you have received as gifts from Mr. Collinson. Did you Ms. Malan make such a list and present them to the investigators for the people?"

"I did."

"Is this the list Ms. Malan?" Mr. Donaldson held up a slip of paper to the camera, given her time to recognize some of the items listed on the slip.

"Yes, that's my handwriting," to the judge and for the benefit of the courtroom, Savanna included. The District Attorney waived the slip in the air so all could see then said,

"We've had the chance to appraise such a list and we've valued this merchandise at three point nine million dollars, almost four million dollars. Now that is a lot of money, I mean gifts, excuse me." Savanna allowed the theatrics. She sat and allowed the line of questioning without interruption. The crowd was now in full rhythm as they all calculated which item would cost the most, either the necklace or the ring, the coat or the rug. The District Attorney gave the audience time to soak in to what he had delivered before he said,

"And you mean to tell me, that Mr. Collinson has given all of these gifts to you."

"That's what I mean."

"Ms. Malan, could you tell us, have you ever seen Mr. Collinson in possession of any narcotics of the resalable amount and if so, how much? And is Mr. Collinson in court today and if so could you point him out to us?"

"I don't know but a lot and yes, he's there." She pointed to the only available defendant.

"Take a couple of guesstimates if you will."

"I don't know maybe two hundred pounds or enough to fill up a whole trunk, I'll say."

"Oh, that is a resalable amount ain't it?" Mr. Donaldson's eyebrows gave him the I'll be darned look.

"I never saw him use any of it, I mean if that'll tell us anything."

"Hmm," said the DA, but to Savanna he said, "No more questions at the time Your Honor."

"Oh-oh," Nigel whispered to Savanna "girl tell me that you've drawn something up for this lady. She is all and every bit of what you said that she would be, good and a hired gun because if I didn't know any better Ms. Lady, I would have sworn that she just shot me from under the table."

"Counselor!" The Honorable Judge Walker said interrupting the conference between client and attorney, "Anytime you are ready," she said impatiently.

"Sorry Your Honor," Savanna said to the judge and to Nigel she said "would you please get a hold of yourself, gosh." She walked over to the podium where she would stand to deliver her questions through the same microphone, which was uncomfortable looking for a moment until she settled into her line of questions, she said.

"Ms. Malan you said that you were in a serious relationship with my client?"

"I wouldn't say serious no, but I have been of acquaintance with your client yes." Now that was a nice dodge if Savanna didn't say so herself and she knew that she done well for herself because she hit

Savanna with her "nice try" smile. In return Savanna remained composed and accepted her maneuver like a champion, and said.

"Oh-kay, so you were an acquaintance of my client, is that better?"

"Much better."

"Oh-kay, so how long has this acquaintance been going on if you don't mind me asking?"

"I'll say seven years."

"So you'll say that it took you seven years to gather such an extravagant list of merchandise, then."

"It was worth the wait," she said exuding her avaricious nature.

"I'm sure it was Ms. Malan, I'm sure that it was. So, seven years, that's a mighty long time isn't it, I'm sure that you have to behave in such a way to receive such a fine list of glitzy things." Savanna's smile gave away the miss direction only it was overlooked or totally missed by Ms. Jessica Malan. The star witness, who took the bait and said in her vanity,

"Oh yeah, just so happen that I'm good at what I do." Instantly they all knew that Ms. Malan was talking about her sexual prowess. So the crowd became jubilant.

"Well, I'm sure that that'll be helpful information for the next contestant but what I was referring to and I should have asked a better question. I do apologize and I'll promise not to allow that to happen again." Disarming Ms. Malan by admitting her faults Savanna set her up for the next line of questions. "What I meant to say Ms. Malan, you know, with me being a female and all, that sometimes I like to reward my man friend with gifts too. I mean, only if I'm feeling that he's doing right by me, this not being a financial issue but a females yearn to shower her man with the finer things. So, I must ask, did you spend a lot of time with my client or was he just foolish like that?" Oh, my God it's a trap is what the DA was thinking because there is no way, would a foolish man have had the brilliance, enough to fool law enforcement for so long. So that leaves only one answer and sure enough Mr. Donaldson heard it once Ms. Malan said,

"Oh yeah, I spent a lot of time with Nigel, and why not he was my fiancé if you could believe that or not." Savanna smiled for the cameras and let out a giggle then apologized to the court, and to Ms. Malan she said,

"So, you two were going to get married?"

"Yes, we were, I don't see what's so funny."

"Sorry, so tell me how'd you do it, a man of my client's stature, a loyal acquaintance you're telling us?" The trap had a nice piece of bait on it and the DA saw it all coming.

"I'm always a loyal acquaintance." The DA was now sick to his stomach.

"No men on the side you mean?"

"Nope, never."

"Straight up and up, is that what you're saying?"

"Yes," she answered. Mr. Donaldson was curious to where the young attorney was heading with her line of questioning. The one thing that the DA had surrendered already was the fact that he was dealing with an amateur. He knew with certainty that his opposition was just as seasoned as anyone else that he had encountered in a courtroom continued to listen on. Though he was getting the sneaky feeling that Savanna had sucker punched him somehow, still he listened.

"No extra luggage on the side? No sneaky late night flings? Just straight up and up you're telling us." The witness nodded her answer.

"Ms. Malan, you do know that perjury is a very serious crime don't you? One sentenced to jail time right?" This was the loaded question that Savanna had to ask in order to draw Ms. Malan's attention towards another direction. It's like the magician who uses a puff of smoke to distract while the hands work the twist as unnoticeable as humanly possible. There was no way, and no how Savanna could have proven that Ms. Malan had an affair on the side and she gave the witness credit for knowing as much. So she smiled when the witness said,

"Yes, I'm aware of that, I have no reason to lie. I have nothing to hide."

"Ms. Malan I have been given such a list of your possessions. Tell me, did you know that if my client is found guilty that those possessions would be confiscated and no longer belong to you?" Savanna saw the alarm ringing in the witness eyes when she hit her with the knuckle pitch and this again was another miss direction that Savanna needed her witness to focus on.

"I object Your Honor, the people has an agreement with Ms. Malan that she shall keep her belongings under the amnesty clause," said the DA. a swing and a miss though because Savanna was already in her zone.

"Oh, I wasn't aware of any amnesty agreement," said Savanna winking into the camera now.

"Me either," said Judge Walker then, "Your objection is overruled and we must tend to such items that are on that list. Ms. Malan not necessarily saying that we would confiscate them but the counselor is right in saying that your possession is in jeopardy." Then to Savanna Judge Walker said, "You may continue." Savanna smiled at the witness through the camera and said.

"Sorry Ms. Malan but as I said before I have been given such a list of fine jewelry do tell me where were you present when my client purchased any of these gifts or you don't know if they were pawn shop merchandise or whatever?" Again a loaded question and again the witness weighed her worth by the disbursement of costly possessions.

"No, they were not pawn shop gifts at all." She snapped now hating Savanna.

"So this means that you didn't buy them yourself from the pawnshop, and that my client spoiled you rotten with all kinds of precious gifts?" Again Savanna smiled.

"Exactly," she said sharply.

"Not on your salary as a hairdresser?"

"No."

"Which means that you were present when the purchase of such a fine quality of material was being tallied up?"

"Sometimes, not all the times."

"Are you employed right now?" Again Savanna changed direction.

"Now I'm not!" Savanna could now sense the attitude decided to press the gas.

"Oh, so you're laid off?"

"No, I was forced to quit."

"This was on my client's somewhat suggestion, then?"

"Like you mean when he got into trouble?"

"Oh-kay, I'll take that. Is that when you quit?"

"Yes."

"Gosh, and I was just looking for a hairdresser, but do tell us," Savanna froze and gone to the table and picked up her pen and pad then said, "Do tell us, where was this hairdresser's shop located." Savanna saw the witness grow fidgety.

"Your Honor, our witness has already confessed to no longer being employed, so she is not at risk by providing such an answer." Savanna said to the judge.

"Ms. Malan you must answer the question." said the judge.

"Never mind, you don't have to," said Savanna then, "But Ms. Malan do tell us at which times were you with my clients to swipe his credit card or to even pay cash to buy you a ring that is now appraised at seventy thousand dollars? We now trace this ring back to the Tiffany Co. we even have the date of purchase. Would you please tell us from which store that such a beautiful necklace was purchased from, so that we could run a check for ourselves, granted the ring we know but the necklace is our mystery?" The witness grew quiet again. "Your Honor," Savanna said the two words again. It was clear that she had the witness on the ropes.

"Ms. Malan you were going to say?" The judge said, the uneasiness was seen for all to see, it was apparent that this witness was now being a hostile one.

"Your Honor, maybe she doesn't remember," said Savanna. "But we have here a pelt which scores at eleven thousand dollars just purchased over a month ago. Ms. Malan has it listed just right under the necklace. Maybe she could remember that purchase, even though I'm sure that it would still be fuzzy, her memory I mean. So I won't ask that question because as it stands both me and my client have grown awfully tired of being ignored. But I will ask, of the seven years Ms. Malan that you've been in acquaintance with my client where did the two of you live, how many residences?" Into the camera Savanna held her note pad up and at the ready,

"Counselor," The judge said to the DA. "I believe this is your witness?"

"Your Honor I withdraw my questions at least this way we won't have Ms. Malan listed as a flight risk, but I too have a list." Savanna walked over to the defense table and picked up a folder then removed a slip of paper. She came back to the podium and said, "Your Honor I know that I'm not supposed to present anything considered evidence on behalf of my client, but for the record just in case Ms. Malan proves to be a flight risk I would like permission to show her a list of names." Savanna knew that she'd gained favor with the judge by her performance.

"Let me see what have you counselor?" Asked the judge who followed Savanna as she approached the bench and handed her the sheet of paper and waited while the judge read, then to the DA, "Mr. Donaldson." She waved the sheet, and from what Savanna could tell the District Attorney hadn't done his homework completely or the District Attorney was now leaving his witness out on an island all by herself, shrugged his shoulders. Picking up that there would be no objection from the people, the Honorable Judge Walker granted permission for Savanna to show the sheet of paper to the witness.

"Ms. Malan," Savanna re-established connection then said, "I am with the understanding that you know a lot of names, Donna Karen, Tiffany, Manolo, Fendi, Prada and Victoria, comes to mind here, but tell me do you recognize any of these names?" She put the paper close enough to the camera and watched for the witness reaction. Savanna showed her one crime family after the next crime family that she had been the star witness for one DA or the other.

"Now, Ms. Malan I could tell that you now recognize where I'm going with this. Your Honor may we get the stenographer to go back a few questions, please?"

"And where would you need her to go?" Asked the judge,

"Back to where Ms. Malan had confessed to being an acquaintance of my client," the stenographer searched through her works then said. "Oh-kay so you were an acquaintance of my client is that better? That was the question." Said the stenographer,

"Is that the one counselor?" Asked the judge who was now curious to how the young attorney would deliver her next punch line.

"No, the next question please." Savanna uttered.

"Oh-kay, so how long has this acquaintance been going on if you don't mind me asking? That was the question." Again said the stenographer,

"And the answer please," Savanna asked the now very eager stenographer.

"I'll say seven years, that was the answer."

"Thank you," Savanna said then walked over to the defense table and materialized with another sheet of paper. She walked over to the judge's bench and handed the Honorable Judge Walker the sheet of paper and to a very stunned audience, one that has now grown mortuary quiet during the whole line of questioning were all thunder struck and non-believing as if Savanna had just stabbed the witness with a Navy Seal maneuver right in front of the Judge. She struck methodically and with the efficiency of a ninja she moved soundlessly in for the kill. She chiseled and sculpted one of the most creative monuments ever. One question after the next one each one feeding off the other one, and never had she ever derailed or swayed away from her main intention and that was to leave the aura of mystery. Savanna knew that she must always keep the mystery in it, and that alone would be enough to become worthy, of at least a listen. Now that she had everyone's attention, Savanna had turned her swagger up to a zillion and in her anger, due to the despicable nature of which this case was built upon not to mention the threat to her new family and friends. Savanna walked over to the District Attorney and eyed him so all could see and simply said,

"That is your Witness!" Before she turned her back on Mr. Donaldson and walked away to join her client where she collapsed heavily into her chair and crossed her arms with the show of disgust. The judge was now reading the one powerful piece of mystery. Everyone wanted to know. No, everyone needed to know. What was the document that Savanna had handed to the Honorable Judge Walker? Who shook her head when finished reading then said?

"I'll call a recess, we'll break for lunch, bailiffs please remain with Ms. Malan this way she would not consider taking a flight as the counselor suggested. The sound of the gavel dropping was like the gun going off to release a row of sprinters. The noise dismissed the courtroom which poured out into the hallways with Juice leading the way. He got a jump on the rest, followed by the press who all knew that positioning was everything and they needed anything that they could scoop from the young attorney who would disappoint them by not making an exit, but chose to remain seated at the defense table studying and preparing for the next witness, and this was exactly how Savanna patiently waited.

Chapter 45

April sat at the desk in her office where she began her day with a prayer and a cup of coffee which eventually gave way to a bottle of Cognac. She took one shot after the next awaiting the information that would either break her heart or fill her with glee. All she knew was that Savanna and her very, very important client was backed up against a brick wall of maliciousness, and knew that winner would ultimately take all. She knew that courtroom twenty-six would play none more than the Roman Coliseum where Gladiators from all walks met up only to rid one another of their lively hoods. April heard the phone ring and it startled her. She knew that the call would come through and she feared that 'this call' would be the call that would break her heart.

"Hello?" She toughened up,

"Mom," it was Juice calling.

"Boy, what's going on over there?" April said impatiently.

"You sound anxious," Juice replied noticing his mother's uneasiness, decided to toy around with it a bit.

"Anxious! I'm a nervous wreck right now; boy I done ate all my fingernails with a Hennessy chaser. So, what's going on over there, is everything oh-kay?"

"The girl is too much for 'em, like way too much I'll tell you."

"Oh, what do you mean, please spare me the wait. Boy don't do this to me."

"Mom she's got that line in her back, she got that ain't taking no prisoners look, she's got everybody in there scared to breathe, and if they do she better not catch them doing it or she's gonna charge at them and ram her horns in 'em. I'm telling you she's too much for them."

"Boy, who, who's too much?"

"Somebody need to step in and stop her unless they gonna book her over there and she'll be sitting right next to Nigel."

"No!"

"Uh hun."

"What did they do so far? Are they going to hang Nigel or what?" April needed to cut to the chase. She had some concerns and would have loved to address them all simultaneously. "Where is Savanna?" she asked as if they decided to book her over there and have her sitting next to Nigel as her son said.

"She's in the courtroom still. I'm trying to tell you we had to run up out of there to save our own lives, after a while she just started charging at everybody… me included, she got to be stopped!"

"Oh," April smiled. "Is that right, and why is that?" She figured that she'd play along.

"Because she done started butchering the innocent people too, we still don't believe what's going on in there. Right now she's on some new shit, I mean she's sticking to the stuff, but she done started Pimp-provisioning, we ran to lunch only Savanna never broke for lunch, they say she's is there swinging her guillotine taking practice shots at the witness stand right now, some would even testify to that."

"Ha, that's my baby," April said excitedly then, "You sound like you're proud of her."

"That's because I am, and mom I'm trying not to miss anything, besides I'm the coroner I need to remain close by, I mean the way she's in there stacking them up I could be late already."

"Oh-kay, quickly do you see Nigel getting hung anywhere?"

"I've been trying to see it, and I can't see it, in fact I could see him getting released before the night's over way before I see him getting hung mom."

"Oooh, boy don't tell me that, don't you say that to me, you know that I'm getting old my heart can't take it."

"Well, it's true but I need to go. I'll see you soon and I love you."

"Oh-kay, now let me know what's going on the minute that it's over do you hear me?"

"Yes ma'am," then the line went silent and April whispered her three favorite words, "Thank you God."

The courtroom re-assembled after lunch, the press felt let down by being avoided by the young attorney who was now known as the young female Picasso. The spectators and the security of officers were now in place and viewing the defendant in a new light now because of this young attorney. Many were beginning to believe that the elusive and hard to capture villain was still in operable condition. While the world looked towards this court presiding, the real villain was still roaming free and still knocking down the big people.

What a huge mistake the state could be making spending large chunks of taxpayers' money attempting to prosecute the wrong man they were thinking. By the looks of things, the wrong man brought the right attorney, a real prize fighter, the no nonsense type of gal who would fight to the bitter end, and continue to be a squabbler even after that.

The judge made her entrance all of business like, it was clear to see that she was furious and on the verge of punishing with extreme chastisements now that she had her mind made up. She came from her chambers taking brisk and powerful steps in the direction of her bench. Her robe was blowing in the wind as the quickness of her steps created a gust that was too much for such a fabric to accommodate. The Honorable Judge took to the steps of the bench. The Bailiff was beginning to announce for all to hear that court was now in session only Judge Walker cut him off before he was able to inhale the correct amount of air to form such words with, by saying.

"No!" And to the District Attorney and to Ms. Clayton the judge said "In my chambers, now!" Then retracted her steps, and with the same forcefulness was how she led the two warriors back to her quarters.

"Please take a seat." She demanded. Savanna had noticed upon arrival that gone was the equipment that was setup to accommodate the witness, one who was granted the rights of protection. She took her seat next to Mr. Donaldson, but across from the judge who'd gone straight to the meat and to the DA she said,

"You're getting killed out there, is there anything on your list to convince me not to release Mr. Collinson right this instance? Seeing that your last witness is headed to the county jail on perjury, and we'll file to freeze her assets seeing how you failed to mention amnesty to me or to Ms. Clayton." Said the judge,

"I have another witness that I will grant immunity because the state believes that his past testimonies had in the past, even now, would be reward enough to repay its debt to society."

"I'll take it that this isn't something you wish to discuss further. Ms. Clayton I need to ask you and you better tell me the truth or so help me God I'll wring your ass out to dry so quick, how much did you know about Ms. Malan coming in today?"

"Your Honor, I am going to have to say no comment to your request." Savanna adamantly sat in her decisions not to give up a source or findings of facts.

"Counselor, in case you haven't been paying attention to the world around you. In the past week two men has been slain, one on a California highway and one in a strip mall, both which were murdered in the same fashion to which your client stands accused. Now you come in here with Intel that of which could either clear your client or dig a deeper hole for him, and you hold at no comment?" Savannas silence was plenty. For the judge knew Savannas thoughts. You either book her client or take him to trial with what you have.

"You're protecting your resources is that it?" Asked the judge and again the silence played its part in frustrating the judge, "oh-kay," the judge relented then said to the District Attorney. "Shall we continue with the preliminary, really I'm having a hard time being convinced enough to set a trial date," but to Savanna she said, "On the other hand no way and I mean without a doubt, do I want to be put in a position to release a murderer back to the society to which it corrupts. Do you understand that Ms. Clayton?" Savanna stared at the judge and shrugged her shoulders then said,

"Well, let's go and finish the preliminary and we'll see what we have after that."

"Which will be?" Asked the judge even though Savanna knew the question to have lead in it she still gave her what the judge needed to know.

"Nothing!" She said, "At the bottom of it all. The cameras, the clowns, the tight ropes and the smoke and all of the mirrors you would only have… nothing."

"And you're sure about all of this." The District Attorney finally came to life.

"You could try me if you like sir." Savanna spoke softly yet she was well polite when saying, "It'll all die right here."

"You think you have all the answers do you, you think you have it all figured out don't you." The District Attorney was now on his feet. His composure was sold at a bargain.

"I done said what I said already," Savanna said looking to the judge allowing her to know that it was her call and not one that the overheated District Attorney should make, but the one Honorable Judge Walker herself must make.

"Take a seat counselor and lower your voice while in my chambers. You see there's a decision that we must make, and to make it we must discuss it at this table. Not the ones three floors down, but this one. Now to continue with the preliminary there's a chance that Ms. Clayton will continue to wrap her rope around you until she has the sock in your mouth, then what? I'll tell you my hands will be tied too and can't help you or the public in the event that Mr. Collinson is really a public enemy as you say he is and truthfully I have a nagging feeling in my gut that I can't put my finger on. Unfortunately, I can't convict people on a gut feeling or I'll have Ms. Clayton cuffed and escorted to the main jail for the information that she has that may or may not have come from some underworld connection which means that she'll have insight to some very, very horrible crimes. So tell me, Mr. Donaldson, what should I do?" Finished the judge,

"I'll say we finish what we started," said the District Attorney and immediately Savannas eyebrows lifted, her ears pricked and her tail shot straight up preparing to attack. The District Attorney never saw this, but hell if the judge didn't, and it was she who grew instantly sick and said,

"Ms. Clayton, if we finish this preliminary is it your intention to later ask for a dismissal in the event you set forth another performance like the last one?" Again Savanna allowed her silence to be her loudest voice.

"Well, since you put it like that," said the judge I'm gonna have to grant the people the opportunity to prove a case against your client. I will waive the rest of this hearing and we'll go set a trial readiness date." The judge stood, but not before Savanna who lead the trio out to the courtroom. The DA sported a dignified look, for he still got what he wanted even in a losing effort. The judge wore a look of contempt and concern, but what these two didn't know was that Savanna still had that line in her back. She still had the blood of a warrior running through her veins, because to her the fight was never over, not until everyone surrendered, and this was the only way for her to determine.

The courtroom had grown impatient; the three were missing long enough. It was time for some action, for some bloodshed and no matter whose. Nigel had also grown impatient because the longer he waited the more nervous he had become. So to see the three take to their rightful positions and the judge granting permission to the Bailiff, the courtroom settled and waited for the bell to ring. Which would mean the fighting would resume, were now disappointed when the Honorable Judge Walker said.

"I have the right to make a decision at this time to waive the rest of this hearing and to still find reason to bound Mr. Collinson over for trial which I will do..."

"I object Your Honor," Savanna snapped with the same ferociousness as she held before break, "It is the preliminary that was asked to be waived during arraignment, but you allowed the people permission to hold such a hearing to show evidence of my client's guilt that or participation of guilt which the people has not done. We have every indication that my client is not guilty and should be released this minute. Giving your right to remand my client and ask him to stand trial for crimes that you or the people are convinced of his guilt is now a prejudice." Nigel had fallen in love with Savanna's suggestions instantaneously but it was evident that Savanna had made an enemy in the Honorable Judge Walker, who said.

"Motion to dismiss is denied..."

"Then I object to the waiving of such a hearing where we are gathered here today to discover if there is enough evidence to bind my client over for trial. We have not produced sufficient enough evidence to warrant a trial or maybe our next witness could produce, either that or I cry severely the scream of prejudice," Savanna interrupted the good judge again who said,

"I will note your objection, but still I will exercise my rights and ask that we find a date suitable to all of those involved to have a trial readiness conference..."

"At this time Your Honor I must ask that my client receive his right to a bail, one suitable for the innocent and with that since it's so obvious that my client would not under any circumstances that or condition receive a fair trial. I must also ask that the court grant us permission to achieve a change of venue as well."

"Why counselor, do you now question my integrity is that it?"

"I'm only saying what I'm saying is all," the audience, all who had showed up on this day knew the same thing at the same time, that Savanna has now wrapped her rope around the judge as well. If she continued to exercise her rights she would now show prejudice to the one and only Nigel Collinson also known as the possible Raymond Buchannon, which in turn would turn into a public outcry once Savanna refused a trial date until she received the change of venue. Which indeed would not only remove one of the biggest cases in California's recent history from her courtroom, but it would be handed to a judge who would throw the case out right away. The people had yet to establish any fault finding or guilt on Nigel and everyone would have all of this for intelligence before the night was over. The Honorable Judge Walker was put on the spot, she shook her head and looked down on the young attorney. Then to the people's bench she said,

"Counselor, do you object to the request of a change of venue or the bail?"

"Heck yeah, I object to both request," said the DA.

"Well, I must rule and I rule to overrule the request for a change of venue, Sacramento is where we will remain on the other hand the people have not established any substantial amount of evidence against Mr. Collinson, but is assured to produce in the event a trial date is set, it is because of this does my ruling now come with complications. To release Mr. Collinson to the street could prove to be no different than me releasing Barabbas the known killer only to crucify Jesus no, it is a ruling that I must make. So instead of us scheduling a TRC a trial readiness conference, we will at this time set a bail hearing, which is the best that I could do." And all of this was said with Judge Walker never taking her eyes away from Savanna.

"Do you have a date in mind Ms. Clayton?" The judge asked.

"I will lobby for the sooner the better," Savanna responded searching the calendar.

"Mr. Donaldson?" Asked the judge,

"I object Your Honor, we believe Mr. Collinson to be flight risk, and we believe him to have the means and the resources to avoid capture if released..."

"And if you could prove any of that then do so at the bail hearing your objection is overruled. It's the date that we are interested in right now counselor." The judge said with finalization. The time that the bail hearing date had been agreed upon the judge released them all by saying,

"Well, we'll meet again on the thirtieth of this month. Court adjourned." At the sound of this Savanna whispered to Nigel and said, "You should be getting released soon, ten days. I need to go, does Juice need to bring everyone back it's getting crazy out there?" Nigel nodded and allowed the deputy to remove him from the courtroom minus the cuffs, at least until he was out of the sight of the courtroom.

"Well," Savanna soliloquized, "here we go." Savanna noticed that Juice had never left the room, he awaited her and the two made their exits together. Once the courtroom door opened Juice and Savanna were bum rushed by reporters and cameramen. The two were asked for statements and exclusives. Savanna continued to speak the same two words. "No comment. No comment, no comment." Each question flew by them in blurs, "No comment," she would say even to the blurs. All the while Juice scanned their faces until he found his favorite reporter. Her blonde hair made her stand out from the rest. Her conservative dress spoke business; her stance was one that spoke dominant for she was highly pissed off. Juice received her attention and to him she strolled over to possibly gain access to an interview with Savanna and to scold them for standing her up for lunch said,

"Counselor, is your client going to be able to post bond if you win the bail hearing?"

"I sure hope so," said Savanna, the other reporters gathered around Savanna and Juice whom was very interested in giving them the exclusive rights to interview both him and Savanna.

"No one is now believing that the right guy is asked to stand trial after your performance, Ms. Clayton is your client guilty?"

"No, he's not!" Then Savanna had gone into what she believed to be an all-out alert for everyone in hiding to come out of hiding she said, "see we don't have to hide anymore, nobody's guilty, though it's a tough time what my client needs is support, right now, from all of his friends and all of his family wherever they may be. He needs them the most and the sooner the better for they may even deny my client bail and lord knows what would become of Mr. Collinson then." Said Savanna,

"Which to my knowledge would be hard to do, for I never heard anything in the way of evidence, what do you think about that?" Asked the reporter,

"I think that it's a miscarriage of justice the ways of these proceedings, but it is what it is."

"Ms. Clayton, there has been two reported homicides in the past weeks, folks are beginning to wonder with the death of the attorney, a Mr. Minor Dixon that Raymond Buchannon was showing to the world that we do have a miscarriage of justice, do you get that to be...."

"I must say no more questions at the time." Juice interrupted the reporter and gave her his conspiratorial wink and grabbed Savanna by her arm and pulled her past the reporters and headed to the rental, a Chevy Blazer that would carry them away from the Roman Coliseum where Savanna had proven that she was indeed a high powered gladiator.

Chapter 46

Filbert Gilbert saw when the police officers fell upon a group of pedestrians and thought for a spell that J-Dog had been captured. Instead of making his getaway he was forced to double back and investigate the matter. One individual in dark clothing was stretched out on the ground with a Shepherd barking uncontrollably at him. The officers formed their perimeter around the suspect, and were behaving aggressively.

"Shit, shit, shit," Filbert Gilbert said to himself then turned to make his getaway. "Fuck," he thought and began to walk away from the scene and head towards safety. He was desperate and nervous so he walked in haste towards the unknown. He passed by the still burning van. He could hear the fire departments sirens blaring in the distance, concluding that soon the van would be burned completely, and the need would grow small for the Fire Department, more like work for a tow truck, he summed up. "Psst," Gilbert heard, but couldn't locate the direction, "Filbert?" Gilbert looked around and still couldn't locate the voice that he was oh so familiar with.

"My nigga, I need you to just follow me." He said loud enough for J-Dog to hear then, "Walk slow and come with me you hear me?" Said Gilbert,

"Is it good or no?" Asked J-Dog,

"Not yet, but when I walk past just blend in with me," Gilbert said now locating the direction that J-Dog took for concealment. The two caught a break when the Fire Department showed up to create a large enough commotion for the two to make their move, and they did and by the hair of their chinny chin, chins if you were to ask them.

"Dog, listen to this shit?" Gilbert cradled the telephone receiver. "The dough had cleared for us last night; could you believe that shit?" J-Dog couldn't believe the money in the briefcase how the hell was he supposed to believe anything else that was taking place. Although he once heard that the secrets to having a whole bunch of money without driving yourself nuts was to look at the money as a bunch of zeros and never mind the numbers next to them. J-dog laid on the bed that he assigned to himself once the two checked into the motel, which didn't make much sense considering that they were now at "home" in Stockton California, and could have easily gone home to their families.

"What did they say?" He asked Gilbert.

"They say that the key was cleared to fit box two four three and that a password would be available to enter the chamber of boxes for Gilbert and James, of Stockton California."

"What, you called the bank or something, how do you know that it's been cleared?" J-Dog finished

"Because, I got the email over an hour ago, we've been invited to come and have a few drinks, Mrs. Raymond said something about the way you let your hair down being exactly what the club needed. Then she went on to give us the password." Smiling J-Dog said,

"Which is?"

"Victor."

"Victor?"

"Yelp, so what you want to do?"

"The fuck kind of question is that?"

"How about we give it a day or so and let everything cool down before we make the trip?"

"I'm not tripping; I'm thinking that we should just take me down to the dealership right now, one that does the gangsta contracts. Do you know any of them?" J-Dog made his mind up, it was time to ball. "Prince got that BMW off of March Lane or we could ride out to the Bay in a rental and come back like twins."

"Now you talking, I'm thinking twin Benzes' or twin Porsche's or something that niggas would give us some respect around this motha fucka with."

"Oh-kay but now there's this other email, it came in today just after the password."

"Mm, and I'm supposed to guess what it said right?"

"Not unless you want me to tell you."

"It's from Mrs. Raymond?"

"Yelp."

"She was saying thank you?"

"Nope, she was asking if we were satisfied, so?"

"So, what you mean by, so?"

"So, are we satisfied is what I'm asking?"

"Hmmmm…"

"I mean we could close the laptop and toss the bitch in a river and keep it moving. We could cash out, nigga that's bread for a long time what we got right now."

"But?"

"But, nothing I didn't say but, I'm only seeing if you were satisfied, because I would at least talk to her before tossing this bitch in the river."

"So,"

"Am I satisfied? Bro I don't know, I've never been satisfied before, I'm only saying though, shit."

"And, you're scared to be satisfied now?"

"Yeah, crazy as hell but, yeah."

"Then don't be, dog you can't be scared of yourself, if it's meant for you to get dough, then get the dough daddy."

"So, I send her a message saying hell naw?"

"Exactly how I'll put it."

"Alright," Gilbert typed the message and sent it off right away.

"So what did you say to her?" Asked J-Dog noticing that his friend tapped more keys than what were needed for the "hell naw" that they agreed upon.

"I said hell naw, then asked her if she knew where you and I could cop twin Bentley at."

"What! What you think she knows about that shit?"

"I don't know; it was worth a try though."

"Don't seem like it to me, I mean they got dough, but do you think they got floss on theirs?" J-Dog tried to visualize the lady in a Rolls Royce and Juice in a ride other than the classic Mustang that seems to be his only wish was to have a convertible classic ride and nothing else.

"Hold on, here goes nothing, we got mail." Gilbert scanned over the message and then he looked as if he had just gotten shot in the stomach.

"What the fuck did she say that got you going all pale and shit with your black ass?"

"My nigga, she holla back and said that Bentley wouldn't become us."

"Told you that she wouldn't know about the nature of the floss, the art of a stunna, nothing about the blingy bling, they all old fashion and shit."

"Well, did you want to hear the rest, or did you want to wait here until I get back?" Filbert Gilbert stood to gather his jacket and other merchandise for his mind has been made up for him. J-Dog wasn't foolish enough to overlook the details, put Gilbert's movements together with the gunshot that came from the laptop and gone over to read for himself. The message read,

"A Bentley! A Bentley! You two sound like senior citizens, trust me, a Bentley doesn't become of you guys but I'll tell you that I have a dealership here in Sacramento that offer high end vehicles. I was thinking Ferrari or twin Lamborghini's for the two of you. Have some fun for a change why don't you. To get this go to Luxury Auto Plugs on Fulton Boulevard and use the same password that I gave you earlier and do come and show me your selection, for I fear that you may have developed bad taste."

"What the fuck," J-Dog exclaimed then said, "Ain't this about a bitch? My nigga now correct me if I'm wrong but did she just say that she has a dealership?"

"She ain't lied so far, I fuck with it."

"I thought we were gonna wait a few days before we head that way."

"Do that mean that you're gonna hang out until I get back or no?"

"Hell to the naw," J-Dog began collecting his things and less than an hour later the two were pulling up into the dealership. An establishment that either J-Dog or Gilbert would have ever believed that they would ever be fortunate enough to pay such a pleasurable visit to, were now with the belief that they had found their very own heaven, one that's been hid on earth.

"My nigga, go and tell them the password and make it do what it do baby," said J-Dog eying a lime green milked out Lamborghini Gallardo.

"You ain't have to tell me no shit like that I'm on that right now. I need to see if "open says me" is really the password." Gilbert said then headed towards the showroom section feeling as if he would find someone to help them inside of the glass structure that spoke luxurious the moment that he entered the building.

"How may I help you sir?" Said the gentleman in the business attire that was oh so different from the sweat shirt, jeans and K-Swiss that Filbert Gilbert wore, which was misplaced in such a luxuriant place, such as Luxury Auto Plugs.

"Well, me and my brother was sent here by Mrs. Raymond, she's a friend of ours and she told us to come and offer up a password, do you need that?"

"Yes, I know Mrs. Raymond and the password she gave is what again?"

"Victor, though I never told you, but Victor is what she told me to tell you guys."

"It's what she told me too, she also said that she would collect the cash from you later. So all I need's a couple of John Hancock's and you have the keys to the city." Filbert Gilbert had never walked so fast nor moved as light as he done on this day while heading to collect his partner in crime.

"My nigga, we just need to go and sign some shit and we gone."

"That's what I needed you to say. How much we need to bust out?"

"She say that she'll get the dough from us later. My nigga it's sign and release, on anything on the lot." Five minutes later the two heard their powerful motors come to life and just as they dreamed of, twin Lamborghini's left the lot one trailing the other where J-Dog followed Gilbert straight to the rim shop. This way they could put some nice shoes on such a fine ride. LeBron's on both of them, sleek and unique.

"Now this is what the fuck I'm talking about, what you wanna do, race back to Stockton?" Asked J-Dog,

"Hell, naw nigga you could go back if you want to. I owe myself a shopping spree. I'm gonna feel free to fill up the whole passenger side with shit. If I'm gonna be in this bitch it's gonna look just like I belong in this bitch."

"I heard the fuck out'ta that, I done fantasized so long about a pinky ring, ooh that bitch is gonna be a fatty baby, watch."

"I mean; I'll race your dog ass to the mall though."

"You'll never win that one, because that's where I believe that my pinky ring is at."

"Try me and the two bolted towards their brand new rides looking like the thoroughbred hustlers that they always said that they would one day become.

Chapter 47

The Dixon family mourned for Minor Dixon, and during this process what most people needed to know was just how did Minor meet such a horrible fate. There was no one that needed this answer more than Minor Sr. Nothing that he could fathom was suitable enough of an answer to why was his only son gunned down like a hoodlum. He looked for many avenues that would bring Minor Jr. back to life but he couldn't. He reflected back to the day before the procession of cars that followed the motorcycle escorted motorcade to Camille's memorial lawn where Minor Sr. would walk away from his only son after plucking flowers from his casket. With tears burning in his eyes, he walked away not knowing the answers, to why. No one at the firm could prove anything convincing, Minor Jr. was not robbed and this they distinguished, so possessions wasn't the motive and a very early dismissal of reasoning.

Minor Jr. sported an oyster perpetual diamond bezel Rolex and Minor Sr., had collected Minor Jr. Possessions from the morgue, and the watch and more than two thousand dollars in cash was in Minor Jr.'s belongings. Right away, Minor Sr. knew that a robbery gone badly was not the issue, the violent and hateful manner in which Minor Jr. had passed spoke intensities, screaming that this deed was not of the business nature, but of the personal variety. Minor Sr. could not explain to his wife Melinda the reason but even she knew that it had to be one because no one dies in this fashion or just because. Not being able to explain to his wife the "whys" for the loss of her son, her darling, darling first born and the pride of her heart. Minor Sr. decided that it was time to take a peek into his son's personal life. For the first time ever, he invaded Minor Jr.'s privacy, not even when Minor Jr. was a teen and living under the roof of his parents was privacy invasion an issue. For Minor Sr. has always instilled trust as part of family values. Arriving at the firm the following day Minor Sr. took the elevator to the fourth floor where the junior partners took their offices, just hours after watching his son lowered into the ground did he follow the hallway to his sons' office.

"Oh-kay kiddo, talk to me and tell me something." Minor Sr. rummaged through his late son's desk, not knowing where to start or what to look for, but hoping that something would jump out at him. Not finding anything of irregularity so he walked over to the file cabinet and there he spent hours combing through one file after the next, one drawer after the next until he was now at the bottom, the last and final drawer. Here he used the same magnifying glass to comb through the remaining files. Not knowing with any certainty what it could be that he was looking for exactly, but Minor Sr. has always known a rat when he smelled one, now very old and his senses growing dull, thought he may not smell a rat exactly, but he smelled something awfully furry and he knew it. There was absolutely nothing that went down the chains of commanding works that he didn't have knowledge of except for this. Every Secretary, every mail room employee, every vending machine refill, every case from an auto accident gone bad to custodial clean up, every civil litigation to every criminal defense attorney and their hours billed, but not this. Nothing had gone unnoticed by the boss, so as he sat in his son's chair and leaned back and studied the pile of folders that sat on top of his son's desk which had nothing to do with any client on the records of Dixon, Juan and Dixon. Minor Sr. looked at the folders again as if the gunman was hidden deep inside of the lines of one of those folders. He feared that if he was to open the folders a bullet would leave the lines on the page and claim him as well. Minor Sr. felt his anger began to rise, was the reason his son deceased inside of these folders again he asked? He scooped up the folders and hid them inside of his son's' desk, then depressed the button on the intercom saying,

"Ms. Kramer would you come in here right away please?" Ms. Kramer was the secretary for Minor Jr. and she was everything a partner needed. She was cute, witty and always available and on time.

"Yes, Mr. Dixon," Ms. Kramer arrived with a tint of paranoia washed across her facial expression. Minor Sr. looked at the young lady as if she was the culprit. As if she was the only person who could have stolen the churches money. Ms. Kramer felt very uncomfortable in the presence of the boss, even so as of lately.

"Ms. Kramer, have a seat please," Ms. Kramer rushed to her seat as if this time the game of musical chairs had taken on a deadly nature, like the last one standing must drink the poison.

"Now, you've been working for Junior for how long?" Ms. Kramer already accustomed to the fact that the boss always referred to his son as Junior said,

"Nine years now sir."

"That's what I was thinking too, now my son would no longer need a secretary where he is," Minor Sr. looked upon the little lady attempting to read her mind.

"Is it that you are releasing me sir?" She asked, this was the same thing he was thinking she would say.

"Not at all, well not yet, I'll leave all of this up to you."

"Oh-kay," Ms. Kramer became confused.

"Ms. Kramer, there's one thing that I despise and always have, Ms. Kramer and that's a liar, so don't lie to me or so help me God, I would fire you so quick."

"Mr. Dixon?" Minor Sr. sensed the nervousness of Ms. Kramer, but no kind of way did he care one iota about the feelings of Ms. Kramer.

"Do we understand each other?"

"Yes sir," Ms. Kramer shivered and it was visible to Minor Sr. who said,

"I have a reason to believe that my son has been conducting other business ventures on company time and on its dime, true or not?" Ms. Kramer grew fidgety and this too didn't go unnoticed by the boss.

"Yes Sir." She uttered.

"I also have reason to believe that you aided him in these ventures is that also true?"

"Sir..."

"True or not!" Ms. Kramer was interrupted immediately by Minor Sr. who really didn't have the patience for explanations. With her head held low Ms. Kramer confessed,

"It is true sir giving my position."

"Then maybe you could define these ventures that I am oh so interested in?"

"Ah…"

"Ms. Kramer."

"Maybe this would go better if I know what it is that you are interested in Mr. Dixon."

"Only the truth is all." The attorney saw as the secretary inhaled and exhaled deeply before she rambled off a thousand words a minute, making it hard for any stenographer to keep up. It was time for all minority workers to clock out. Ms. Kramer a secretary who indeed was a minority worker was at the moment, too busy trying to save her tomorrows than to worry about clocking out today. Once her story was complete Minor Sr. continued to rock in his chair, never taking his eyes off of Ms. Kramer. The one thing that he knew was that the frail lady had spoken the truth.

"Ms. Kramer if I turn this computer on could you get me into Junior's files?"

"Yes Sir, I am the one who created all of the passwords and installed and upgraded all the software's, unless he has changed them then I should be able to get you inside." He had one hope and that was that Junior had kept his passwords the same. The gamble was a good one, no need for his son to have changed anything, there was absolutely no sense in hiding anything from your secretary because it would be the secretary who would dictate, transcribe, take calls and protect a wayward husband from a snooping wife. Minor Sr. watched as the desktop came to life and saw as Ms. Kramer pecked at the keys and maneuvered the mouse until she was now revealing to the boss his wishes.

"Thank you Ms. Kramer, tomorrow I need you to come in early. I want this office cleared out and the files sent upstairs, it looks like a lot of work so I'll send someone to aid you, perhaps seven." Ms. Kramer who felt the sense of relief said,

"Yes Sir."

"I'll be here when you come in you'll drive safely, won't you?" This being the dismissal and Ms. Kramer knew it said,

"I will," then left the office and gone to check out nearly three hours late. Minor Sr. poured himself into the files of his late son and occasionally he'd lean back to ponder, then he'd pour himself in some more until every file was now printed and copied before he shut down the computer and left the building, it was 12 o'clock a.m.

Chapter 48

"I told you she was trouble, I sat there and told you that it was something about her that I didn't like, she sat there and took pictures of us all, she waltzed right up to us and ruined every single one of our plans." Roberto Garcia shook his head and smiled then continued by saying,

"You think that's something, she hops out of a Limousine and buys the building and I'm willing to bet anyone in here that she's gotten her cash back, all five hundred thousand dollars." Roberto couldn't believe it, but he had to respect it and to all of whom were present which was the bosses of the Munoz family, all three of the Mendez family heads and also in attendance sat Juan Salazar. The powerful attorney and the mastermind behind all of this failure and then Roberto himself who found humor because never had he saw so much disaster happen to one simple plan. Never has he ever seen such weakness in a boss as he had now.

"Well, we came this far is there any reason why we shouldn't continue with our arrangements?" Asked Jesus Munoz,

"By came this far you mean what exactly," asked Roberto. "You mean by drawing up the courtroom fiasco, is that what you mean by far or is it that we all underestimated the power of Nigel. I'd like to know who this

Mr. Buchannon gentleman is myself, wouldn't you like to know Juan? I mean you are the one who told us that this city, this town would be easy pickings once we remove Nigel, ain't I the one who said that we should have just killed him, ain't I the one?" Roberto finished.

"And that would have proven what exactly? In jail, in the morgue still no results, no easy pickings, only problems," Raymundo Mendez shook his head at the reality then said,

"Only problems, nothing but problems, no, we didn't come here for problems, we come here for the easy pickings as promised. Two thousand pounds we bring, countless of dollars we spend," only the way Raymundo spoke he made dollars sound like "dough-lurs" but still everyone knew what he was talking about, even more so when he nodded towards the one and only Mr. Juan Salazar only to see Pedro stand and shoot twice in the direction of Mr. Salazar. Both shots scoring real big for the three .357 python put a hole in Juan's chest, and the next shot sent chunk off the top of Juan's skull flying into the air. No one moved, no one even inched to wipe away the blood which was now filling the table and dripping to the floor. Raymundo spoke again, he stood then said "problems, I don't like problems because of problems, we could all do without. Still we have problems! Do we run back to Mexico risking and spending for it was expensive getting the junk over here, risky as well or do we bring war to the streets of Sacramento where we would later do our business?" This question was asked to everyone present and everyone present had the same somber thoughts in common. No way would they enjoy risking the trips of taking their product back to Durango, Mexico or to Mexico City, Mexico, but on the flip side this guy who was called "The Panther" all throughout Mexico, no matter where one may have looked. There was a Panther in California they would say, hard to see and hard to contact. This panther would hunt, and he would destroy. So, this would be a really big decision that had to be made and everyone knew it.

"Before we decide, Raymundo you have the biggest family out West, tell me do you see a successful conclusion if we brought war?" Asked the elder Munoz, the soft spoken gentleman who never got excited, who never panicked, not even with a slowly decaying corpse spotted for all to see just right in front of him. What he needed to know, just like everyone else in attendance was did they really have enough man power to declare war on "The Panther," whoever this man may be. For they were all convinced that this man, The Panther was not Nigel.

"I have no guarantees to offer Alberto, none whatsoever. Though, I would like to I am not that kind of man who makes fabricated guarantees like this rascal who lays there. As I would like to go on record saying that I have not guaranteed anything. I only speak of risk and of expense. Although, I must also rationalize with everyone here today for this man, this "Panther" we all despise, really because he won't let us "Wet," which is the only reason we despise him. His tactics are sophisticated, and his intelligence is those of a genius, we should love him though in our hearts we wish him dead. Although we can all collectively respect this kind of gentleman, we must agree that our anger, our collective angers comes from him not letting us, Wet." Finished Raymundo,

"If only he would let us Wet our beak we wouldn't even have this for a problem. Not even the Zapatta family was able to wet their beaks. No one has ever Wet their beaks here and war has not solved this issue." Alberto swept his hands across the fallen attorney then continued, "This was foolishness, I agree we were sold on the idea because of the quiet times that we've observed here. Mislead or not, I don't say that run away like sissy guys, like cowards I don't suggest. Not now not ever, but we must ask do we stay and fight and risk more dead, and we all know that there would be more dead or do we pack up and leave and live to fight another day. Since it is you Raymundo who has such a large family of soldiers here on the west coast I must ask you this question. I ask because if there are more to die they would be the dead of your own decision, of your own soldiers and of your own reputation." Raymundo was nobody's coward. Raymundo in fact was built for battle, a warmonger at heart, had stood and said to everyone in attendance on this night. “We must rid ourselves of the Panther.” The quiet that swept over the room was a dead silence until Alberto said referring to the cadaver that was once an attorney, “Roberto, get rid of this jerk would you?” Roberto nodded his head then said,

“Sure, and the girl, tell me would she lead us back to “The Panther,” to this Mr. Buchannon?”

“No, the girl would only lead us back to Nigel can’t you see that Roberto, you’re disturbed because Nigel has made the best move under the circumstances. I like Nigel, he withstood the circus and look he doesn’t crack, he has balls. I like men with balls Roberto,” Alberto said punctuating his words with a pat on the cheek of Roberto, as if sending a message that everyone has already known that Roberto was indeed a rat, a bona fide hope to die snitch and the thought gave way to more hatred. The need to kill anything about Nigel has grown more of an obsession than anything else. If it took the last piece of his being, he would revenge his family. His last sight on earth must be the sight of Nigel falling to his finish. Snitch, yes this was degrading but as long as Nigel lived was way more humiliating to Roberto. “So, we will assemble here again tomorrow night to discuss formations and participation’s. We’ll discuss the end of “Raymond Buchannon,” the end of “The Panther” and find a way to allow ourselves to Wet.”

Raymundo spoke the words, and he sounded pretty convincing, probably too convincing for the rest. His words were already past the stages of conceit and leading more towards an underestimation. An over exaggerated belief that no one shared at the moment, a belief that was never found to be mutual. Not only did anyone not believe they’ll leave unscathed nor did they believe that they would live to ever fight another day, but all of them believed that Raymond Buchannon or the Panther was already the Victor because no one has ever met him at all.

“Yes, we will meet here tomorrow to discuss our new life here in America, here in California, and here in the State’s Capitol,” said Alberto failing to let the sincerity of his words ever to reach his eyes.

April spent all day fielding calls the following morning of the preliminary hearing, oh my God she thought, this was sinuous work. She needed arms like a craw fish to keep up with this phone, and that phone. Phones that would fail to quit, nevertheless she found a pleasure in such a task. Her son had conquered the task of bringing their family back to Sacramento.

Juice received the newspaper with eagerness. Savanna handed it over pleased at what she had read.

"Hmm" Juiced hummed after seeing the bold lettering of the headline. "Oops, perhaps the SPD has made yet another mistake," it read. The paper captured the hearing in full detail, bypassing nothing. Juice read the last statements that was passed on to the blonde reporter. "We are not guilty; we don't have to hide anymore." What the reporter didn't know was that those statements were the call to arms. No different than the printed poster that read "The army wants you," scrolled across the top. In the event the soldiers missed the message on the news the other night, they were sure to capture such a message in the newspaper. In this Juice was indeed proud of the reporter and vowed to always grant her exclusives, as much as he could.

Juice watched as his mother took one call after the next; it seemed as if everyone had decided to all call at the same time. The morning started off in a heated rush, there were pick up arrangements from the airport. There were seating arrangements to be made in the VIP section of Club Pepe's where everything must be conducted in privacy and under the normal procedures. The scheduled meeting gave everyone time to catch flights and haul some serious ass back to Sacramento for the desperate cry for help was indeed, truly a desperate cry.

"Looks like your plan has worked out just fine," said April hanging up the phone for what she felt and hoped would be the last time.

"Did you doubt my skills mommy dearest?" Juice said then the phone rang.

"No I didn't, in fact I liked the idea, hold on?" April took the call, and right away Juice and Savanna knew that it was an awkward moment by the expression that April sported while she listened on then said,

"Oh no, he'll be here, just ring for him once you arrive I'm sure that he'd spare a moment for an old friend, oh-kay, yes sir, oh-kay, see you when you get here." Then she replaced the receiver.

"Who the hell was that?" Asked Juice,

"Mr. Dixon," April responded.

"What! Are you serious, what did he want?" Asked Savanna shaking her head in disbelief,

"He called from his car, said he'll be here in five minutes," April assured them both then continued, "He said that he needed to talk to the kid and we all know that means you Dominic. Would you please tell me what could he possibly want with you?" April asked and waited, but Juice had absolutely no idea, just shook his head and walked over to the bank of monitors and watched over the club and what he saw he couldn't believe.

"Mom," he said terror stricken. Both Savanna and April recognized the look on Juices' face and both came rushing over in time to see a figure make an exit out of the club.

"Boy what, scaring me like that," for an answer Juice went over to the computer and recalled the footage from the camera that hovered over the bar and replayed it for his mother to see, then pointed at the screen and said,

"Now that should scare you"

"Could say that again," said Savanna then, "What he doing here?" Juice took Savannas accusatory stare.

"You looking at me like I know," said Juice then, "but I bet you this ain't all the way friendly." Savanna and April watched as Juice had gone to his drawer and retrieved his forty caliber pistol then took to the stairs concealing his weapon in the small of his back. Then later saw him resurface into the screen on two of the monitors. They watched as he'd gone to the bar to question the bartender. Then saw as he turned to meet the Elder Dixon by extending his hand to accept the grip of the powerful attorney.

"Let's have a seat shall we," said Juice and the two took a seat then he said, "How can I help you Sir. First my condolences, now how may I help you?"

"I'll be straight up with you; I come because I believe that you could help me understand why I had to bury my son the other day."

"And, umm, how can I help you with that Sir, I'm confused," Juice looked sincere,

"Well, you are friends with Mr. Collinson and my son has gotten involved with some terrible things and I believe one of these things were the conspiracy to do away with your friend. Though I don't know the reason completely, but I fear that your friend has reached out in revenge for his present condition."

"Sir, I respect a person of your stature and I too mourn the loss of your son, so I will speak oh so sincerely when I tell you that I fail to see how Nigel could have contributed to this horrible tragedy," Minor Sr. stared into Juices' eyes and Juice returned his stare.

"Son, could you assure me that this man has nothing to do with my son's death?"

"I could assure you that I don't see how. As we know his phone calls are well recorded and monitored which means that his only clean line of communications would be through his attorney. Do tell me, are you suggesting that she carried out his message to a killer?" Minor Sr. again held Juices eyes and again Juice held his, waiting on the powerful attorney to accuse the attorney of such treachery.

"You see, I have no other way of knowing the "why" of it, like why would such a person die so violent. My son or anyone else's for that matter. It all indicates hatred and criminal and Nigel has every reason to hate my son…."

"Are you saying that Nigel has the criminal means to do such a thing Sir?" Juice asked.

"Son, don't mind me, I'm desperate for understanding is all."

"In that case Sir, I am awfully busy," Juice said dismissively.

"I'm sorry to have intruded," the attorney stood as Juice had stood and the two shook hands once more before Juice saw the attorney to the door.

"What the hell was that all about," asked April the minute Juice returned.

"Well, the guy in the camera came in asking about the girl who he described to be Savanna and Mr. Dixon wanted to know if Nigel killed his son."

"What?" The two women said in unison, but for obviously two different reasons. April couldn't believe that the lawyer came expecting information and Savanna couldn't believe that the Mexican man came to the club looking for her.

"Yeah, this seems like a nice morning don't it," he said removing his pistol and leaving it on the counter top then gone to the phone.

"What are you doing?" Asked April trying to figure out why is it that her son was acting like he was just invited to a prize winning Easter egg hunt and not behaving like a killer had just walked out of their establishment and home, and a ruthless killer at that.

"I'm calling Benny," he said.

"What you calling Benny for?" Asked April,

"To see if Benny could send his tech over to see if that motha fucka put a bomb in my car or Savanna's rental."

"Oh! Well call Benny and ask him if his tech could come and stop me from being scared to death," said Savanna.

"Me too," said April.

Chapter 49

While the Mexican Cartels were busy strategizing their attack on Oak Park where they believed Raymond Buchannon operated his illicit business dealings. In Oak Park there was also a Cartel, only this one was built of brotherhood and there in the "P" they assembled all neatly packed in the VIP section of Club Pepe's. Every family member was present except Savanna because Savanna was not a sworn member, not by oath nor by bones. No feelings were spared in this regards. Still, she was given an important job and that was to watch over the club through the eye in the sky. Although Filbert Gilbert and J-Dog weren't brotherhood they have bones for the cause of being brothers so they were in attendance. Benny held up his shot glass and was followed by everyone in attendance.

"Brothers," he said and nodded towards April who understood that he would address her as well "and sister, time has come. Let me say what an honor it is to be surrounded by family and friends again. Man I miss you guys." The VIP section erupted into a hearty laughter. For this was a mutual feeling, one felt throughout the whole club. Gilbert and J-Dog spent most of the evening with their heads on a swivel. They looked around and saw quality in everything. They saw quality in clothing, quality in jewelry. They saw quality in personality and they felt the quality of the killers. They both heard the togetherness, the closeness and became awestruck when they saw April take control of the meeting and how she spoke highly of the two who she called friends. Everyone at the meeting turned to them with honor. They saluted them and held them in high admiration and this made the two very nervous. No one had known how April had pulled it off and stayed alive while spending her time tending to and fighting for their comrade. Vulnerable, yet she survived, she survived while tending to their wounded which was Nigel. For everyone knew that she had every means to leave. If that was what she so chose to do. To now discover that two kids, two young men were the prime reasons for the true survival of their family, they were guards that set against the threat of their brother. So, to the two the shot glasses again had gone airborne.

"Now, to the business at hand," everyone tuned in to April as she explained to her family and its friends the threat and the strategy that their enemies were forming to take over, the responsible perpetrators and their reasons. She explained to them all the locations of these perpetrators and their soldiers. She explained to them the trucks that brought in the perpetrators supplies of drugs and guns. Most of all she explained to them the positioning needed to lunge any successful attack. April looked around for questions, and even though he didn't know that he was doing it because he was caught up in the moment, but J-Dog had raised his hand seeking permission to speak. April acknowledged him with the permissible nod and heard when J-Dog said.

"And…. Umm, when is this all going down?" He heard everything else, in fact he grew more excited by the minute because the lady that he calls Juices' momma was now speaking his damn language, but as soon as he asked the question he became instantly embarrassed when everyone turned to him and not one face sported any symbol of friendliness. Still April came to his rescue by saying,

"Oh-kay, that's not a bad question because you didn't know, but when we get together like this, it only means that everything else had failed to work. So, the answer to your question is let's say the next thirty minutes." Oh at first J-Dog was excited, now his excitement had taken on a whole other kind flavor. Filbert Gilbert was relaxed and relieved because the one that he called Mrs. Raymond had come immediately to his friends' rescue. He elbowed J-Dog as if getting him to hush the fuck up while all of these grown folks and all these very dangerous folks were talking.

"All I wanted to know," said J-Dog then he had done what his friend had suggested and hushed the fuck up. They all saw as April operated her slide show of pictures, those of the warehouse and of the soldiers who manned the warehouse. Each one saw footage of the trucks that pulled up to the warehouse and had Gilbert been a rookie, rookie, and not the rookie of the year. He would have raised his hand too. Instead he was now whispering into J-Dogs ear his discoveries that there was the very same kind of freight liner parked right outside of the club. He was sure of it because he hid his brand new car on the other side of that motha fucka, and just like he thought and as soon as Mrs. Raymond finished narrating the captured footage she explained the need for the truck. Whoa, was this lady screwed! J-Dog swore that when he grew up he needed a woman just like her. He heard her, only he couldn't believe her or a minute of the shit that she was talking about. He wanted to but he couldn't. He even heard when she told them that the supplies were to come back with them. As soon as J-Dog shook his head for the umpteenth time April spoke again.

"All of our arms are equipped with army issued suppression's, so carry out as you like with the real understanding that we would also need time to load the truck up." April walked over to the bar and removed the cloth from the counter top revealing the assault rifles, and other firearms to be equipped as she said, with silencers. There were twenty-six brothers in attendance. On the counter there were twenty-four fully loaded weapons with extra magazines. Brand new out of the box were AR.10s, AR.15s, HK, MP5s and MP5SD sub machine guns. Also on the counter top were Glock .40 calibers with magazines extended to thirty shots. There laid also a twin set of Mac 11s also with extended magazines. No one had known it plus he was scared to reveal it, but J-Dog was in dog heaven and was willing to race anyone to the counter top that held his passion.

"Easy Tiger!" Benny who has been eying J-Dog and Filbert Gilbert ever since the meeting started received their attention and sat them down next to him and Raul, another longtime member of the brotherhood family and said, "Listen, we understand that there is a need here in the club. This is the most important place on earth, do you hear me?" Benny asked the suspicious looking friends who both nodded their understanding. "This place is in danger; do you understand me?" Benny asked and again the two nodded.

"Oh-kay, so we are gonna go and hit this place and relieve them of their goods. While we're doing that we need you two to make sure that nothing happens here, do you understand that?" Benny spoke very slow and was as calm as he could be under the circumstances saw as the two friends nodded again their understandings.

"Oh-kay, the two women is in your care; the older one is more important than the Queen of England and the younger one, is running a close second. Little brothers tell me that you understand me?" Again the two nodded, this time more vigorously for they were indeed with understanding.

"If while we are gone this place gets stormed by some two piece suits, some greasy hair slime balls we need you guys to kill them all. Every last one of them, again, do you still understand me?"

"Hell yeah, we understand you." Filbert Gilbert was now completely in rhythm with Benny. So much that Benny held the young man's eyes for he knew that the eyes were windows to the young man's soul. Seeing what he needed to believe he then turned to J-Dog who had kept his eyes on the firearms so Benny dismissed the soul searching that he needed for this particular young man then continued.

"Upstairs is your arms, they are maybe the variety that you are accustomed to or maybe not, but they are of the variety that is needed to protect this club. Upstairs is where you two would sit with the two ladies, however you conduct yourself do it knowing that the safety of these women are first and foremost do you have any questions?" Asked Benny,

"So, umm, what kind of firepower did you leave for us to protect this joint? I mean if they may storm this place I want a chance you know." J-Dog spoke without wavering nor taking his eyes away from Benny, who said,

"Upstairs there is an M-4 carbine and an M-203 both is equipped with a Grenade Launcher. The red trigger is for the rocket, the black one is for you to spray the place with pepper. None of those are equipped with suppressors so therefore it could be a lot of noise and the need to get to safety could be a hurried one, just needed you to know. Do you understand all of that?" The two nodded their understandings and once more Benny felt the need to do the soul searching.

"Oh-kay," said Benny as he walked away from the two, Raul was next to add his concerns he said,

"The only time they dead is you must too be dead, then is good. They died you no dead is no good, yeah? I like you, but I will kill everybody you know, don't mean to sound this way, but it's true." Without waiting for an answer Raul joined the rest of the brothers who all waited until April, Gilbert and J-Dog was safely upstairs before making their exit through the rear and out to the truck as discreetly as they could under the circumstances, for the club was indeed in full swing.

Raymundo was also in full swing while he paced in front of the impassive expressions. He showed streets and footage of the hustlers that serviced their clienteles on these streets. He relayed to the whole room the importance of gaining information in regards of the most distinguished gentleman of question, Raymond Buchannon.

"It is these guys who protect the streets of our Panther. It is these guys who will hand over this Raymond Buchannon or they will die," said Raymundo the head of the Mendez family who operates in Colorado, Utah and Nevada.

"Are you sure about this Raymundo?" Again Salvatore spoke. He still needed the guarantee that Raymundo was refusing to give him.

"It is the only sensible thing left. Now is the time to run, anyone who wish to run away shall do so now." Salvatore had been painted into a corner and he knew it. He chose to sit and remain silent. Though his gut was telling him to grab his hat and get the hell out of there, still he knew that to stand and make his exit was to return home to a bad reputation and there he must endure more wars, wars of a different kind. Seeing that Raymundo now had everyone's attention again he stressed the message with emphasis on the need to capture the whereabouts of Raymond Buchannon and to fall upon such a man with deadly force. The gentlemen studied every tactic, every maneuver and every word as if their very own lives were depending on it. So concentrated were they that no one heard the beeping of the truck as it was placed into reverse and backed its way into the loading dock.

Benny backed the truck up with confidence in his ability to handle such a big rig. He backed the truck up to the same port that he had viewed many of times before. He backed the truck up knowing that he may also have to spit fire at the two soldiers who occupied the tiny office next to the warehouse. It was documented that the two soldiers were known to interview the driver of the truck before alerting the other soldiers who were concealed within the space of the warehouse, exactly where? No one knew, and because no one had known this was indeed a risk that each one of them had to take. Benny waited a moment and then the two soldiers made their presence felt. Both waved their confused gestures towards each other which was all the time that Benny needed to swing down and spit his consecutive rounds at the fully armed soldiers. The barely audible sounds of five rounds were more silent than the grunts and the collapse of the two soldiers. The tap on the side of the trailer was the signal of everything being clear and because of that the rear door slid up as quietly as possible and twenty-three masked men hit the ground running. Each one running towards their assignments, for each one had known that to lag was to create more risk and eventually lagging would ultimately mean to lose. Benny had taken his seat at the wheel of the truck. He played his mirrors trying to catch anyone of the soldiers attempting to raid the truck where he knew that to try was to die. It was through these very looking glasses did Benny see the fire flying from one weapon after the next one. He saw men being slaughtered in the hallways, on the docks and those who tried to escape he saw them die in the yard of the warehouse and in the parking lot. With ferociousness and treachery was how they fell upon the warehouse. The signal was for a flashlight to hit the windshield, symbolizing that the warehouse had been cleared. A signal that had taken twenty minutes to come, what Benny didn't know was why so many beams made their way to him. This being so new to him, so not part of the plan that in frustration Benny climbed down from the truck with weapons at the ready, and made his way towards his brothers.

"What the fuck was that?" Benny said in regards to the many signals.

"We got a big problem, a big problem," said Lamarcus, one of the brothers who had proven himself over and over again. So much that he was now deep into the folds of the family.

"That's what I was saying when I saw all the fucking lights, we need to be as discreet as possible remember?"

"Yes, but check this out?" Lamarcus lead Benny and the other brothers through the warehouse and to another office where Benny saw the men who've come eat in the very city that offers no food what so ever to strangers. The sneer creased his lips. He shook his head and to Juice he said, "Kid we're here with you," and the answer that Juice provided was a good one. Without words he walked over to Tomas, the chubby mobster who was caught trying to make his getaway and placed the .40 caliber handgun to his head from the rear and there he sent Tomas' brains to flying.

"That's all you had to say," said Benny before following suit. Before the night was finished a dent has been put into the powerful Mendez family and before the night was finished some very powerful men now lay in the ruins of their very own waste while a number of masked men loaded all of their merchandise on to the trailer of a big rig.

"Dinky, find the box that has the tape and bring me the tapes." What Benny saw was a bank of monitors that had captured all movements inside and outside of the warehouse. Dinky followed the wiring until it led him to another room and from there he resurfaced with three VHS recording tapes and then and only then did the brothers board the truck and make their exit. Three of them were shot but none were life threatening.

Chapter 50

Savanna was the first to spot the intruders, it was three of them. They came inside of the club and took their positions in various areas of the club. She revealed their whereabouts to Gilbert and April then later to James.

"Oh-kay the moment has come," said April who walked over to the cabinet and retrieved her pistol and Savanna to everyone's surprise took a hold of her man's pistol, a very high powered one and said,

"Seeing that they came for me, you know, I may as well do it fighting for mine." Then she gave a subtle laugh.

"I heard the fuck out of that," was all that J-Dog was able to say before the club was indeed stormed. April was the first one to the door. "No!" shouted J-Dog who took April's place at the door. He looked to Gilbert and the two nodded to each other. Then J-Dog swung the door open and Gilbert was the first one through the door.

"Stay behind us, don't stop!" Said J-Dog over the loud thundering gun blast and the two women followed closely behind their guards. Gilbert began to fire in a sweeping motion the room not really caring who was hit and by his side J-Dog stood aiming in the opposite direction until he saw Gilbert go down. Then the echoes came from the small arms that the women were carrying. J-Dog chased down one slime ball after the next; he was caught reloading by one of the slime balls that looked to have gotten the drop on him until a hole appeared where his Adam's apple used to be. Looking up he saw April who came to his rescue then allowed for him to take the lead again. More and more slime balls came into the club and there they would lean towards the entrance, then fall in dead.

"Find your way to the rear!" April screamed over the burst that J-Dog offered.

"No, it may not be good, follow me!" J-Dog scooped up Gilbert into his arms saying, "You alright my nigga?"

"Hell naw," Gilbert said to the relief of the other three.

"Dog could you walk?" J-Dog asked his friend of many years.

"Could you run is the question," April said.

"I need a little help," said Gilbert.

"Where are you hit?" Asked Savanna,

"By my balls," said Filbert Gilbert.

"Oh yeah, you need some help," said J-Dog.

As they scanned the club they now saw the many innocent bystanders that died next to a group of slime balls.

"My nigga we need to get out of here, we can't stay do you know what I mean?"

"Hell, yeah go get us a car and hurry back to get us," said Gilbert then, "We need a big car."

"Oh-kay, oh-kay just hold on a minute, ma'am I need to get us out of here do we have car that we could run to?" J-Dog asked the lady that he call Juice's momma but Savanna answered,

"I have a car only the keys are upstairs."

"Go get them and hurry!" Shouted April,

Savanna took to the stairs in a heated sprint then returned sorting the keys until she found the one that would grant her easy entry into the vehicle.

"Are you ready?" J-Dog asked the ladies "Oh-kay," he said then "I'm gonna need one of you guys to carry my brother and where are you parked?"

"Right out front," said Savanna.

"I got this boy," said April and then to Gilbert she said "If we are trapped I will drop you and I need you to crawl or do what you have to do to get inside the car," Gilbert nodded to Mrs. Raymond.

"Oh-kay let's go," J-Dog led the way out of the club to find a car that was parked just right outside of the door, "Down!" Was all he said before he squeezed the red trigger that launched the Grenade, sending its explosion to the car that was full of slime balls. More slime balls were waiting across the street from the club and J-Dog accompanied by Juice's momma sent bullets in the direction of the slime balls until the slime balls were felled. Everyone heard the sirens coming in a heated rush.

"Hurry child!" Screamed April to Savanna who finally slung the doors open giving everyone access before she ran around to the driver side and started the rental grateful and relieved, that there was not a bomb inside of the vehicle.

"This boy needs a doctor!" April shouted from the rear seat.

"Where to, should we go to the hospital?" Savanna asked and all three of them said,

"No!" A chorus that came simultaneously.

"Mrs. Raymond, I need some water," said Filbert Gilbert.

"No son, you need a doctor, girl get on the freeway and take us to 47th Avenue and to our man. I left my phone, is there a phone in here anybody?" J-Dog dug into his pocket and brought out his phone and gave it to Juice's momma who dialed the number quickly.

"Hello, Brian I'm sorry if I woke you, but I got a kid in my lap who's been shot, I need you to help me right away. Oh-kay no it's a below the waist shot. Oh-kay, in ahh, I think the testicles. Oh-kay, I will. I need a shirt, a towel, anything!" Shouted April, who received J-Dogs shirt, she pressed it firmly onto Gilbert's testicles after pulling down his trousers.

"Oh-kay I'm back. I have pressure on him. Oh-kay, oh-kay we'll arrive shortly." April hung up the phone then said, "Girl could you drive this thing any faster."

Chapter 51

Juice, Benny and a hand full of brothers turned the corner of MLK Boulevard and saw the emergency lights.

"Oh shit," said Juice after swinging the door open to the minivan and there he hit the ground running. There were many EMTs. There were also many police officers and of the many there was one special group that sported a patch reading ORBITT. This group of officers paid fine detail to every broken glass; they had canvassed every section of the club. They had followed the crime scene investigators everywhere they went. Pictures were taken at a rapid rate. Tweezers were used to pick up tiny pieces of what everyone would love to call, evidence.

Every officer stopped what they were doing to the sound of a loud commotion that was taking place outside.

"Take your hands off of me." Yelled Juice, he was attempting to gain entry into the club which was also his home.

"Sir, I have my orders to secure this area and that goes for anyone," said the young officer.

"What's going on here?" Asked the Captain surprised to see the spot shooting bartender, he said. "Mr. Raymond, what's going on here?" Asked Captain Wynn,

"I need to come in with you. I need permission to come inside sir." Said Juice refusing to conceal his eagerness,

"And just why is that?"

"Because I believe that my mother and wife is inside."

"Oh, oh shit, come with me but don't touch anything do you got that or I'll haul your ass out'ta here, do you follow?" Juice nodded his understanding then followed the Captain inside of the club.

"Do you think she's inside?" Asked Raul to Benny as they watched from the vehicle,

"I sure hope not, it doesn't look good though," said Benny then, "shit, shit Raul, shit!"

"No, no don't worry brother." Said Raul,

"Raul I swear, she bet not be in there I swear, I swear, I swear," Benny banged on the steering wheel, emphasizing each promise.

"Don't worry brother, she no inside." Raul smiled to Benny then patted him on the shoulder to relax him.

"How you know Raul, how could you know for sure that she's not inside, brother how the hell could you know, man?"

"I don't know for sure but it looks good so far no, I think she get away." Raul pointed to the yellow tape across the street where there were other crime scene employees taking pictures, then said.

"If she no get away, why those guys and look," Raul pointed to the car that was blown to bits then said, "See, she gets away. Just like us brother, we fuck up something, we really fuck up something." Raul finished then leaned back into his seat and continued to smile. Then to his delight he drew a smile from Benny who had overlooked the details surrounding him. Happy to arrive at the conclusions that in order for the car to look like it did, a rocket had to hit it. Then there was the yellow tape across the street which meant that whoever gunned them down did so once they had made it outside of the club. Smiling Benny said,

"Yeah, when we tear it up, we tear it all the way up." And this made everyone in the van happy and laughter had filled the vehicle for the first time since they had pulled up on such a horrible scene.

Inside of the club Juice followed the Captain until he had for evidence nothing of which he was looking for. The Captains strategy which was to shake the young man up by showing him one dead body after the other, had failed the Captain severely. Juice saw his mother's friends motionless around the room, he saw many soldiers as well. He watched as one medical tech turned over a body of one of the soldiers. Juice concealed his anger, but barely as he recognized the man to be the very same guy from the pictures. The man had been identified by Juice as Roberto Garcia. Juice had felt the stare of the Captain on to him, and heard when the Captain said.

"Do you recognize anyone in here?" Juice didn't know if the Captain was then asking a loaded question, or one with a double meaning. So he turned to the Captain and said "Yeah. I do."

"Oh, would any of them happen to be anyone that you are looking for?" Not yet thought Juice,

"Any place that we could talk for a minute son. I really have things that I need to discuss with you."

"Not right now," said Juice, then looked over the club. Bottles were broken and every mirror was shattered, cards and chips were soaked in blood on the same tables.

"No son I'm afraid this could not wait, you see, I have been made a fool of long enough, now I must gently ask, what is going on here?" Juice looked to the Captain then shook his head and said,

"Sir, I respect you. I really do, but you need to know, from the bottom of my heart, that just because I respect you, it doesn't mean that I trust you."

"I'll accept that, granted that I know your history. I would've sure liked to have seen you play every Sunday, sorry for your misfortune. Son, just know that I'm as straight as they come ..."

"Which doesn't say a whole lot, considering." Juice interrupted then asked. "Have you been upstairs?"

The Captain have been waiting on this question said, "Yes, we've been all over this place." The light hit the kid's eyes. The Captain had saw this and shook his head then said,

"I'll give you one; if you don't see your wife and mother here then chances are that they made it out. How, is what I'm interested in?"

"Maybe they weren't in when all of this took place?" Said Juice,

"No, don't play. I said that too, only the door upstairs was found wide open, we looked everywhere up there, and this is what I think." The captain leads the kid to the stairs and halfway up the Captain turned around and pointed to the kid and said, "See, those bullet holes tell me that whoever was up here came down the stairs firing," the Captain led Juice down the stairs then said,

"And whoever came down those stairs, you know the ones that I believe came down firing, well, they stopped right here and pointed his or her weapon in that direction, look at the holes there, same ones found all over the club. What I'm saying young man is that more than one gun came down those stairs. So far we believe two. Now that's a whole lot of offense. You see those guys; you could separate them from the rest. They look like wise guys, depending on who you ask, had run into this club only to be out matched by at least two gunmen, but you did say your wife and your mother is missing right?" Juice followed the rest of the Captains' summations and he had to agree that the Captain had really turned in a good supposition. Only he knew that suppositions would never hold up in court. Juice also knew that he needed to make it up the stairs to see if the computers had been seized as evidence.

"Come, follow me." Juice lead the Captain down the stairs, the Captain was so eager, for now he believed it was the time to separate the shit from the sugar. Juice lead the Captain to one of the corpse then stopped and said, "We need someone over here to take the sheet off this guy.

"I thought you'd recognize him," said the Captain.

"I know you did," Juice said, but really he was hoping that he had gotten away with the look of satisfaction once he saw the dead body of Roberto Garcia. Captain Wynn was back with an emergency tech and ordered the sheet to come off.

"This Mr. Wynn is Roberto Garcia. Have you ever heard of him?"

"Uh uh, and how should I know him?" Asked the Captain,

"Well, he was on the witness list. I thought you might want to know that I really don't trust you," said Juice.

"Ahh shit son what gives," So much for closer, Juice had turned and headed for the stairs with the Captain hot on his heels. Once inside of the living quarters Juice saw that there was no blood and that everything was intact. The computer was turned off, which was almost never.

"So, who turned off the computer?" Asked Juice,

"You tell me, hell I'm the guest here."

"Well if you don't know who turned it off how the hell should I know, I just got here remember?" This is what Juice had said with his lips, but in his mind he said, "So, this is where they saw them storm the place." Immediately he had known that Savanna had done as instructed. For if the place was to get infiltrated by the enemies while they were in the meeting to turn off the computer which would then stop recording the very instant.

"Son, there is a lot going on here. What I need to know is how much of this has to do with Ms. Clayton? We had gotten a tip from an owner of a restaurant that her client had supposedly gone into business with. Later we found our tipster shot to death on a California Highway. He too was on the witness list. Later we find an attorney fatally shot in a downtown strip mall. He was of Dixon's, the biggest law firm in town. The crazy thing is now that we find another attorney floating in the Sacramento River. A Juan Salazar now we could fuck me to tears, but Dixon, Juan and Dixon had lost two partners, a Dixon and a Juan. Now maybe I'm reaching but this is the address where I can locate another attorney you get what I'm saying," finished the Captain.

"Yeah, you wanted to know how much of this has to do with Ms. Clayton. Then you blew a hole into that theory by suggesting that maybe Nigel had launched an attack against his own attorney. Even after the stellar performance that she displayed for him while getting him a bail hearing. Why would he off her when it's starting to look as if she'll now get him a dismissal?" Juice began wandering around picking up things that he was sure to need. He figured that he would be permitted as long as he kept talking, and part of his possessions were both cell phones, his Mother's and Savannas. Now knowing why neither one answered their lines when he placed dozens of calls to each.

"What I was suggesting was simply the read that I get from the streets. You know I've been here so long, young man I know this place inside and out. I get a tip and I'm sure of this guy Nigel. Then this place is crowded with mob figures. Oooh scary, I mean none of this has ever gone down before. The streets were quiet, and peaceful. We were beginning to think that Mr. Buchannon had passed away. You know, there was always the wonder. Somewhat like the guy who left Alcatraz, always the wonder, is he dead or is he out there somewhere. Then we get your friend to surrender, crazy but he surrendered just right down those very stairs. You want to know what's even more disturbing, the guy who once owned this club he had done work for us then we find him cooked "well done" inside of a car. Killed by Mr. Buchannon who I am now thinking is either your friend or that Mr. Collinson knows this fine person, it's one of those, no other way around it. It's one of those, and then we find that not one, but two attorneys of the same firm had now met their end. Now what am I to think? You know with the holes in my theory and with such a fine performance and all?" Finished the Captain,

"I'll tell you what you should think. I would say now that you have everything figured out like you do, then get your warrants together, make some arrest and then and only then would we see in court. If you think the last performance was something try us with this new shit that you are drumming up."

"Oh-kay, so where would your mother and wife be right now? I mean we would like to talk to them."

"I don't know, if and have I find them before you do I'll let them know and I will accompany them believe me."

"Oh-kay, I'm good with that, just one more question, Sir where were you during the hours of ten o'clock and the time that I encountered you down stairs?" This question froze Juice at the door.

Chapter 52

April had driven herself crazy, she had called her son twenty times, and not receiving an answer had only made it worse.

"Mom, would you sit down, you're making me crazy right along with you, gosh." Savanna couldn't take it anymore, "I've been calling that boy over and over," said April who sat down for two seconds then she was back on her feet pacing in the doctor's office while her on call doctor had taken both young men into his sterile operating room.

"Well did you think to call Benny?" Asked Savanna noticing that Benny had never crossed her mind,

"No! How come I didn't think of that?" She said then dialed quickly and quickly she was answered.

"Hello," said Benny.

"Benny this is April."

"Oh my God, girl where are you at?" He asked with his excitement building up he said, "We are at the club, man it's so much going on right here."

"Where's my son? Is he with you?"

"He's oh-kay, right now he's inside of the club where are you?"

"We're at Brian's."

"His house or what?"

"At his Practice."

"Is it bad?" He asked.

"I don't know we're in prayer right now, it's hard to say." This was enough to get the minivan started and headed in the direction of 47th Avenue. What no one knew nor did Benny ask was who was hit and possibly laying on their deathbed because if it was the girl, the kid would lose his mind and they all knew this. Ten minutes later found Brian's medical practice filled with some very concerned men. Right away upon entry the brothers knew that one of their friends if not both of them were in surgery because it was Savanna who opened the door for them to come rushing in.

"Where's Dominic?" She asked after not seeing him.

"We left him at the club, the cops got him."

"The cops got him!" She snapped.

"Not like that, they're asking a lot of questions, too many for us. What's going on here?" On cue Brian the PHD medical man who held his private practice on 47th Avenue walked out with a very emotional and nerve thickened J-Dog, they all gathered around them.

"Well, shit Brian, tell us something man," shouted Benny who was the first to have grown tired of the suspense, "I'm saying," said Lamarcus. It was always Brian's specialty to allow the concern to grow panicky before announcing his brilliance, shook his head then said,

"He's gonna live," Benny scanned the presence of the younger man, seeing his depression said,

"But?"

"He only got one of his... You know," J- Dog chose his words carefully considering that there was the presence of women.

"He got shot in the balls," said April.

"Oh my God! Are you serious?" Benny flinched at the thought of this incident. Raul walked over to J-Dog and put his arms around him and said,

"Now you, I really like you, you good man, I know that you could do it. Scary yeah," for an answer J-Dog shook his head and replayed the moments for them outside of earshot. He showed them the motion he used to get all of the slime balls.

"I let that rocket go then ka-boom the tire left first, twenty feet in the air." Was how he finished.

"Don't mean to bust your bubble little daddy but did you say that one of them caught you slipping though?" Asked Lamarcus,

"Hell yeah, I ran out of bullets..."

"Then what happened?" Asked Lamarcus,

"Juice's mama had to come and get me." Everyone turned and looked at April who caught them looking at her shook her head and signaled that the boy was crazy brought everyone to laughter.

"Yeah, first I don't think so, but I like you. Your friend one ball is bad yeah, but lucky one ball better than no ball, no?"

"Yeah, one ball better than no ball, dog who are you, and who taught you how to talk like that," again the room broke into laughter then Raul said,

"I'm Raul, your brudder from an udder mudder."

"Brudder from an udder mudder, what mother is that?"

"The one in Puerto Rico."

"If you say so," said J-Dog then Benny came to J-Dog and said,

"Young man if he says so then trust me on this one, I mean you could be knee deep in shit and guess who would come and get you."

"Nah."

"Yeah, would put his life on the line every time, so much that it'll become boring after a while." J-Dog was young, but he was far from dumb, accepted Raul as he said a brudder from an udder mudder.

"Man my car is at the club still," said J-Dog then "So how do I get that back?"

"With a tow truck?"

"You know what kind of car I got?"

"Yeah, a Lamborghini right?" Lamarcus stated flatly,

"Yeah, how you know?"

"It was a dead giveaway; it says new money all the way around it."

"Is that right, well new money or old money my car is at the club and I want my new money car, so how do I get it back?"

"On a tow truck, little daddy you are gonna have to learn to trust your ears." Said Benny getting in between the two for he had known a long time ago that Lamarcus had very little patience for foolishness.

"I saw two sport cars. The other one I'm a take it belongs to him in there." Benny pointed towards the rooms while punching numbers in his phone.

"Hello, Greeny, I got two sports at the club that belongs to some friends of mine. The club is surrounded by police and all kinds of stuff is going on over there. The cars were for a video shoot and were supposed to be brought back to Luxury Auto Plug. Could you pick them up for me...? No, the keys I got. Oh-kay come through Brian's and I'll wait for you. Yeah on 47th Avenue. Oh-kay." Then Benny hung up the phone,

"It must be nice." Said J-Dog,

"What's that?"

"To be able to pick up a phone and order anything you need."

"It is son, you got to get you one of these." Benny said holding up his phone.

"Hardy har, har, har," said J-Dog.

"I know, I know, yeah it is pretty good when you have a lot of connections, but come here and I'll tell you a secret." J-Dog came close enough to hear Benny say,

"We got a shit load of junk at one of our storage places. A shit load I tell you, uncut and raw. I took a test tube to it myself. Off of one pound I could make about three on the extras. Do you know anything about that stuff?"

"I'm pretty sure that I do."

"Well guess what?"

"I'm listening."

"We're gonna all split it."

"Nuh uh."

"Yes sir."

"You're playing with me."

"Never would."

"But, I know there's a but somewhere."

"No buts." J-Dog eyed Benny then said,

"A shit load of it?" J-dog needed reaffirming.

"Mmm hmmm."

"Oh-kay, well, thank you then."

"No, no the appreciation is all of ours. You did well, we are all proud of you. Now tell me where would you go from here?"

"What are my options?"

"Well, you could get a phone like mines or you could get a phone like yours."

"Uh uh, I think I want a phone like yours. My phone only knows the pizza guys, your phone knows who's gonna pick up my car and something is telling me that I'm gonna need a phone that's gonna help me pick up my car a lot." Said J-Dog,

The past few days were an experience Savanna just couldn't seem to get off of her mind. She stared at the judge's bench. The Honorable Judge Walker is what it read on a tag just near her bench. One would have to strain to see it, but it was there. Savanna sat in her seat a full hour before anyone arrived. Knowing that a million people wanted to see her, cops included.

"Counselor," it was the Honorable Judge Walker. "You're a mite early aren't you?"

"It's a zoo outside," said Savanna.

"Even bigger than the last showing I suppose," the two knew the judges meaning.

"I would think so." Savanna shook her head then said, "I have a feeling they will show more so for your words than for me or mines this time."

"I suppose so, so tell me how much of this has affected you?" The judge was genuinely concerned.

"Well I've had an attempt on my life. I've endangered my mother in law and ruined her business and home all because I picked to be an attorney." Savanna was milking everything that has been wrote in the newspaper. For everyone loved the young attorney. No one suspected her of foul play at all. The paper had targeted the death of two attorneys and connected them somehow to the attempt on Savanna at her mother in law's place of business. Savanna shook her head then said, "I came here for a bail hearing."

"But," interrupted the judge.

"I'm gonna ask for the full ride."

"I figured as much," the judge said. Then Savanna left to study her files. Really Savanna had no studying to do. She could only reflect to the previous day when Gilbert was wheeled out of his home. One that Juice found following the trace of a Lamborghini. The minute Juice laid eyes on him the two just stared at each other. Then Juice walked over to Gilbert to simply say,

"Thank you." Even though Juice didn't think it was possible, but Gilbert stood up and the two embraced.

"Thank you my nigga, thank you for looking out for my mom's man."

"Nigga fuck that I need a Remy for that, you should have saw it that shit was crazy. Bitch ass nigga your mom's is a fool with it. Now that's my motha fucka. I like you, but I really like her." Savanna was so preoccupied with thought that she didn't even notice that the bailiff had brought her client in and seated him.

"Girl what the fuck, no visit or anything, and what the fuck is going on out there?" She knew that Nigel wasn't speaking about the reporters.

"Trust me, you don't want to know."

"Of course I do." The crowd came rushing in sending the press to their post. The spectators were on first come, first serve basis and that was the seating arrangements. The bailiff called the case and Savanna stood and headed to the District Attorney and handed him a motion 995 to dismiss. By the time she made it outside of the courtroom the reporters stormed around her aiming one question after the next in her direction and all that she could say was,

"No comment."

"No comment," to whether or not she'll survive the night. It was no comment to the good law enforcement who were in desperate need to make an arrest, but were scared to death by the thought of asking Savanna to turn around and place her hands behind her back. What had happened at The Club Pepe's is what everyone wanted to know. Savanna knew that she would be investigated long after this case was over, but she was more confident in the system built around her and had more faith in that than she did in such a system where it was becoming more and more complicated to determine the friends from the foes. At least on the streets one knew where their enemies were not so when the ones who write the law exploits it, corrupts it and rearranges it so much that somehow even God's law has become buried under such a miscarriage. No, Savanna thought. Handcuffs or plenty space, one was gonna have to be given to her. So, when she saw the Captain arriving with a heap of officers in tow she allowed his approach without concern.

"Counselor," said Captain Wynn.

"Officer."

"Ma'am we would love to ask you a lot of questions."

"Yet, I will only give you one answer," Savanna responded.

"Yeah, and just what would that be counselor?" Asked the Captain,

"No, comment."

Authors Notes: PM Don is the author of other fictional works including the prolific title, T*he Geto Love Song*. Also, the author of *1.6 Million, The Paper Boi* and *A Hint of Jasmine* which is due to arrive soon. PM Don is a native of Sacramento, California where he studies Theater Arts and is a Cinematographer student. His histories consist of long intensive years in both creative writing and song writing. His library of other authors that motivates him and his writing abilities listed are Dan Brown, James Patterson, Donald Goines and Alex Haley. When asked what motivates him the most? Simply to show a generation that there are other methods to be successful then to fall victim to the poison injected into our inner cities and our youths.

PM Don resides in Sacramento where he is hard at work writing other novels and fulfilling the promises of bringing feature films to the City of Trees.

www.ingramcontent.com/pod-product-compliance
Lightning Source LLC
Chambersburg PA
CBHW050020030726
47506CB00001B/42
* 9 7 8 0 9 9 7 8 3 0 5 0 7 *